'Absorbing . . . no run-of-the-mill
The Times

'Universal truths . . . an unbuttoned sense of humour . . .
engaging and eventful'
Wall Street Journal

'Good atmospheric writing . . . moments of chilling horror
. . . a fine example of tartan noir'
Allan Massie, *The Scotsman*

'You'll have a blast with these'
Ian Rankin

'A top talent, and one to be cherished'
Quintin Jardine

'Spellbinding . . . one of the UK's most loved crime writers'
Sunday Post

'Satisfyingly twisted plot'
Publishers Weekly

'Touches of dark humour, multi-layered and compelling'
Daily Record

'If you like Rankin, MacBride and Oswald,
you'll love Meyrick'
Sunday Mail

'The right amount of authenticity . . . gritty writing
. . . most memorable'
The Herald

'The remote peninsula and the claustrophobic nature
of small-town life are perfectly painted'
Scotland on Sunday

A note on the author

Denzil Meyrick was born in Glasgow and brought up in Campbeltown. After studying politics, he pursued a varied career including time spent as a police officer, freelance journalist and director of several companies in the leisure, engineering and marketing sectors. Denzil lives on Loch Lomond side with his wife, Fiona.

Also by Denzil Meyrick

Terms of Restitution

DCI Daley thriller series
Whisky from Small Glasses
The Last Witness
Dark Suits and Sad Songs
The Rat Stone Serenade
Well of the Winds
The Relentless Tide
A Breath on Dying Embers
Jeremiah's Bell
For Any Other Truth

Tales from Kinloch
A Large Measure of Snow
A Toast to the Old Stones

Short stories
One Last Dram Before Midnight

For more information
www.denzilmeyrick.com
and www.birlinn.co.uk

THE DEATH OF REMEMBRANCE

A DCI DALEY THRILLER

Denzil Meyrick

First published in Great Britain in 2022 by Polygon, an imprint of Birlinn Ltd.

Birlinn Ltd
West Newington House
10 Newington Road
Edinburgh
EH9 1QS

www.polygonbooks.co.uk

1

ISBN 978 1 84697 585 1
eBook ISBN 978 1 78885 501 3

British Library Cataloguing-in-Publication Data
A catalogue record for this book is available on request from the British Library.

Typeset by 3btype.com, Edinburgh

For Fiona, this decade and for ever

'To improve is to change; to be perfect is to change often.'
—Winston Churchill

PROLOGUE

Glasgow, fourteen years before

Chief Superintendent John Donald stopped his black Audi A8 outside the disused workshop in Glasgow's Townhead. All manner of new buildings were rising from the ground, as cranes, diggers, vans, lorries and battalions of men in hard hats and fluorescent jackets went about their business. Donald barely recognised the place where he'd walked the beat what seemed like a lifetime ago.

Now, it was all so different – apart from his destination, that was. Like the last dog turd in the street, it stood out because of dilapidation and decay. Once white walls had faded to dirty grey, slathered in the exotic scrawl of gang tags and familiar obscenities. Cracked drainpipes led to fractured gutters, from which sprouted incongruous clumps of grass and the odd drooping dandelion. The pavement that ran along the full length of the tumbledown building was cracked, the road almost gone. He regarded this remnant of the old city's decline with distaste. Superintendent John Donald's world was all about the future, his rise and rise. But there were hurdles to be overcome.

Donald left the cocoon of his car and sniffed at the air. It was a fetid mix of diesel fumes, brick dust, damp earth and a hint of urine. He neatly sidestepped a used condom as he walked towards a steel security roller-shutter, within which was located a much smaller wicket door, lying ajar, a small gap affording a glimpse of dim yellow light within.

He stopped, passed a hand over slicked-back hair and pushed his way into a large empty space. All was dim apart from a pool of yellow light from a single unshaded bulb hanging over a table in the centre of a pitted concrete floor.

Donald could see the silhouette of a man sitting beside the table. Though only his back was visible, the superintendent knew this individual all too well. He cleared his throat by way of an awkward intimation of his presence.

'You got the cold, big man?' The voice was deep, rough, from what had been the wrong side of Glasgow's tracks, the lines of which had long since blurred. This city was now a place where businessmen shared streets with barrow-boys on the make. Judges and felons parked their cars alongside one another. Whores and churchgoers lived cheek by jowl with dignitaries and drug dealers in some of the best properties the city had to offer, while living entirely different lives. Glasgow was becoming the meritocracy of which everyone had once dreamed. But the nature of merit had never been specified. So now, as long as they had plenty of cash, the city no longer segregated its less desirable citizens in crumbling tenements, swaying high-rise flats or dolorous schemes. A healthy bank balance was all you needed to share the same rarefied air as those who considered themselves the cream of society.

Donald ignored his host's sarcasm and strode towards the light. The only chair at the table was occupied, so he stood before the man who had summoned him like a recalcitrant schoolboy before a headmaster. Not a sensation he enjoyed. Making people feel small was his job.

The senior police officer could see his host's features properly now. And despite himself, a shiver of fear went down his spine.

'It's been a long time, Johnny, eh?'

Donald cleared his throat again, not this time to announce himself, but from discomfort. 'It has. How have you been?'

'Oh, just dandy, my man, just fine and dandy. Living on the profits of my hard work and ingenuity – taking it easy for a while. Have you missed me?'

'Do you want an honest answer?'

The man laughed. 'An honest answer fae a polis? Aye, there'll be green snow and yellow hailstones the day that happens.'

'What do you want?'

'*What do you want?*' He mimicked Donald's acquired accent. 'I want my money's worth, that's what I want!' He banged the table with a clenched fist. The sound echoed round the empty space.

'What did you expect me to do? I can't control your men – particularly Frank MacDougall.'

'You could have had him arrested!'

'I thought that's the last thing you'd want.'

'Aye, well, you thought wrong. No' for the first time either, arsehole! Too busy with your new friends in Eastern Europe from what I hear.'

'I don't have to listen to this.' Donald turned on his heel, ready to leave, but the click of the safety catch on a weapon stopped him in his tracks.

'Your good lady's one for the self-improvement, eh?'

3

Donald spun back round to face his interlocutor. 'Sorry?'

'She likes learning – never oot that night school, is she? Every couple should have a family – kids. It's important to pass something down. You know, something of yourself.' He paused, a salacious smile spreading across his face. 'You've no weans, I hear. You no' keeping her happy, big John? In between the sheets, I mean. Needs to amuse herself wae extra-curricular activities.' He laughed.

'Fuck this. You asked me to come here for our *mutual benefit*. I don't see anything beneficial about being abused by you. I've had too much of that in the past!'

'Remember how you managed to climb the greasy pole, Johnny boy.' The man got to his feet and walked over to where Donald stood. 'Never turn your back on me again, you piece of shit.' He rammed the barrel of a pistol into John Donald's ribs, making him double over in pain.

'I don't know what you want me to do,' he gasped.

'I want a favour – for services rendered, let's say. Let's call it an apology for letting my auld friends get too full o' themselves when I was busy being somewhere else.' He towered over the bent figure of the police officer. 'Read this.' He dragged Donald towards the light and thrust a piece of paper under his nose.

Donald squinted at the page, scanning its contents. 'I can't do this – it's not my job. I have no influence over this department!'

The man returned to his chair. He held the pistol in one fist, resting it on the table, one knee bouncing up and down with clear irritation. 'You know why I really asked you to come here?'

Donald looked round in the darkness. 'To intimidate me, I imagine.'

4

'Aye, that's true. But I mean *here* specifically – to this place. Man, you seem to have a short memory.'

'How so?'

'This used to be a garage, remember? My garage, in fact.'

'Oh yes, I remember now. So what?'

'This is where you took your first bribe from me. A Sierra Cosworth, I seem to remember. Nice motor. I can mind how chuffed you were wae it. It's also a place I had to get off on my toes quick smart, because of you being shite and doing what I asked you.'

'Yes.' The policeman lowered his eyes.

The gun was now pointing at Donald's head. 'Well, remember what I'm saying right now. Do this thing for me or you'll be down one wife. Do you understand?'

The superintendent made to speak, but his tormentor put a finger to his lips to quieten him.

'No excuses, no shit – just get it done. We go about this properly – the way we should have done the first time round. Let's face it, that little plan backfired big time.' He yawned. 'Now, get tae fuck. I'm a busy man.'

'I do have something else to offer you. I'm sure you'll like it.'

'Aye, I'm listening.'

'Daley and Scott.'

'What about those pair o' bastards?'

'They'll be taking the low road to somewhere out of the way soon. I'm just waiting for a suitable opportunity.'

Machie narrowed his eyes at the policeman. 'Daley's one too many for you, eh?'

'Nothing of the kind. But not having him looming over everything will be a welcome break. And his little dog, Brian Scott.'

5

'That bastard. He was someone else's little dog once.'

'Yes, how can I forget. But down there, well, they're sitting ducks.'

Machie shrugged. 'They'll keep for a while. Just make sure my old pals don't get the chance to turn on me now I'm back, got it?'

'Yes, I've got it.'

'Good. Now, do one.' Machie turned away, meeting over.

Donald swayed from foot to foot, desperately wanting to argue, to remind this man that he was no longer a mere sergeant on the beat who could be ordered about by a thug or kept loyal with petty bribes. After all, this was the gang boss whose own lieutenants had turned their backs on him in his absence. He was nothing now, nothing!

But Donald's courage failed him. Meekly, he trudged away, back through the wicket door and across the pavement to his Audi.

The chief superintendent drove a few streets away to where he'd once trodden the beat. There was barely anything left of Parliamentary Road, he noted. In fact, the whole Townhead he'd once known was almost obliterated; it was as though Glasgow had removed one head and another had been surgically implanted. This was the world he wanted to be part of, not the one he'd left moments ago – the throwback to a time he dearly wanted to forget.

Donald parked his car close to the Northgate building and grabbed the phone from its charger on the dashboard. He dialled a number from memory and waited impatiently for a reply.

'What can I do you for, Mr Donald?'

'It's what I can do for you, Frank.'

'Oh aye. Well, that makes a change. And how much will this largesse cost me?'

'I'll give you this for free.'

Frank MacDougall laughed. 'You retiring or what?'

'No, but *you* are. James Machie's back. It's time to cut that deal.' John Donald waited for a reply, but the laughter had stopped. The line was dead. Frank MacDougall had gone.

1

The present

The Douglas Arms in Kinloch was busy. Bottles sparkled on the gantry and polished beer fonts stood tall on the bar as a young woman busied herself serving customers while her white-haired boss took his time, idly washing glasses whilst talking to one of his pals – *floating about*, as his overworked employee preferred to think of it.

This was karaoke night, and a good turnout was guaranteed. It was that few seconds of fame that people craved. Getting pissed on lager, whisky or vodka and stepping up to the mic. To everyone else, most participants were a source of amusement. But with a brain freed of inhibition by alcohol, closed eyes and even the tiniest imagination – for a moment – anyone could be Elvis, Beyoncé or Frank Sinatra.

The man stood unsteadily on a tiny stage made of upturned beer crates and a sheet of stout plyboard. He was in full Sinatra flow. 'New York, New York'. His suit was dishevelled and there were stains down the front of his shirt.

The pool room wasn't big, but it was packed with people shouting words of encouragement, or indeed the reverse.

Regardless, the singer carried on, perspiration dripping down his face, the notes in a higher register as flat as a pancake.

Brian Scott missed the bridge by three beats and was soon desperately trying to catch up with the words as they scrolled across the screen in front of him.

'Away tae fuck!' shouted a disgruntled punter, his hand cupped at his mouth by way of an improvised loudhailer.

Scott, having given up on his race to catch up with the rest of the song, squinted in his direction. 'What did you say?' he slurred.

'Ho-ho,' shouted his tormentor, nudging his friend with an elbow. 'Look at that polis, he's steaming!'

A chorus of laughter accompanied this remark as the man in charge of the karaoke machine decided enough was enough, cut the music and tried to grab the microphone from Scott's sweaty hands.

'Hey! What's your game, pal?' said Scott. 'I've no' finished my song yet.'

'By public demand, you have!' The host managed to wrest the mic from Scott's grip, and the policeman was sent flying.

This was great sport for the rest of the drinkers in the Douglas Arms. They'd come to either partake in the karaoke or watch their friends make fools of themselves; seeing a drunken detective sprawled on the floor was more entertainment than they could have possibly wished for.

A kindly woman brushed her chortling husband aside and kneeled over Scott. 'Are you okay? You took a right tumble off thon stage.'

'Aye, I'm fine, doll.' Scott tried to get back to his feet, but fell backwards again, hitting his head against the wall.

'Malcolm, give me a hand with this poor bugger, will you?'

'And spoil all this fun – are you mental, Helen?'

Helen scowled at her spouse and leaned back over Scott. 'That's blood. You've cut your heid.'

For Scott, the room was now spinning due to a combination of his liberal alcohol intake and the blow he'd just taken. He could see the woman's lips move, but he couldn't hear what she was saying. This was partly down to the rabble, but also to the state of confusion in which he now found himself. He couldn't focus on the bodies that loomed over him, mouthing things he couldn't understand from sneering faces. Scott was suddenly back in the playground at school, lying on the ground as the older and much bigger Frank MacDougall laid into him with punch after punch. The crowd of children had formed a circle around the pair, shouting and screaming with each blow. Some of the girls turned away, upset by the violence, while the boys – anxious to be in notorious bully MacDougall's good books – roared encouragement, glad it wasn't them taking a beating on the rough concrete of the playground.

Scott lashed out at Helen with a bunched fist. She fell backwards trying to avoid the blow, the contents of her handbag spilling across the sticky floor. Thinking he had beaten off Frank MacDougall, Scott forced himself up the wall to his feet, just as a large man with a beer gut caught him by the collar.

'Hey, take your hands off me. I'm a police officer.' He tried to focus.

'I don't care if you're the chief constable, you bastard. You've just floored my missus.' The man aimed a punch at Scott's face, but even in his state of drunkenness instinct bred in the cobbles was enough for the policeman to sway his head to one side, ensuring his attacker's fist made contact with the plasterboard wall, leaving a neat dent in it.

'Machie, you bastard!' roared Scott. He drew back his head and butted his attacker on the cheek.

People piled in, some intent on breaking up the brawl, others anxious to get in a kick at one or other of the combatants. What had started out as a tuneless night of karaoke had turned into a fully fledged pub brawl.

Willie Archibald, the owner of the Douglas Arms, now saw fit to intervene.

'Hurry up, man!' shouted the karaoke host, standing with his arms outstretched in an effort to protect his equipment from those caught up in the mêlée. 'This shit costs a fortune. And you're paying for any damages, Willie.'

Old Gavin MacKenzie, deaf as a post, had been sitting near a speaker in order to appreciate the abysmal quality of the singing. He was now alarmed to see it toppling towards him. Inebriated as he was, he managed to dive away from the tumbling piece of equipment, but it pinned him to the floor by the ankle. Sadly, his cries of pain went unnoticed amidst the turmoil.

'Right, that's enough!' shouted Willie as he waded into the action, his white beard and hair seemingly at odds with his black eyebrows. He pushed his way forward to Scott, who seemed to be at the centre of the battle. 'Right, Mr Scott, time you were away home.'

'Fuck off, you fat bastard!' shouted Scott as he pushed away the man who'd punched the wall. He was about to square up to the proprietor of the hostelry when two uniformed police officers appeared.

'Right, sergeant, time to go.' Scott felt himself being dragged by powerful arms through the unruly clientele of the Douglas Arms.

'I'm an inspector, you duffer,' he shouted as his colleagues ushered him from the pool room where the karaoke was being held and out into the main public bar.

'You got busted back to sergeant, don't you remember, Brian?' This voice was almost a whisper.

Scott narrowed his eyes as he looked at the man who had just imparted this unexpected information. 'Shaw, it's yourself. Away and arrest that fucking Machie. He tried tae punch me right in the coupon!'

'We're going this way,' replied Sergeant Shaw as he and Constable Murphy hauled the wriggling detective past the regulars at the bar.

From Scott's perspective, everything was still a tumble of confusion. He looked along the line of drinkers as he was being manhandled out of the pub. Most, being no strangers to the odd altercation in this premises, were ignoring what was going on, while others just laughed, talking to drinking companions behind their hands.

But one man stuck out.

As Scott stared, the old man raised his head. His face was long, thin and drawn, his pallor an unhealthy grey, combining to make his high cheekbones look even more prominent. The expression in his striking blue eyes was sad. He looked almost lost, defeated somehow.

'Hey, stop! I know that guy.' Scott stared wide-eyed at the old man.

'Come on, Brian,' said Sergeant Shaw, and with the help of the younger cop he managed to force Scott out of the Douglas Arms and into the fresh, cold air of a winter evening in Kinloch.

2

A date night: this was a place they'd come to in their marriage. But the couple had decided they wanted to take the advice of their counsellor, so here they were. The restaurant was on the corner of Main Street and Long Road. It was good, the very best Kinloch had to offer, but between the pair at the corner table the genial atmosphere was lost.

'Forty-two.'

'Forty-two – what do you mean?'

'That's how old my uncle Walter was when he died. I've been thinking about him lately.' Daley patted his chest. 'His heart – of course.'

Liz raised her eyes and sighed. 'Is this all we'll ever talk about from now on, your heart?'

'No, I was just trying to make conversation. It's not as though you're saying anything, is it?' The big man stuck his fork in a piece of fish with intent.

'Fabulous. We're arguing about nothing now.' She looked across to a table where a young couple, clearly besotted with each other, were sitting. As the young man spoke, his girlfriend looked almost entranced, her mouth moving in a silent echo of what he was saying.

'Look over there, Jim. We used to be like that.' Liz nodded to the table across the room.

'I was like that, you mean.'

'Sorry?'

'I was the one with the puppy-dog eyes. You – well, I don't know what you were doing.'

'Meaning what?' Liz's big eyes were suddenly ablaze.

Daley shrugged.

'No, I want you to tell me what you mean by that.'

'I just said it. It doesn't *mean* anything.'

'Everything you say means something. You're as deep as the ocean. I never know what you're thinking. It's always been the same.'

'Aye, but I've always got a good idea what you're thinking, and it's not about me,' Daley said under his breath.

Liz sat back in her chair, shaking her head. 'Oh, here we go. It always goes back to the same thing.'

'What?'

'You accusing me of infidelity, while you're still mooning after that poor dead girl!'

The four people at the table next to them stopped talking momentarily and stared at the Daleys.

'Sorry, can I help you?' Liz said sarcastically.

Quickly, the foursome looked away, muttering, while making sure not to make eye contact with this outspoken woman for a second time.

Daley leaned across the table. 'Do you have to?'

'Oh, I forgot, sorry. My husband has a position in society of which we must be mindful. It wouldn't do for anyone to know he was fucking one of his colleagues. That she died driving to break it off with her boyfriend in order to take up

14

with a man twice her age.'

Daley slammed the knife and fork down on his plate with a clatter. 'I'm not going to go through all this again. I'm not going to retaliate, because there's no point. You clearly think that you've never put a foot wrong in our marriage. Though I can't imagine why you've come to that conclusion.'

'So, that was you not retaliating?'

'I mean, I'm not going into specifics. In any case, there're too many to count, never mind talk about.' Daley reached for his wine and drained the glass.

Silence reigned for a few moments as Liz picked at her salad.

'And round we go again.' Daley filled his glass almost to the brim with red wine.

'You don't want this to work, do you?' For the first time that evening there was a look of hopelessness in Liz's eyes, a genuine sadness.

Jim Daley shrugged. 'We just go over the same stuff, over and over. I tried to say that to the counsellor, but neither she nor you were listening.'

'I want another baby.'

Daley stared at her for a few moments and then burst out laughing.

'Wow! That's the first time you've laughed at anything I've said for years. I'm flattered.'

'You really think that us having another child is going to fix things? If it wasn't for the wee man, we'd have split up long ago.'

'I've never thought that way.'

'Liz, we were apart, remember?'

'That was down to you – *remember*?'

'We might as well get the bill and leave. All we're doing is ruining the night for everyone else here.'

'You agreed to come.'

'You wanted me to, so yes, I did agree to come. But I knew it was a waste of time – and money, by the way.'

'Oh, drag yourself out of the council estate, will you? You'd think we were living hand to mouth the way your family did. We've got plenty of money.'

'No thanks to you.'

'I bring up your child, or hadn't you noticed?'

Before Daley could say something he knew he'd regret, he spotted the distinctive figure of Sergeant Shaw winding his way between the tables in the busy restaurant.

'Here we go,' said Liz, following her husband's gaze. 'Calling all cars.'

'Alasdair,' said Daley with a forced smile. 'What's up?'

Shaw leaned in to Daley. 'I'm so sorry to bother you, sir – Mrs Daley.' He smiled across at Liz, who chose to take a drink and ignore him completely. 'We have a situation.'

'One that needs me there right now?'

'I think it would be for the best, sir.'

'What is it? Surely you can give me a clue?'

'It's concerning – the problem is to do with DS Scott, sir.' Though Shaw related this awkwardly, the look on his face said it all.

Liz sighed and raised her hand to attract the waiter.

'Yes, madam? How can I help you?'

'Can we have the bill, please?'

The waiter looked at the half-empty plates with some dismay. 'I hope there was nothing wrong with your meals?'

16

'No, I have to attend to a police matter. The food was beautiful,' said Daley.

'My husband has to deal personally with every drunk they arrest,' said Liz with a very false smile.

DCI Jim Daley left the police car and punched the entry code into the security door at the rear of Kinloch police office. Liz had gone home in a taxi without further comment. He stormed along the corridor to the family room, where he stopped and kicked the door open, a flustered Shaw in his wake.

On a long sofa lay Brian Scott. One of his shoes was discarded on the floor alongside his jacket. The room stank of stale alcohol and echoed to the sound of Scott's loud snoring.

Daley, his face set in anger, shook his DS vigorously. 'Brian, wake up!'

One of Scott's eyes opened, then the other. He mashed his mouth and grimaced, putting a hand to the back of his head. 'Fuck me, I feel as though I've been kicked by a horse.'

'Sit up!' Daley commanded.

'Okay, calm your jets, big man. Hey, Alasdair, any chance o' a coffee, buddy? I've got a heid like Barrheid.'

Before Scott could reply Daley leaned over and grabbed his shirt collar. A button shot off and landed on the carpet beside Scott's shoe and jacket. 'You've done it this time, Brian. And there's not a thing I can do!' He looked furious as he stared into Scott's puffy face.

'What are you on about noo, Jimmy?'

'You were in a fight earlier. Do you remember?'

'Nah, I went tae the Douglas Arms for a wee drink, that's all.'

'Yes, that's where you were fighting. You threw a punch at a woman and head-butted her husband. Does that jog your memory?'

'Ho! Hold the bus, big man.' Scott blinked into Daley's face. 'Aye, and take your hands off me while you're at it.'

Daley stood, his face still florid with rage. 'You don't remember, do you?'

'Ach, gie me a break. You would think you were Snow fucking White, the way you go on. Lucky I'm no' a dentist, eh? I'd be lying half deid on a boat. Does that jog your memory, *sir*?'

Daley turned to Shaw. 'Get him out of here and put him in a cell until the morning.'

'Sir?' Shaw looked perplexed.

'Just do as I say!' Daley stormed out of the room, almost taking the door off its hinges as he went.

'Who rattled his cage?' said Scott, still blinking in the bright light of the room.

'This isn't funny, Brian. That MacConnachie bloke made a complaint. You know as well as I do what happens now – especially these days.'

'It's my word against his – so what?'

'There are over thirty witnesses, Brian.'

Scott lay back heavily on the sofa. 'I need a coffee before I can cope wae this shit.'

'Okay, but I'll need to take you to one of the cells. You heard the gaffer.'

'At least get me the coffee first, eh?'

Shaw sighed and headed off to fetch it.

Brian Scott massaged his temples. His head was aching, and he felt the familiar squeamishness and sense of impending doom that always accompanied the onset of one of his mammoth hangovers.

He desperately tried to remember the events that Daley had described, but all he could recall was entering the Douglas Arms and chatting to a man at the bar. After that, everything was a blur.

'I miss you, Annie,' he whispered to himself, aware that the dead barmaid from the County Hotel would never have allowed him to get into such a state. He wiped a tear from his eye at the memory of her.

These thoughts brought on the post-drink melancholy to which he was well accustomed. The familiar feeling of dislocation and anxiety was making his head ache even more. Then something occurred to him. A face passed before his mind's eye. A face from long, long ago. The memory had penetrated the fug in Scott's brain, but it gave him no pleasure.

He rushed out into the corridor. 'Jimmy, Jimmy, where are you?' For the first time in a long time, Brian Scott felt the old fear.

3

The big man was sitting in Ian Macmillan's office at the top of the County Hotel. He was tall and broad-shouldered, a scar on his right cheek. He looked around the well-organised room and nodded with pleasure. A large computer screen sat on an antique desk next to a bundle of papers neatly stacked by a stapler, almost as though it had been meticulously measured into place. Pens, pencils, a short ruler and a pair of scissors stood to attention in a black box beside a landline telephone. The keyboard in front of the computer was of the expensive mechanical variety, with keys colour-coded to ease typing. At the far side of the desk was a photograph of a good-looking middle-aged woman sitting on a leather chair, flanked by a younger female and a teenage boy.

'Your family?' Vernon Teague didn't so much sit on a chair as lounge on it. He was tall – almost six feet four inches. He had tidily cropped dark hair and, despite the passage of a hard life, his pale face exuded no little intelligence. Though he looked relaxed, something about the man was quietly threatening, intimidating, almost.

That was the way Ian Macmillan felt, at least. But he knew more about Teague's background than most, and he cursed the day he'd met the enforcer.

'Yes, it's my ex-wife and children.' Macmillan felt his throat constrict. He wished he'd had the forethought to put the photograph in a drawer before his visitor arrived. He'd always tried to keep his personal life as far away from the criminal fraternity as he could, but it had been a hopeless task. He tried to compose himself.

Teague leaned forward to pick up the frame and held it before him. He ran his finger across the glass, hovering over the image of Macmillan's daughter. 'She's a pretty gal, eh?'

Macmillan cleared his throat. 'Yes, she is.' He could hear the tremble in his own voice and hated it.

Teague placed the picture back on the desk, making sure that it was in the same position as before. 'That's what you want from a family: a beautiful daughter, a strong son and a wife far away!' He laughed heartily at this observation.

'My wife and I are estranged.'

'I know.' The statement was flat, delivered with no emotion.

Macmillan felt as though enough time had been wasted in this pointless small talk. In any case, he was anxious to move the conversation away from his family. 'I've done as you asked. The room has been altered to your requirements, by tradesmen from Glasgow, not Kinloch. Paid for by cash, as you wanted.'

'That is good. But I worry about this place. Like all small towns, people want to know everything – they have big noses, yeah?' He tapped his own nose by way of emphasis.

'I keep myself to myself.'

'Not true, my friend.'

'Sorry?'

'Your manager – her death – got everyone talking.' The Londoner sighed.

'You can't blame me for that!' Macmillan could feel his colour rising.

'I can blame you for what I want.'

'She thought the place was hers, not mine.'

'What's done is done, Ian. The milk is spilled, so no point crying over it. But remember, we want no undue attention on this place – on you. You are supposed to be a respectable businessman returning to his family home – saving this hotel for a grateful community. We want people to like you, to trust you. This is not how I feel things are at this moment. Small communities always take an interest in new people, especially when they appear to be rich.' He smiled broadly. 'But we both know that you're not rich. In fact, if it wasn't for us, you'd have no money at all. No money to spend on your lovely family, for instance.' He nodded to the framed photograph back on the desk. 'No money to pay for your divorce, or to spend on your strong son or pretty daughter.' He let his gaze linger on the image again. 'That doesn't come cheap – none of it.'

Macmillan sighed. He stared at the frozen face of his wife. They had been happy once, a partnership in every sense of the word. She was as ambitious for her children and their trucking business in Canada as he had been.

But his happiness had soon waned when Kristina began to mix with other prominent business folk in Toronto. Suddenly, she wanted expensive holidays, cars, designer clothes. She'd persuaded him to buy a house they couldn't afford on the lake. Yes, it was a beautiful home, with stunning views and acres of land where the children could be children and they could relax as a couple. But leisure and relaxation had never been high on Ian Macmillan's list of priorities, and in any case Kristina just wanted the place to show off to her friends at endless dinner parties.

In the end, he supposed, all Kristina aspired to was the high life. Meanwhile, he wanted to expand a business, to be successful – to be the best. Too many late nights in the office, too many business trips, too little time spent with his family. It was an old story, with the old almost inevitable consequences.

And still he'd failed. Now here he was with a man who terrified him, in a place – regardless of family history and blood ties – he could never think of as home.

'Why here and not Canada, Vernon? If you want somewhere something won't be noticed, there's no better place.'

'It has to be here, in this country. Your job isn't to worry about things like that. It's to do what you're told. We need places for our people to go when things get tough in London, or Berlin or Paris – wherever. After all, who is going to look for anyone in this shithole town?' He stood, looming over Macmillan, who cowered in his chair. 'Make things right in this place. Do you understand? No more *suicides*. Do you get me?'

'Yes. I'm sorry. I was just thinking aloud.'

'That is a dangerous habit to form.' The big man's face brightened. 'In any case, I've frozen my bollocks off for too long. I don't want to do the same thing in Canada.'

'I just don't like it here. My employee – the one who died – that's made me unpopular. I've even had the police asking questions.'

'We know. That's why you have the satellite phone and access to our encrypted sites on the dark web.'

'Yes, but I'm still not sure that I can make it work – whatever it is,' he added in a rush.

In a flash, Vernon Teague swung his arm through the air and caught Macmillan with a vicious back-handed slap to the face, knocking him from his chair. The hotelier yelped in pain and put his hands out in front of him to fend off any further blows. None came.

Teague kneeled over him, propping himself up on one of his long limbs. 'You can do this – you *have* to do this. Don't work too hard trying to turn this place into the "destination" I read about in your brochures. This is a quiet country hotel with a few visitors, the emphasis being on *quiet*. But I don't need to tell you this, do I?'

He stood back up to his full height. 'Now, I have some distilleries to visit. I love malt whisky. And after all, I am a tourist in your *lovely* town. I must leave you to get on with the many things you have to do. I'll be in touch.' With that, he swept out of the office and closed the door quietly behind him, leaving Ian Macmillan lying on the floor, wiping blood from his lip.

Vernon Teague left the hotel and strolled down Main Street. His sheer presence turned heads. But, as had been drummed into him long ago, the trick to hiding in plain sight was to be courteous and pleasant. This in mind, he nodded cheerfully to a pair of elderly ladies. 'It is a lovely day, don't you think?'

The women returned his smile, though not quite agreeing with him on the weather. For them, it was cold, with a biting wind. But for Teague it was a welcome break from the big city.

The Londoner walked to the harbour. The smell of diesel, fish and the tang of the sea was strong. He looked out across the loch to the distant island at its head. As a former sailor, he appreciated what a fine haven this was for craft seeking safety in a storm. He idly wondered about the depth of the water in the narrow channel through which the loch was accessed. Once a sailor, always a sailor, he reasoned.

He pulled a basic-looking mobile phone from his pocket and pressed the screen twice.

'Hello.'

He recognised the voice immediately. And though he'd never met the person on the other end of the call, it was hard not to smile. This little sideline was making him more money than he'd ever expected. He'd soon have the holiday home in Spain. Yes, Ian Macmillan was an asset, a pawn in a dangerous game. But for now, he was little more than a sleeper, lying in wait for the time he could be of use. And who cared, or would ever know, that he, Vernon Teague, was using that spineless man to earn some extra money?

'All is in hand,' he said now. 'Whenever you want to begin, you begin. I have a secure location.'

'You're sure?'

'Ha! What do you think I am? Of course it's ready. Take the time you require, but as soon as you wish. And remember, if you need any other little favours, I'm at the end of this phone – day and night.'

'Good.'

'The money – the next instalment. I want it in my bank no later than tomorrow.'

'It will be with you within the next two hours. Check it.'

'To be sure I will.'

Teague was about to say more when the line went dead. He shrugged, checked the time on his Rolex Explorer and decided to take a walk along the loch. This was the easiest money he'd ever made. Though he couldn't fathom why anyone was willing to pay such a sum for his services, he didn't really care. If anyone took a fall, it would be his paymaster or Ian Macmillan. Some parts of what he'd had to do had been distasteful, but that was his business. There was little room for sentiment in his world.

Teague breathed deeply and set off on his walk. Still, he thought, it wasn't the worst place in the world in which to hide.

'Scotland the bloody brave!' he said to himself, attracting a questioning look from an old man. 'You okay, sir?' He smiled, and went in search of a distillery.

4

Ella Scott was trying to keep busy. Anything to avoid thinking about her husband, because thinking meant worrying, and she was all worried out. Yes, she'd married a man she'd known to be a heavy drinker. Brian Scott's family all drank too much ... well, most of them did.

But these were different days. The busy pubs of yesteryear were as quiet as the tomb now. People had found other ways to entertain themselves. They sat in front of Netflix or YouTube rather than going out on the batter every night and arriving home with a fish supper or a kebab. Come to that, the world had changed; there was no doubting it. Drunkenness had once been part and parcel of existence. Everyone Ella had grown up around had a social life predicated on a *couple of drinks*. It was a euphemism nobody really believed, but the whole thing was unremarkable, and few paid any attention to warnings from the government about their levels of alcohol consumption. The fact that Glasgow had one of the highest rates of premature mortality in the western world was put down to poor genes, hard work, tough living conditions or simple bad luck.

These days, though, everybody knew more about every-thing. All anyone had to do was type 'dangers of alcohol abuse'

27

into a search engine and a ghastly parade of prose and images flashed before their eyes: diseased livers, domestic abuse and poverty. Broken lives, ruined health, premature death. The happy nights of yesteryear down the pub now seemed like the gateway to hell.

For anyone with any sense – and Ella Scott was by no means stupid – the message was clear. Drink too much and you'll die. This only fuelled the worries over her husband.

But Brian Scott had always been a happy drunk. He didn't come home and abuse his family like many men she knew. Yes, sometimes he could barely stand and blethered a lot of nonsense, but her own father had done the same. She remembered picking up the change he'd dropped on the floor when in his cups and spending it on chips, or the latest record in the charts, when she was a teenager.

That he'd died in his late fifties was unremarkable. Most of his friends looked much older than their years, many with early onset morbidities. That's what happened; it was the way of life. While the bereaved mourned, nobody gave it a second thought, not really. The fact their loved ones could have added another twenty years to their lives had they been able to curb the need for booze and fags was rarely, if ever, considered.

He liked a good time, eh? Aye, he was grand company. Nothing wrong wae a dram now and then. Man, he lived life to the full.

These bon mots were regularly imparted with a wink to the women in widow's weeds. But *living life to the full* really meant staring into a glass of some description while listening to the same old stories, older jokes and inane patter. This wasn't living life, it was watching it pass you by.

28

Ella Scott knew now what she hadn't thought of then. She was also well aware that her husband was hitting the bottle again, no matter how hard he tried to hide the fact. She'd found a half-empty bottle of whisky concealed at the back of the wardrobe amongst a pile of old shoes just the other day. Brian Scott only hid drink when he'd something to hide. She saw it for what it was, the tell-tale behaviour of an alcoholic. Someone who knew they were doing wrong but couldn't help themselves. Someone who was out of control.

Ella's mobile rang, taking her mind off the whole thing for a few precious seconds. But when she saw 'Liz Daley' written in bold letters on the screen, she almost didn't take the call.

'Hello, Liz. How are you?' she said with a forced smile in her voice.

'Take a wild guess.' The woman on the other end of the phone was well spoken – posh, many would have considered. But Ella knew her well – had known her for more years than she cared to remember. Their relationship had often been frosty, only perpetuated by the closeness of their respective husbands. But Liz's suffering at the hands of an attacker had brought them closer in recent years.

Even so, Ella knew what that this call would consist of: her making the right noises while Liz trotted out her marital woes. Usually, she would have just shrugged this off, congratulating herself for doing at least something good for someone. But today she just let Liz ramble on about the state of her marriage to Jim Daley without really listening. She'd heard it all before, and as long as she made the appropriate sympathetic noises when Liz paused for breath, there was little need to focus her mind fully on the one-sided conversation.

'But I shouldn't be bending your ear, Ella. I know you've got enough on your plate after Brian's antics at the weekend. I don't think I've ever seen Jim so worried about him.'

Ella, who had been thinking absently about a new washing machine, was suddenly brought straight back to the here and now. 'Sorry, what did you say, Liz?'

'Oh, I know you're used to it. And let's face it, Brian is like the Teflon man when it comes to surviving these things.'

'Sorry, I haven't a clue what you're on about, hun.'

Sensing she'd put her foot in it, Liz tried to back-pedal and change the subject, but Ella Scott wanted to hear just what *antics* her husband had been up to at the weekend.

'Listen, I shouldn't have said anything. It's none of my business. It's just that Jim and I were out for a meal when it happened.'

'*What* happened?'

'I'm sure it's nothing.' Liz was desperate to find an excuse to hang up, but nothing came to mind.

'In the name o' the wee man, just tell me what you're on aboot?'

Ella Scott listened as Liz revealed the events of the previous Friday night. The detective's wife had thought nothing of her husband's arriving home at six in the morning looking tired and dishevelled. He was a police officer and unusual hours were the name of the game – always had been. She would never have guessed that he'd been in a bar brawl, despite an obvious cut on his head.

'I'm sorry, Ella. I shouldn't have said anything. I hope I haven't upset you.' Liz paused. 'You didn't hear this from me, okay?'

'Aye, don't worry aboot it. Listen, I'll need to go.' Ella ended the call without waiting to hear any more of Liz's pleas to keep her name out of it. She sat down heavily on the sofa, her head in her hands, an ache of despair in her throat and a tear in her eye.

'Here we go again,' she said balefully.

5

Moving to a new place was always stressful. He knew that better than most, for in his long life he'd had to move on much more frequently than was desirable. First, moonlight flits, as they called them. His mother, desperate to escape her creditors, would wake him and his younger sister in the middle of the night. Before they knew it, the place that had been home disappeared in the rear window of a taxi or a friend's car as they headed to a new one, often in another town.

But that was a long time ago – a very long time ago.

He turned on the hot tap on the bathroom sink, passing his hand underneath the flow of water to make sure it was warm enough for his shave. He squeezed the top of the can and watched as the white shaving foam curled into his left palm, then dampened his face and applied the foam to his stubbly chin. Only at this point did he look in the mirror.

He'd always imagined that growing old would be accompanied by mute acceptance. Elderly men he'd known when he was young – workmates, drinking buddies and the like – always appeared to be content, despite the wrinkles, absence of teeth, rheumy eyes, bent backs and fingers twisted by arthritis and hard work.

But this quality had passed him by. Every time he looked into the mirror, he recoiled, recognising only his blue eyes in the face of the old man who stared back, mouth agape.

To combat this melancholy, he'd begun to think of the image in the mirror as someone else entirely, not his reflection. Another tactic was to screw up his eyes, to make the unwelcome image before him harder to see. But that only ended in an accidental nick to his cheek with the razor.

The thought of growing a beard had also crossed his mind. But when he'd tried, the patchy grey whiskers that sprouted from his face made him look even more ancient. They were soon removed before anyone else had the misfortune of having to take in the full horror of it all.

Shave over, he rinsed his face, dried it with a towel and rubbed a wrinkled hand across his chin. Where once there had been taut smooth flesh was now loose, broken and blemished skin, hanging in folds from his scraggy neck.

It was another of the cruel tricks that life played on you, he thought. As a child, a teenager and even a young adult, the world and all it had to offer seemed endless – filled with possibilities, excitement and thrills. But as the years went by, two notable things happened. The reality of existence was living from hand to mouth, day to day, week to week. If you could scrape together enough money to feed, clothe and house yourself and your family, you should be grateful. But by the time that was done, the only refuge was sleep and booze.

He thought back to Monday mornings a very long time ago. Grey-faced men had trooped into the Glasgow shipyard where he'd learned his trade. Canvas satchels slung over their shoulders contained a life support system: a flask of tea, some meat paste sandwiches in a plain bread wrapper, baccy or a packet of cigarettes.

Simple pleasures for hard times.

The man buttoned on a shirt that had seen better days, then pulled a woollen sweater over his head. This flat had central heating, but even so, the winter chill made his old bones ache. He walked through to the living room, where too many boxes sat still unpacked, though many could stay that way. Sitting on a threadbare armchair, he pulled one towards him. Discarding a pile of rolled-up newspapers, he eventually came to the important contents of the box. These were his precious things: not expensive ornaments, beautiful works of art or gold and silver adornments. No, just a few photographs he took everywhere with him. One by one, he removed them from the box.

In a black and white image, a tall thin young man stood with his arms round a pretty girl, both of them smiling broadly. His hair had been worked into a DA cut, curling up like an ice cream cone and held in place by lashings of Brylcreem. Her hair looked fair in monochrome, but he could remember its deep golden lustre. He could still smell the sweet scent of the shampoo she used. How he loved to bury his head in her hair, to luxuriate in it and the closeness to the woman he loved with all his heart.

What would she think of him now, he wondered.

There were five framed photographs in all. Little moments in time, remembered forever on flimsy, crinkled paper: the only thing that saved them from oblivion, from the death of remembrance. He held them in a pile in one hand and forced himself out of the chair with the other to the sound of the cracking of his knees. Taking his time, he placed these little pieces of his life around the sparsely furnished room: on the cracked mantelshelf above the cheap electric fire, the scratched table that sat beside his chair, the cabinet with the stain on its side, a broken-down sideboard from another time that was riddled with the tell-tale pinprick holes left by woodworm.

He stepped back, looking from one photograph to the next. At least this sad shithole of a place had something of his life in it now. For what that was worth.

He sat back down on the chair. There were two items left in the box. One was a large wooden crucifix. He'd converted to Roman Catholicism almost two decades ago. He placed the crucifix on the floor, taking time to study the tortured face of the man on the cross. He'd have to find a nail on which to hang it over the fireplace.

The last thing he removed from the packing case was a metal box roughly the size and shape of those used to carry new shoes. He delved into the pocket of his trousers, panicking as always that he'd lost the small key. But there it was.

The old man turned the tiny key in the lock of the strongbox. The lid creaked as he lifted it open. Inside were the documents he'd fought to save from another. He stared at the box for a moment, then closed and locked the box. Could good come of all these years of pain? He hoped so.

He thought back to the weekend. He'd been careless, but how was he supposed to know he'd stumble into one of the only men for miles around who was likely to recognise him?

But such was life. It didn't change anything. In any case, though the drunkard being carried out of the bar by the two burly policemen had stared at him, he had seen no sign of recognition in his gaze, despite the man's protests to the contrary. Such was his state of inebriation, it seemed unlikely this face from the past would remember anything about it when he woke the next morning.

He sat back and looked at his photographs again.

6

Scott was sitting in the canteen at Kinloch police office when his mobile rang. He noted Ella's name and decided to ignore her. The atmosphere between them had been frosty to say the least over the past few months. She wanted him to stop drinking, but he didn't want to – it was a clear stand-off.

But Brian Scott had more to worry about than conflict with his wife. Daley had summoned him earlier that morning. None of the usual banter had passed between them. It was almost as though they were strangers. His superior wanted him in the office at ten o'clock sharp, and that was it.

Scott knew that he was going to be lectured about his behaviour at the weekend. But as far as he was concerned, all he'd done was defend himself, though the exact details of what had happened in the Douglas Arms that evening were hazy, if he was being honest with himself.

Brian Scott was no stranger to heavy seas. He'd been carpeted before more senior officers in his early days in the job than most police officers saw in an entire career. This was just more heavy weather that would, eventually, blow over. He and Jim Daley would be back on good terms before the end of the day, he was sure of it.

But something darker, deeper, was nagging at his mind.

Scott sighed as he took another sip of hot coffee, mentally preparing himself for the first roar of the storm.

Inside Daley's glass box, the atmosphere was not one of resigned acceptance. On the contrary, one look at the big detective's face was enough to confirm that his current mood was dark.

'Oh, come on, sir,' he shouted into the phone. 'It was a scuffle in a bar. From what I've managed to glean, DS Scott was the innocent party. He was defending himself.'

Superintendent Saunders, the senior officer in charge of discipline in their division of Police Scotland, notoriously lacked empathy. Yet again he was proving it. 'The rules on this are clear, Jim. A complaint has been made and it will be addressed. It's as simple as that.'

'Yes, by all means investigate the matter. But I promise, you'll come to the same conclusion I have.'

Saunders sighed on the other end of the line. 'But this isn't just an isolated incident, is it? I nearly gave myself eyestrain reading DS Scott's disciplinary record yesterday. It took me the whole bloody day.'

'So, you'll also be aware of his commendations and the fact he's been shot twice in the line of duty?'

'Yes, yes. I'm very aware of Brian's heroism; that's never been in question. But that doesn't excuse him from his many misdemeanours. The fact we had to remove his acting inspector rank only a few weeks ago is testament to the fact that we have an officer who is out of control. Surely you must see that, DCI Daley?'

'That was just a misunderstanding. The woman in question was Swedish, and she misinterpreted what Brian – DS Scott – was saying.'

'She was Danish, and her English is probably much better than ours and certainly better than DS Scott's. She knew exactly what "stupid cow" meant.'

'We've only got her word for that. Anyway, she was driving on the wrong side of the road – she could have killed someone.'

'As you well know, our rules and regulations are there for a reason. I know you have extra responsibility with Chief Superintendent Symington's extended leave, Jim. But it is what it is.'

'You sound like some cardboard gangster.' Daley's tone was dismissive.

'I sound like some cardboard gangster, *sir.*' In return, Saunders's tone was as dry as dust. 'If it's worth anything, I was absolutely against retaining you in your current role after your little incident with the dentist a while back.'

'Just as well you didn't make that decision. But I've noted what you've said, and I'll be contacting my Federation rep.'

'Enough of this nonsense. I don't have the time for it, DCI Daley. DS Scott is suspended as of now. I'll send a team down to investigate the matter. I expect you to afford them any support and courtesy required.'

Daley was about to reply but the line was already dead. Though he'd done his best to defend Brian Scott, he'd known there could only be one outcome. He picked up his mobile and dialled Scott's number.

'Aye, Jimmy, what's the score?'

'I hope for your sake you're somewhere in this building, Brian.'

'Aye, I'm in the canteen.'

'Well, get your arse in here – now!'

Daley drummed his fingers as he awaited Scott's arrival.

He'd been genuinely angry with his old friend on the night Shaw had carried him out of the Douglas Arms. But he realised that shouting at Brian Scott was unlikely to have any lasting effect. It was time to address the real problem, not just dance around it.

A knock rattled the door. Scott appeared in the glass box looking sullen and tired. Huge bags under his eyes were exaggerated by dark circles. His pallor was unhealthy. Daley noticed his hands tremble as he placed his mobile on the desk.

'Well, it's finally happened.' Daley was stern but calm.

'What's happened, big man?'

'You're suspended. I'll need your warrant card.'

Scott stared at Daley as though he'd never seen him before. 'Are you serious?'

'Deadly.'

Scott shook his head. 'There's nae justice in the world. You half kill a man and you're still sitting in the big chair. I defend myself and here you are dishing out the tawse to me.'

'Oh, don't worry. I've heard all about my lucky escape from Superintendent Saunders already this morning. When I was trying to defend you, incidentally.'

Scott lowered his head. 'Sorry, I shouldn't have said that.'

'No, you shouldn't. But let's be honest, we both know that you've been doing a lot of things lately that you shouldn't.'

'It's been a rough time, you know that.'

'Annie, you mean?'

'Aye, Annie, of course. But Willie, too. My boy could have been killed or jailed for life. Dae you think that doesnae matter to me?'

'I know it does.' Daley leaned forward in his chair. 'But tell

40

me – be honest now – at what point in your life, or the lives of anyone you know, has drink make a bad situation better?'

Scott pursed his lips, staring into space. 'These buggers that get lost in the snow, what aboot them?'

'What?'

'They big dugs get sent oot tae rescue them. There's a wee barrel o' brandy roon their necks. If it wasnae for that, you'd have folk lying deid all o'er the Alps. That's a fact, Jimmy.' Scott nodded his head vigorously in confirmation. 'Aye, and look at thon snooker player. Couldn't hold a cue unless he'd had a scatter o' bevvy. Likely, he'd have ended up stacking shelves in Tesco if it wisnae for a drink or two.'

'You're not fighting for your life in the Alps and you're not a snooker player. You're a police officer, remember?'

Scott didn't reply.

Daley opened a drawer in his desk and removed a small bundle of booklets. He thrust them across the desk at Scott.

'What's a' this?'

'Read them. Personally, I think this might be the last chance you get to save your job, Brian. Maybe the last chance you get to save your life, even.'

Scott took his reading glasses from the inside pocket of his jacket and placed them shakily on the bridge of his nose. He peered at the booklet, eyes widening in disbelief. 'Alcoholics Anonymous! Are you at the madam, big man?'

'No, I'm absolutely serious. If you show willing by knocking the drink on the head and get your shit together, then maybe – just maybe – I'll be able to convince them to keep you on.'

'Bollocks! I did nothing that cops across the country don't dae all the time. I had a night oot. Aye, maybe I'd a few too many. But how many times have you seen that, eh?

There wouldnae be a polis left on the street if every bugger got their jotters for taking a refreshment.'

'*A refreshment*? You've always loved a euphemism, Brian. Your drinking is out of control again and you know it. I can't force you to get help. And I can't save your job, either.'

Scott looked puzzled. 'What makes you think I like they tuba things?'

'A euphemism, not a euphonium!'

'Oh, right.' Scott sniffed. 'So, you're washing your hands of me, eh? I never thought I'd see the day – especially after the shit we've been through together all these years.'

Daley's temper broke. He stood and punched the desk with his fist. 'Don't come here with the nostalgia, Brian!' He managed to take hold of himself and sat back down. 'You know that's not true, Bri. But you have to listen. If not for me, for this job – for your family.'

Scott stared disdainfully at the booklets scattered before him. 'Okay, you might be right. But I don't need a room full o' alkies tae help me stay off the booze. I'll do what I did the last time. That's all I'm saying.' He gathered up the reading material and threw it back across the desk in Daley's direction.

'It's up to you, Brian.' The DCI shook his head, a sorrowful expression spreading across his face. 'And while you're busy throwing stuff, pitch me your warrant card while you're at it. I'll need your mobile, too.'

Scott shook his head. 'It's at home somewhere – my warrant card.' He slid the phone gently across the desk.

'I'll need it before the close of play today, Brian. And your car keys – now!'

Scott produced his keys. 'Aye, you'll get my warrant card. And dae you know what? You can keep it!'

'I know you're angry. But I'm not the enemy here.'

'I know fine. But I've had it wae a' this shit, Jimmy. This is the last straw. I'm going to cash in my chips. That's what these bastards want anyway. It's bright young things wae degrees and posh voices they're after nowadays. Me and you are over the hill. I hope you'll remember that.'

'Think carefully, Brian. You'll need to speak to Ella.'

'That's my business.' He stood and straightened his jacket. 'I'll leave the warrant card wae Shaw later. Can I go, *sir*?'

'Yes, you can go. But you know the score. Don't speak to anyone about what happened in the Douglas Arms, and don't approach anybody who has any connection with it. Okay?'

'Ha! Remember who taught you the ropes, Jimmy boy.' Scott made for the door but stopped short of opening it. He turned to Daley. 'And what aboot that other thing?'

'What other thing?'

'Big Hughie, that's what.'

'Oh, aye. You get pissed and you start seeing bogeymen round every corner. Hugh Machie, my arse. What on earth would he be doing here in Kinloch? In any case, the man must be in his eighties, if he isn't dead. Which is by far the most likely scenario.'

'I grew up wae these folk, remember? I know James Machie's faither when I see him. Watch your back, Jimmy. That's all I'm saying.'

Scott turned on his heel and left Daley's glass box, slamming the door behind him.

7

DS Shreya Dhar was busy at her desk in the crime campus at Gartcosh, the hub of Police Scotland's operations. Her job revolved round the growing problem of organised crime and its detection. This could be anything from the very worst fraud perpetrated across borders to hate crime targeted at an individual – anything. Extortion, prostitution, people-trafficking, drugs. Each month it seemed that such criminal activity increased. For their department, it was akin to standing beside the sea, trying to force back the tide by sheer force of will alone – or that was what she felt, at least.

Yes, they achieved success in many instances. But for every crime they solved, another ten would pop up in its place. Despite this, Shreya enjoyed her work, and had become especially devoted to helping the victims of racism and abuse. That she'd had some success in this made her proud, but she knew that the pride was fleeting. She had much more to achieve, she was certain. She had a real goal in mind, a passion.

For a start, though Dhar found her job interesting, it was a means to an end. She longed to be out amongst the public – away from the room of twenty or so officers, many of whom were lecherous middle-aged men, whose eyes she could feel follow her round the room. The more people convinced themselves that they now lived in a different world, the less convincing it became.

Not only was Shreya Dhar pin-sharp clever, she was young. And some older men were drawn to young women as if to a magnet. No matter how happy their lives, the yearning for something new drove them on, it seemed.

She'd grown to despise some of her colleagues, who, over the last eighteen months, had done all they could to ask her out on dates by telling stories about their masculinity. As soon as a tale began with something like *Did I tell you about the time . . .* she instantly switched off, knowing this yarn would be one of bravery and derring-do designed only to impress her.

There were some good folk about. She had especially taken to Inspector Alana Spence, who oversaw the section. She was business-like, but friendly and approachable. Dhar owed her much by way of advice and instruction.

Shreya Dhar was in the process of switching off her computer when Inspector Spence called her to the office.

Dhar closed the door behind her and stood in front of her superior. 'Take a seat, Shreya,' said Spence. She was in early middle age, married to the job and carried hard years of police work on her pale, weary face. 'You've been with us for a while, haven't you?'

'Nineteen months, ma'am,' Dhar replied.

'And before that you were in Ayrshire, then Govan, am I right?'

'Yes. I served out my probation in North Ayrshire then moved to Govan, ma'am.'

'Lovely. I'm sure you saw the other side of life?'

'Ma'am?'

'After being a student, I mean.'

'Oh yes, it was certainly a different experience. I sat my master's in criminology, but I knew I didn't want to be shackled to some desk somewhere.'

'Yet here you are shackled to a desk, Shreya.'

'But I'm learning, ma'am. And helping people.'

'That's important to you, isn't it?'

'For sure. That's why I joined up.'

'With your skills and qualifications, you could have made a lot of money in the private sector. That must cross your mind.'

'Yes, I could. But what life would I have? There's more to life than money, and I'm very happy with my salary.' Shreya eyed her boss, wondering when she'd get to the point.

'Okay. Well, we think it's time you had some more practical experience of policing under your belt at a more senior operational level. You've been promoted to DS since you've been here. It's time to take your stripes to some new places, a different challenge for a while.'

'Oh, I see.'

'Don't look so crestfallen.' Spence leaned forward. 'We need more people like you in Police Scotland. Clever, motivated, caring – it's what the job is all about. And the placement we have in mind involves the kind of work you've been doing here. And we listen. We've listened to you.'

'That sounds interesting.'

'Have a look.' Inspector Spence gestured to the large screen on the wall behind Dhar, who turned her swivel chair round to face it.

On the screen was a blown-up image of the west coast of Scotland. A portion of the map was shaded in red.

'You're looking at Argyll and some of the islands of the Inner Hebrides. I'm sure you recognise it.'

'Yes, ma'am.'

'You identified a situation here. A hotelier, I believe.'

'Yes, that's right. Ian Macmillan is his name.'

'In short, we want you to take this further. I've read your reports, so has the boss. Impressive and persuasive, I must say. It's the kind of intuition that's all too sadly lacking round here.'

'But this type of thing is usually investigated by the local cops – initially, anyway.'

'Yes, but we could do with a subtle approach in this case.'

'How subtle?'

'Very. There are a couple of old stagers down there. They have their own methods, let's say. Don't get me wrong, fabulous officers. But this might not be for them. Especially considering what you've reported.'

'So, what do I do?'

'You don't stick out. You play the game of small-town policing. But all the while, I want you to gather anything you can on this Macmillan. His phones and internet have been tapped for months, as you know.'

'Yeah. Just inane chatter about his kids, arguments with his wife and various creditors back in Canada.'

'That's it. So, he's off grid, somehow. It'll be the usual: burner phones, dark web. We need you to do the groundwork. If you're right, this guy could turn into a major asset. And we need to take down some big names – soon.'

'Okay.' Shreya Dhar shrugged. 'I can go there whenever you want.'

'Tomorrow?'

'Wow! I mean, yes – why not?'

'I was hoping you'd say that.' Spence searched about on her desk. 'Ah, here we are.' She picked up a sheet of paper and scanned it. 'The police office at Kinloch are looking for a temporary number two. They've just had a DS suspended.'

'For what?'

'Getting pissed and fighting in a pub, by the look of things. But I know the officer concerned, and if anyone can get away with something like that, he can. Brian Scott. He's a bloody legend, as well as being a dinosaur.'

'Stegosaurus?'

'No, much less sophisticated. But a bloody good cop.'

'Who's the gaffer?'

'A DCI – Jim Daley.'

Shreya looked puzzled.

'Yes, the one that's not very fond of dentists. And I don't mean missing appointments.' Spence nodded by way of confirmation.

'Oh – that DCI Daley. Yes, I've heard of him.'

'Everyone has. He and Scott come as a double act – have done for years. But that might be coming to an end if what I hear sticks.'

'Sounds like a scary partnership to break up.'

'Don't worry. This has all happened at just at the right time. DCI Daley will be briefed as to why you're really in Kinloch. But as far as everyone else is concerned, you're just filling in for a miscreant officer until things are resolved one way or the other.'

Shreya thought she detected a note of caution in Spence's voice. 'Problems?'

'Just go carefully, okay? Any sign of trouble, you pull out and we send down the heavy mob. If this is happening, it won't be small beer.' Her expression brightened. 'But then, it might just as likely be a diversion, and we've fallen for it.'

'Which is why it's best to keep the locals in the dark?'

'You've got it in one. I know Daley and Scott. We might get our man Macmillan, but it won't be low-key.' Spence shrugged. 'And it's your pigeon, you identified Macmillan. It will be good experience for you, even if nothing comes of it. Daley is as good a detective as they come. He should have gone further. I've never really understood why he didn't. I suppose his association with Scott hasn't helped. He's real old school.' Spence stood and held out her hand. 'Good luck, DS Dhar.'

8

Glasgow, 1978

The scheme in the north of Glasgow was unremarkable in many ways. Some boarded-up windows, gang tags, broken bottles, rubbish, dog shit and all manner of detritus strewn along the potholed roads.

Most of the accommodation comprised three-floor blocks of flats, some with a narrow veranda in front of single-glazed windows. A few homes – the most sought-after – were two- or three-bedroom houses, with proper back and front gardens. They were so coveted that many of the proud occupants kept their gardens neat and tidy, with freshly painted doors, a scatter of rockeries and even the odd garden gnome.

In other towns and cities – perhaps even in some parts of Glasgow – little details like this, signs of care and pride in the community in which they all lived, would be despised. But not so here. On this street, the spirit of the old Glasgow still flourished. This was a place where people held their heads high and one family helped another, despite the poverty into which they were thrust by strikes, redundancy and general decline. Neat lawns sat next to derelict properties covered in graffiti. The latter was the city council's problem. But if you

chose to try to make a decent home – in this area, at least –
you could remain reasonably confident that gangs of youths
wouldn't target your property. Some of the hardest men in
the city lay in wait behind newly painted windowsills, trim
hedges or expensive curtains.

But the scourge of illegal drugs and the mindless violence
and crime that accompanied them were always just in sight,
both physically and metaphorically. A few streets away, the
roads looked like bomb sites.

It was a warm summer afternoon, and many were out on
their verandas or little patches of garden. Loud music – the
latest New Wave offering – was blaring out from an open
window in one of the top floor flats. An elderly gentleman
walked his dog along the pavement, wiping his brow clean of
perspiration with a grey hankie. Two women chatted over a
garden fence, while an overweight man, dressed in brown
slacks held up by braces over a tatty vest, struggled up and
down a small rise in his front garden with an old push-pull
mower. A trio of teenagers – one girl and two boys – sat on
the pavement, one of the boys idly bouncing a football on the
hot tarmac, the heat proving too much even for the young.
The ball was like a heartbeat, its syncopated rhythm echoing
down the street off buildings and the few cars that were parked
at intervals along the way. A cat jumped into a hedge, its front
paws held out as though in flying prayer. In reality, the creature
was anxious only to make prey of a thin sparrow that took
flight just in time to avoid the deadly grasp of its sharp claws.

Apart from the fabulous weather – a rarity even in summer
on the west coast of Scotland – all was normal, humdrum.

Then, as though choreographed, the music stopped, as did
the man mowing his lawn. He coughed and sat down with no

little struggle on the low bank on which he'd been toiling. He wiped his forehead with the back of his hand, breathing heavily after his exertions.

It was in this relative silence – apart from the ever-present underscore of distant city traffic – that raised voices could be heard. The women stopped gossiping and turned their eyes to number thirty-three, one of the houses with a neat garden and newly painted front door.

The shouting grew louder – clearly two males arguing, the language they used not for the faint-hearted. There was the crash and tinkle of smashing glass, followed by the yell of a woman who was clearly trying to put a halt to whatever stramash was taking place behind closed doors but open windows.

The teenagers a few yards down the street stopped bouncing the ball and listened intently. They, like everyone else, knew to whom the raised voices belonged, and eagerness to learn the outcome of this battle of expletives overcame any flight response that would have perhaps been more practical.

When silence broke out, one of the women shook her head over the garden fence at her neighbour. She was about to speak when, with a crack that sounded almost like the report of a rifle, the red front door of number thirty-three burst open and the slim figure of a young man tumbled down two steps and on to a garden path. Behind him followed a tall man, his muscles bulging under a white open-necked shirt. Even from across the street where the two women stood gaping, the pulse of a vein on his forehead was apparent.

As the younger of the two tried to struggle to his feet, the man launched a vicious kick into his ribcage. The lad rolled over on to his side with a groan, though not emitting the yell of pain that could have been expected under the circumstances.

Somehow, the youth got back to his feet, bright blond hair shining in the summer sun.

But no sooner was he upright than the older – and by far the larger – of the two took a step forward and threw a punch which connected with the blond lad's chin, sending him flying over the hedge and on to the pavement at the other side.

Calmly, the man whose fading fair hair was an echo of his son's opened the gate and made his way out on to the pavement.

'Get up, you little bastard!' he yelled.

'Fuck you,' was the weak yet defiant reply from the bloodied mouth of his victim.

The tall man with the bulging muscles kicked his son again, this time sending him rolling on to the road. 'This will keep coming until you shut the fuck up and get back in that house and apologise to your mother!'

There followed a pause. The man stood with his fists bunched, watching for another sign of defiance from his son. A woman in floods of tears appeared in the doorway. She took one look at the scene before rushing to grab her husband, desperately trying to prevent him from launching another attack on her son.

'Hughie, that's enough. Jamie can't take any mair. You've half killed him!' she wailed.

Her husband pushed her away with one arm, almost sending her tumbling to the rough ground of the path. 'Stay oot o' this! He has to learn.'

As he turned back to face his son, a look of surprise showed briefly on his face when he realised that the youth was back on his feet.

'Fuck you, Faither.' Jamie swung his arm through the air like someone throwing a javelin. Encased in his grip was a small boulder he'd found by the roadside. The blow caught the older man firmly on the side of his head, sending him staggering back in a spray of blood.

Taking his opportunity as his father staggered to keep his balance, James Machie took aim again. This time the rock he held in his fist drove into the side of his father's nose, the sickening crack of bone audible across the road. One of the women turned her head away, this scuffle no longer mere entertainment.

Now helpless, the big, strong man lay dazed on the pavement in front of his home. His son discarded the boulder and kneeled over his father. He lifted a balled fist in the air and swung it hard. Again and again the blows rained down on the older man to the syncopated sound of his son's voice.

'I-have-nothing-to-learn-from-you!' The young man forced himself from the rough pavement, taking deep breaths. He stood over his father and aimed one last kick at the side of his head. 'And my name's James, no' fucking Jamie. James Machie, okay!'

He spat on the broken figure before calmly turning on his heels and stalking down the road in long strides, like a prize fighter who'd just won the battle of his life.

But for James Machie, there were many more battles to come.

9

Brian Scott took the long route home. He had a lot to occupy his thoughts, and he knew that when he explained to Ella what had just happened between him and Jim Daley, the likelihood of getting peace to think was a remote one.

He stared at the loch for a few moments. The water was grey and cold-looking, typical for the time of year. There were no leaves on the trees, and a chill wind blew off the loch, itself tipped with white horses. The sky was grey and sullen, resentful, almost.

Scott pulled his suit jacket tight across his chest with both hands. Had he known that he'd have to walk home, he would have worn his overcoat. But the more he thought about it, the outcome of his meeting with Daley had never been in doubt. He'd gone too far, run out of rope and luck. Something in his heart told him that this was the end – the end of his career as a police officer.

Still holding his jacket tight around him, Scott leaned into the wind and turned up a narrow path that meandered deep into a steep bank of thin trees. It had once been a railway cutting and was now his quickest route home. He was cold, and now regretted taking the much longer way round to get here in order to clear his head. He'd resolved nothing he hadn't realised back at the office, and now he was chilled to the bone. At least the steep banks offered some respite from the chill wind.

Up ahead, the cutting opened out on to the road that took him past the hospital and its helipad. In another few minutes he'd be home. The main problem he faced now was how to break it all to Ella.

Ella Scott sat on her favourite armchair, a cup of untouched cold tea by her side on a small table.

As she'd been unable to reach her husband on his mobile, which was now switched off, she decided to call Kinloch police office. Shaw sounded rather sheepish as he told her that DS Scott had just left the building. When she asked where he was headed, the bar sergeant said he had no idea, though something told her he wasn't being entirely honest. Still, she was used to police officers and their ways. After living with Brian Scott for so long, nothing came as a surprise.

But he was in trouble – again – and she knew it.

Ella stared at the photograph of her son and daughter on the wall. So much had changed since that was taken. One child in America studying, the other struggling to come to terms with events that could have cost him his life or liberty.

Thinking back over the problems Will had caused himself through naivety and misplaced affection, she wondered whether she should be thankful rather than sitting alone nursing her wrath. But, Ella reasoned, one problem couldn't cancel out another. They all came along with their own particular challenges – and in her family, all too often.

She heard the key turn in the lock of the front door, and automatically reached into her handbag and lit a cigarette, before taking a drink of her tea. It was stone cold; she'd been too caught up in her own thoughts to track the passage of time. She spat it back into the mug.

'How are you getting on?' asked Brian as he appeared in the living room. He looked cold, and immediately walked across to the fire and held his hands out to warm them.

Ella had decided to say nothing, to wait and see what web of lies her errant husband would tangle himself up in before he came clean. He could have no idea about her telephone conversation with Liz Daley. Catching him in a lie would make her feel a whole lot better – for a while, at least. 'I'm just thinking about oor Will.' She paused. 'I've been trying to call you.'

'Aye, bugger me but I cannae find that damned mobile.' He was about to embellish this lie when suddenly a wave of tiredness washed over him and he slumped on to the sofa, devoid of energy.

'What's up wae you, apart fae too many late nights on the drink?'

Brian Scott gathered his courage. 'Ella, I've something to tell you.' He stared at her earnestly.

'Oh? What is it?' She tried her best to sound as innocent as possible.

'I want to leave the police – go somewhere. We've often talked aboot Spain. I'll have a pension, and we've a wee bit o' money put by, what wae my compensation payments for being shot so many times.'

'Twice.'

'Eh?'

'You were shot twice, Brian.'

'Aye, I do remember, Ella. It's no' the kind o' thing you forget in a hurry.'

57

'Well, I'm just saying, twice isnae *so many times*, is it?'

'It's twice too many, thank you. You try it and see how you get on!'

'So, what's brought all this on? Surely no' another mid-life crisis. Bugger me, you'll be having them in the auld folks' home at this rate.'

'I'm just fed up, that's all. It's been a long time.'

'Aye, it has. Good times and bad, eh?'

'A lot o' good times, right enough.'

'Apart fae a' those times you got shot.'

'Apart fae them.'

'So, that's just it. You hand in your jotters, and we jolly off to Spain. I've got to say, I wisnae expecting this.' She thought for a moment. 'What are we going to do when we get there? We might have your pension and a few bob, but that won't be enough to live oot the rest of oor lives.'

'I don't know. Maybe start a wee business o'er there.'

'Oh, what did you have in mind? A tea shop?'

'Aye, maybe.' Scott stared into space for a few moments. 'Mind you, I'm no' sure how keen they Spanish are on tea – mair coffee, is it no'?'

'And wine. They like their wine o'er in Spain.'

'Good thinking, Ella. Why don't we go the whole hog and buy a wee bar there? Wae oor savings, like.'

'A bar – you? That would be like leaving Lizzie Daley in charge of a male modelling agency! Anyway, what's Jimmy saying to all this?'

'Och, you know him: Mr Happy. The usual gloom and doom. *You cannae just up and leave me after a' these years*, that type o' thing.'

'Right, I see. So, it's nothing to do wae the fact you were

hauled oot o' the Douglas Arms at the weekend after assaulting some poor bugger?'

'What are you on aboot?' Though he tried to look earnest, Brian Scott couldn't hide the truth in his eyes.

'Brian, I had herself on the phone this morning. The usual moans aboot how miserable her life is and how Jimmy doesnae feel the same as he used to aboot her. Man, I was near cutting my ain throat.' Ella forced a smile. 'But lo and behold, just to brighten things up, she decided to tell me you were in the soup again. This time it was serious; some bugger is wanting you charged. Imagine, she thought I'd know.' Ella turned her expression into one of mock surprise. 'I don't know what made her think that, especially when you're such a lying bastard!' She picked the mug of cold tea from the table beside her and flung its contents over her husband.

'Wait a minute, Ella! You've soaked me and it's all over the sofa.' Scott tried to brush away the tea with one hand.

'Buy a bar, he says. Aye, great idea. An alcoholic wae a bar. That's bound to be a success!'

'Come on, at least hear me oot. Surely I'm entitled tae a defence?'

Ella shot out of her chair. 'No, Brian. I've made my mind up. I'm going to New York to see oor Martha.'

'That's a good idea. A wee break would fair clear oor heids o' all this hassle.'

'No, Brian. I said *I'm* going to New York. Frankly, I'm past caring what you do. Now, if you'll excuse me.'

'What? You mean you're going now? You'll have to book a flight, fill in forms. You cannae just hop on a plane to America like jumping on the number fifty-three to the Gorbals!'

'I'm going to stay wae my sister for a few weeks while I sort it all oot.'

Brian Scott stared at his wife. 'But what aboot me?'

'Huh! What about you? I'd recommend having a good bevvy and getting arrested. That's your usual solution to any problems.'

'No, I mean – I can't remember when I wasn't wae you. I wouldnae know what to dae. I love you, Ella. Plus, I cannae work that washing machine, and as for the cooker . . .'

She didn't let him finish. 'Maybe you should have thought o' that before you opened that bottle o' whisky you had hidden in the wardrobe.'

Ella strode out of the room and took the stairs two at a time, rubbing the tears from her eyes as she went.

10

Hamish looked out of the dirty window of his little cottage at the head of the loch. He had a mug of tea in his gnarled old hand as he took in the white-tipped breakers out in the sound beyond the island. As a youngster, it was the kind of weather in which he'd loved to sail. But as the years went on and mistaken notions of his own invincibility diminished, he longed for a flat calm. In this part of the world, that was by no means a regular occurrence.

He dragged himself away from the view and took a seat by the fire that roared in the hearth. On a worn red rug at his feet, Hamish the cat was curled into a ball. Even this half Scottish wildcat was getting too old to face the cold winds and the promise of heavy rain.

Hamish's gaze moved from his pet to the mantelpiece above the fireplace. Four framed photographs were arrayed along its length. His first and only love, the girl his mother had encouraged him to reject, stared out at him in monochrome. He remembered the day that picture had been taken as though it was yesterday. It was 1966 and she was standing outside the town's old cinema. She'd been the one – of that he had no doubt. But his mother was strong-willed, and he'd caved in to her stories of the imagined criminal behaviour of her family.

In the end, she'd married another fisherman and not long after emigrated to Australia. He remembered meeting her in Kinloch about twenty years later. She was tanned and plump – he barely recognised her. But still Hamish was hypnotised by her beautiful dark eyes.

That was the thing about the past – it never really went away. Any trip to a funeral would be bound to bring back memories of those who were no longer there. Meeting a son or daughter – or, more likely in his case these days, a great-grandson or great-granddaughter – with the echo of a face he'd known so well happened all the time.

He looked at the next two photographs, both black and white. In the first his mother and father were walking arm in arm down Main Street. It was back in their courting days, long before he'd been born. He loved this picture: his mother looked so beautiful and happy, his father young, strong and healthy: not the man wasted by addiction to alcohol he'd known.

The next frozen image always made him smile. There, with the *Girl Maggie* in the background, stood Sandy Hoynes, his old skipper. As always, a pipe was clenched between his teeth, almost hidden within his bushy white beard, and a curl of smoke rose above his head. The man had taught him so much about fishing and life. Hamish wished now that he'd listened to his advice on finding a wife and settling down. The moment never seemed right. And though he'd courted other girls, his heart always belonged to his first love.

And now, here he was. An old man sitting with his cat in a run-down cottage, with only memories keeping him sane.

That thought made him take in the last photograph on the mantelpiece. It was the only one in colour. He was in the bar of the County Hotel, Annie enveloping him in a tight embrace.

She was smiling broadly at the camera, while he looked mildly agitated. No doubt I was after another dram, he thought. He'd give anything to see that smile again – to see all these folk just one more time to tell them how much he loved them.

Photographs were ten-a-penny these days. He remembered the time when getting your picture taken was a real event. He recalled trying not to cut off the heads of his subjects when he struggled with his old Box Brownie camera. Hamish wasn't sure he'd ever mastered it.

But scanning the images again brought a tear to his eye. Now, it felt as though he had nothing – not even a happy place to visit for a yarn and a dram. He refused to go back into the County Hotel as long as Macmillan owned it. In any case, it could never be the same without Annie behind the bar. And while there were plentiful licensed premises in Kinloch, he never felt at home or welcome, not the way he had done with Annie in the County. These days, though he still went for the occasional refreshment, he found himself annoyed by jukeboxes, fruit machines or some of the younger clientele. It was more of a chore than a pleasure.

He picked up a paperback from the coffee table he'd made himself, adding differing numbers of old beer mats under three of its four legs just to level the thing up. The story was about a journalist on an island that he'd never heard of seeking the truth behind the disappearance of one of her ancestors. It was good, but he thought the lassie was terribly depressed. But, like him, he supposed, she had every reason to be.

As he pondered on the merit of the book, and indeed on his own worth, he started at a loud, official-sounding knock at the door. Struggling out of his chair, cursing, while Hamish the cat hissed loudly, he was ready to give any passing salesman or Jehovah's witness a piece of his mind. But when he opened it, he was pleasantly surprised to see the hulking figure of Jim Daley framed in the doorway.

'Man, it's yourself! Come away in and take a heat by the fire.'

Daley crouched under the lintel and made his way into Hamish's cottage, the familiar smells of pipe tobacco and age strangely comforting. Though the cat knew him well – the pair had stayed for a while at Daley's house on the hill – the animal still saw fit to bristle as the policeman sat on a rickety armchair that he always feared he'd break.

'You behave!' Hamish chided his namesake in between puffing his pipe into life. 'Noo, is it a cup o' tea or that damnable coffee you're after, Mr Daley?'

The policeman reached into the inside pocket of his bulky windcheater and produced a bottle of Glen Scotia malt whisky. 'I thought you might like to share a dram with an old friend, Hamish. And stop calling me "Mr Daley" – it's Jim.'

'Aye, Jim, just so. Och, I'm no' used to calling a man in such a particular job as your own by his Christian name. But I'll try.'

Daley smiled and handed the bottle to Hamish, who shuffled over to his sideboard – another piece of unlikely DIY – to find two small glasses into which he poured large drams.

'You'll be off duty, Jim? And no car, I see.'

'Yes, to both. I needed a walk, Hamish.'

'Cold day for a wander, I'd say, eh?'

'Good for clearing the head.'

'Aye, like that, is it? I had a notion you'd be in the glums after the weekend, right enough.' Hamish handed Daley his whisky and sat stiffly back in his chair.

'So, you heard about Brian?'

'I did. I took a wander over to the Island Bar yesterday. Big George is always good wae the local gossip. As you'll be aware, a' the lawyers go in there for a refreshment, and a more loose-lipped bunch wae a drink you cannae find. I'm sad to say it, but Brian has the same weakness for the drink my own faither had. It's a curse when a man cannae enjoy a good dram now and again without wanting to repeat the process the next day and the next again. Or until he canna stand or behave the way the good Lord intended.'

Daley nodded with a sigh. 'He's in bother this time. And there's not much I can do to help him.'

'Malcolm MacConnachie, that's the bugger he was scrapping wae, I hear.'

'Yes, so it would seem.'

'A sleekit bugger – och, his grandfaither was worse. Malcolm's always on the lookout for the main chance. I canna mind the number o' times he's fallen over in the street on cracked pavements or potholes. Aye, every time looking for the compensation fae the council.'

'Oh, is that the way of it?' Daley looked interested.

'A big claim at his work, too. He was a baker wae Michael Kerr for a whiles. Tried to take them to court when he near choked on a rock bun at his tea break.'

'Was he successful?'

'No, he wisna. He managed to swallow the thing, unfortunately. But it turned out that he'd no' paid for the bun, so he got his jotters for stealing before he could head up the hill to Campbell the lawyer. Och, he's drifted fae job tae job all his days. Trouble follows him like an auld dug.'

Daley took a sip of whisky and sat back in the chair. 'Well, that's encouraging, at least.'

'Any sheriff that takes anything MacConnachie has to say seriously shouldna be in the job, and that's for certain sure.' Hamish eyed Daley over his glass. 'But your troubles don't end wae Brian Scott, I'm thinking.'

'Sorry?'

'I know it's none o' my business. But since we're on the first-name terms now, I just thought I'd mention your good lady.'

'What about her?' Daley looked confused.

'Apparently – aye, just that, mind – you and she were at the argument in the restaurant where the auld Kinloch bar used to be. This would be just as Brian was getting tae grips wae MacConnachie, I'm thinking.'

Daley laughed. 'You should be the detective, not me, Hamish.'

'You know fine what this place is like for rumours. It doesna take the likes o' the lassie fae the book I'm reading tae hear what's what.'

'Any good?'

Hamish held up the paperback. 'No' bad. No' as good as thon fella wae the funny name, mark you, but entertaining enough. Though it's no' a book the likes o' yoursel' should read, I'm thinking.'

'Why?'

'You're depressed enough.' Hamish clenched his pile between his teeth. 'Noo, what's that other fella's name again? His books would fair cheer you up.'

Daley shrugged. 'No idea, sorry.'

'Och, it'll come tae me. Anyway, you've mair to worry you, eh?'

'I have. And you're right. Me and Liz aren't getting on well. But what's changed?'

Hamish took a long puff of his pipe. 'But when you had the problem wae your heart, I swear the lassie looked lost.'

'She did?'

'Aye, she did. And by the same token when you had your wee stramash up at the yacht marina. Well, you were hardly doing it for nothing. Nobody puts their job – aye, and their life – at risk jeest for no reason. I would haud on to my ha'penny if I were you – before taking any drastic steps, I mean.'

'You think?'

'I do. Folk that spend a lot o' time together – well they have the habit o' taking the other for granted.' Hamish's gaze drifted to the picture of Annie and he had to quickly blink away a tear.

'How are you holding up, Hamish? I feel as though I barely see you these days. I'm not out much – well, since what happened at the County, you know.'

'Aye, hellish, so it was. But that's what I'm on aboot. Don't have regrets. I know you understand what I mean, Jim. There's bags o' time left for you. Rushing at a gate never helped a man grab a coo.'

Daley nodded, a whole parade of thoughts crossing his mind. 'Yes, you're right, I suppose.'

'And I'll tell you something for nothing. You don't want to be sitting here like me, an auld man wae jeest a cat, fire, whisky and memories for company. And memories fade and die, like we all dae.'

Daley took another drink, this time draining his glass. He got to his feet and walked over to the sideboard. Taking the bottle, he filled his own glass then topped up Hamish's. 'And tell me. What am I going to do with Brian?'

'Apart fae wringing his liver oot wae a mangle, you mean?'

'Very funny.'

'Och, take people like you and me. We go through oor lives wae all kinds of troubles hammering aboot in oor nappers.' He tapped his head for effect. 'And then you get folk like Brian Scott. Aye, they fall plenty times – bad falls, too. But bugger me, dae they no' jeest come oot it all as though nothing had happened? Neither up nor doon. Let Brian sail his own course for a while. Man, we've all to navigate oor ain waters in the end.'

'You're right, Hamish. Of course you are.'

Suddenly, Hamish's whole body shook, as though he was in the throes of a fit. Daley sat forward anxiously. 'Are you okay?'

'Och, just shivering wae cold, Jim. I'll need to poke that fire.' But as he said the words and looked at Daley with a smile, he hated the lie.

11

Scott was at his desk in the CID office at Kinloch when his phone burst into life. Apart from himself, the room was gloomy, empty of people, so the sound seemed to echo. He reached over and answered the call.

'Aye, how are you?' he responded to the caller. 'Eh? You must be joking! Seriously?'

Scott threw the phone on to the desk and rushed into Daley's glass box. There was no sign of his old friend, and the place was a mess: papers scattered across the floor, an upended computer monitor and a coffee mug smashed against a wall, a pool of its former contents meandering towards Scott's feet.

'Ach, where the hell are you when I need you, Jimmy?' he mumbled to himself. 'This place is a coup!'

Scott rushed out into the corridor. It was dark outside, and the low lighting gave the place an eerie feel, ethereal almost. He made his way along empty passages to the front desk. There was no sign of Sergeant Shaw, and like Daley's office the space was a shambles: the same discarded paperwork spread hither and thon, a broken telephone and a police officer's bunnet, peak half melted, a neat hole the size of a bullet just beside the cap badge.

'What in the name o' Andrew Sloan is going on?' he roared. He reached under the high front desk and removed a key. It was of the old-fashioned mortise variety with an ornate head that wouldn't have been out of place in a Florentine palace. With it clutched firmly in his hand he ran down another dark corridor. The old oak door before him was stout, a formidable barrier. Scott used the big key, and though he had to put his shoulder to the door, it opened with a loud, low creak.

It was pitch black inside, and he stumbled about before his hand passed across the light switch on the wall. When he pushed it, a bare bulb glowed dimly in the centre of the room. It hung by a long, corded flex, and swayed as though propelled by a breeze.

At the end of the room, Scott was faced by three long steel lockers. As he took this in, he realised that he didn't have the little keys needed to open them. Desperately, he took a step back and forced the sole of his boot against the lock of the first. Once, twice – he only left a dent. But on the third attempt he was successful. The door came off its hinges and fell with a clatter to the floor.

Scott peered at the contents of the locker. A vicious-looking cutlass with a basket hilt and an old truncheon broken in two.

'Bugger this!' He removed the sword and carefully threaded it through his belt. It was clear he'd have to kick open another locker to find what he was looking for.

He was more successful this time. The door crashed open on the second thrust of his boot. There was only one item here: a pistol, a long silencer attached to its barrel.

'You and they silencers, Jimmy.' Scott shook his head as he removed the weapon from the locker. He looked around in the gloom. Boxes of ammunition sat on a shelf under a cracked Police Scotland logo. He stared at the fractured jaggy thistle for a moment before filling his pockets with rounds. For what he faced, he knew he'd need all the ammunition he could carry.

With the long cutlass swinging at his side, he rushed out of the room and into the corridor. But to his dismay, the lights had failed and the whole office seemed to be cast in the dim blue glow of the emergency lighting. Scott stumbled along the corridor, trying desperately to find the front door. He had to get out on the street as quickly as he could. He felt panic rise in his chest as, with each step, he seemed no nearer to the exit. 'Bastard!' he roared as he turned another corner with no inkling of a way out.

'Daddy!' The voice was disembodied and came from somewhere up ahead.

'Martha? Is that you, dear?'

'Yeah, I'm in a closet, Pop. I need your help!'

Scott hesitated. 'Didnae take you long to pick up an American accent, hen.'

'We ain't got time for this – you need to get me out. He locked me in here.'

'Who locked you in?'

'Uncle Jimmy, who else?'

'Wait, I'm no' getting this at all. You're saying oor Jimmy locked you in a cupboard?'

Before Scott's daughter could reply, he was almost blinded by a bright light as a door swung open, crashing against a wall with such force that its brass handle was dislodged and rattled along the floor. Steam billowed from the room behind.

'Jimmy, what's up wae you?'

Daley looked huge in the doorway, silhouetted by the blinding light diffused by the steam. 'You, that's what's wrong with me!' Daley shouted at the top of his voice. His words were slow, his voice low and echoing down the corridor.

'What are you banging on aboot? Have you been drinking, big man?'

'So, what if I have?'

'You're always on my back for it! You're nothing but one o' they hippo thingies.'

'Hypocrite is the word you're looking for, Brian. I don't know how you got into this job in the first place.'

'Aye, so you said – often. I telt you, my faither was in the lodge wae the Duke o' Kent.'

'I never heard that story, Pop,' shouted Martha from the cupboard in her newly adopted American twang.

'Aye, that's another thing, Jimmy. Why have you locked my lassie in that cupboard?'

'She stays there until you sober up. Nothing I can do about it, order from Emperor Donald.'

'Eh? The job has gone tae the dogs since this Police Scotland nonsense started. I was happy in the Glasgow polis.'

'You've never been happy. That's why you get drunk every day!' Daley spat out the words.

'Never mind me. Do you have any idea o' what's going on outside?'

'Of course, that's why I'm in here, you arsehole.'

'Enough o' the language in front o' my wee lassie.'

'Pop, you cuss every day of your life. I grew up with it, remember?'

'That's enough fae you, queen o' the Bronx.' Scott turned

72

his attention back to Daley. 'You're frightened tae face Machie, is that it?'

'Of course. He shot you twice – I was there, remember?'

'Aye, I kinda remember too, believe it or no'. But you have to get a grip, big man. Frank cannae hold him off much longer.'

'Frank Di'Angelo?' enquired Martha from the cupboard.

'No, Frank MacDougall. Who are you on aboot?'

'Just a guy I know from school. Don't blow a gasket, Pop. He's got a cute ass.'

'He can have a cute donkey, for all I care. We need tae get oot o' here – all three o' us! Jimmy, you need to get your heid together.'

'Or what?'

'Or Machie will kill us all, that's what!'

'You're lying, Brian. You've always been in league with them – MacDougall, Machie, the lot! You're a plant.'

'Oh aye, like thon film?'

'Yes, just like the film – *Star Wars*.'

'Nah, that's no' the one, big man.'

'I can't breathe over here. Could you, like, do something, Pop?'

'Right, I've had enough o' this, Jimmy.' Scott drew the cutlass from his belt and flourished it before him. 'Lock my wee lassie up, would you? Just wait until you get a taste o' this bastard!'

'That's not a sword,' said Daley nonchalantly. 'This is a sword!' He brandished a huge blade in front of Scott's face. It flashed in the light coming from the room behind.

'It's no' the size, Jimmy, it's what you dae with it!'

'Oh please, that's, like, disgusting!' Martha wailed.

'We'll see, Brian.' In one quick, flowing movement, Daley swung his huge sword at Scott, who managed to parry the blow just in front of his face. They were momentarily locked together, blade against blade, face to face. Daley's eyes seemed to blaze with hatred as he clenched his teeth, staring down at Scott, who returned his glare with a defiant expression.

'You'll need to be quicker than that, big man.' Scott took a step back and elegantly pushed the point of his cutlass past Daley's defence, piercing his right shoulder. Then, in a flash, he pulled back. 'Remember, I'm fae the East End. We grew up wae shit like this.'

Daley roared in pain, but simply transferred his sword from one hand to the other and rained blows down on the shorter man. Scott managed to meet them all, the blades clashing over and over as he was driven back into the darkness of the corridor.

'Help me, Pop. You're my only hope!' wailed Martha, as steel clattered on steel.

'You shouldn't have come back here, Brian,' said Daley, his breathy voice now deeper and more menacing as it echoed down the empty corridors. 'Time to join me on the dark side.' He swung another massive blow with his sword.

'Go tae Partick CID? You must be joking!'

Though Scott twisted, turned, parried and thrust, Daley's sheer strength was too much for him. He slipped and landed on his back, the cutlass falling from his hand.

Daley loomed over him, a huge figure swathed in darkness.

'Come on, Jimmy. How did it get tae this, eh?'

Scott could hear his own scream as Daley, sword held out before him in both hands, point facing down, thrust it mercilessly into his chest.

Brian Scott shot up in bed, his body dripping with sweat. He was gasping for breath, desperately trying to shake the nightmare from his mind and pull himself back to reality. In a few moments, he began to calm down, his breathing slowed, and he reached to his side to touch the reassuring figure lying beside him in the bed.

'That was one hell o' a nightmare, Ella.'

She stirred into wakefulness. 'You okay, darling?'

'Darling? I see you've forgiven me after oor wee argument today, eh? I don't think you've ever called me that in all these years.'

She giggled. 'Well, there's a first time for everything, isn't there?'

Scott felt a hand slide up his thigh.

'Haud your horses, Ella. I'm dead beat after that bad dream, I just want to get some kip.'

Effortlessly, she threw one leg over him, straddling, pushing him down on the bed.

'What's up wae you, eh? One minute you're heading off to America, and the next thing it's like a French brothel in here.' He reached out and clicked the light on his nightstand into life. But as he stared into the face of the woman who was now squirming on top of him, he screamed.

'Oh, come on, Brian, you and I both know this should have happened long ago.' Liz Daley leaned in to his face, searching out his lips with hers.

'No, no way, Liz! Get off, get off me – Lizzie, no!'

Brian Scott was woken by the light on the ceiling of his own lounge. He was lying on the sofa, Ella now standing in front of him in her leopardskin onesie, both arms firmly planted at her sides – the double teapot.

'Well, this is where we're at noo. You roaring in your sleep. I'm affronted. You'll have woken up the whole street. I have to admit, I never thought you were holding a candle for Lizzie all these years!'

'It was a nightmare, Ella. I was trying to get away fae her.'

'Aye, the same as me juking oot the road o' Brad Pitt when he turns up wae the bedroom eyes – nae chance!' She stormed into the kitchen.

'Aye, a nice wee cup o' tea, that's what we both need, hen.'

'If I make you a cup of tea, it's going straight o'er your heid, Brian Scott!'

Scott lay back on the sofa. He was still dressed in his shirt and trousers, though one sock dangled from his right foot. There was an empty bottle of whisky on the coffee table. He gathered his thoughts for a moment. 'Hey, see oor Martha, has she picked up a New York accent? I've no' spoken to her for a while – you always hog the phone.'

Ella leaned her head out of the kitchen. 'You're having the DTs again.' She slammed the door, leaving Brian Scott with an aching head, dry mouth and a feeling of impending doom.

12

Shreya Dhar drove into Kinloch for the first time. The journey had been longer than she'd expected. The road twisted and turned, one minute a meandering passage beside a loch, the next a high climb into the hills, where the drop to the valley below made her dizzy.

The last part of the journey saw the road skirt the Atlantic. She could see islands looming on the grey horizon. The day was cold and wet, and the ocean looked dark and unwelcoming. Dhar wondered what this place might look like on a bright summer's day, but found it hard to conjure the image up in her mind, such was the nature of the almost oppressive view from her car.

Dhar was looking forward to meeting Jim Daley more than she'd anticipated. Certainly, he was a legend amongst the cops she'd spoken to. A contradiction: a man of high principles who thought nothing of beating his wife's attacker half to death. A risk-averse senior officer who actively sought out the assistance of DS Brian Scott, a police officer who'd broken almost every rule there was to break. There could be no doubting the pair's bravery or indeed efficacy in terms of cases solved. But every success seemed to come at a price.

As she drove past a little industrial estate with a car showroom and small factory units, she wondered what it must be like to live in such a small, isolated community. Dhar had grown up in cities; she loved as many things about urban living as she despised. Glasgow was a strange, wet and miserable place when she'd first arrived – as was Kinloch, she thought, as she checked her satnav on the way through the town. But her mother had been forced to move from the sub-continent for reasons she hadn't understood at the time. Now that she'd grown up herself, it made more sense.

The time spent getting used to a new culture, a strange new country, had been difficult. The hardest thing of all had been the casual racism she faced every day, whether at school or with her friends. It just seemed part of life, shrugged off as banter or *just the way things were*. But every jibe cut her to the core. Shreya Dhar was no shrinking violet, but she found the relentless nature of it all simply exhausting.

Hey, little Paki, what are you looking at?

Those were the words that had first greeted her in the school playground in Glasgow. Over the years things had improved, but that same abuse was still around; now whispered rather than given full voice. A nudge, a wink and a laugh rather than a cruel jibe. The emptiness of feeling unwelcome, even in the homes of some of the children with whom she'd made friends, was still there. Not every family looked down their noses at her, but too many did.

But as she got to know her surroundings, it dawned on Shreya that immigrants like her could have no hope of being universally accepted in a place where the locals themselves were hopelessly divided by religion and politics. Those who bullied or shunned her, called her names or laughed behind her back, were just as likely to turn their malice on someone from their own street – their own people.

The satnav announced that she'd reached her destination. She saw the sign that read *Shandy's Guest House*, an arrow pointing to an ascending gravel driveway. When she had to work away from home, Shreya had learned to hate hotel life. In her experience, guest houses were altogether quieter, more intimate places. In any case, she had simple needs. Somewhere to sleep and bathe – that was it, really. She didn't drink, and the last place she wanted to be was a hotel bar with unleashed husbands on the pull.

Shreya Dhar knew she was attractive to the opposite sex. She'd used it sometimes, first at school and uni, then in her new role as a police officer. Shreya had read about the 'halo effect' during her sociology studies, part of her degree that was a respite from criminology. It was another quirk of humanity: the way others treated good-looking people so differently from those less blessed. But a handy tool. However, although she dressed well and took care of herself, Shreya Dhar didn't crave expensive cosmetics, body treatments or exclusive handbags. Hers was a quiet, natural beauty – inevitably the most attractive of all, in a man or woman.

She knew Jim Daley was reputed to have an eye for the ladies. A beautiful but wayward wife and a tragic affair with a young detective. There were no secrets in the job . . . well, not many, she smiled to herself.

Shreya took the twisty driveway carefully and stopped outside the large house on the hill. She'd chosen well. The guest house was perfectly positioned, with an elevated view of the loch. She looked across to the twin piers, the pontoons and the main part of the town beyond. This place hugged its loch as a mother hugs her child. She'd made it her business to learn a little about Kinloch in the hours before she'd arrived. A fishing town, famous for the creatures of the sea and for the distilling of whisky. Certainly, now she took in the place, it looked better than it had on the road in.

She jumped out of the car, grabbed her bags from the boot and made her way up the front steps. Pressing a brass button, she heard a distant bell then movement behind the frosted glass of the door. A small woman of early middle age opened it and greeted her with a smile.

'You'll be Miss Dhar. I'm Shona MacBride. Please, come in – let me help you with those bags.'

Shreya followed Shona into a broad entrance hall, a winding staircase at its far end.

'I'll take you up to your room, dear. You have a sea view. I thought you'd like that.'

'Yes, very kind, thank you. But you shouldn't have bothered. I'll probably be spending much of my time in Kinloch at work.'

Shona cocked her head with an interested expression. 'And what is it you dae?'

'I'm a police officer – a detective sergeant.' Shreya returned her smile, knowing full well that her host would become instantly more inquisitive following this revelation.

'Oh, that's nice. A pretty lassie like you. I thought you would be a model or a film star,' said Shona as they took the winding staircase.

Shreya Dhar laughed. 'Thank you, you're too kind. But I prefer the police.'

'You'll be working with Mr Daley, I take it?' Shona had stopped outside a large oak door bearing the number 3 on it in polished brass.

'That's right. I'm just down to assist for a while.'

Shona opened the door to Dhar's room. It was large, with a double bed set against one wall, a small sofa and a compact little writing desk behind the door. The usual wardrobe was joined by a neat chest of drawers, all sitting on a deep pile carpet in a faded beige. A TV was secured to the wall opposite the bed, beside the bathroom door. A tall bay window afforded even better views across the loch. The place smelled as fresh and clean as it looked.

'I hope this is okay for you?' said Shona, placing Shreya's bag on the floor beside her bed. 'We have wi-fi – the password is in the drawer beside your bed.' She paused. 'Mr Daley just lives up the hill – a wee bit further down the road. Nice man.'

Though Shreya took in her smile, she thought there was something disingenuous about it. 'I've never met him. I'm looking forward to it,' she decided to say.

'Oh, I'm sure he'll be delighted to meet you.' Shona had a knowing look on her face, which Dhar ignored. 'You'll be here to replace Sergeant Scott?'

'I'm afraid I can't really talk about my work, Mrs MacBride.'

'Aye, of course. I understand. He's a fool to himself, that's all I'll say.'

Dhar smiled weakly by way of a reply.

Shona looked around, just to make sure all was in order, or in case her new guest was willing to reveal any more about the recalcitrant detective. Realising that she wasn't, she handed her the room keys. 'Just you make yourself comfortable. If you need anything, give me a shout. My husband Andy works on the rigs, so it's just you and me in the house.'

'Is that why you call the house Shandy's?'

'No wonder you're in the polis, eh? Smart as a tack, so you are. That's it, Shona and Andy – Shandy. You'd be surprised the folk that don't get it.'

'I'm sure.'

'Now, I'll let you get settled in. As you know, we don't do meals. But I have no objection if you want to bring your own food in. There's an Indian restaurant doon the front, just along fae the pictures.'

There it was – the unthinking comment. It was innocent, but all part of the same mental process. 'I'm not too fond of Indian food, as it happens. But I'm sure DCI Daley will keep me right about places to eat.'

Shona took this in before leaning in to Dhar, whispering into her ear as though they were in a room full of people. 'Jeest keep your hand on your ha'penny, that's all I'm saying.'

'Sorry?'

'Och, you know what some men are like.' She sniffed and changed the subject. 'Right, the small key is for the front door. Come and go as you please, but make sure you lock it behind you.'

'Don't worry, I'm very security conscious.'

'Aye, stupid me. Of course, you a polis and all.'

'As we discussed, if you can make up a bill for two full weeks, I'll get it paid upfront by Police Scotland.'

'That would be great. Only here for two weeks?'

'I've no idea, but we'll take it a fortnight at a time, if that's okay?'

'Aye, absolutely – that's much appreciated. Things get right quiet this time o' year. And it's nice to have somebody else in the house. Especially a policeman – woman,' she added quickly.

When Shona MacBride had scuttled off, Shreya unpacked her bags and organised the contents into the wardrobe or chest of drawers, as appropriate.

That done, she stood at the window and took in the view. 'I wonder how long I'll be here,' she whispered to herself.

13

Glasgow, 1982

Three young men sat in a car opposite the bar in the city's East End. The street was unremarkable: a bookie's shop shuttered up for the night, tenements with lights on in some curtained windows, others boarded up. Graffiti flowered in patches here and there: beside the dark fish and chip shop, on the roller-shutter of the newsagents and under flaking paint on a window frame of a ground-floor flat. Recently, following a trend in America, graffiti was coming to be thought of as legitimate art. Certainly, it was the only splash of colour to be seen amidst the drabness. A dog cocked its leg against a lamppost and then trotted off purposefully.

The driver of the red Peugeot was a thin, sharp-featured individual with bad acne. He pawed at the wheel nervously as they sat parked by a tumbledown kerb. The man beside him looked eager rather than trepidatious, while the occupant in the back of the car smoked idly, looking in the opposite direction to his companions.

'Did you no' have a wee toot before we left, Chaz?' he said, addressing the driver.

'Nah, I don't like it when I'm driving, man. I want to have my wits aboot me, take it all in, so I dae.'

'Fuck's sake, we're no' on a Sunday school picnic. It'll calm you doon. You're making me nervous twisting at that wheel.' He looked at the driver with disdain. This man hadn't been his first choice, but a job needed to be done, and he was the only decent wheelman available.

'Gie Chaz a break, Jay? He's bad enough as it is, without you making him worse.'

Jay sniffed, eyeing up an old camera in the window of the pawn shop next to where they were parked. 'Mother Frankie Teresa, eh?' He inserted the sneer into his voice on purpose. While he liked Frank MacDougall in an abstract kind of way, appreciating his guile and street smarts, he tired of his mouth. But Frank had lots of friends, something he lacked. James Machie had never sought out friendship. He was happiest on his own, reading a good book or listening to music. He often found people his own age tedious, shallow and unappealing – half-formed, he preferred to think. They all wore the same clothes, bought the same albums, went to the same nightclubs, took the same drugs, lusted after identical women and had the same boring, pointless jobs. Wage slaves, working from nine to five for someone else's profit. He hated the endless conversations about football and fanny. It bored him rigid. His taste in the opposite sex went beyond the group of girls dancing round their handbags, taking fly sips of vodka from a ginger bottle in some fleapit club.

'When are we going for it, Jay?' said Chaz.

'When I'm ready.' The reply was curt.

'Didn't you know, Chaz? Nobody can take a shit unless Jay gives the thumbs up,' said Frank MacDougall.

Machie made no response to the tame wit. Anyone else, he'd have punched in the back of the head. But Machie realised that Frank MacDougall knew his limits, as well as his worth. He ran with the pack, hanging out in the snooker hall they'd made their base of operations, or the pub the gang used as though they owned it. The publican was able to run his business in peace, free from the various factions in the East End happy to get drunk and wreck bars. James Machie was his guarantor, but Frank was the happy face of the business. And such was Machie's reputation for unalloyed violence, made in only a few years, Frank MacDougall was the man people wanted to see, not his boss.

'I've got a bird on the go tonight, I hope this bastard gets a move on. She'll no' stay warm until tomorrow.'

'I'm sure she's a real classy lady, like the rest o' them,' Machie replied.

Frank MacDougall shrugged. 'I'm no' going tae walk her doon the aisle next week, if that's what you mean.'

'Mair like up the back passage than doon the aisle for you, Frankie boy, eh?'

Chaz's laugh was cut short by a glare from MacDougall. Still working his hands on the wheel, the driver leaned forward, peering into the acetylene glow of the streetlights. 'Hey, lads, there's a polis coming!' As though by instinct, the sight of a police officer made him shrink down in his seat.

'Get a grip o' yourself,' said Machie. 'You're like one o' those auld grannies that cannae see over the wheel. Have some fucking balls, man!' He leaned over and punched Chaz on the shoulder to reinforce the point.

As the policeman made his way towards them, it soon became clear he was no older than the young men in the car.

MacDougall turned round in his seat. 'That's oor man, Jay.'

'Okay, do the business.'

MacDougall got out of the car and walked towards the constable.

'Oh, no fucking way, man!' The sudden change in Chaz's pallor made the boils on his face look even more pronounced.

'What now?' said Machie irritably.

'If yous are going to take oot a polis, I'm off.'

Machie leaned forward. In his right hand, sharp steel flashed under the glow of the acetylene. He pushed the tip of the blade at the back of Chaz's neck, making him yelp in pain. 'See, if I want tae take out your mother, you'll sit there and say fuck all, okay?'

'Aye, right, okay, Jay! That's sore, man!'

Machie leaned back, placing the flick-knife back in his jacket pocket. 'Good, that was the correct response. Now, just shut up and don't speak again until I tell you to say something.'

Machie looked on as MacDougall approached the young constable. The man in the uniform nodded and looked over his shoulder nervously. A few words passed between the two, then MacDougall made his way back to the car.

'So?' said Machie when MacDougall was back in his seat.

'All as planned. He's going in now.'

Machie turned his attention to the policeman, who crossed the road in front of them and entered the pub. 'I hope that prick Alec is in there.'

'Ha! Cracker, man. They bastards will be flushing their shit doon the toilet.' Chaz guffawed.

Machie drew back a leg and kicked Chaz's seat forcibly.

'Hey!' The driver yelled out in surprise.

'I told you not to say anything until I told you. Are you incapable of following simple instructions, twat?'

MacDougall shook his head and held a finger to his lips to encourage Chaz not to reply.

The three of them sat in silence for a few minutes. The door to the pub swung back open and the policeman emerged. Again, he crossed the road in front of their car. He looked at Frank MacDougall and inclined his head a fraction before heading back down the street in the direction he'd come.

'Okay, we're good to go,' said MacDougall. He fished in his pocket and pulled out a balaclava that he quickly pulled over his head. He and Machie – also wearing a balaclava now – slid out of the car, both carrying baseball bats, held tightly in their gloved hands.

Chaz looked on, almost paralysed with fear, not failing to note that James Machie's bat was studded with nails hammered in along much of its length.

MacDougall opened the door, and the pair ran inside.

The pub had a dozen or so customers, ranging from two old men in the corner playing dominoes to a courting couple who stopped pawing each other at the sight of the men in balaclavas. Three middle-aged men dived off their stools as Frank MacDougall thumped his bat on the bar and ran it along to the end, scattering glasses to the linoleum-covered floor, where they smashed one after the other. A large tin ashtray, adorned with the laughing cavalier trademark of a brewery, spun through the air like a frisbee, crashing against a table where no customers were sitting.

The scene was chaos. The old men abandoned their game of doms and got stiffly to their feet. Along with the courting couple, other customers fled the bar, the girl screaming at the top of her voice. There were only four people left in the room now: Machie, MacDougall, a man lying back in a chair unconscious with drink, and the barman, brandishing a golf club behind the beer fonts.

Machie stood before him, only the bar between them. 'You can always tell a classy pub fae a shite one: the good ones don't have Buckfast on the optics.' In one swift move, he placed an arm on the bar and vaulted it, the baseball bat still held tightly in his other hand.

The barman tried to dodge away, but Machie caught the golf club and batted it out of his hands. The bald man, dressed in white shirt and dark trousers, was now defenceless. He backed as far away from his tormentor as he could, until he found himself wedged in a corner below the gantry.

'Take it – take the money in the till. Just press the red button to open the thing!' he shouted, his voice trembling.

'That's very kind of you,' Machie said calmly. MacDougall stood on the other side of the bar amidst the broken glass, spilled drinks and discarded cigarette ends.

Machie opened the till and, with one hand, stuffed notes into his pocket as the man whimpered in the corner. 'No' very busy tonight, Alec – judging by this miserable offering, anyway.'

'Listen, I can get you mair. It's nae bother. I can lay my hands on near a grand – tonight!' He held his hands out in front of his face.

Machie walked slowly towards him, bat trailing at his side along the sticky linoleum. 'Batter on some music, buddy,' he called to MacDougall.

In the far corner of the room, just before the door to the gents, was a wall-mounted jukebox. MacDougall fed a few coins into it. 'What do you fancy?'

'Me? A bit o' Frank Sinatra.'

MacDougall scanned the song selection, pressing a button to move on to new choices. 'He's no' got any Sinatra.' MacDougall turned to the barman. 'What kind o' place is this – nae Frank Sinatra?'

Alec shrugged his shoulders, his hands still trembling before him.

'How many years have you had this shithole for now, Alec?' said Machie.

'Near ten.'

'Ten years and no Sinatra on the jukebox.' He shook his head. 'You're turning this place into one o' they trendy wine bars or what?'

'The people who own the machine, they fill it up wae the records, no' me.'

'Right, that's fair enough. Just stick on some ABBA, big man. Surely you've got them, Alec?'

'Aye, aye, there's ABBA on there. That lassie that was in, she had them on just a while ago.' He laughed nervously.

Suddenly the strains of 'Waterloo' sounded in the bar.

'Oh! No' loud enough, Alec. I like my music blasting, man.'

'The switch – it's just beside the till.'

'This one?' When Alec nodded, Machie turned up the volume to full and started singing along to 'Waterloo' at the top of his voice.

'The polis, they was just in here. They'll still be aboot!' shouted Alec above the din.

'No, they won't.' Calmly, with one hand, Machie pulled the balaclava up to reveal his face. He smiled broadly. 'You remember me now?'

'No, no! Please, Mr Machie – it wisnae my fault!'

90

'You've been telling every bastard that I'm just a pussy and you're no' paying up.' Machie paused for a moment, as though deep in thought. 'Dae I look like a pussy to you?' he roared above the music.

Baseball bat now in both hands, Machie swung at the screaming, cowering man again and again. First his hands and arms took the blows. But as the nails bit and ripped at his flesh, he fell forward and curled into a ball, desperately trying to protect himself as his own blood pooled darkly beneath him.

Mercilessly, Machie brought the bat down on his helpless victim. His white shirt was now punctured and crimson. After a few more agonising moments, his body went limp and he was still, sprawled over the bloody linoleum.

'Have you killed the bastard?' shouted MacDougall.

'Nah, he's still breathing.' Not content with the damage he'd already done, Machie aimed a vicious kick at the unconscious figure's head, which lolled backwards like a boxer's on the ropes, replaced the balaclava over his face and nodded to MacDougall. He vaulted back over the bar and the pair ran out into the street.

Chaz was scared, but he wasn't stupid. He'd turned on the engine the minute they'd entered the pub and kept it running; there was nothing worse than a getaway car that wouldn't start. As soon as his accomplices were safely back inside, he revved the engine and shot off.

'Ho! Watch your speed,' said Machie from the back. 'Dae you want the cops to pull us over?' He'd removed his gloves and the balaclava, as had MacDougall. 'Just take us back to oor motor. And what's that smell, by the way?' Machie curled up his nose at the offensive odour.

'Sorry, big man. I pished myself. It's just the adrenaline, you know?'

While Machie looked disgusted, MacDougall edged away from the driver, holding his nose.

Chaz drove down a warren of East End backstreets – past ruined houses, empty factories, building sites and run-down rows of tenements, the odd shop dotted amongst boarded-up premises – until they came to a piece of waste ground, where once a cement factory had stood. A black Audi Quattro was sitting at the edge of this muddle of churned-up earth and broken bricks. In the shadows the silhouette of a bulky figure was just about visible behind the wheel. Chaz was careful to drive to the very back of the waste ground, well away from the orange glow of the streetlights and the other car.

'Right, out!' shouted Machie. Leaving the baseball bats, balaclavas and gloves discarded in the vehicle, the three of them jumped out. While Machie and Chaz slowly walked away. MacDougall lifted the boot and removed an old rag. He unscrewed the petrol cap and thrust the rag into the tank, leaving only a couple of inches free. He produced a Zippo lighter from his pocket, set the rag alight and walked briskly away from the red Peugeot.

Machie was smoking a cigarette, leaning against the Audi. 'Slick work, Frankie boy.'

'Right, pay the man and let's get to fuck,' said MacDougall, jumping into the passenger seat of the Quattro.

First there was a pop, followed quickly by another, then a clump that shook the ground as the petrol in the tank of the Peugeot caught alight. A ball of flame erupted into the night sky, illuminating the buildings around the waste ground.

'Okay, here you are,' said Machie. He handed a bundle of used notes to Chaz, who was still shaking at the whole experience.

'Right, thanks, man.' Chaz turned to hurry off, away from the crackling, bright flames of the burning car and the man who scared him so much.

'Hang on – here's a wee something extra.' In a flash, Machie produced the blade from his pocket and slashed Chaz down his left cheek.

For a moment, the erstwhile driver looked bewildered. He stared first at Machie then at the bloodied knife. He put his hand to his face, felt the open gash and fell to the ground screaming.

Machie jumped into the car and tapped his new driver on the shoulder. The car pulled away, leaving the stricken man kneeling on the waste ground framed by the flames of the burning car.

MacDougall turned round in his seat. 'What the fuck did you dae that for?'

'Because he was an annoying prick, that's why. What kind o' man pishes himself, eh?'

The Audi sped off into the night.

The policeman walked towards the bar he'd been in only half an hour before and made his way inside. The place was wrecked, broken glass and spilled drinks across the floor, the jukebox silent. The man he'd seen asleep before was still snoring in his chair as though nothing had happened.

'Hello, is anybody here?' he shouted. When no reply was forthcoming, he walked over to the bar, his boots crunching down on broken glass.

It was then he saw the barman lying in a pool of his own blood.

The constable ran round the bar and kneeled over him, the cloying damp of drying blood soaking into the knees of his uniform trousers. He felt for a pulse. It was weak, and he could hear a high-pitched wheezing sound coming from the victim's throat.

He ran back into the street, pulling the radio mouthpiece from the lapel of his tunic. 'Two-four-eight! Code twenty-one at McGarry's Bar. Badly injured man at the locus, over!'

As the controller calmly asked him for more details, the young police officer leaned forward and vomited on to the pavement.

14

Having unpacked, Shreya Dhar locked the door of her room and took the winding stairs back to the entrance hall. She heard a woman humming tunelessly and pushed open a door marked *Lounge*.

'Oh, is that you unpacked already? That was quick,' said Shona.

'I'm used to it. Can you give me directions to the police office, please?' Shreya knew she could use her satnav, but she was weary after the long drive and figured that the place couldn't be that hard to find.

Of course, like anyone answering such a question about the place where they lived, Shona gave a rambling set of directions, naming shops and even the homes of some of her friends. But Dhar thought she could decipher a recognisable route from the extraneous information.

She looked round the large bright room. 'This is nice.'

Shona sighed. 'Yes, me and Andy thought folk might like to come down and pass the time of day with their fellow guests. We were going to put a wee bar in the corner.'

'You didn't though, I see.'

'Nah. Guests just want to stay in their rooms wae tablets and phones. I was quite disappointed. They arrive, you see

95

them coming in and oot, they pay their bill at the end o' their stay, and that's that.'

'That's a shame.'

'I was expecting a wee bit o' chat – some gossip. Like I said before, it's lonely here when Andy's away on the rigs.'

Shreya found this bewildering. She'd always preferred her own company but supposed that she spent most of her time at work surrounded by people. Being alone was bliss after a long, busy shift. 'I'd better go. Thanks for the directions.' She smiled at Shona.

'You'll be late back, I suppose?'

'No idea, to be honest.' Shreya shrugged and left the room.

The drive through Kinloch was just about as easy as she'd imagined, though she was slightly disconcerted when a woman pushing a pram ambled over the pedestrian crossing against the red man, seemingly oblivious of Shreya's car.

But as she wound her way up the last stretch of Main Street, she saw that, despite the cold, cheery-looking folk were milling about the shops. The town reminded her of places she'd been in Aberdeenshire. For her, at least, it had an old county town feel. Somehow, it was reassuring not to see the high street names: coffee shops, clothes franchises, mini supermarkets. But, with internet shopping taking huge bites from those places, this was the shape of things to come. A return to the high streets she'd seen in pictures from the fifties and well before. It was the old adage: the more things changed, the more they stayed the same.

Kinloch police office was situated at the top of the hill looking down over the town. She parked her car as close to the place as was safe, crossed the road and took the few steps to the front door. Inside, a harassed-looking sergeant was busy on a call. He smiled at her and gestured to the chairs opposite the front desk.

'But this isn't the first time Charlie has been away all night, is it?' The sergeant looked exasperated as he listened to a tearful reply. 'I know you're worried, Mrs Thomson, but I'm sure he'll be back soon. It's just the way the male of the species can be. I can't count the times our Paddy's disappeared for days on end. You know how it is, he arrives back looking knackered and sleeps for two days. No females safe when he's about, eh?' He smiled again at Shreya Dhar. 'If he's not back by tomorrow, we'll see what we can do.' He paused again to listen for a few seconds. 'Okay, Mrs Thomson, 'bye.' The sergeant put down the phone with a shake of his head.

'Not her husband, I hope?'

He looked puzzled for a moment. 'What? No, no – her cat. And Paddy is our tomcat.' He laughed. 'I suppose that must have sounded quite odd when you didn't know the context.' He leaned on the front desk. 'Now, how can I help you?'

Dhar got to her feet, produced her warrant card and handed it over the desk.

'Oh, DS Dhar. We've been expecting you. I'm Sergeant Shaw – Alasdair Shaw, desk sergeant.' He leaned across and shook her hand. 'Not to be confused with Alistair the butcher.'

'A local ned? Sounds nasty.' Dhar looked surprised.

'No, a local butcher. Oh, it's a Kinloch thing, sorry. I've probably been here too long. People and their jobs are sometimes indivisible in a wee place like this. Especially when you've so many Johns, Davys, Billys and Bobbys – all with a small selection of surnames.' He looked embarrassed. 'Sorry,

I'm rambling. You'll be looking for DCI Daley. He's just popped out.' Shaw looked at his watch. Dhar noticed it was cheap, with a cracked face – an old Casio. 'He'll be back any time. Follow me, please.'

Shaw took Dhar along a warren of corridors and up a short flight of stairs. He pushed open the doors marked *CID* and led her through a familiar-looking room of desks and computers. One detective was busy studying a long list of numbers on his screen, while another sipped at her cup of coffee and smiled at Dhar as the DS was led into Daley's glass box.

'It's from here that DCI Daley captains the ship, if you know what I mean.'

'I thought he'd have his own office – being sub-divisional commander.'

'Yes, he does, but he leaves that for the divisional commander when she's about. But she's on leave at the moment.' For a second, Shaw looked uncomfortable. 'DCI Daley is more at home in the CID suite. Old habits die hard, and all that. Just take a seat here.' He pulled out a chair beside Daley's large desk. 'As I say, the DCI won't be long. I'll call to let him know you're here. Sorry, I can't leave the front desk unmanned for too long. Can I arrange a tea, coffee – something?'

'I'm fine, thanks,' replied Dhar. 'I have a bottle of water in my bag. It's no problem.'

'Great, well, I'll get back to randy cats and the like.' Shaw dashed off, still looking flustered.

The first thing that struck Dhar was the size of the desk before her. In this run-of-the-mill office, it looked huge. Daley's chair was also huge. Here worked a man of no little presence, she thought. There wasn't much of a personal nature to be seen around the place. One single framed photograph sat on the desk, which was a muddle of papers, pens and the ubiquitous computer. Dhar leaned her head across the desk to have a look. A striking woman and a small child were frozen in the image. The young boy looked happy, his face bearing a broad grin. On the other hand, there was something about the woman that – despite her beauty – made her look unhappy. Vulnerable, almost.

But Dhar knew that the camera often lied. People, caught in a moment of time, could look one way and be entirely different in the flesh. She remembered a photograph that always sat on the table beside her mother's bed. It was the last thing she'd asked to see before she died, her body eaten away by illness and the hard grind of the years. Shreya had placed the picture before her mother. The dying woman had leaned as far forward as she could and kissed the glass, a tear meandering down her skeletal face. It was a picture of the only man she'd ever loved.

It was a moment Shreya Dhar would – could – never forget, no matter how much the memory pained her.

'Make him proud,' were the last words her mother said. It was typical of this clever, kind, thoughtful woman to think only of someone else in the moment she passed into eternity. Dhar's tears welled up, but she managed to choke them back.

Just as she reached into her bag for a drink of water, the door burst open. She turned to face a bear of a man framed in the doorway. Though she'd seen pictures of Jim Daley, he looked different, she thought. Not as bulky. She knew he'd been ill. Even so, he was still an impressive man: tall, with an open, kind face, something that rather caught her off guard. But looks were often as deceptive as photographs.

He bounded over to her and held out his great paw of a hand. 'Jim Daley, pleased to meet you, DS Dhar. Am I saying that right? Hopeless with names, sorry.'

'Absolutely perfect. But please, sir, call me Shreya.'

'Right, Shreya it is then. And when nobody's about, please call me Jim.'

She nodded her head and took in his eyes. They were rather faded and bordered by dark rings. Here was a man who loved joy but rarely found it, she thought. Unlike photographs, eyes could never lie. In her experience, at least.

Daley landed on his chair with a creak and a sigh. He was wearing a shirt and tie, almost hidden by a thick jumper. He yawned. 'I do apologise. I've not been sleeping very well. We've had a bit of an upheaval.'

'Can I ask, is this because of DS Scott?'

'Ah, you know about that.'

'Yes, I was briefed by my DCI. Please, don't feel as though you need to talk about it. It's just handy for me to know what's going on now I'm here. I don't want to put my foot in it or anything.'

'Not at all. You're here to fill in for him – amongst other things, of course,' Daley added quietly. 'To be honest with you, I could happily strangle him. But best not to make a bad situation worse, I think.'

'You've worked together for a long time, I'm told.'

Daley nodded and stared into space for a moment. 'Yes. Maybe too long.' The regret in his voice was plain. 'Anyway, we can discuss my old pal and pain in the backside later. I'm really interested to hear about your work.'

She shrugged. 'Could be something, but most likely nothing. That's why I'm here. We've managed to gather some information on your new hotelier. It's worth a look. But not a job for special branch yet, I don't think.'

'Oh, please. I've had enough of them to last me a lifetime.' Dhar noticed Daley's face darken.

'Not a fan?'

'Not particularly.'

It was clear he wasn't going to elaborate, so she carried on. 'If – and I say this with a very big *if* – there is an issue here, then it shouldn't be too hard to get an inkling.'

'But how easy will it be to prove – to find something?'

'I think you know how it should play out. But new technology is appearing almost every day. My guess? He's using the dark web, burner phones and the like.' She shrugged.

'Okay, well, I'm afraid I can't help you much with IT, but we'll be here for anything else you need. Ian Macmillan isn't the most popular man in Kinloch, that's certain. Let's see what we can do.'

'You're very kind, sir.'

'Jim, remember?'

'Yes, Jim, sorry. What a beautiful family you have. Sorry, I just took a peek at the picture on your desk.'

'Yes, I'm a lucky man. The wee lad's just started school. It's frightening how time flies.'

'And your wife, she's very beautiful. What does she do?'

A shadow passed briefly across Daley's face. 'Oh, she's very talented. Design, photography – that kind of thing. Been pretty full-on with our son over the last few years, mind you. You know what this job's like – I never get enough time to

101

spend with them. Never enough time to do anything, as it goes.'

Dhar could see confirmation of what she'd been told. This was a man at odds with himself, perhaps looking for things he'd never find. She'd seen it so often. People who should have been content with their lot always looking over at the other side of the fence. But, of course, there could be any number of underlying reasons for this. If the stories she'd heard about Daley's wife were true – well, maybe he couldn't be blamed for being restless.

'Okay, come on and I'll give you a tour of inspection of our little town.' Daley got to his feet.

Shreya Dhar followed him out of his glass box.

15

Hugh Machie groaned as he towelled himself down. The warm bath had been welcome. Though this house had been advertised as being centrally heated, it was soon apparent that while the radiators grumbled and groaned, they delivered very little in the way of warmth. And much as the two-bar electric fire in the living room crackled and sparked, it by no means made up for the lack of heat.

He could remember a time when he'd barely felt the cold. He recalled walking the streets of Glasgow in midwinter in his shirt sleeves. Hugh had been fit in those days. Tall, strong and handsome. He'd remained so until his forties; then his lifestyle began to take its toll. In a city notorious for premature death, and like many of his fellow citizens, he suffered one illness after another as a result of too much alcohol, tobacco and a bad diet. By the time he was in his mid-fifties, his quick, bold stride had been replaced by a rather more sedate trudge. Where once he never left the house without a packet of Woodbines, it was now the small blue inhaler he patted his pockets to find.

Hugh Machie stood in front of the mirror in his new bedroom. He didn't recognise the man who stared back. To him, the wrinkled face was an aberration. Where once had been solid muscle, his old bones now showed, each rib visible above a sunken belly. At least I'm not fat, he reasoned. But the vision of the old man in the mirror still disgusted him.

In a fit of temper, he pulled the mirror off the wall and flung it to the floor. He didn't need to be reminded of the ravaging passage of years. He had struggled through every one of them and the memory was plain. When he thought about it, memories were all he had – and most of them were bad. Of course, he knew he was to blame for much of the misery that had blighted his life. But by no means was he completely at fault. There were others – one in particular – who had caused him heartache that was still too hard to bear. And, as misery loved company, he easily recalled other faces he despised. All confederates of the person who had turned him into a shadow of the man he'd once been. The shadow he'd just seen in the mirror, now lying cracked on the floor.

Hugh pulled on a pair of faded trousers and made sure to wear a vest under his shirt, over which he pulled a V-neck jersey. Even his clothes hung off him. He'd had to pull his belt in another notch. But the cause of this was no fad diet or passing malady. Before long there wouldn't be enough notches left in the belt. Soon, his heart wouldn't be sore, his head full of hatred and regret. But before that, he had one last, meaningful thing to achieve. Something that, as he lay taking his final breath, would soothe his soul.

He had to sit back and draw in a few deep breaths after he'd tied his shoes. Hugh propped himself up by his thin arms on the bed, looking absently at the ceiling. The long crack spread from one end to the other, an almost perfect diagonal. He tried to work out what could be the cause of this, but only concluded that everything came to an end, whether it was bricks and mortar or skin and bone.

He shrugged on his jacket, patted his trouser pocket to make sure it contained his inhaler, pulled the door and left the flat. The building was unusual, but not unfamiliar. On an open landing sat a little brick structure, boarded up, the door replaced by a stoutly riveted sheet of metal. It was an old steamie. A place where woman had chatted and laughed as they washed their families' clothes. The advent of washing machines and tumble dryers in every home had made such amenities redundant. Convenience was all that mattered now. But how many lonely people now stared out of their windows, desperate for human contact?

In his lifetime, so many things had improved. But that improvement – in Hugh's view, at least – always came at a price. Increasingly, folk were living solitary, compartmentalised lives. Even the pubs he'd known and enjoyed to the full were rapidly becoming a thing of the past. Back then, they'd been places where company could always be found, a laugh and a joke guaranteed. Though he'd visited a couple of Kinloch's hostelries since his arrival in the town, he was disappointed to find that they all suffered from the same decline that afflicted the bars in his native Glasgow. Either one or two old men sitting in the corner of an almost empty room, or a place more dedicated to food than to booze; pool tables and dartboards replaced by dining tables, chairs and chef's specials scribbled on blackboards. It was just the way things were. The younger generation seemed happiest holed up in their rooms living a virtual life on screens of one description or another. It was something he would never understand.

But Hugh Machie didn't understand a lot of things.

He pulled the flat cap tightly down on his head and made

his way gingerly down worn stone steps that spiralled two floors on to Long Road.

The cold wind hit him like a blow to the face as it funnelled down the street. There were one or two people about, a few cars parked here and there, but otherwise the place was quiet, which suited him well.

He had taken a couple of days to get his bearings in the small town that was his present, and probably last, home. It hadn't taken him long to find the places he required. He pulled the collar of his long, shabby woollen coat up round his face, turned right and huddled into the wind to make his way down Long Road until it terminated at Main Street. He then took a right and plodded up a hill, past some shops, the town hall and a hotel. The road got a bit steeper the further he went. He stopped and took a couple of puffs of his inhaler. He spotted the police station at the top of the brae, and shrugged further into his coat, crossing the street to his destination.

The lawyers' office was a small red brick building that stood on its own ground beside a bank. How ironic, he thought, as he made his way up the path to the front door of the building. The two establishments seemed handily situated. It surely meant the lawyers need go only a few yards to bank the latest loot they'd squeezed from their hard-pressed clients. But the legal profession had its uses, he reminded himself.

Hugh stepped into the warm office. He removed his cap and with one hand tidied the few wisps of faded grey hair left on his head. Lawyers' offices were all much alike, in his experience. Wood-panelled walls, thick red carpet. The smell of money and old books. This place was no different. The young lady behind the desk was on the phone, but she acknowledged his presence with a nod.

'Yes, sir? How can I help you?' she said as she put the phone down.

'I've an appointment with Mr Campbell at three,' said Machie.

The woman bent over a computer, clearly checking Mr Campbell's diary for the day. 'Mr Forsyth?'

'Yes, that's me.'

'Excellent, I think Mr Campbell is free now. I'll just give him a quick buzz.'

Machie watched her as she simpered over the phone to her boss.

'Okay, Mr Forsyth, he can see you now. The last door on the left at the end of the corridor.' Happy that she'd done her job efficiently, the receptionist began typing quickly at the computer.

Machie made his way along the passageway, removed the inhaler from his pocket and took another quick puff before knocking the door lightly with the knuckle of his forefinger. He reflected that the whole process, from front desk to office, was designed to put him in his place. This man knew he was coming and that he was likely to be a paying client. But instead of opening the door to welcome him, he made Machie wait until he was called.

'Come.' A voice sounded from within the room.

Swallowing his irritation, Machie turned the brass handle and was soon in a plush office lined on three sides by shelves of thick, leather-bound books. At the rear of the space, underneath a window, a florid-looking man sat behind a desk of which an American president would have been proud. It was wrought in highly polished oak and covered with green baize like a snooker table. On it were scattered some files, papers and a laptop computer. A vague odour of good cigars hung in the air.

'Please, take a seat, Mr Forsyth.' Campbell the lawyer struggled up from his seat, leaning across the desk to shake his prospective client by the hand. A small gesture of civility, crumbs from a rich man's table.

This formality over, Machie sat down. Though he was grateful to take the weight off his feet, he also noticed that his chair was considerably lower than Campbell's. Everything had been choreographed to make the visitor to this room feel subservient.

'Now, Mr Forsyth, what have you been up to?' Campbell loomed over him across the desk, a sarcastic smile playing on his flabby lips.

'Sorry?'

'I mean, how can I help you today?' His expression became more serious.

'I'd like to make a will, please – sort out my estate.'

'Right, well that's a very wise decision, I must say.' Campbell looked surprised. 'People think these online wills are sufficient unto the day. I must tell you, they're not. I don't know how many disputes I've had to deal with because of them. Never too late to visit your lawyer, as I'm sure you know. Now, what are the details?' Campbell pulled the laptop closer, clicked a few keys and looked back at the man in front of him.

Machie reached into the inside pocket of his jacket and was delighted to see the lawyer flinch. He produced a few sheets of folded writing paper and handed them across the desk to Campbell. 'It's all on there. Excuse the handwriting, by the way.'

Campbell unfolded the few pages, donned a pair of glasses and began reading. Machie took great pleasure in noticing the surprise on his face as he read on.

Not halfway through Machie's notes, the lawyer removed his glasses and cleared his throat. 'Now, I can see we're talking about considerable sums here, Mr Forsyth. This is no straightforward will and testament. Have you appointed an executor? I know the temptation may be to hand this job to a close friend or family member, but I must advise you that this arrangement rarely works out well. You know how difficult some family members can be – especially at a time of bereavement,' he added quickly.

'Oh aye, I'm well aware how difficult families can be, Mr Campbell. I'd like to make you the executor, if that's okay?'

A broad smile spread across Campbell's face. 'Well, yes, of course. It will be my honour to perform this service for you.' He hesitated. 'You'll want a cup of tea or coffee on a cold day like this. I can have one brought through now. What's your preference?'

'It's fine. I'm no' staying. Things to get on wae. You'll find all you need on there. If you're after more, I've written my mobile number on the last page. Now, I'll let you get on wae your day.' Machie stood.

'Well, now, hold on, Mr Forsyth. This is an estate . . . well, it's complex. I'd like to ask you a few questions, if you don't mind.'

'Like what?'

'Well, for a start, I'd like to know how you happened upon such a large sum of money?'

Machie stared at him for a few moments. Now he was looking down on the lawyer. 'It's none o' your business,

Mr Campbell. It's an executor I'm after, no' a forensic accountant.' Campbell opened his mouth to speak, but Machie raised his hand. 'Listen, it's quite simple. Do you want to do this for me or not? Last time I looked, there was nae shortage of solicitors about.'

'No, no, of course I'm very pleased to be able to help you.' Campbell donned his glasses once more. 'I see you have a list of beneficiaries.'

'Aye, all there – names and addresses.'

'I must warn you, an estate of this size – well, we have to take a percentage, by way of payment, you understand.'

Machie smiled. 'I do. I also know what the going rate is, too. So, if you'd just do the necessary, I'd be most obliged to you. You know how to get in touch.' Machie turned on his heel and left the office. 'Hey, doll,' he said to the receptionist on the way out. 'Better get your man in there a cup o' tea. I think he needs one.'

Back outside, he replaced the cap back on his head. 'Fat bastard,' he mumbled under his breath with a smile. For the first time in a long time, he felt good about himself.

16

Glasgow, 1983

The room was reasonably long, with some tables and chairs scattered about. A girlie calendar was pinned beside a vending machine where tasteless beverages could be purchased in exchange for a few coins. At the opposite end of the room some police officers were huddled into a group. Chatting and eating, they were enjoying time out from their shift, or piece break, as it was known in the city. One young cop struggled to navigate a doner kebab into his mouth without its red sauce dripping on to his uniform shirt. His collar was unbuttoned and the black tie with its false knot and metallic clip slung over one shoulder. Beside him, an older constable looked on, chewing lazily on a corned beef sandwich, punctuated by slurps of tea from the plastic mug that accompanied the tartan flask on the floor at his side.

Radio traffic sputtered into life now and again. But each officer was so tuned in to his or her shoulder number and the codes that could see all of them rush from the room to help a colleague, it looked as though nobody was paying attention.

The older cop finished his sandwich and addressed his colleagues. 'This yin here, eh? Looks as though he's no' been fed for a month.' He nodded at his young colleague eating the kebab.

'Where he lives, they don't have any shops,' said PC Angela Cootes.

'Aye, they eat their ain weans in the schemes.' Alex Hughes finished his chips and wiped his drooping moustache. 'When's the last time you had a square meal, son? Your girlfriend will be too busy selling blow jobs to make the dinner, eh?'

As the rest of them laughed, Constable Brian Scott finished chewing on his strip of kebab meat. 'Bet you cannae remember your first blow job, Alex?'

'Aye, I can.'

'Honestly? You'll remember how long it took the bloke to come, then?'

Angela laughed into her hand, while Jock Mears replaced the mug on top of his tartan flask. 'Too quick for you, Alex.' He turned to face Scott. 'You're good wae the jokes, son.'

'He'll no' be so quick wae them when I've knocked all his teeth oot,' said Hughes, still staring at Scott, who was now carefully trying to wrap what was left of his kebab into a ball without making more mess than he already had.

'I hear Discipline are coming to interview us all tomorrow night,' said Mears.

'What for?' asked Scott.

'That shit at thon pub the other night. I hear the barman lost a kidney.'

Suddenly, Brian Scott wished he hadn't eaten anything. 'He was in some state, right enough.'

'Aw, poor Brian,' said Hughes. 'Is that the first time you've seen a man that's taken a good beating? If you don't like it, you've joined the wrong job, son.'

'Are you careers advice?' Scott snapped. Though he was by far the youngest police officer in the room, he wasn't going to take any of these barbs lying down. It seemed as though it was a kind of initiation into the job. In their first few weeks, young probationers were seen and not heard. Their tutor cops, the experienced police officers tasked with showing them the ropes, would employ diverse tricks to rid themselves of their young charges. Scott had experienced this himself, having been locked in a police box for three hours. But he'd grown up in a hard school and wasn't going to back down now he had some time under his belt.

In any case, he had other things on his mind.

The back shift, from two in the afternoon until eleven at night, was the most hated. It seemed to drag on for hours. His break over, Scott made his way back on to the beat, feeling as though the weight of the world was on his shoulders. News about the Discipline Branch hadn't improved his mood.

He attended a few calls: a shoplifter had made off with a pile of papers from outside a newsagent's shop, a woman in the high flats was worried that her son might be on drugs, and there were reports of an assault outside a bookmaker's. It was clear from the off that the newspaper thief would never be caught; red hair and a pair of denims was a description that could have covered half of the East End. He'd assured the woman that he would have a word with her son, but felt sorry for her. Most of the young teenagers in that area dabbled in something, but the thought of her own precious offspring being so tempted had clearly come as a shock to the mother. And by the time he'd reached the bookie's, there were no signs of a disturbance. Predictably, nobody had seen a thing. That happened a lot where Brian Scott walked the beat.

He checked his watch: almost nine thirty p.m. Scott made his way into a phone box and fed a few coins into the slot.

'Aye, who are you and what dae you want?' Scott could hear the click of snooker balls, raised voices and the clink of glasses.

'Is he there?'

'Who wants to know?' The man's voice was coarse.

'Just tell him it's Brian fae along the street.'

'Oh aye, I'm sure he'll want to speak to you.' Nonetheless, Scott heard Frank MacDougall being called to the phone.

'Scooty, my man. How are you?'

'No' so good, Frank.'

'Why so?'

'The other night – you know fine.'

'That's enough!' MacDougall paused. 'Careless talk, an' all that.'

'The Discipline Branch are coming tomorrow. Guess who'll be the person they want to speak to?'

'Listen, where are you now?'

'At work. I know that's not something you're used to.'

'Cheeky bastard. You finish at eleven, right?'

'Aye.'

'Nae bother. Come to the usual place – about half eleven.'

'I'm meeting Ella at my mother's.'

'So gie her a phone. I want to help you, but I need to see you face to face – you know what I mean, Scooty. I don't trust phones. We'll sort this, don't worry about it.'

'How?'

'Just be there at half eleven.' The line went dead.

*

The rest of Scott's shift was quiet. He spent it wandering round the streets, fretting. He called his mother to let her know he would be a bit late back from work, and to tell Ella, his girlfriend, to wait for him.

Work over, he wandered out of the station and into the maze of the East End. Scott didn't have a car, so it took him time to get to the place MacDougall wanted to meet. The tenement block was run down. He trudged up the worn steps in the gloomy close to the second landing. The flat opposite had been boarded up by the council, but the door on the right-hand side of the landing was painted bright red, and light of a similar shade shone through the fanlight on to his face as he rang the bell.

After a few moments, a woman opened the door. She was dressed in a skimpy leather skirt, high black patent boots, fishnet stockings and a revealing blouse. Her face was thickly caked in make-up. She looked him up and down. 'Hi, son. A blow job is a tenner and full sex is twenty. Money on entry – intae the flat, I mean. Aye, and it's no' me, by the way.' She held out her hand and gave him a weak smile.

'I'm here to see Frank,' said Scott.

'Aw, okay, hun.' The woman shrugged and opened the door, all interest in her visitor gone. 'He's through in the lounge – straight ahead.' She gestured down the red-lit hall.

Scott could hear a woman groan as he walked past one of the bedrooms. He shook his head. Here he was in a brothel, with only a leather jacket covering his white uniform shirt and epaulettes.

He pushed open the door to the lounge. He'd been expecting MacDougall to be surrounded by the usual acolytes, but was surprised to find the figure with the dark hair and trendy clothes alone.

'Scooty, my man!' MacDougall jumped off a threadbare sofa and greeted the young policeman with a companionable slap on the back. 'How was walking the beat today?'

'The usual. I'm more worried about what happened the other night.'

MacDougall shrugged, his expensive Italian leather jacket creaking with the movement. 'I hear you. You know what he's like.'

'You were supposed to be going to pick up money – that was all. I didn't think *he* was going to be there. That's what you said.'

'That's Jay all over. He changed his mind. I swear, we were supposed to go in, get the cash he owed us and bugger off. We ended up leaving wae fifty quid and change. He lost the plot, as usual.'

Brian Scott sat down on an easy chair. 'The guy's lost a kidney.'

'I heard.'

'Don't you care aboot that, Frankie? If you don't, I dae. I'm supposed to be protecting these people!'

MacDougall followed Scott's example and sat back down. 'Look at you wae the shiny boots and the polis troosers. Why the fuck did you join that mob, eh? You could have come and worked for me. You'd have made ten times as much.'

'You really have to ask me that?'

MacDougall shook his head. 'Right, I get it, you've got a social conscience – good for you. But why did you choose to become a polis on your ain doorstep? You must have known what would happen.'

'You don't get a choice where you're put.'

'Then you should have joined another force – got the fuck

116

oot o' this place. You surely realised you were asking for trouble. Especially coming fae where we do.'

'Lucky me.'

'Listen, that bastard's been trying to avoid us for weeks. Every time we sent somebody he wasn't behind the bar.'

'Why didn't you send in one of your own men to case the bloody place?'

'Come on, Brian. He knows them all.'

'So just send in a polis tae put him at his ease, aye?'

MacDougall shrugged.

'I'm out! I'm no' doing this any more. If oor friend has a problem wae that . . . well, I'll nail him for the other night.'

'Scooty man, don't be mental. He'll do what he said, you know he will.'

'If that bastard lays a hand on my faither, I'll kill him!'

'Have you any idea how much dosh he owes us, your dad?'

'Lots, I'm guessing.'

'Aye – a pile.' MacDougall leaned over towards Scott. 'Every time you do us a wee favour – well, a chunk comes off the principal.'

'My father owes that money, no' me.'

'Like I said. You should have gone somewhere else to pound the beat or whatever it is you do.'

'Between a dock and a hard place.' Brian Scott shook his head.

'Rock, Brian.'

'Eh?'

'It's between a rock and a hard place, no' dock.'

'How's that important right now, Frankie?'

'Lesson in life – it'll stand you in good stead.'

'Aye, in Barlinnie. That's where I'll be standing before long.'

'Listen, don't worry aboot anything. Machie has it covered. You won't even be asked a question.'

'What dae you mean?'

'Trust me.'

'Aye – look where that's got me.'

'You and Ella. You're looking for a flat, right?'

'If you think I'm moving her in here, you can think again. She'd go radio rental!'

'I'll sort you out. One of oor other places.'

'I'm only doing this for my faither, no' for money or any other favours.'

'I'm telling you, Brian. You fuck this up and you know he'll do it. And you know I cannae stop him, neither.'

Disgusted, Scott got his feet. 'And what aboot you, Frank? How dae you think all this is going to end for you? That bastard is mental. He'll probably end up killing us all.'

'Nothing lasts for ever, Scooty. Know what I mean?'

Brian Scott attended work the next day with a heavy heart. The moment he appeared through the door Sergeant Logan called him aside.

'Nice wee treat for you, Scott.'

'What?' Scott was still nervous about the Discipline Branch, and it showed on his face.

'Largs.'

'Largs? Sorry, sergeant, I'm a bit confused.'

'Nothing new there, son.' Logan stroked his moustache and continued, 'You're off for some work experience. You'll be aide to CID down at the seaside. Wish it was me.'

Brian Scott thought for a moment, remembering the conversation he'd had with Frank MacDougall the previous evening. 'So, just like that – I'm off?'

'Yup, just like that. One o' the boys will drive you down in half an hour or so.'

'And how do I get back?'

'Two choices. You can jump on the train, for which you'll be compensated.'

'Or?'

'There's a nice wee flat down there. One of ours. It's especially for people like you. You know, young cops who have to move fae place to place. It'll get you out o' the East End.'

Scott thought for a moment. 'You know I'm engaged, sir.'

'Aye, I do. The lassie passed all the family checks.'

'What does that mean?'

'It means that if you want her to move with you – well, whose business is it but yours? I'm no' going to say anything.'

'Right. Thanks, sergeant. I better go and get my stuff.' He paused. 'What about Discipline? I heard they were coming today. About what happened the other night, I mean.'

'They can read your report.' Logan shrugged. 'Nice to have friends, eh? Do yourself a favour and stick in down there. You never know where it will lead.' He plodded back into the sergeants' room.

Brian Scott stared out into the street. Last night he'd been ready to be asked very awkward questions about a man beaten half to death in a back-street pub. Now, he was about to move to Largs and team up with the CID. Not to mention having a flat of his own to share with Ella.

Though he felt no little relief, the bile still rose in his throat.

17

Ella Scott was sitting in her kitchen. Even at this distance, she could hear her husband snoring loudly upstairs. It was already after ten in the morning. She took a sip of tea and a bite of the toast and jam she'd made for breakfast, chewed miserably for a few moments, then pushed the plate away.

It was her worst nightmare. Though she'd threatened to leave her husband and head to New York to visit their student nurse daughter, she knew that it was irresponsible. Ella was the only person who could keep Brian Scott remotely near the straight and narrow when he hit the bottle. This time, having been suspended from his job, it was as bad as she could remember. The sight of this funny, daft, beautiful man now with stains down the front of his shirt, a bloated face and pinprick, red-ringed eyes broke her heart. Though she'd resolved to be less accepting of his behaviour – more censorious – she was at a loss as to what else to do.

Ella lit another cigarette and stared at the screen of her computer. Her son Will had arranged for home movies, photographs and other bits and pieces to be digitalised. She watched her life parade before her eyes to the backdrop of her and Brian's favourite songs.

There they were on a beach. It was Largs, she remembered.

Brian had just been made an ADC. A smart little police flat near the seafront came with the position. At first, she'd not dared mention to her father that she was moving in with her fiancé, making the excuse that she was on a new college course in Ayrshire. She remembered shaking when she finally plucked up the courage to tell him. Because Ella was his favourite, and despite his feelings for the police, her father gave her his blessing. He liked Brian. It had been one of the happiest times of her life.

He looked so good in a suit as he headed off to work from their new home. But she remembered worrying about him even back then.

When they'd first met, he liked a couple of drinks, but growing up with an alcoholic father had been enough to warn him off excess. Since he'd joined the police, though, she'd noticed a change in the carefree youth she'd first known.

While Brian insisted that it was the pressure of the job that was taking its toll, she knew there was something else. But try as she might, she could never get to the bottom of what was the real cause of this descent into binge drinking and melancholy: something that had blighted his life every now and then since.

The next picture was of Brian's father, Willie. He was standing holding a baby, his namesake, their son, Will. Even though the image on the screen was faded, she could still see the haunted eyes, the yellow hue of his skin. The man was a frail shadow of his former self, even in the time she'd known him. A few short weeks after that picture was taken, Willie Scott's best friend alcohol had accompanied him on his final journey – to the grave.

Naturally, her husband was devastated by the death of his

father. Gradually, as though the manner of his demise had served as a warning, Brian began to rally. He stopped drinking. He also moved on in his career and began to flourish. In return, he was awarded a full-time position as a detective constable. The job was back in Glasgow. Ella was so proud of him. And much as she missed the sea air and friendly folk of Largs, she was happy to be back amongst friends and family.

Ella heard Brian snore once more and sighed. She'd seen Willie Scott's haunted eyes again the night before. Only this time they belonged to his son.

Needing another cup of tea, Ella got to her feet just as the phone rang.

'Hello?'

'Hi, Ella.'

'Jimmy. How are you?'

'You know, the usual.' Daley sounded as he always did – weary.

'If you're after your friend, he's still in bed.'

'How bad?' said Daley without preamble.

'About as bad as I've seen him. All this at work isn't helping either, by the way.'

Hearing the admonishment in her voice, Daley wanted to tell her that there was nobody to blame but Brian himself, but managed to hold his tongue. He knew that Ella would be suffering enough because of his old friend's drinking. 'About that, I'll need him to come in tomorrow.'

'He's suspended. Why would he come in?'

'To help with the investigation about what happened in the Douglas Arms.'

'Ah right. Okay, Jim. Sorry.'

'Nothing to be sorry for – in fact I should be apologising.'

'Why?'

'Liz. She had no right telling you about all that.'

'Ach, no' her fault.'

'No, the man upstairs is firmly to blame for it all.'

'Eh? God, dae you mean?' Ella sounded puzzled.

'No, Brian – you said he was still in bed. I assume he's upstairs. Or did he not make it that far?'

'Aye – he's up in the spare room. Where he's been for quite a while.' Ella thought for a moment. 'So, how are you doing without him? I'm sorry, you'll be run off your feet because my husband cannae behave like a normal human being.'

'They sent a replacement – temporary,' Daley added quickly.

'Yous don't hang about, eh?'

'She's not just covering for Brian. She's a specialist. I can't say much more.'

'Right. So, what time tomorrow?'

'Eleven, sharp. Though I could do with having a word today, if he's up to it?'

'Well, I'll try. Maybe he could make it in this afternoon. Once I've drawn him a bath and wrung his liver oot wae a mangle, that is.'

'Okay, that's great, Ella. How are you holding up?'

'You know me, Jimmy. Nothing I've no' seen before.' She took a breath.

'But?'

'I don't know. It's different this time.'

'How so?'

'Talking about handing in his cards. Wants to move to Spain. Buy a wee bar, would you believe?'

'That would be a disaster.'

123

'You're telling me! I caught the bugger pishing in the sink last night.'

'He might struggle, you know.'

'He certainly wouldnae be able to be at that kind o' nonsense in Spain. Places we've been to are spotless.'

'No, tomorrow – with the investigation.'

'Aye, I suppose so. As you say, Liz filled me in wae all the gory details.'

'I might be able to help. I'm going to see someone later.'

Ella shrugged, though she knew Daley couldn't see her. She was resigned to the fact that her husband had run out of rope as a police officer. Goodness knows, he'd come close enough on many occasions in the past. They had a house up the road, his pension and a little money put away. But the man she knew and loved would drift without the bustle and companionship he found in his job. And that could lead to only one thing.

'Hello? Are you still there, Ella?'

'Aye, just daydreaming, Jim.'

'That Brian was back to normal, you mean?'

'Nah. That Brad Pitt just arrived at the door and got me the fuck oot o' this.'

Daley laughed. Ella had the same wit as her husband. Probably what drew them together in the first place. He couldn't imagine them apart. 'I'll see him this afternoon – hopefully.'

'Aye, I'll dae my best. If it's a no-go, I'll gie you a bell.'

'Thanks, Ella. I'll see you soon.' Daley ended the call.

DS Dhar knocked at the door of Daley's glass box just as he was putting down the phone.

'Yes, Shreya? How can I help you?'

'I think a visit to the hotel would be a good thing, sir – Jim.' She smiled.

'Just to check it out, you mean?'

'Yes, try and get an impression, that kind of thing.'

'Good idea. I'll say one thing for Macmillan, he's certainly done wonders for the menu.'

'Would you like to join me? For lunch, I mean. Just as a cover, of sorts,' she added quickly. 'I don't want some desperate travelling salesman hitting on me.'

'Don't worry. Everyone will know who you are by now.' Daley stroked his chin.

'Oh, of course. A small place like this. I understand. And you won't want people talking, either. I should never have asked – didn't think, sir.'

Daley smiled. 'So, news of my marital situation is still the talk of the town?'

'No, not at all. My mistake.' Shreya Dhar turned to leave.

'It's my fault. I'm just being stupid. I knew the member of staff well – the one who died. We all did.' He gestured airily.

'And you haven't been in there since?'

'No, I haven't.'

'It's fine. I'll ask DC Potts.'

'No, this has to be done. It could be part of an investigation. I'll have to do it sometime, might as well be now. About twelve? Brian is coming to see me later this afternoon – hopefully.' Daley grimaced.

'Twelve it is, Jim.' Dhar smiled and closed the door of Daley's glass box quietly behind her.

18

Hugh Machie was back in his flat warming up following his trip to the lawyer. He really fancied a drink, but the events in the Douglas Arms had put him off the local hostelries. The sensible thing would have been to buy a bottle of whisky and some cans of beer from the supermarket to consume at home. But he hated drinking alone. It was something his father had told him never to do, as it was the last step before alcoholism. And, unlike his own son, Hugh had always listened to his father.

Stiffly, he kneeled to reach under the bed and remove a small leather case. He unzipped it and took out an old Webley MK II .455 revolver. He'd owned it for so many years that it sat perfectly in his hand, the handle and trigger worn to fit after years of practice. Hugh was a fastidious man and had kept the weapon in almost mint condition. Funny, he thought, that this firearm had been with him longer than he'd been married to his wife. She'd been taken from him; now he would use the gun in his hand to help him make the journey back to her.

But he had one last thing to do before then. Another wrong to right. And nothing would stop him, because he had nothing to lose.

Machie oiled, polished and tested the unloaded weapon. As always, it was as sweet as a nut. He laid it on the bed and stood back to admire his handiwork. He'd always been fascinated by real craftsmen – men like those who had made this gun, long before the mass-produced, computer-designed, robotically fabricated shit that everyone lusted after now. Like a good mechanical watchmaker, gunsmiths spent their lives perfecting their skills. Experts in the field could match a weapon to an individual workman. They all left a hint of their identity in the way they'd worked.

Now everything was uniform, mostly untouched by human hand. This new world made him recoil. He was glad to be leaving it.

Machie placed the gun back in its neat case and made for the door. If he was to do what had to be done right, he would have to practise, feel the revolver in his hand and reacquaint himself with it. Some people took it for granted that if they could do something well once then that would always be the case. But he remembered his time in National Service. The sergeant major had them take their weapons apart, maintain them, fire them, sleep with them, until caring for the gun you used was the most natural thing in the world.

He shrugged on his coat and left the flat. This time he turned left out of the close and then left again down a side street. The car was old and modest, a creaky little Toyota, which, like him, had seen better days. It was parked a few feet from a barber shop. When he ducked in and sat behind the wheel, he could smell oil and damp. But the car only needed to last as long he did, and that time was shortening by the day.

Machie had studied maps of the area. He wanted to be able to practise with the gun as often as he could, which meant not having to drive miles in order to find a suitable place. Too much wasted time, he reasoned. And Hugh Machie didn't trust farmers. Sharp, inquisitive men and women, in his experience. All with a nose for those who dared trespass on their property. So much time spent on the land they farmed that the mere fall of a pin would alert them to something awry.

He took the south coast road out of the town. Shops and flats soon gave way to spacious, expensive homes overlooking the loch. When they thinned out, he passed a graveyard as the road meandered along the loch.

The island at the loch's head he'd seen when he first arrived looked larger than he'd imagined. Eventually, he arrived at a lay-by. As he'd expected, it was quiet; his was the only car to be seen. He'd driven past this place four or five times, and on each occasion it had been deserted. Machie picked up his case, left his car and went through a small gate that led on to a patch of grass. With stiff knees, he staggered down a sandy bank and out on to a sliver of rocky shoreline. He made his way along carefully; the rocks and boulders were slick with weed and seawater. In a few more paces he turned a corner, and a small bay opened out in front of him. Still, almost stagnant water was trapped between the shore and a rocky causeway that twisted to the island. The tide was high, and he only had a couple of yards of beach on which to stand. Nonetheless, the roaring surf echoed around the place, the sound almost deafening. Certainly, had he anyone to speak to, they'd have had to shout to each other. This was the perfect place. He looked out over the grey waves with their white-horse tips. No boats or other sailing craft to be seen.

Machie turned and examined the inevitable detritus that had been discarded in the little bay by heavier seas. As he expected: some old fishing buoys, rusting cans that had once held soft drinks or beer. He picked a few up and made his way to the shoreline. Carefully, he placed them on the water. Slowly, by force of wind and waves, three old buoys and four empty cans were washed away from him, their presence a flash of colour on a grey sea under a dull sky.

Calmly, Machie unzipped the leather case. The Webley was already loaded. He held it out before him with both hands and took aim. Quickly, he fired off six shots. Only one found its mark. He sighed, reloaded and tried again. As the floating targets were getting further away by the second, his task was becoming more difficult. He took aim again. Five shots this time, three hits. The reports were carried off on the wind, adding little to the tumult.

Though he was pleased with himself, he felt the strain of holding the weapon. His forearms ached already, and he'd only managed to fire a few rounds. If this is to be done, it'll have to be done at close range and quickly, he thought.

Hugh Machie was about to reload again when movement at the corner of his eye made him instinctively turn to face whoever was coming. An old man wearing a fisherman's cap and smoking a pipe was heading towards him along the shore.

The man took one look at the revolver and took a step back. 'What are you at?' he said, a look of concern spreading across his leathery face.

'Just a wee hobby of mine – target practice.' Machie pointed to the cans and buoys floating out in the bay. The gun was still in his other hand, directed at this unexpected visitor.

Where there had been bewilderment, there was now panic, as the old fisherman reached for his chest. His mouth drooped open, and he made a groaning noise, his eyes wide.

'What's up?' Machie shouted against the churn of the waves.

The man dropped to his knees. 'Help me,' he said weakly, before collapsing on the sand.

Hugh Machie rushed over to him. He placed two fingers on the old man's neck but could find no pulse. He struggled for breath as he turned the dead weight of the body over and attempted to administer CPR. But Hugh Machie was frail, and the task proved too much for him. He rolled away from the still figure in the sand, gasping for breath.

When he'd recovered, Machie stared at the body. All colour had drained from the man's face, and his lips were blue. His life had ebbed away.

Machie thought for a moment. He'd seen more than his fair share of death, but this was different. This death was natural, probably a heart attack, no doubt prompted by meeting the ghost of a man that Hugh Machie now was, pointing a gun.

'Fuck!' Machie swore loudly. He rushed across the sand, jumped on to the machair and hurried to his car. He pulled a key from his pocket and opened the boot to reveal a small shovel. Looking around, he removed it from the boot and stumbled as quickly as he could back on to the sand.

The hole he dug was little more than a foot deep. Groaning with effort, he rolled his victim into the impromptu grave, then fetched the pipe that lay where it had fallen and placed it on the dead man's chest before beginning to cover the body, first with sand, then with a few loose boulders he found lying about that were light enough to carry.

He could have left the body on the beach. But it would surely have been discovered, and soon the police would be looking for a battered old Toyota. Hugh knew how these things worked, and he needed time. Not much, but some nonetheless.

He stepped back to assess his handiwork. The beach looked much the same as it had when he arrived. Machie was breathing heavily. He gathered as many of the shell cases that were scattered around the place as he could find and put them in his pocket. He stood for a moment over the pile of boulders. 'I'm sorry. I don't know who you were, but probably you deserved much better. It's people like me who should be buried in the sand.'

Cursing his and the dead man's luck, he made his way back to the car. He placed his hands on the steering wheel, but found he was trembling uncontrollably. So much death; but this unfortunate soul struck at his heart like none other. Machie knew he didn't have much time left, that soon, his would be the colourless face with the blue lips. It had all been so quick, so random. But he supposed he'd seen that many times. People whose run-of-the-mill day had ended in their death.

But he remembered what he had to do. Gathering himself, he turned the key in the ignition and drove away.

Back on the beach, all that was left was an almost imperceptible mound in the sand.

19

The County Hotel was as quiet as Daley had seen it. He knew that most of the locals were shunning the place. Indeed, Macmillan had received death threats, both via the internet and in person. Though Daley sympathised with Kinloch's citizens over the tragic loss of one of their own, he'd had to be firm, but he hadn't gone further than a caution.

When feelings ran high in this town, the whole community gathered together. In a way, it was like one big, extended family, something he admired very much. But it was his job to keep the peace. Daley liked to think that the locals, if they did not love him, did at least respect him. More than many incomers could hope for – certainly in his position. But he knew that he could live in this place for decades and never be considered a true part of it. That took generations.

He and DS Dhar took a seat in the centre of the empty dining room. They had to wait ten minutes before a waitress appeared to take their order. Where once only locals had worked, the staff these days was a hotch-potch of Eastern Europeans, Glaswegians, Australians and New Zealanders. Nobody from Kinloch would work for Ian Macmillan now.

Dhar chose macaroni cheese, while Daley ordered a seafood pasta. Since his heart problems had been discovered, Liz had ensured that he steered clear of red meat. It had become a habit.

Quietly he observed Dhar. It was clear that she was taking a careful note of her surroundings, from floor to ceiling. Here's a thorough detective, keen on detail, he thought. Though he was alone in knowing the real reason for her temporary posting to Kinloch, he still couldn't work out what she would be able to uncover about Macmillan that he had been unable to find. He supposed that she had access and information to which he was not privy. This notion irritated him. How many bad people had escaped justice just because one department guarded its knowledge rather than sharing it? It was a perennial problem.

But Dhar was very forthcoming. And though he hadn't yet, he believed that if he were to ask her just what she suspected Macmillan was guilty of, she would tell him.

'You like shellfish?' she asked.

'Oh yes,' replied Daley, dragged back from his thoughts. 'I had a little health problem a while ago. Had to look at my diet, and all that good stuff.' He shrugged regretfully.

'I'm a vegetarian.'

'Because of your religion?' Daley knew he'd said the wrong thing immediately.

Dhar stared at him, blank-faced, then at the tablecloth.

'I'm sorry – I didn't think.'

Dhar burst out laughing. 'You don't need to apologise, Jim. Because I look a certain way, people just put me in a box. An Asian woman eating the vegetarian option on the menu – she must be a Hindu, or some other exotic religion. The logic is there, but no real thought, I'm afraid.'

'No.' Daley looked sheepish. 'I suppose we are all racists, and we don't even know it.'

'You're not racist, sir. I've met real racists, red in tooth and claw bastards with only hate in their hearts. I know one when I see one. It's a look – the eyes. I don't know.' She took in her new, if temporary, boss. He was holding up despite the ravages of time and so long spent in the unyielding, unforgiving job they shared. That there was much sadness in his eyes was obvious. But she also sensed regret. 'How do you think things will go for DS Scott?' she asked.

Daley sighed. 'I don't know. I have one chance to help him. The guy he is supposed to have assaulted is one of those people who trip over traffic cones or cracks in the pavement and try to get money out of the council.'

'I know the type.'

'I shouldn't, but I'm seeing Brian this afternoon, then the guy who made the complaint.' He hesitated. 'Forget you heard that, Shreya.'

'I've been in the police long enough now to know how things work, Jim. I'd like to come with you to see this guy, if that's okay?'

'Are you sure? I mean, we won't be taking many notes.'

'I'm sure. We all stick together, right?' She smiled.

Daley thanked her. Strangely, there was something in that smile that was fleetingly familiar. He puzzled on it for a few moments before putting the notion down to the detective's tendency to always see a connection somewhere. It came from years of trying to pair villains with crimes, and it became habit. 'Tell me about yourself. They didn't send much in the way of background – I suppose because of your line of work.'

'Not much to tell. My mother came to Scotland from India. She never told me the real reason, and I never asked. We moved about and landed in Glasgow. There were already people from her part of India living in the city. I suppose she made it a home from home – or at least tried to.'

'Why the police?'

Dhar's expression was suddenly serious. 'Growing up – well, I saw a lot, you know? I was brought up to believe that everyone has good in them. But I now know that isn't true. I realised it a long time ago.'

Daley was about to ask another question when the doors to the dining room burst open. Instead of staff members bringing their meal, the tall, elegant figure of Ian Macmillan strode across towards them.

'Hey,' said the Canadian. 'Mr Daley, how are you? I haven't seen you since . . .' He paused. 'Well, since . . . you know.' He lowered his head.

Daley, determined to be civil and not give Macmillan any clues that he was under suspicion, forced a smile. 'Yes, it's been hard – coming in here since then, I mean.'

'Oh yeah, I understand. I can't get the whole thing outta my own head, if I'm honest.'

'What happened?' said Dhar guilelessly.

'Sorry, this is my new sergeant. Shreya Dhar, meet Ian Macmillan.'

Daley looked on as the pair shook hands. While Macmillan held her hand for rather too long, Dhar looked cool and untroubled. She knew about what had happened to Annie and yet acted as though it was all news to her.

'A member of staff. Sadly, she decided to take her own life.' Again, Macmillan lowered his head.

Daley wanted to shout, to yell at the top of his voice. *You caused it! You took away everything that was important to her just when she was at her most vulnerable.* But he remained silent, still determined not to raise Macmillan's suspicions. He found the hardest thing to do was to keep his expression neutral. He remembered Liz smiling at Macmillan when he had just taken over the hotel. He saw Brian Scott frown at his wife and realised once more that his friend had his back – always – professionally and domestically. The thought made him feel guilty. He had been very cool with Brian the last time they'd met. He resolved to make up for that in their meeting later that afternoon.

'You're from Canada, Mr Macmillan?' said Dhar.

'Yes, from Toronto.'

'It must be a very different experience living here?' She cocked her head.

'Oh, I don't know. My folks were from Kinloch. I like the place.' He glanced at Daley. 'Despite everything.'

'We all make mistakes,' said Dhar.

'I've never made one with those consequences. I never want to do it again.'

'Here's hoping,' said Daley, damning himself for thinking out loud. Hearts and sleeves – he couldn't stop himself.

'Surely running a truck company is very different from owning a hotel?' said Dhar.

Daley was surprised by her directness. She was here to investigate the dapper man who was standing by their table, that much was true. But this investigation was supposed to be covert, and the DCI was surprised that she was willing to reveal how much she knew about Macmillan.

'Very different. But business is business, you know. I've made mistakes, sure.' Again, he glanced at Daley. 'I have to remember that truckers are a different breed from folks who work in hotels, I guess.'

Involuntarily, Brian Scott's likely riposte to this comment crossed Daley's mind, but he focused yet again on keeping his expression neutral.

'What about your family – you must miss them?' Dhar patted her chest and excused herself. 'I'm sorry, I'm assuming you have family.' She displayed no emotion as Macmillan bridled at the question.

'My wife and I are estranged, DS Dhar. My children? Well, kids are kids, if you know what I mean. Your kids will be young, I guess?'

'I don't have children. It's not something I've thought much about, to be honest.'

'Take my advice, keep it that way. They're a drain on your pocket and your resolve. And it never stops.'

'I love my wee boy,' said Daley.

'Hey, I'm not saying that I don't love them. But your little guy, for instance; just wait until he grows up, becomes a teenager. It's like living with an alien. I don't have to tell you guys about the dangers out there. Drugs, crime – all kinds of shit, right?'

'You must feel quite helpless – being so far away, I mean?' said Dhar.

Macmillan stared at her. 'I keep a close eye on things. We have the internet in Canada, you know.'

'Yes, but it's not like being there, is it? All the drugs and crime you're talking about. It must be a worry.' DS Dhar smiled benignly.

'My wife might not talk much to me any more, but she still loves her kids.'

'But there's nothing like having a father about. I know. My father left us high and dry when I was just a child in India.'

It was Daley's turn to look at Dhar. She wasn't afraid of revealing her own vulnerabilities, that much was clear. He admired the way she was toying with Macmillan, probing, waiting for him to slip up, with the use of what seemed like merely innocuous questions.

'Too bad. I do feel guilty sometimes – with the distance and all. But they know where I am, and I speak to them every day. Comes a time when the birds have to leave the nest, yeah?'

Dhar nodded but didn't reply.

'Okay, guys. As I say, it's lovely to see you here – nice to meet you, DS Dhar.' Though he smiled, his eyes were saying something else. 'I'd better get going. Enjoy your lunch.'

Daley watched Macmillan leave the dining room, his stride almost imperceptibly less jaunty than when he'd arrived. 'Well done. A masterclass in searing understatement,' said Daley, genuinely impressed.

'That's a man under pressure, I'd say.'

'I would agree.'

The waitress brought their meals. Daley tucked into his fish with great relish. He'd been arguing with Liz that morning and had skipped breakfast, settling for only a mug of coffee. He knew he needed something in his stomach before facing Scott later in the afternoon. That was bound to ruin his appetite. 'How's your meal?' he asked.

Shreya Dhar shrugged. 'I'd rate it slightly above average.'

Taking this in, Daley couldn't help thinking that this was not only how she felt about food, but also about most people: *slightly above average.*

20

Glasgow, 1984

James Machie was sitting alone in the back room of the pub he used when he wanted to impress people. Many of his associates were next door in the lounge or the public bar. He didn't really care for pubs. Noisy places where empty vessels could make a noise. Places where stupid people could feel good about their miserable lives with the aid of alcohol and the company of like-minded idiots. But he knew only too well that it paid to show face now and again.

The room was spartan. Like most pubs in Glasgow's East End, little attention was paid to decoration or adornment. This was a place where people came to get drunk – when Machie wasn't here, that was. The room was lit by weak sunlight coming through two slit windows high on the back wall, bars guarding them from the outside. One single strip light was the only other form of illumination, and consequently the place managed to be both stark and gloomy at the same time.

James Machie sat behind one long table, abutted at each end by two shorter versions. Chairs, cigarette ash and discarded beer mats were scattered across the stained linoleum floor.

The thud of the jukebox mingled with the noise of the street beyond, a mix of traffic and the chatter of pedestrians.

Frank MacDougall opened the frosted glass door. 'He's here, Jay.'

'Gie him a drink and make him wait for half an hour.'

'It was you that wanted to speak to him, big man.'

'And?'

'We've got that other thing, remember?'

'You'd have made a great secretary. "Come in, Miss Smith",' Machie said, mocking his lieutenant.

'You know what he's like wae the stories. That's all I'm saying.'

'Oh aye, he's always been good wae the stories.'

'Well?'

Machie sighed. 'Okay, bring the bastard in.'

MacDougall stood his ground.

'I know that floor is a disgrace, but you're no' stuck tae it, are you?' Machie said.

'I was just wondering, when was the last time you saw the big man?'

'My faither?'

'Aye.'

'When we were busy burning my mother in the crematorium.'

'Oh.'

'Just say what the fuck you're going to say and let's get on wae oor lives, eh?'

'Things haven't been good between you pair for a long time.'

'They took a downturn when I battered his heid in wae that rock, aye.'

'That's a few years ago, Jay.'

'No' that many.'

'I'm just thinking, dae you want me in as well? You know, when you're speaking to him.'

'Why?'

'I know he's your faither and that. But as we know, he's no' too auld to gie you hassle. He's the hardest man I know.'

'Shite!'

'Eh?'

'I'm the hardest man you know.' Machie smiled. 'And if he gets difficult, he'll get this.' He reached under the table and produced a long sword with a vicious-looking blade that had been concealed there.

'You would stick your ain father?'

'Aye. I'd stick anybody. You know that, Frankie.'

MacDougall shrugged and made his way out of the room. In a few moments, the shadow of a tall man was framed behind the frosted glass. He chapped the door loudly.

'Come in!' Machie shouted.

The door swung open to reveal his father. He was broad-shouldered, the muscles of his arms bulging through the cut of his unfashionable grey suit. His hair was brushed back, faded blond turning grey at the temples. But the death of his wife had aged Hugh Machie. His face was lined, his eyes sorrowful. He had the puffy features of someone too fond of alcohol.

'James,' he said, his face expressionless.

'Grab a chair, Faither. We don't want you keeling o'er, eh?'

'Fuck off, you wee shite.'

'That's no' a nice way to greet your only son.'

'Shows you how much you know.'

'It's okay, Da. I know you couldn't afford to keep me and my brother. Wasn't I the lucky one?'

'You were brought up fine. Fed, clothed – your mother spoiled you. That's why you live the way you do.'

'I take after you, and you know it.'

'Nah, son. You're just a thug.'

'Who tried to kick his ain son's head in? Wait, that was you.'

'You deserved it. The way you treated your mother.'

'I never got it though, did I?'

Instinctively, Hugh Machie passed his right hand through his hair, feeling the deep scar there.

'Still hurt?'

'Nah.'

That's good.' James Machie leaned forward on his chair. 'You know MacLafferty wants his money.'

'He'll get it when I can pay him.'

'No, he's past that stage, Faither. You're oot the game if he doesn't get paid – aye, like last week.'

'Fuck him.'

'I know me and you haven't always got on too well.'

'The understatement o' the fucking century.'

'Listen to me!' James Machie banged the table with his fist. 'Personally, I don't really care what happens to you. But that's no' what this is about.'

'What's it about then?'

'I'm no' going to let some cheap loan shark off my faither. It would make me look weak.'

'So, you're going to pay him. That's good o' you, son.'

'Nah. You're going to kill him.'

'Eh?'

'You've still got that Webley from your National Service?'

'Aye.'

'Good. You come to work for me. All debts to whoever and his weans are cancelled. I'll pay you regularly – more dosh than you've ever had in your miserable life. That's the deal.'

'Oh aye – or else?'

'I'll have to kill MacLafferty myself.'

'And then I'm off the hook wae the money. So what?'

'Then you owe me the dosh.'

Father stared at son, their piercing blue eyes almost identical.

'Be honest. It's the only thing you've ever been able to do. Kill folk or batter them. You've no' got my mother to navigate you through a pittance any more.'

'You bastard. Leave your mother out of this.'

'I wish I was – a bastard, that is. Then I wouldn't have to be ashamed of you. You'll dae this, then you'll make yourself useful whenever I see fit, okay?'

'I'll think about it.'

'Good. That's the sensible thing. You've got until ten tonight to think about it. Frank will give you a number to call.'

Hugh Machie swallowed hard. 'I've no' got a phone.'

'Then you phone us. You've heard of phone boxes, aye?'

Hugh turned out his trouser pockets. 'Empty, see?'

James Machie stood and thrust his hand into a pocket in his leather jacket. He pulled out a handful of change and threw it on the floor in the general direction of his father. 'There's money for the call. You can spend the rest on a poke o' sweeties.' He leaned on the table and stared at the man who'd given him life. 'Your call. Either way, I'm no' really bothered. But you're no' going to embarrass me again. You work for your keep.'

21

Malcolm MacConnachie looked surprised when he opened the door to find Daley and a young woman he'd never seen before standing on his doorstep.

'Mr MacConnachie, I'd like a word with you, please,' said Daley.

'Oh aye, here we go.' He sneered at the police officers.

'This is DS Dhar. I'm DCI Daley, as you probably know.'

'Aye, I know fine about you, Mr Daley. Who doesna in this toon?'

'We'd like to come in, please.'

MacConnachie shook his head. 'No can do, I'm afraid.'

'Sorry?'

'My lawyer – Mr Campbell. He said yous would try an' put pressure on me to withdraw my complaint. He telt me to have nothing to do with any of you.'

'That's not Mr Campbell's privilege. Now, are you going to let us in, or do I have to come back and arrest you?' Daley realised this was pushing it, but with Dhar straight-faced beside him he knew he'd wrong-footed MacConnachie.

The man in the faded jumper and jogging trousers sniffed and rubbed his index finger along his nose. 'Okay, come in. But I know what's happening here, and if yous try to put pressure on me I'm straight on the phone to Campbell.' He stood aside to allow the detectives into his home.

A narrow hallway led on to a lounge. A three-piece suite that had seen much better days and a huge flat-screen TV dominated the modest room. Against one wall, a unit displayed some whisky glasses and various photographs. In front of a gas fire sat a coffee table, on which a copy of yesterday's newspaper folded to the racing pages, scattered with little pencil marks, was spread.

'You enjoy a bet?' Daley asked.

'Is that a crime now? What man doesna like the gee-gees?'

Daley shrugged. 'Can we sit?'

MacConnachie plonked himself down on a chair and pointed at the sofa, gesturing that they take a seat. 'Be my guest.'

'Is your wife in?'

'No, she's at work, Mr Daley.'

'And your work is?'

'I'm between jobs, at the moment.' It sounded rehearsed, as though he was in the habit of being asked the question and it irritated him.

'You worked at Michael Kerr the bakers, yes?'

'And?'

'You tried to make a claim against them, I see.' Daley was consulting his notebook, but the page he had open in front of him had nothing to do with MacConnachie. Nonetheless, he looked as though he was reading all about the incident.

'Pardon me, but I'd have thought the polis had better things to be at than me near dying on a Danish pastry.'

'A rock bun, I think. Or am I mistaken?'

'Rock bun, Danish pastry – who cares? What's this, *The Great British Bake Off*?'

'But you failed in your attempt at compensation? In fact, the bakery accused you of stealing the item on which you *choked*.'

'That was never proved because it wisna true!' MacConnachie sat forward in his armchair.

Daley turned a page of his notebook. 'And you've made no less than eighteen claims to the council regarding injuries due to poor maintenance of roads and pavements?'

'The state o' this place – everybody knows that.'

'And you sprained your ankle in the local paddling pool, I see.'

'That's another disgrace. The bottom o' that pool is like a skating rink.'

'Surely, it's a facility intended for children not adults?'

'I never saw any signs aboot that. Anyway, it was a hot day. A man canna have a paddle to cool down now?'

'I'll be honest with you, Mr MacConnachie. We're beginning to see a pattern emerging.'

'Aye, the roads and pavements are shite, the paddling pool is a death trap. Also, you'll no' find me eating anything fae Michael Kerr's. No' a Danish pastry, rock bun or fuck all else.'

'I wasn't referring to your luck – or lack of it – more the fact that you appear to have been unsuccessful in any of these actions, to date.'

'Not true!' MacConnachie had a triumphant look on his face.

'Really?'

'The time I got whacked on the heid wae a golf ball at the pitch and putt. Aye, they admitted that they were at fault. Folk out too close together.'

'And you received compensation?'

'Aye.'

'Which was?'

'A free round for two any time we wanted for the rest o' the summer.' MacConnachie sat back, clearly delighted to have proved Daley wrong.

'I see. Still, I want to look further into this. I'm just giving you fair warning.'

'Aye, do your best work.'

Daley closed his notebook and placed it back in his pocket. 'I'll be in touch.' He moved to stand, but DS Dhar spoke, so he stayed in his seat.

'You enjoy cannabis, Mr MacConnachie?' She smiled at the man in the faded jumper.

'Eh?'

'I can smell it, sir.'

'Nah, you'll be smelling my aftershave.'

'You won't mind if we took a look around? If it's just your aftershave, that is.'

'Nah, I've had enough. Go and get a warrant if yous want to search my place.'

'Okay, fair enough, Mr MacConnachie.' Dhar got to her feet. 'We take the use of illegal substances very seriously.' She looked at Daley.

'Yes, absolutely. I think you can expect another visit – soon.'

'Ach, on yous go.' MacConnachie made a dismissive gesture with his hand.

Back in the car, Daley started to laugh. 'Classic. Well done, Shreya.'

'I try my best, sir. I hope it works.'

'We can't lean too heavily on him. But you never know. You must have some sense of smell. I didn't catch it.'

She looked at Daley. 'Me neither.'

When Daley stopped laughing, he turned to the DS. 'Are you sure you weren't trained by Brian Scott?'

Daley drove into the car park at Kinloch police office, spotting Ella Scott's car in the parking space Brian always used.

'He's here,' said Daley.

Shreya Dhar stared at the car. 'I know this sounds pathetic.'

'What's pathetic?'

'Well, I've always wanted to meet him – both of you.'

'Well, now's your chance. But given the situation, I'd better talk to him myself about MacConnachie. But I'll introduce you.'

'Great! I must admit, you are both legends up the road.'

'Well, it's the old story. Never meet your heroes, it's always a disappointment.'

Shreya gazed at Daley. 'Not so far.'

He parked neatly and they made their way through the office from the rear security door. Shaw was at his desk. Daley leaned over and asked where his old friend was.

'I put him in the family room.' Shaw lowered his voice. 'He looks as rough as a badger's arse, Jim. Apologies, DS Dhar.'

'Oh, don't mind me. I've been in this job for nine years. I've heard and seen . . . well, what you would expect.'

Dhar followed Daley along the corridor to the family room, usually a place where worried relatives were accommodated. On this occasion, an unkempt figure was sitting in an armchair, head bowed in sleep, snoring quietly. Brian Scott did indeed look like a badger's arse. His hair stuck up in salt and pepper tufts, he hadn't shaved for two or three days, and the distinct odour of stale alcohol filled the room.

'Brian!' Daley shouted to wake Scott up.

'Eh? Where's the fire, big man? Is it raining ootside?'

'What?' said a bemused Daley.

Scott rubbed his face with both hands and yawned with a sigh. 'Sorry, Jimmy. Just dropped off, you know.' As he blinked into the light, he saw Daley had company. 'Sorry, dear. I'm no' at my best.'

'You said it,' said Daley. 'This is DS Shreya Dhar. She's here on a temporary basis.'

'So, you're the new me, eh?' Scott reached out and Dhar shook his hand.

'Pleasure to meet you, DS Scott.' She smiled.

Scott cocked his head. 'Have me and you met before?'

'No, I don't think so.'

'You would have remembered, DS Dhar. Few ever forget the first time they meet this one.'

'Cheers, Jimmy, you're a pal.' Scott blew his nose loudly on a crumpled handkerchief he'd produced from his pocket.

'Well, as I say, it's great to meet you. I'll leave you to it.' Dhar nodded to them both before sweeping out of the room.

'Aye, dangerous waters there, Jimmy boy.'

'What do you mean?'

'Well, she's a cracker. And – I'm no' trying to be unkind, but you've got an eye for the ladies, as we both know.'

Daley sat on the sofa facing Scott. 'Brian, come off Planet Whyte & Mackay and listen to me. Don't spend your time worrying about me and members of staff. You've got a lot more to fret about.'

'No' really.'

'What do you mean?'

'Well, it's a scuffle in a pub. I'll get a slap on the wrist fae a court – aye, in the unlikely event it gets that far.'

'You're forgetting something. You're a police officer, remember?'

'How could I forget? I've been at it for an eternity.'

'Listen, I've just been to see the guy you had the fracas with.'

'Fracas? I've enough problems wae English, never mind German.'

'It's English.'

'Aye, whatever.'

'This guy is called MacConnachie. He's a jumper.'

'He's going tae top himself? Well, that's good news.'

'No. Jumper, as in falling off pavements and cracks in the road to try and get compensation. Do you get my drift?'

'Here, it was me that ended up on my arse that night.'

'It doesn't matter. Shreya and I put some pressure on him. I'm trying to get him to withdraw the complaint.'

'Well, that's very good of you, Jimmy, but you're wasting your time.'

'I don't know what you mean.'

'I mean I've had it. Aye, up to here and beyond.' Scott held his hand above his head. 'This job – we both know the score. It's been shite for years, and it's getting worse.'

Daley sat back on the sofa. 'So, you're just going to sink into a bottle and spend the rest of your life like your father did?'

'No, I'm no'. Me and Ella, well, we've got plans.'

'Is this the pub in Spain?'

'No' necessarily a pub.'

'What then – a plumber?'

'Me, getting my hand doon a U-bend? Don't be ridiculous.'

'It's not as ridiculous as the thought of you running a bar in the Costas.'

'Oh aye, you know everything. I know I'm drinking. But it's only the stress o' this bloody job that's caused it.'

'So you're going to cash in your chips and head for Spain. You, the bright sun and a bar full of booze. Perfect.'

'Bobby Cowan did all right.'

'As in Bobby Cowan from "A" Division CID?'

'Aye.'

'He got pished and drove off a cliff!'

'That was an accident – a tragedy, right enough. But he was doing fine up until then. Him and the wife was lapping it up, so they were.'

'Until they were scraping him up off the rocks.'

'Me and Ella went tae the place when we was on oor holidays, remember?'

'Yes, I remember,' said Daley wearily.

'See the tan he had. Aye, and Bobby was always right peely-wally, tae.'

'Fabulous.'

'You know, I had a dream aboot you the other night, Jimmy.'

'Oh yes?'

'You locked my wee lassie in the stationery cupboard. Then you came at me wae this great bugger o' a sword.'

'Okay. Well, that sounds just the kind of thing that would happen.'

'Fighting all the way doon the corridor, we were.'

'So, you had a sword too?'

'Oh, aye. No' a massive, big bastard like yours, mind. Hey, but I was giving as good as I got.'

'Booze dreams, Brian – the DTs. It's not as though this hasn't happened before, is it? How did it all end?'

Scott remembered the end of his dream: waking up beside Liz. 'Och, that bit was pure nonsense.'

Daley shook his head. 'And the bit where we were having a sword fight down the corridors of the police office just after I abducted your daughter seemed quite reasonable?'

'It's a meta-thingy.'

'Eh?'

'When something means something else. You've been banging on aboot it for years.'

'A metaphor.'

'Aye, that's the one. You and me are always battering oor heids together aboot something. That's what the sword fight was a' aboot.'

'And Martha – why did I lock her in the cupboard?'

'I've been thinking about that. It was fear aboot those close to me. They're in danger.'

'Not so much Kant as cannae.'

'What?'

'A philosopher. Never mind.'

'No, I'll tell you what's at the heart o' it all, Jimmy. It's Hugh Machie.'

Daley sighed and rubbed his forehead in frustration. 'Not this again. Why on earth would Hugh Machie be here?'

'Revenge, that's how. You killed his boy, remember?'

'He's in his eighties. We've been through this.'

'I saw him, I'm telling you!'

'Right, listen to me, Brian. You and Ella are coming up to ours tonight. We're going to have a civilised meal and talk this all through.'

'You'll need to pass that wae Ella.'

'I have. I want you there, and I want you sober, okay?'

Scott shrugged. 'Aye, you're the boss.' He thought for a moment. 'Is Lizzie going to be there?'

'Yes, of course.'

'Right.' Brian Scott grimaced as the end of his dream came back to him in unforgiving detail.

22

Glasgow, 1984

Patrick MacLafferty had closed his bookie's shop for the evening. It had been a good day, and he was pleased to have hedged some heavy bets from a couple of serious punters with the national bookmakers. It was all too easy to get stung.

The back room contained a sink, a toilet and a washroom hidden behind a door, a card table and a few easy chairs. One bar of the old electric fire sparked as MacLafferty counted wads of notes at the table. His friend and 'collector' Thomas Selkirk sprawled on one of the armchairs, sipping at a small glass of whisky. The big man yawned as he watched MacLafferty count. 'We'll be here all night, Paddy.'

'Shut up, Tam. You'll make me lose my place. Do you want to be paid or no'? Drink your dram, I'll no' be long. I'll bag this and you can drive me to the night safe.'

'Then what?'

'You can go home to Flora and gie her a good time.'

Selkirk looked doubtful. 'I've no' had a good time wae Flora since nineteen seventy-four.'

MacLafferty sighed and kept on counting, as the electric

fire sparked again. Selkirk stared into it absently, the glass of whisky in his fist.

The bookie had almost finished tallying up when he was disturbed by a loud knock at the front of the shop.

'Who the fuck is that?' said Selkirk.

'Eh, hang on . . .' Patrick MacLafferty closed his eyes as though he was concentrating on something. 'No, it's gone.' He glared at Selkirk. 'How the fuck should I know who it is? Go and find oot!'

Selkirk blew out his cheeks and levered his large frame out of the chair. He knocked back the dram and placed the empty glass in the drainer beside the sink. Through in the shop it was pitch black, the steel shutters blocking all but a sliver of light from the street beyond. Selkirk flicked on a switch and two fluorescent strips flashed into life. He made his way to the door.

'Aye, who is it?'

Silence.

'Are you deaf? Who the fuck is there?' He made his way behind the counter and retrieved a baseball bat, and was about to call again when he heard a voice.

'It's me, Hughie.'

'Which Hughie?'

'Hughie Machie.'

'What the fuck dae you want? Oor man's no' happy wae you. You've got some balls banging on the door at this time o' night.'

'I've got his money. I'm here to pay up.'

Selkirk put the bat back behind the counter. He'd known Hugh since school. Machie was older than him, but he liked and respected the man, even though he had gambling and drink problems that made him unpredictable. But so were most of the people Selkirk had to deal with daily. It was a part of the job that he disliked, watching lives being steadily ruined every day by men – it was mostly men – who were willing to bet everything they had on a sure thing, then resorted to the solace of alcohol when fate dealt them yet another cruel blow. It was a mug's game, and he'd never gambled as much as a shilling on dogs, horses or anything else.

'Right, hang on.' He took a large set of keys from his pocket, and opened three locks, two bolts and then the padlock that held the roller-shutter door in place on the concrete floor.

Sure enough, when he pulled it up with a noisy clatter, there was Hugh Machie. His old school friend was huddled into an overcoat, clapping his hands in the cold night air.

'Hurry up, Tam. I'm freezing my bollocks off here.'

'Have you been ill?'

'Why?'

'You look like shit, that's why, Hughie.' Tam kneeled back down to secure the roller-shutter. 'Too much time spent in places like this. Aye, and shitty pubs. I don't know—' Thomas Selkirk didn't get the chance to finish his sentence. Machie brought the hilt of the revolver down on his old friend's head, three swift blows.

'Sorry, Tam. It could be worse,' he whispered.

Machie knew the place well. He'd been gambling at this bookmakers since MacLafferty senior had been in charge. Putting the Webley back in his pocket, he made his way behind the counter and through into the back room.

Patrick MacLafferty was busy applying thick rubber bands to large wads of bank notes. He stared at Hugh Machie with distaste. 'Where's Tam?'

'Away for fags.'

The bookie looked his errant customer up and down. Machie was wearing a shabby long coat that he'd once filled. Now it looked as though the garment belonged to a much bigger man. His face was grey and drawn, though his blue eyes were bright and still bore a hint of menace. Though MacLafferty too had known Hugh for years, he was still annoyed that his right-hand man Tam had chosen this moment to succumb to his nicotine habit. When money was involved, people did strange things. 'I hope you're here to pay me, Hughie – in full.'

'Do you think I'd turned up just for a wee chat?'

MacLafferty shrugged. 'I've no' seen you for a while. I was beginning to worry – you owe me nearly four grand.'

'Come on, you know I'm good for it.'

'Oh aye. I was thinking that maybe you'd had a word wae that boy o' yours. He's making a right name for himself, eh? No' a pleasant one, neither.' As he finished speaking, he heard a groan coming from the front shop. 'What the fuck is that?' He got to his feet.

At the same time, Hugh Machie reached into his pocket, pulled out the old Webley revolver and fired two shots. Both hit MacLafferty in the chest. The bookie looked bewildered. He stared at Machie wide-eyed, then staggered back, fell over his chair and landed on the floor in a fluttering shower of bank notes, like confetti at a wedding in his wake.

But Machie had underestimated Thomas Selkirk. The big man, though unsteady on his feet, emerged from the shop and caught him a vicious blow to the head with his bunched fist, roaring at the top of his voice as he did so, the guttural yell of a man fighting to survive.

For Machie, the room began to swim. He had to bite

through his lip in order to stay conscious. He blinked his eyes back into focus just in time to see Selkirk bearing down on him once more, blood running down his face from the blows he'd sustained at the front door.

Though he'd taken a hefty blow himself, Hugh Machie was still quicker. As the bigger man swung a right hook, Hugh pulled back, leaving Selkirk to stagger forward when his punch didn't connect. He fumbled the revolver into position and fired a shot. It was a lucky one for him, but not for Thomas Selkirk: it caught him in the temple and he slumped to the ground like a puppet with cut strings, the life gone from his eyes.

Calmly, Hugh Machie walked over and shot the man he'd known since they were children through the heart. He then made his way round the card table and administered a similar shot to the motionless MacLafferty.

Job done, Hugh rushed from the room and out through the front shop. He stooped to lift the roller-shutter door and hurried out into the street. He scanned the road desperately for a few seconds, until, from a side street, a black Audi Quattro emerged. It screeched to a halt in front of him. Hugh Machie flung himself into the passenger seat, and the car roared off.

Hugh laid his head back and gulped deep breaths. He was still groggy from Selkirk's blow. He screwed up his eyes, hoping to ease the thudding pain he felt in his skull.

'Did you get any dosh?'

The voice from the back of the car surprised Hugh. He hadn't noticed anyone there when he'd flung himself into the car. Come to that, he hadn't even taken note of the driver.

He swung round in his seat to look at the rear passenger. 'James,' he said with quiet disgust.

'That's me, Daddy.' James Machie was his usual sarcastic self. 'So, you came out of there with nothing?'

'I had to kill MacLafferty and big Tam.'

'And?'

'I've just killed two men. I'm no' in the mood to recount it all for your entertainment.'

'Fuck me. The only man that goes into a bookie's shop, kills everyone and comes out without so much as a fiver.'

'Don't worry. I'm sure you'll be able to fill the void MacLafferty leaves.'

'And I'm sure you'll be happy to owe me money instead o' the bookie, eh?'

'What?'

'It's just a change of ownership – the debt still stands. If you'd had any sense, you'd have filled your pockets full of cash and you could have paid me.'

'Fuck you, son. I've just killed two people to get you a new business.'

'Honestly, I'm very grateful. It'll make up for all the Christmases I missed out on when I was a kid. But don't worry. I'm sure I'll think of something for you to do – in lieu of payment, I mean.'

Hugh Machie sat forward in the front seat of the Audi. He realised that he'd made a pact with a devil, and that devil was his own son.

23

Ella brushed something from her husband's jacket as they stepped out of the house.

'What are you at?' said Scott.

'I'm trying to make you presentable, that's what I'm at. It's been a good while since we've been invited to Jim and Liz's for a meal. The way things are for you just now, we're going to make the most o' it.'

Brian Scott was heading for the driver's seat when he felt his wife pull him back by the collar.

'My car, I'll drive, thank you.'

'Eh?'

'You think I'm going to let you drive me aboot after the three distilleries you've put away o'er the last few months? That'll be right.'

'Oh, that's good. It means I can have a few glasses o' wine at Jimmy's.'

'For one, Brian, do you really think that man will give you as much as a thimbleful o' alcohol?'

Scott shrugged. 'I suppose not.'

'Plus, I intend to have a couple, so you can busy yourself driving back.'

They took their seats in the car.

'So, it's okay for me to drive you later? What aboot all they distilleries I've drunk dry?'

'I'll be suitably anaesthetised by that time, so it'll no' bother me so much.'

Brian Scott shook his head as his wife started the car. He wasn't looking forward to this evening at all. For a start, he wouldn't be able to drink. And though he'd spent a few dry years following his previous problem with alcohol, he'd never quite become accustomed to social situations without a glass in his hand. The solution had been – apart from trips to the County – to stay away from whisky as much as he could. Which, he reasoned, hadn't exactly been a bag of laughs for Ella. That made him feel bad, and he wanted a drink to counteract the guilt. It was a vicious circle.

Ella backed out of the driveway, and began the short journey across to the Daleys' house on the hill. 'Anyway, why are you so uptight? You've known them for decades,' she said.

'I'm no' into these cosy dinners, Ella. You know that. Aye, and Liz can be a right handful when she's on the sauce.'

Ella almost steered off the road. 'The pot calling the kettle black doesnae even begin to cover that.'

'Right, fine – I know I've been drinking a wee bit too much, lately. But gie me a break, eh?'

'Too much? May I remind you, you're suspended from your job, you're about to go to court, and you've got a liver the size of a small country. If you're going to get a break, it'll be me breaking your neck.'

'I need tae tell you something.' Scott looked sheepish.

'Oh, surprise me, Brian. You've taken up the drugs now. Aye, just go for it. Nae bother, I can cope.'

'Nah, don't be so stupid. Anyway, what is it wae you and the drugs? You had oor Willie on them a wee while ago.'

'He was behaving strangely. And it's no' as though he'd be the only junkie in your family, is it?'

'My family again. Anyway, it's nothing to dae wae drugs. If you must know, it's Liz.'

Ella slammed on the brakes and the little Nissan squealed to a halt. 'What dae you mean, *it's Liz*?'

Scott looked uncomfortable. 'It's no' what you think.'

'The famous last words of any philanderer. In this case, your very last words – ever!'

'It was a dream, that's all.'

'A dream?'

'Aye, a dream.'

'I thought men got o'er that type o' thing when they were teenagers.'

'What type o' thing?'

'You know . . .' Ella nodded her head impatiently.

'I know what?'

'Wet dreams!'

'Eh? Wet dreams, my arse! I'd been having a sword fight wae oor Jimmy. The bugger had Martha locked in a cupboard.'

Ella Scott's mouth fell open. 'You've lost it, nae question whatsoever.'

'Wait, you've no' heard it all yet.'

'I don't think I want to!'

'I thought I'd woken up – you know, fae this dream wae Jimmy laying intae me wae a sword and that.'

'What aboot Martha?'

'What aboot her?'

'You just left her there in the cupboard? Your ain flesh and blood?'

'She wisnae in a cupboard – it was a dream! Anyway, wheesht a moment while I tell you the whole thing.'

'Oh, I cannae wait.' Ella glowered at her husband,

'So, I wake up in bed. I nudge you and tell you what a bugger o' a dream I've just had. But it wisnae you.' Brian Scott folded his arms.

'You were in bed wae Liz. This is what you were having the wet dream aboot. Fuck me.'

'It wisnae a wet dream! How many times, woman!'

'Well, I'm right glad you telt me this just before we go up there for dinner. How will I be able to look that hussy in the eye?'

'She'd nothing to dae wae it.'

'Liz Daley in bed wae my husband and she wisnae up to anything. That will be shining bright. Do you think I'm demented?'

'I give up. I was just trying to tell you that it will make me feel awkward, that's all.'

'And now we'll both feel awkward. Thanks, Brian.'

'I was telling you about a dream I had. Bugger me, I'd hate to see how you'd react if I telt you I'd had an affair.'

Ella glared at him once more. 'Lizzie Daley. I thought you had better taste.'

'I need a drink,' said Brian Scott flatly.

They made the rest of the journey in silence.

'I wish you'd given me more notice, Jim,' said Liz, as she polished off a glass of wine.

163

'I'm cooking, what are you worried about?' Daley carried on stirring the tomato sauce he was making to accompany a pasta dish. He whizzed up a carrot and some celery, a tip he'd picked up from an Italian friend years ago.

'But I've still got to be here, haven't I?'

'Not if you don't want to.'

'How would that look?'

'I think Brian and Ella are fully aware how difficult things are between us, don't you? After all, I thought Ella was your new confidante?'

'She's somebody to talk to. Somebody who listens. You're always working, and when you're not you just mope about.'

Daley turned to face his wife, a wooden spoon coated with bright red sauce in his hand. 'I know what happened to you. I think about it every day. But you're not the only one with problems.' He pointed to his chest.

'And what about this Dhal woman?'

'Dhar – Shreya Dhar. She's just here to fill in for Brian. She's young and alone in a new place. It's the least we can do, don't you think?'

Liz stared into space. 'She's pretty, I suppose.'

Daley sighed and went back to stirring the sauce.

'No comment, is that it?'

'I'm not going where you want to go, Liz.'

'Well, let's hope you can restrain yourself this time.'

Daley stopped stirring the pot for a few seconds. He wanted to reply to his wife's taunts, but he knew that would be pointless. His affair with Mary Dunn would never be forgiven. The fact that Liz had been unfaithful on countless occasions didn't seem to matter – in her mind, at least.

The doorbell rang. Daley continued to stir the sauce. It was thickening now; just a bit more seasoning, some basil and a pinch of sugar needed, he reckoned.

'Aren't you going to answer that?' Liz asked.

'I'm a bit busy, as you can see. Surely you can get the door?'

Liz shook her head and stomped off into the hall. She could see the silhouette of a woman in the frosted glass of the front door. When she swung it open, Shreya Dhar was standing there, the porch light shining off her black leather jacket.

'Mrs Daley?'

'Yes.' Liz forced a smile. Jim had told her that his acting sergeant was young. He'd omitted to tell her that she was also beautiful.

'I brought these for you.' Dhar handed Liz a bouquet of flowers. 'I brought a bottle of wine, too. I hope it's the right thing. I don't know much about wine, I'm afraid.'

There followed an uncomfortable pause. Liz was motionless, staring at the flowers, while Dhar stood waiting to be invited in.

'I'm so sorry,' Liz said eventually. 'I love flowers. These are gorgeous, thank you.' She stood back and ushered her guest into the hall. 'Let me get your jacket.'

Shreya Dhar shrugged it off and handed it to Liz.

'Just take a seat through in the lounge. I'll be with you in a moment. What a lovely jacket – the leather is so soft. Is it Italian?'

'Yes, I think so. It was a gift. I'm about as clueless with clothes as I am with wine. Through here?'

'Yes. I'll just make sure Jim isn't ruining the dinner.' Liz's laugh was false, and it sounded so. She watched her husband's new colleague walk into the lounge. The DS was tall and elegant, dressed in black denims that matched her black knee-length boots. Her blouse was of floating chiffon, a striking blood red in colour. Oh, you know nothing about clothes, my arse, Liz thought to herself.

She flung Dhar's jacket none too gently over a hook on the coat stand and marched off to speak to her husband in the kitchen.

24

For Hugh Machie, the walls of the small Kinloch flat seemed to be drawing closer. He had a large measure of whisky in his hand as he lay back on the grubby couch. He felt miserable and ashamed. He had come to this place to right wrongs, to rid the world of the last of those who could ruin his life.

The time had to come for the random killing to stop, and yet here he was again, with still more blood on his hands. Even though the whole thing had been a tragic accident.

He thought of the man he'd killed lying in a shallow grave on the rocky beach. That had been an act of nature. But what followed was always the same: deep, unrelenting guilt that made him feel sick to his soul. He cursed himself for having swung round with the gun in his hand. It had been too much of a shock for the old man's heart to bear, he was sure of it.

Hugh had killed first when he was little more than a boy. It was the war that Britain forgot – Korea. Like most other lads his age he'd been dragooned into National Service. The Second World War was long over. Most of his contemporaries saw Korea as little more than a great adventure. A way to get out of the cloying poverty and grime of Glasgow. A way to see the world and maybe find a new life away from the shipyards and factories that might have put food in their mouths but blighted their lives with hard work and illness, while making their bosses rich. But any notion of a paid holiday soon disappeared when you were squatting in a foxhole deep in the killing grounds of that far-off country.

The face of the first man he'd put to death still haunted him. The Korean soldier was small, his head shrouded in a brimless helmet. But Hugh Machie could see the hate in the eyes of a man he'd never met who jumped into the hole in the ground where Machie was sheltering from the bullets and explosions. Seconds before, the Scot's only thoughts had been focused on how he could avoid the hell that was happening all around and turning his mind to jelly. He was desperate to save his own skin. Nothing else mattered.

The Korean's rifle was tipped with a vicious-looking bayonet that flashed in the warm sunshine. He screamed words that required no translation as he pulled the trigger, his weapon only inches from Machie's face.

For a split second it was as though they were both frozen in time. The noise of battle disappeared as the soldier who wanted to take Hugh's life looked at his jammed rifle, a confused expression on his face while Machie moved his hand to the pistol lying at his side.

The roar of battle was back. For seconds they stared at each other: young men from different worlds, connected only by the will to kill their enemy and survive themselves.

The Korean soldier's face hardened. He yelled again and made for Hugh with the bayonet. At point-blank range, the teenager from Glasgow couldn't miss. The force of the bullet hit the Korean soldier in the middle of his face, blowing his head apart in a flash of crimson and sending him flying backwards. Despite the din, Machie heard his victim's neck snap as he landed awkwardly on a boulder.

For the young man he'd been then, the shock was palpable. He forced himself back as far as he could into the foxhole as a live round screamed overhead. All he could do was stare at the man he'd just killed. He felt no sense of relief or vindication, even though he knew events could have easily ended up the other way.

They say once you've killed for the first time, the act becomes easier. But not for Hugh Machie. Yes, he'd taken many lives from that day to this, but with each death a little piece of his soul slipped away. Now an old man, he was almost an empty shell, spiritually bereft.

He swirled the whisky in his glass, staring at the spirit as though trying to divine the future. But no answers were to be found there, only the numbing of the mind, a short respite from the malevolent ghosts that followed him everywhere. All that remained of those whose lives he'd taken.

But there was only one more life left to take – he hoped.

He took a large gulp of whisky to banish the thought, but it went down the wrong way. He started to cough – a rasping wheeze that became so persistent it made breathing difficult. Hugh sat up on the couch, desperately trying to draw in air. He pulled the tattered handkerchief from his trouser pocket. Dark blood again.

Machie staggered into the bathroom. In a small cabinet he cast about for his pills. After spilling his razor and toothbrush into the sink, he laid a hand on the bottle and desperately tried to prise off the lid. It was of the variety designed to stop children from accidently ingesting the contents. He cursed the whole notion as, again and again, he pushed down and twisted the cap to no avail. He tossed the little brown bottle into the sink.

The coughing had stopped now, but his breath was still a loud wheeze. He could barely draw a breath. He sat heavily on the toilet seat and fumbled a white inhaler from his pocket. After two shallow breaths he felt slightly better. He used the inhaler again. This time he could take a deeper draw. His breathing eased, but his heart was still pounding.

Hugh Machie looked at the hankie. The blood was drying black into the faded grey of the material. He lowered his head. His time was short. He had to do what had to be done – and soon.

25

The atmosphere chez Daley was convivial enough. Everyone was chatting away companionably, despite Liz's state of insobriety and a peculiar reticence from the Scotts. But as the host brought through the large bowl of pasta in sauce, he couldn't help but notice Ella. She looked nervous, unhappy – something that surprised him. Brian's wife was usually the life and soul of any party. He put it down to her husband's predicament at work.

'Right, grub's up,' he said as he placed the bowl in the middle of the table. 'We don't have a seating plan, so just arrange yourselves as you will.'

'I'm sorry,' said Liz. 'My husband has no idea how to give a proper dinner party. I mean, *grub's up* tells you all you need to know.' She staggered forward, almost spilling red wine from the large glass in her hand.

It was Daley's turn to conjure up a fake smile. He stared at his wife, whose eyelids looked heavy as she smiled at Brian Scott. 'Liz is only joking, don't worry. This is a casual meal with friends – old and new.' He smiled at Shreya Dhar.

'Well, if I don't sit down, I'm going to fall down,' opined Liz, grabbing Brian's hand. 'Come on, Bri, us black sheep must stick together.' She hauled him over to the table.

'Haud your horses, Lizzie,' said Scott, trying to pull away from her while at the same time not wanting to make it obvious. Daley caught what he was sure was a look of extreme irritation on Ella's face. Again, it was something he wasn't used to . . . well, at least not in these circumstances. Finally, Liz succeeded in dragging Brian on to the chair beside her, where he sat looking like a condemned man.

Ella plonked herself down at the head of the table, glaring at her spouse.

Shreya Dhar stood behind a chair across from Liz and Brian. 'Will I take this one, Jim? Lets you get to the kitchen more easily.' At Daley's nod, she sat down, glancing at Liz, who was leaning into Scott and whispering something into his ear.

'Now, is everyone happy?' said Daley.

Liz stopped whispering to Brian. 'I've not been happy for years – in fact, I don't know if I've ever been happy,' she said drunkenly.

'Here we go,' Ella muttered under her breath.

Daley took the seat beside his new detective sergeant and reached forward to hand her the bowl. Shreya helped herself to some of the pasta, before passing it on to Ella.

'Thanks, dear,' said Ella. 'What a lovely shade of red that blouse of yours is.'

'A femme fatale,' murmured Liz.

'I found it in a charity shop when I was in Edinburgh. I guess some people just buy clothes, wear them once and then give them away. It certainly didn't look worn.'

'You're filling it out nicely now,' said Brian, immediately regretting it as he glanced at his wife and caught her glare.

'You'll have to forgive Brian. As we all know, he's going through a difficult time right now,' said Ella. 'It appears as though he's regressing to his teenage years. I'll no' tell you why.'

Liz grabbed Scott's arm. 'Good for you, Brian. I wish I was back in my teens. I'm bloody sure I'd do things differently.'

'Here, if you can manage to peel yourself off my husband, take your dinner.' Ella held the bowl out to Liz.

Daley watched as his wife served herself a tiny portion before handing the pasta on to Brian. Given his old friend's current problems, he'd asked her to stay off the wine. Clearly his plea had fallen on deaf ears. 'I thought – since Shreya doesn't drink – we'd have some sparkling water with our meal.' He smiled guilelessly round the table.

'Bugger that,' said Ella. 'He's the designated driver tonight.' She turned to Dhar. 'I would like some wine, if you don't mind, dear?'

'Oh, please don't worry on my account, Mrs Scott. All of my friends drink – it can be quite funny actually.'

'That's very kind, Shreya. When my Brian agreed to drive home, I thought I might as well take advantage o' it. Not something that happens every day. In fact, hardly ever.'

'What a nice surprise,' said Dhar.

'A bloody miracle,' said Ella.

'I didnae have much choice,' mumbled Scott.

'I'm with Ella. Go and grab the wine, Jim. I need a refill.' Liz smiled defiantly at her husband.

Daley sighed as he walked into the kitchen. He'd bought a fancy cheesecake for dessert, and they had biscuits and cheese if anyone wanted them. But it was already clear to him that Liz was going to be a problem. The aim of the whole evening had been to make Brian feel as though he hadn't been discarded. Daley knew the man so well, and realised that his suspension and the possible case hanging over his head were almost bound to send him tumbling further into the bottle. All the signs were there.

Maybe her husband's predicament was also impacting on Ella. She certainly didn't look happy. But with Brian in his cups most of the time, he supposed that was no surprise.

He grabbed a bottle of white from the fridge, picked up what was left of the red Liz had been drinking and took them through to the table. 'Water for you, Shreya?'

'Yes, that would be lovely, thank you, Jim.'

'Brian?'

'I suppose a beer is oot o' the question?' said Scott.

'I don't have any beer.'

'Cider?'

'Nope.'

Scott sighed. 'Just a Coke then, Jimmy.'

'Good choice, what with you driving, eh?'

'You can sip my wine, Bri,' said Liz, then sucked up a long strand of spaghetti with a giggle.

'He's fine!' said Daley and Ella almost in unison.

'Aw, they're cruel to you, Brian. So what if you battered some yobbo.'

'I didnae! He assaulted me first.' Scott looked indignant.

Daley hastened back to the kitchen, returning as quickly as he could with a bottle of water for Dhar and Brian's Coke.

'This is lovely, Jim,' said Shreya as her host poured her water into a stemmed glass.

'Thank you.'

'It's my husband's thing, Shreya,' said Liz. 'He doesn't do it very often, but when he does, he's very, very good. Aren't you, darling?' She pouted a sarcastic kiss across the table.

174

'Fuck's sake,' muttered Ella.

'Who's your boss, Shreya – up the road, I mean?'

'Chief Inspector Spence,' replied Dhar.

Daley looked at Brian. 'Hewer,' he said.

'Steady on, big man – that's a bit harsh, eh?' said Brian.

'Hewer was her maiden name. We worked on that murder on the golf course case with her when she was a DS out in Rutherglen, remember?'

'Oh aye. I've got you now, Jimmy. Nice lassie. Fine set o' . . . clubs,' said Scott as he caught Ella's baleful gaze once more.

'I bet she didn't have balls like yours, Bri,' said Liz.

Ella had had enough. 'What's up wae you tonight, Lizzie?'

'I'm just trying to add some life and soul to this dinner. I've had a better time at wakes.' Liz sat back in her chair and squinted at her husband and Shreya Dhar. 'What a lovely couple they make. Don't you think, Ella?'

'I think you should shut up, Lizzie,' Ella replied.

Liz leaned across the table towards Dhar. 'Do you know my husband is fond of young detectives? I mean *very* fond, if you get my drift.'

Dhar smiled back at her hostess. She wiped her mouth with a napkin, then turned to Daley. 'Can I use your bathroom, please?'

'Sure, just down the hall, second on the left,' he said sheepishly.

There was silence as Dhar made her way to the bathroom. But as soon as she was out of earshot, Liz shook her head. 'She says she doesn't know much about clothes, Ella. That's a lot of shit, for a start. She looks as though she stepped off a catwalk. I'd love to knock that simpering smile off her face.'

'And I'll stick this bloody fork in your eye if you don't take your hand off my Brian's leg!' snapped Ella.

Liz made a gesture with both hands flapping under her face. 'Woo, I do believe Ella's jealous. What a surprise – I mean, a real surprise. It's Brian, not Brad Pitt.' Liz leaned into Brian, who tried desperately to back away. 'Don't be shy, Bri. Your wife and my husband may think you're a crashing drunk, but I still love you.' She kissed him on the cheek.

'Right, that's it!' Ella picked up her wine glass and propelled the contents into Liz's face.

'You bitch!' Liz staggered to her feet and with a desperate lunge pushed Ella's chair backwards. She stumbled round the table, and soon the pair were rolling about on the thick carpet.

Jim Daley and Brian Scott rushed to stop the fight. Liz had grabbed a handful of Ella's hair, while the latter had one hand round Liz's throat.

Just as their respective husbands tried to pull them apart, Shreya Dhar arrived back in the room. It didn't take her long to discern all was not well. The Daleys and the Scotts froze, like a bawdy scene from a William Hogarth print, Liz still holding a clump of Ella's hair, Ella with her hand clamped to Liz's neck.

'Oh, I'm sorry. I've just remembered I have some paperwork to do for the morning. It's been lovely, Jim – Liz,' she said, keening her head over the table in an attempt to make eye contact with her hostess.

'It's lovely to meet you, Shreya,' called Ella from her recumbent position, pinned down by Liz Daley.

'Yes, you too – all of you.' She turned on her heel and was shrugging on her leather jacket by the time Daley appeared in the hall.

'I'm so sorry, Shreya. I really am.'

'Don't be, Jim. It's the most fun I've had in years. I'll see you tomorrow. Thanks again.'

Daley ushered her to the front door and waited until her car pulled out of the driveway. When he returned to the dining room the others were back in their chairs. Liz's blouse was ripped and stained, while Ella's hair was standing on end as though she'd been electrocuted.

'Well, I hope you're all happy now. What an embarrassment.' He shook his head. 'How long have we known each other?'

'You cannae blame this one on me, big man,' said Scott. For the first time in a while, he felt rather pleased with himself. 'See how easily a wee misunderstanding can escalade, eh?'

'Escalate, Brian,' said Daley.

'Right. This all makes sense, mind you.'

'What makes sense?'

'This dream I had . . .'

'Don't you dare say another word,' said Ella.

26

Glasgow, 1984

Brian Scott was sitting at the counter of an up-market wine bar in the city's West End. The place was full of young people like himself, but they were from the other side of the tracks. Some youths in shiny suits guffawed in a corner, glasses of champagne in their hands. A group of young women were sitting at a table behind him. Their accents made them sound as though they came from a different country, not merely a couple of miles across the city.

Scott sipped his bottle of beer wishing he was anywhere else but here. But this place served a purpose; he was anonymous. Not only was the clientele alien, the chances of anyone recognising him were minimal. And on this occasion, Brian Scott desperately didn't want to be recognised.

There was a flurry of activity at the door as three men arrived in the bar. They were dressed in trendy suits, the sleeves of the jackets rolled up to the elbow, pleated trousers, pixie boots and fashionable haircuts. In fact, they fitted in very well with the company – until they opened their mouths.

'Hey, Gerry,' said the shortest of the three, a man of average height with dark hair cut in a mullet. 'It seems that champers is the bevvy o' choice in here. Grab us two bottles, eh? You gie him a hand, Sean.' His accent was straight out of one of Glasgow's schemes. He scanned along the bar until he noticed Brian Scott.

'Ho! Brian, my man. How's it going?'

'Frank, I thought you were coming alone – just me and you?'

'Don't worry about big Gerry and Sean – you know them. Sound as a pound, by the way.'

'Aye, but the whole point o' this is us being discreet – low profile – remember?'

'This is me being discreet, Brian.'

'Hey, Frankie!' Gerry shouted from further down the bar. 'Guy's asking what kind o' champagne you want. I just thought it was a' the same, man.'

'What dae you think, numb-nuts? The most expensive shit they've got!'

Scott glanced round the room. 'Really keeping it low key, Frankie.'

'See you wae that torn coupon all the time. You'll end up in an early grave, so you will. Lighten up, man!' He raised his head and looked behind Scott. 'In the back – there's some spare tables. C'mon, we'll go and get a seat, eh? These pixie boots are killing me. There's no place tae put your toes, know what I mean?'

With a shrug, Scott left his stool at the bar and followed Frank MacDougall. He winced as his companion shouted to his friends to follow them with the champagne.

To get to the space at the back of the bar, MacDougall and Scott had to pass through the group of raucous young men already drinking champagne. They were drunk, laughing and joking in their Glasgow University accents – the rugby crowd. As MacDougall pushed past them, one lanky youth took exception.

'Hey, watch where you're going. You nearly spilled my drink, you prick.' The other five young men in the party laughed. Brian Scott immediately feared the worst. He'd grown up with Frank MacDougall and knew all about his temper. He also knew that these yuppies had no idea what genuine peril they were in.

MacDougall stopped for a moment. Scott thought there was going to be trouble, but Frank simply raised his arms in a gesture of surrender. 'Listen, lads. Me and my pal here are just out for a quiet drink, know what I mean? Sorry to bother you, an' that.'

MacDougall's deference took both Scott and the tall young man by surprise.

'Just watch what you're doing, pal, okay?'

'Aye, nae bother. Keys, big man. If you don't mind?' MacDougall nodded to where he and Scott wanted to go.

The youth stood aside, a mocking smile spread across his long, thin face.

MacDougall led Scott to a table for two. 'What about Gerry and Sean?' the policeman wanted to know.

'They're big boys. They'll no' be feart sitting on their own.'

As he took his seat, Brian Scott noticed that the group of young men parted like the Red Sea when MacDougall's large henchmen passed by.

'Here, gie me and Scooty two o' they glasses and a bottle. Yous sit o'er there,' MacDougall commanded.

Drinks sorted, MacDougall leaned back in his chair, slipped off one of his pixie boots and flexed his white-socked foot.

'Oh, that's a relief. Pure murder, these bastards. See me, I was quite happy in DMs and a skinhead.'

'I remember,' said Scott.

'I keep forgetting you're a couple o' years younger than me, Scooty.'

'Please stop calling me that. Ella goes apeshit.'

'Under the thumb and yous aren't even married yet? That's no way to start, Brian.'

'It's got bugger all to dae wae you.'

MacDougall made the gesture of faux surrender again. 'Hauld the bus, tiger. It was just some advice. See my woman – fuck me, she's mental, man. You need to start out on the right foot.'

'No left-footers in your world, Frankie.'

'Not true, pal. Big Sean o'er there is thinking o' the priest-hood, so he is.'

'Aye, well, he should think again.' Scott looked at the hulking figures at the table across from them. 'Anyway, why couldn't we have done this over the phone?'

MacDougall bit his lip. 'Our man's worried aboot you. Anything we have to say has to be face to face from now on.'

'Eh?'

'It's okay. I know you're sound as a pound, Brian. But you know Jay. He's as paranoid as fuck.'

'It's all that coke he sticks up his nose.'

MacDougall shrugged.

'Right, what is it you want?' said Scott.

'Tuesday next week. You're on the nightshift, yeah? Can't be that much of a CID presence on a week night, I widnae think?'

'Great to know that if I forget my shift times, I can just phone you. That's a comforting thought.'

'Aye, whatever. Listen, we need a wee diversion.'

'I told you, I'm no' doing this any more.'

MacDougall hesitated. 'You know Jay's got all MacLafferty's shops now?'

'Aye, and I know how he got them.'

'I don't know what you mean.' MacDougall smiled.

'Why should I care? I don't gamble.'

'You're a good lad, so you are. But see, your faither isn't the same model of restraint.'

'What do you mean?'

'He's intae us for near two grand.'

Scott's face turned white. 'I'll pay it.'

'And you getting married? Nah. In any case, Jay won't take your money. After all, it's no' your debt. The big man's fair like that, you know.'

'Bollocks.' Scott stared at MacDougall defiantly as the other man sniffed. Plainly James Machie wasn't alone in his penchant for cocaine.

'Play the game, Scooty, eh? You love your auld man, aye? I've told you before, that bastard's insane. I'm no' kidding. He'll fuck your faither up if you don't do the business. I cannae stop him – we've been through this before.'

Scott sighed. 'What is it you want?'

'Methven Street.'

'What about it?'

'We've got a wee job there. Nothing for you to worry aboot.'

'Oh, aye. Like the pub, you mean? Yous said that then, too. The barman is still buggered. Nearly lost his life, so he did.'

'That was careless, eh?'

'No' funny, Frankie.'

'Here's what's going to happen. Stay on London Road near Methven Street around one in the morning. You'll get a call – a disturbance, some wee neds.'

Scott shook his head. Not for the first time, he realised how naive he'd been to think that he could escape his background by joining the police. His father was a liability, a drunk and a gambler. Machie had taken advantage of the fact, and there was nothing he could do about it. 'Then what happens?'

'You attend, as you're close by – you'll be on your tod, aye?'

'Yes.'

'Good. All you need to do is go to the flat in London Road and sort these wee bastards oot.' He winked. 'When you get there, you make one o' they emergency calls – what is it again?'

'A code twenty-one.' Scott sighed as what they were planning formed in his mind.

'Aye, that's the one. So, you get the uniforms o'er there. We'll make sure they have something to keep them busy.'

'And what do I do? I can't just walk away when my colleagues are taking a hammering, Frankie.'

'Nah. You might have to take a punch or two yourself – just to make it look realistic and keep you straight wae those other bastards you work wae, right?'

'Great.'

'Listen, we appreciate it, buddy. Hey, and it's no' all stick and nae carrot.' MacDougall delved into the inside pocket of his jacket and produced a small box covered in blue velvet.

'I'm already engaged, Frankie. You're no' my type.'

'Aye, good one, Brian. You always were the town clown. Here, take it.'

Brian Scott took the tiny box and opened it. The wedding ring inside was broad and shining gold.

'Eighteen carats, Scooty. Fluted at the edges to make it pop in the light. I'll no' tell you how much it was. But I bet your Ella will light up when she sees that, eh?'

'Fuck off, Frankie. I don't want to know where you got it, but it's no' going on my new wife's finger.'

MacDougall leaned in to him. 'Dae you really want to bring her into this? I'm telling you. If your man doesnae spot that on her hand on your wedding day . . . well, I guess you know what's going to happen.'

'You're a bastard, Frank.'

'You know what it's like, Brian. You follow orders, so dae I. Know what I mean? The only difference is, when you fuck up in your job, they fire you. In mine, you get set on fire.'

Scott shook his head. 'This is the last time. You tell Machie, okay?'

'Aye, sure, Josie, sure.'

'I mean it!'

'Jay reckons yous should have some weans. You know he likes children.'

'Why's he got none of his own then?'

MacDougall shrugged. 'Ours is not to reason why . . .'

'Aye, well, I'm no' for taking any advice fae that nutter.'

'Right, job done.' Frank MacDougall drained his glass of champagne. 'We need to go, Scooty. I suggest you go back to the bar, know what I mean? He glanced over to the group of loud young men including the one who had challenged him on his way to their table.

'Frankie, dae me a favour, just leave it.'

'And let that get out? No' likely. You go to the bar, like I said. If you leave now, someone might recognise you. Maybe put two and two together and get five, know what I mean?

This way, you slip out in the mêlée – easy-peasy. There will be too much going on for folk to take notice o' you by that time.'

'Frankie, c'mon.' Scott tried to dissuade MacDougall from taking any revenge for the earlier insult, but he knew it would make no difference. He walked to the bar and ordered a bottle of beer. He could see the young men in the mirror behind the counter. They were still laughing and guffawing, not a care in the world.

It happened in seconds. Scott saw MacDougall and his associates leave the back room. There was what looked like a minor scuffle. Then the three of them left the bar.

Brian Scott turned round just as a man roared and a woman started to scream. Before a large group of people surrounded him, Scott saw the youth who had challenged MacDougall lying on the floor, a stream of blood coming from a livid gash across his right cheek.

As the staff rushed around for towels and phoned the police and ambulance service, Brian Scott pulled up his collar and hurried out into the street with a host of frightened customers.

27

Jim Daley walked into Kinloch police office still pondering on the shambles that had been his dinner party the previous evening. He could have strangled his wife, who had been the catalyst for the disaster, though he was still puzzled as to why Ella Scott had reacted the way she had.

As he approached the front desk – always his first port of call each morning – wondering how he could explain away their outrageous behaviour to DS Dhar, he noticed that Sergeant Shaw looked troubled.

'Alasdair, good morning.'

'And to you, sir. Though I'm not really sure how good it's going to be.'

Daley sighed. 'Tell me the worst.'

'A body, Jim. Discovered in a shallow grave just near the causeway. A man picking winkles found it early this morning.'

'That's not far from where Hamish lives.'

'Indeed.'

'Do we have an ID?'

'Not yet, sir. But DS Dhar is putting a team together now. I've informed the powers that be up the road. But I think it's safe to say that it's inconclusive, at the moment.'

'He didn't bury himself,' said Daley dolefully. 'You should have called me.'

'I intended to, sir. DS Dhar said she had it in hand until your arrival. She's very efficient, Jim. Took charge straight away – did all the right things.'

'To the manor born. I'll have to watch out for my job.'

'I was thinking more of DS Scott, sir.'

Daley nodded his head and blew out his cheeks. 'PIRC are due down this afternoon. They still haven't given Brian a time for an interview.'

'You'll be delighted to hear that I'm the new Federation rep for this area.'

'Good. At least he'll have someone with some common sense sitting beside him. We all know he's got none of his own.'

'I'll send you in a full summary of events to date, Jim. It's written up, I just need to print it out. We're expecting SOCO in about an hour.'

'Very good, Alasdair. And so here we go again.' Daley bit his lip. 'Do me a favour, please – get Hamish on the phone.'

Shaw looked at him with a concerned expression. 'I've been trying since seven, sir. No reply.'

It was Daley's turn to look concerned. 'Where's DS Dhar?'

'Making sure the locus is secure.'

'And still nobody has identified this man?'

'I'm not sure. If they have, nobody has informed me, Jim.'

Daley turned on his heel. 'Hold the fort, Alasdair. It looks like we're in for one of those days.'

'I think we're well used to them. What will I do if PIRC arrive early?'

'Tell them to sit on their arses. I'm not in the mood for their shit. I've got a dead man to go and look at – again.'

Daley left the building. Only when he was back behind the wheel of his SUV did he close his eyes, trying desperately to control his breathing. He reached for his mobile and dialled Hamish's number from his contacts. Still the phone rang out.

Daley remembered how the old man had been badly beaten for helping the police on a previous case, not to mention his recent experiences in County Antrim. Together, these thoughts made his head swim. He revved the engine and headed for the causeway.

Dhar had secured the locus where the man's body had been found. The entrance to the causeway had been cordoned off, and a forensic tent placed over the remains to preserve the scene. Now all she had to do was wait. The SOCO team and Daley would arrive soon, and she checked off a mental list to make sure she'd done all that was required of her.

It was impossible to know how this man had died. His body had been covered by boulders that had to stay in place until SOCO appeared. She'd expected many things before embarking on her journey to Kinloch, but this wasn't one of them, though she was aware that both Daley and Scott had the unfortunate knack of getting caught up in the thick of things wherever they happened to be. This time, she was taking Scott's place. She knew Daley had worked with many other detectives, and wondered what the dynamics would be now the man who had been at his right hand for so long was gone, even if only temporarily. Come to that, how would the great detective go about his business? She remembered the stories; now it was time to witness the real thing.

She saw Daley duck under some police tape on the machair. 'Which way?' he shouted.

She'd had the three constables who'd attended the crime scene with her construct a pathway of raised plastic platforms across the rough grass beyond the beach, in order to preserve evidence. They pointed this out to Daley, who headed towards her, treading gingerly as he went. Only when he was within feet of her did Dhar notice that his face looked pale and drawn.

'Sir, good morning,' she said.

'Good morning to you too, DS Dhar.' He looked about with a practised eye. 'You've done well. Thank you.'

'Wouldn't be much of a shakes at this job if I couldn't preserve a locus, sir.'

'That's true, though you'd be amazed at some of the poor work I've seen.'

Dhar approached him and spoke quietly so the uniformed constables nearby couldn't hear. 'Are you okay, sir? You don't look well.'

Daley stared at the blue tent marked with the Police Scotland logo. 'Yes, I'm okay. I just want to take a look at our victim.'

'Of course, sir.'

Both detectives made their way to the crime scene tent. Dhar moved to open it, but Daley caught her gently by the arm.

'Sir?'

'What does he look like?'

'Judging by what we could see, old, in his mid-seventies, maybe older, I reckon.'

'Which doctor attended?'

Dhar pulled a notebook from her pocket. 'Dr Britten, sir.'

Daley furrowed his brow. 'I've never heard of him.'

'A locum, I believe. Only his first week in Kinloch.'

Daley stared at the tent. He'd hoped that he'd get some indication as to who was lying dead on the sand, but it was clear that neither Dhar nor the doctor, new to the town, would have recognised the victim. 'What about our boys? Did they know him?' He nodded to the police officers back up on the road making sure the public stayed away. A few cars had passed, slowing down to see if they could get a look. Inevitably, word of what had happened was now common knowledge in the town.

'They didn't see his face, sir. The victim's body is still covered by boulders. I didn't think it prudent to remove them. Thought that was best left to SOCO, sir.'

'Boulders?'

'They'd been placed over the body, sir. The man who found the body noticed some material sticking out of the sand. He disturbed the crime scene quite a bit, I'm sad to say, and the hands and neck were uncovered.'

'Why didn't he look at the victim's face?'

'A boulder, sir. We can't identify.'

'Where is he now?'

Dhar gestured over her shoulder. 'In my car with Constable Howe. I thought it best to keep him here until you arrived.'

To Daley, it was as though the world was conspiring against him. He had hoped that the local police officers would have been immediately able to identify the body and set his mind at ease. But it was clear, through force of circumstance, that was not going to be the case.

'Okay, let's take a look, Shreya.'

The DS unzipped the side and held it open for Daley to look inside.

The detective leaned into the small space. It took his eyes a few moments to adjust to the relative gloom. He could see the tip of a yellow seaboot, dark blue cloth like that used to make dungarees, and a faded jumper, knitted in blue wool, sticking out of the sand.

Daley hesitated for a moment. He wanted to walk into the space and pull the rock from the face of the victim, but common sense and years of training overtook his gut reaction. He withdrew from the tent, breathing heavily. 'Walker!' he shouted to one of the uniformed cops up by the causeway gate. The constable hurried towards him.

'Yes, sir?'

'You know Hamish – where he lives?'

'Yes, of course, sir.'

'Get over there and see if you can find him. Break in, if necessary.'

'Sir?'

'Just do as I say.'

Walker nodded and made off to do Daley's bidding. He took a few steps along the duckboards before stopping. Slowly, he turned to face Daley and Dhar. 'Sir, you don't think—'

'Just do it, please!'

Dhar looked puzzled. 'What's going on, Jim?'

Daley swallowed hard. 'I think this may be a friend of ours.'

'Oh.' She put her hand to her mouth as she watched Daley take the mobile from his pocket.

'He was very close to the woman who took her life in the County Hotel. Accused your Ian Macmillan of killing her.'

'Shit.' Dhar quickly realised why Daley looked so concerned. 'Who are you calling?'

191

'Brian.'

'He's suspended, sir. Do you really think that's a good idea?'

Ignoring her, Daley walked away, the mobile phone at his ear.

28

Glasgow, 1986

DC Brian Scott was in the CID room at Stewart Street police office. He was busy writing up yet another shoplifting case. 'A' Division covered Glasgow's city centre, and much of the crime that concerned theft from shops, pubs or supermarkets was processed here. It was a mind-numbingly boring task.

Most of the team were out of the office. The only other person in the room was Anna Rankin, like himself a DC, who was also submerged in paperwork. He looked across at her neat desk, marvelling at her focus and dedication. Scott himself could barely keep his eyes open.

'No' what you thought it would be like, eh, Anna?'

She looked up from her work. 'I kind of enjoy it. I've been like that since I was a kid. Tying up loose ends – everything in its place – that kind of thing. I mean, when that's what you're into, there're only three jobs that would suit, and two of them are accountancy and banking.'

Scott grimaced; he couldn't imagine anything less appealing than working with numbers all day. He'd a hard enough time filling in his overtime sheet. 'Aye, I see what you mean. You don't fancy getting your teeth into some o' these, do you?'

'Good try, Brian. I tell you what, though, I'm gasping for a coffee – do you want one?'

'Aye, thanks, hen.'

'How many sugars?'

'Four, but don't stir it, I don't like it sweet.'

'Are you being serious?'

'Nah. Just two, please.'

'I don't know how Ella puts up with you, honestly.' Anna Rankin left in search of coffee.

Just as Scott got his head back into report writing, he heard the door open. 'That was quick.' But the heavy tread of the person walking through the CID room made him look up from his work.

The man was thick-set with untidy dark hair, in the uniform of a sergeant.

'Can I help you?'

'You're Brian Scott, aren't you?'

Scott recognised him but couldn't place his name.

'Aye, what about it?'

'You're getting a new pal to play with.'

'What are you on about?' Scott was confused. Any orders he got these days came from his DS or above. He couldn't understand why some random shift sergeant was telling him who he'd be working with.

'You don't know me, do you?'

'I know your face.'

His visitor adopted a haughty expression, at odds with his demeanour and attitude. 'I'm Sergeant Donald – two-shift.'

'You're the guy that swore at the Japanese tourist. She went to the papers. Aye, I remember noo.'

'Fuck off wae that. She was a cheeky bastard.'

'Pity her boyfriend filmed it all, eh?'

'How was I meant to know? Anyway, it doesn't matter.'

'If you say so, gaffer. Anyway, what are you talking about?'

'A cop on my shift – Daley – he's coming to work here as an ADC. You're babysitting him.'

Scott shrugged. 'So?'

'He's clean roon the bend, okay?'

'Why are you speaking in riddles?'

'Why are you speaking in riddles, *sergeant*?' There was the haughtiness again.

'Aye, okay, *sergeant*. I don't know what you want me to dae?'

'Make sure his stay in here is short. Got it?'

Scott leaned back on his chair. 'And piss off DCI Burns? Not likely.'

'That relic. It's time he was put out to pasture.'

'The man's a legend!'

Sergeant Donald perched himself on the end of Scott's desk. He leaned in to the young DC. 'It would make certain folk happy if he was back on the beat.' He winked.

A shiver ran down Brian Scott's spine, though he tried not to let it show. 'Sorry?'

Donald stood up and straightened his tie. 'Just passing on a wee message, that's all.' He turned to leave.

Scott's throat was dry, and it felt as though his heart had sunk into his belly.

'I'm sure he'll only be here for a few weeks. If he's one of those "future boss" types, they'll want to show him round as many departments as possible. It's always the same.' Sergeant Donald stopped and turned back to face Scott. 'Jay was asking for you, by the way.'

This time, Scott froze. 'Jay who? I cannae be bothered wae banter. As you can see, I'm up to my arse in paperwork here.'

Donald smiled. 'You know who I mean.' With that, he swept out of the room, leaving Scott alone.

In the main, Machie had not bothered Scott since he'd ended up in the CID. Though he had wondered at the ease with which he'd managed to get this job when others, much better qualified than himself, were passed over. It suddenly dawned on Brian Scott that he wasn't the only police officer with ties to James Machie. The bosses had told him that they needed someone with knowledge of the East End and its criminals. He'd grown up with the likes of James Machie and Frank MacDougall, so hadn't thought much about it. But now, somehow, the feeling of shame and worthlessness flowed freely again. He'd joined the police for all the right reasons: to do something good with his life, not hang about with a collection of drug-takers, petty thieves, drunks, pushers and the permanently unemployed – most of the kids he'd gone to school with, in fact.

It had turned sour as soon as Frank MacDougall appeared at his side in a local pub just after he'd joined up. That was when the threats to his father had begun.

So far – he tried to console himself – all he'd done was turn a blind eye to a beating of some other criminal, or create a diversion for a cash grab from some recalcitrant gambler with bad, dangerous debt. But the implicit threat to his father was always hanging over his head. Since he'd come out of uniform, they'd mainly left him alone, he'd thought because he was now in the CID. It now occurred to Scott that Machie had been responsible for his move out of uniform. That he was just a pawn, to be used for bigger, wickeder things.

Just as the horror of it all bore down on him, Anna Rankin reappeared with two coffees.

'Is the boss in?' said Scott.

'Don't know. I haven't seen him. Why?'

'I need a word.'

'Brian, you're white as sheet. Here, drink this.' She handed him a mug. 'Is something wrong?'

Scott took a sip.

'Your hands are shaking. Maybe you should cut down on the bevvy.'

It was the perfect excuse. 'I had a few wae a mate o' mine last night.'

'Too many, by the looks of things.'

'Just takes the edge off – you know, after a day in this place.'

'My father used to say that,' said Anna.

'Oh aye, he was a cop, wasn't he? Must be retired now, eh?'

'No, he's dead.'

'Oh, I'm right sorry to hear that.'

'Thanks.' She hesitated. 'Go on, ask me what happened to him – how brave he was in the line of duty – that type of thing.'

'Shit, is that how he died?'

'No. He drank himself to death – I was only a kid.'

'Right. Man, that's worse. I have a father who's busy doing the same thing.'

'Crap, isn't it?'

'Aye, it is.' Scott brought a picture of his father to his mind's eye. He was whippet-thin now. His face was drawn, his eyes sunken, his arms like twigs. Something in the young detective snapped. 'Hey, thanks for the coffee.' He got up from his seat and shrugged on his jacket. 'And thanks for keeping me right, Anna.'

'What do you mean, Brian?'

It was too late. Scott was already on his way out of the door.

When Brian Scott arrived at Ian Burns's office, all that remained of the chief inspector was a thick cloud of smoke. Scott bit his lip but decided that there was no point returning to his desk. After all, once he'd told Burns what the man needed to know, the work he was busy with would inevitably be handed to someone else.

He sat on one of the three chairs placed in the corridor outside his DCI's office and waited.

As the minutes passed, Brian Scott went over the things he had come to say in his mind. He didn't know what it would mean for himself but was pretty sure that he was about to lose both his livelihood and liberty.

Just as his resolve was crumbling, DCI Burns appeared in the corridor. Like Scott's father, he was thin, with a gaunt face under greying fair hair. As always, he had a cigarette in his hand, as though the act of chain-smoking was his only nourishment. Scott stood up as he approached.

'What can I do for you, DC Scott?'

'I'd like a word, if you have time, sir?'

'Surely. Come in, son.'

Brian Scott followed Ian Burns into his office, closing the door behind him. 'Take a seat,' said the chief inspector as he took off his trademark beige raincoat and hung it on the coat stand beside his desk.

Scott's stomach was churning. He liked and respected Burns. The man had been good to him during his time at 'A' Division CID. Though Scott knew his rise in the ranks would never be stellar, he had hoped that at least now he was a detective he could make up for helping Machie, even though the assistance had been given under duress. In fact, he had nothing for contempt for the gangster who had made his life a misery. Scott often fantasised that he would arrive at work to discover that Machie had been killed by some other lowlife. But that never happened. He guessed it never would.

'Right, DC Scott. I don't have a lot of time, so fire away,' said Burns, lighting a new cigarette off the old one.

'It's serious, sir. I need to tell you something.'

Burns jutted his chin. 'Oh yes? This sounds ominous.'

'Sir, I'll no' waste your time. I've been helping James Machie – well, not recently – when I was in uniform in the East End, mostly. He threatened to harm my faither unless I co-operated.' Scott awaited the inevitable explosion and subsequent arrest. All the same, he felt as though a huge burden had been lifted from his shoulders.

Burns sighed and took a deep draw at his cigarette. 'I know, son.'

'Sir?'

'This isn't how I envisaged this conversation, DC Scott, but events have clearly overtaken us. I've known about it since you were sent to Largs as an ADC. I know the man who found you that position, and the rest was easy to uncover.'

'Frank MacDougall?' Scott was so confused that he said the first thing that came to mind.

'No, not Mr MacDougall. Though I have no doubt he has many sins to answer for.' Burns opened a drawer in his desk using a small key he'd removed from his pocket. He pulled out a bulging file and slapped it down on the table. Scott looked at it and swallowed hard.

'This is a file on you, your family and your association with Francis MacDougall and James Machie, DC Scott.'

'I don't understand, sir.' Scott felt as though he was watching a movie – a spectator.

'My colleagues and I have had many disagreements on this subject, Brian. Some of them wanted you to pay for what you've done. I, on the other hand, saw an opportunity.'

'You did?' said Scott with a large measure of incredulity.

'Yes. You were compromised and you did what you thought was right for you and your family – your father, in particular. That isn't a choice most police officers would have been faced with.'

'No, sir.'

'But it does leave you in something of a unique position.'

Scott had heard that Burns was clever – had been studying to be a doctor until he'd dropped out of Glasgow University. His manner was cool and calm, with none of the window-shattering hysterics in which some senior officers indulged.

'So, we have you as a trusted associate of the Machie crime organisation. The man has gone from being little more than a street thug to becoming a scourge of this city. All in a very short time.'

'What's going to happen to me, sir?'

Burns blew a long trail of smoke from his nose. 'I see nothing wrong with your work or intuition as a detective – apart from your report writing, which has to improve, and quickly. That apart, I think you're talented. And you've clearly got guts.'

Scott screwed up his face in disbelief. He was close to affording Burns a close look at his guts – all over the floor. 'Eh?'

'You are now an asset, DC Scott. You report to me – and only me – on every occasion you are contacted by Machie, directly or indirectly. Is that clear?

'Very clear, sir. But what about my faither?'

'Let me tell you something, Brian. I have tape recordings of you in discussion with both MacDougall and Machie. I know that you've had little choice in doing the things you've done. But it stops here, you understand?'

'Yes, sir.'

It will come as no surprise to you that there are people in this job who shouldn't be here. There are a small number of us dedicated to their removal. And you can help with that by bringing down Machie and his cohorts.'

'I understand, sir, aye.'

'Good. But this reprieve comes with caveats.'

'I'm no' sure I like that stuff, sir. Ella says it's fish eggs – disgusting. She telt me it's right salty.'

Burns stifled a smile. 'No, I mean this all comes at a price.'

'Oh, aye – fair enough, sir.'

'You speak of this to nobody – not even your wife – and certainly no police officers, serving or otherwise.'

'You have my word, sir.'

'And I believe you.' Burns stood. 'I know how you and your family have been threatened. It must have been a heavy burden, Brian.' He put his hand on Scott's shoulder. 'But what I'm proposing is dangerous: to you, your family – everybody you know. To lie about that would make me as bad as Machie. Are you willing to do this – I mean really willing, DC Scott?' He stared down at his junior officer with a piercing gaze.

'Yes, sir, I am. Totally.'

'Good. Take some time off, DC Scott – a week. Surprise your wife with a holiday. But get out of Glasgow, understood?'

'I do – I think.'

'In the meantime, things must be put in place to keep you and yours safe.' He stubbed out the cigarette. 'And don't forget. When you come back, you'll be under the closest scrutiny of your life.'

When Brian Scott left the room, he wasn't sure if he'd dreamt the whole thing. But despite Burns's dire warnings, at last the shame he'd felt for so long was gone. He would help bring James Machie to his knees.

29

Daley looked on as Constable Walker appeared at the head of the causeway and made his way along the duckboards towards them. The constable's progress was slow, and Daley tried to contain his impatience. He just wanted to hear what he'd found out about Hamish.

'Right, Walker, what happened?' he said when the constable finally arrived.

'No sign of him, sir. I looked through the windows, front and back. Nothing apart from a massive cat that nearly gave me a heart attack. It jumped up at the window.'

'That's Hamish,' said Daley absently.

'Sir?' Walker looked confused, as did DS Dhar.

'His cat's called Hamish, too.'

'Lack of imagination?' said Dhar.

'No, because he has no children – it's a long story.'

'Here's the cavalry, sir.' Looking up at the road, Walker had spotted DS Brian Scott emerging from a small Nissan.

'Right, Walker, I want you to head down to the pier. Hamish might be there. Let me know immediately if you find him.'

The young officer lingered, staring at the forensic tent.

'Just do as I ask!' Daley barked.

Walker hurried off. Everyone at the office knew and liked old Hamish.

'Jimmy, what's all this, eh?'

'We have a body, Brian. An old man, by the looks of things. Buried in a shallow grave. But we can't ID him until SOCO arrive. Can you chase that up please, DS Dhar?'

Without a word, Dhar walked away from them and soon had a mobile to her ear.

'She's no' happy, Jimmy. It's because I'm here, isn't it?'

'It's not her job to be happy or unhappy. When she gets her pips – and she will – it'll be up to her to make decisions. Until then, the buck stops here.' Daley prodded his own chest.

'Whatever you say, sir.'

'Don't be sarcastic, Brian. I think that might be Hamish in there. You're hereby recalled to duty, on my orders. Stay sober and don't bugger anything up, okay?'

'Hamish? Why dae you think that?'

'His clothes. His age – build.'

'I don't get it, Jimmy. I'm confused.'

'Come here.' Daley led Scott across to the tent that was covering the remains buried in the sand. He unzipped the tent and, as Dhar had done for him, held open the flap for Scott to look inside.

'Right, I see your problem.'

'And you can see why I think it might be Hamish?'

'The jumper and the wellies, right size. Aye, I get it.'

'We can't remove that boulder over his head until SOCO appear.'

'Aye, I dare say.' Scott shook his head.

'Sir, can I have a word, please?' Dhar called Daley from

further down the beach. She had one hand covering the mouth-piece of her mobile.

Daley looked grim as he approached her. 'Okay, what's happening?'

'There's been an accident on the road. At the Rest, sir. They're going to come by another route.'

'The Tarbert ferry. That could take ages. I don't know when they sail.'

Dhar shrugged. 'I don't even know where Tarbert is.'

'What do you think, Brian?' Daley shouted over his shoulder. When no reply was forthcoming, he turned to look back towards the forensic tent. Scott had disappeared.

'What's he doing now?' Daley marched off to the tent, cursing under his breath, Dhar at his heels.

'Are you sure this was a good idea, sir?'

'Please don't ask me that again, DS Dhar.'

Daley stood by the forensic tent. It was as though Scott had vanished into thin air. He was about to call to the officers at the causeway gate to ask if they'd seen Scott when the ripping sound of a zip made him turn to face the tent.

From within, Scott emerged. 'It's no' him, Jimmy.'

'How do you know?'

'I moved that boulder away. It's a big one. I recognise the guy – I'm sure I've seen him about. But it's no' Hamish, I can tell you that.'

'This is ridiculous,' said Dhar. 'Who knows what evidence you've disturbed – destroyed, even!'

'Don't get in a fluster, lassie. I was careful. I moved the boulder wae the toe o' my boot.'

'You shouldn't even have been in there. Is this how things work down here?' Dhar was flushed with anger.

'DS Dhar, go back to the office, please,' said Daley.

'I'm sorry?'

'Please go back to the office and await further orders.'

'So, I'm to be sent packing like a naughty schoolgirl, while an officer under suspension tramples all over a potential crime scene?'

'I've reinstated DS Scott. And in any case, I'm in charge here. So please do as I ask.'

Shreya Dhar's eyes flashed with rage. She looked between Scott and Daley. 'I'm not going to be party to this.' She stormed off back to her car.

'She's sparky, Jimmy.'

'You shouldn't have done that, Brian.'

'Aye, but you're glad I did. I could see that face you'd on. Thon tearing yourself apart that you do. Mind, I've known you for a long time.'

Daley smiled. 'You have.'

'If there's any shite aboot it, just blame me. I mean, this will likely be my last few hours in the job.'

'Shit! PIRC are on their way. They want to speak to you this afternoon.'

Scott looked at him balefully. 'I'm no' for fighting this time, Jimmy. And it's no' because o' the drink. I know that's what you're going to say.'

'What, then? You've been in more trouble in this job than anyone I know. Why is this so different?'

Scott shrugged. 'It just is, that's all. I've been in this longer than you, remember. I'm just fed up pushing the rock up the hill. Or in this case, off the deid punter's coupon. Admit it, that's why you brought me down here. You knew fine I'd do something reckless to save the day.'

'Subconsciously, maybe. I'm used to having you around, I suppose.'

'It's that Jim and Jan thing.'

Daley looked puzzled. 'Do you mean yin and yang?'

'Ach, it's the same in any language, Jimmy.'

Daley managed to keep the smile from his face. 'Don't do anything hasty – this afternoon, I mean.'

'Okay, I'll try.'

'Meanwhile, we need to find out who our man is.'

'Where's SOCO now?'

'Coming on a slow boat from China.'

'Bugger me. I knew things were pushed, but we're calling on the Chinese polis now?'

'No, it was just an expression, Brian.'

'Oh, right. But would you be surprised?'

Daley sighed. 'Nowadays? I don't know what to think.'

'Face it. Me and you – we're relics. This job isnae the same one we joined.'

'You think you recognise this man?' Daley was looking into the tent at the newly revealed face. The man's eyes were staring into the space above him. His skin looked like mottled wax.

'Might have seen him in the County. You know the fishermen liked it in there.'

'Nobody left there that would know him. Folk from the town won't work for Macmillan after – well, after you know what.'

'Annie. Poor lassie. I still can't get my heid roon it.'

'That's why you started drinking again, isn't it?'

'I'm just sick, Jimmy. Sick o' staring at another pair o' blank eyes. All the sadness and cruelty. Folk's lives wasted. It just gets to me. Aye, and you, too – don't lie.'

207

'Big Davie!' said Daley, apropos of nothing.

'Eh?'

'The lad that does the cellar in the County. He's still there. I saw him when I was having lunch with Shreya.'

'I hope you've no' got designs on that lassie, big man.'

'I have one affair, and now every woman under the age of forty who comes to work here isn't safe. Is that it?'

'Oh, steady! You'll gie yoursel' one o' they emblems!'

'Embolisms, Brian.'

'Aye, one o' them, tae.'

'Okay. We leave the boys here and go to the County.'

'Oh. What aboot they PRICs?'

Daley looked at his watch. 'You've got loads of time before *PIRC* arrive.'

'I'm no' sure about going to the County, Jimmy.'

'The drink?'

'Nah. The ghost behind the bar.'

Daley nodded. 'I hear you. But we need to do our jobs. I'll take a couple of photos on my phone. They'll just have to eliminate our footprints.'

'I'd better take the pictures. You'll just get into bother. It's goodnight Venice for me, anyway.'

'Vienna.'

'Aye, early dark there, tae.' He stared at Daley. 'Do you ever get the feeling o' things coming to an end, Jimmy?'

'What do you mean?'

'I don't know, just a feeling.' Daley's phone in hand, Scott disappeared into the tent.

30

Hugh Machie was lying on the bed in his small, rented flat. The bed was old; the springs were hard under the bedsheet. He tried to roll over, but even this small act caused him to cough up more blood.

He lay back and did the best he could to make himself comfortable. But he knew that the blood he produced with every cough was getting worse and the wheeze was louder with every breath.

I need to find the strength to get this done, he thought as he reached for the small brown bottle on his bedside table. They called it Oramorph, but it was basically liquid morphine. Hugh was aware that he was taking too much, but what did he have to lose? In any case it dulled the pain and helped him relax. Most of the time, he was drifting along on a cloud of the medication. Without it, the panic and pain made him cry out. He knew this because he'd tried it. He'd wanted to focus his mind, but doing anything without chemical assistance was now impossible.

Soon, the morphine induced a state somewhere between sleep and wakefulness. Machie was conscious of everything around him in the shabby room, but his mind was free.

He thought of his childhood in Glasgow's East End.

The war had taken its toll on everyone, especially the urban poor. He went to bed hungry every night, his stomach a concave hollow. He remembered his uncle visiting from Perthshire, where he worked as a farm labourer. The very memory of the man always made his mouth water.

The reaction was predicated on the fact that Uncle Charlie always arrived in Glasgow with food. He'd bring cheese, butter, homemade bread, vegetables and rabbits that tasted just like roast chicken. The feeling of being well fed was strange. He membered that his sister had once eaten her meal so quickly she was sick and had to be taken to the doctor. Her body was so accustomed to a meagre diet that the sudden ingestion of lots of food made her ill.

After that, when his uncle visited, they all ate smaller portions. He hated it, but realised that, this way, the Perthshire bounty lasted a lot longer. He could still picture his mother standing at the stove making a pudding with hard cheese and stale bread. She transformed food that many would have thrown away into something delicious.

Hugh was overtaken by another bout of coughing. He struggled to sit up straight in bed. Desperately trying to catch his breath, he looked at the duvet. It was covered with the black blood he'd been coughing up for a while, but this time it was different. The blood was clotted – a sign his doctor had warned him to look out for.

This is an indication that your condition is entering its final phase, Mr Machie. I know you want to cope with this illness on your own terms. But there will come a time when that becomes impossible.

The doctor looked like a boy. The hospital stank of illness, death and decay. Hugh Machie had promised himself that once the end was clear, he'd use the Webley one last time.

He did his best to wipe the duvet clean with a hankie, then reached into the drawer on his bedside table. It contained only two items: another bottle of pills and the gun.

Instead of reaching out for the firearm, he removed the medicine bottle and shook three yellow tablets into his hand. He knew that he was only supposed to take one at a time, but this medication was the only thing that helped him get up and about.

He swallowed them with another slug of Oramorph. Now all he had to do was wait for his energy to return. And even though this strength came from a bottle, he had enough to help him to the end.

Hugh lay back again and the image of the old man who'd died on the beach flashed before his mind's eye. It was the last thing he wanted to happen. But as he'd learned to rationalise, there was nothing to be gained by regret; it was a negative, harmful emotion. If he let it in, its sheer force would surely crush his frail body more quickly than the cancer could eat it away.

His wristwatch had been a present from Frank MacDougall, way back in the eighties. He'd always liked Frank, even though he knew that he was capable of heinous acts. But he reasoned he himself had done plenty of wicked things that matched that description. For Frank, at least, violence was a last resort.

For Hugh's son James it was like the food he'd craved as a boy. James Machie couldn't survive without it. His cruelty knew no bounds, and he demanded to know every detail from his father in the aftermath of a job.

What was his face like when he was dying? Did he cry or scream? Did he piss himself?

To hear of the painful demise of someone whose crime may have been as minor as talking to the gangster out of turn gave James huge satisfaction.

Hugh Machie had faced it a long time ago: the only son he'd got to know was mentally ill. So dangerous that he should have spent his miserable life locked away, if only to keep everyone else safe – including his own family.

Hugh often fantasised about killing his own flesh and blood to rid the world of such evil. But the chance had never presented itself. He was sure his son knew of his murderous intent and ensured that the man who had given him life never had the opportunity to fulfil it.

But though James Machie was dead, part of him lived on – and not just in Hugh's head. Part of the story was incomplete; every tale had to have a beginning, a middle and an end. Every character must play his or her part until the last page. Family was family, after all – it was the way they'd all been brought up. It was all that had kept him going during the years when he was little more than a hired killer, working for his own son.

Everything had to stop somewhere – to every player, their final bow.

As the medicine he'd taken began to kick in, Hugh Machie's mind drifted to a Remembrance Day long ago. The November morning was crisp and cold. Ranks of uniformed men stood to attention, as they had done in parade squares across the world over so many years.

The ceremony had been solemn. Each of them remembered fallen colleagues – dead friends. But in the back of their minds, the silent prayer was always *Thank you for sparing me*. It was a thought that was never given voice, but it was real, nonetheless.

After the hymns and parades, the prayers and the tears, he'd sat with some of his army pals in a London pub. They were the lucky ones; they'd made it home.

Sitting opposite him across a table in the bar was Herbert Fletcher, a quiet, thoughtful young man from Norfolk. Hugh Machie liked him. On many nights amidst the horror of war in Korea, they'd played chess to distract themselves from the death that stalked them all.

Herbert looked up from his pint of lukewarm English ale. 'What happens when we're all gone – a hundred years from now, eh?'

'What do you mean?' Machie had asked.

'Who'll stand in rank and file beside that big hunk of stone and think of us?'

'Somebody, I suppose.'

'No, they won't, my friend. It'll be like a distant memory – all of it. Same with the World Wars. People will get on with their lives, their own problems – and the good Lord knows, people can create horror wherever they go.'

'We'll be long gone,' said Machie.

'And so will everyone who gives a shit. It'll be like another death; everyone who ever died in battle will be forgotten – it's the death of remembrance.'

Hugh Machie had remembered that moment, those words, through all the years since. They were simple and logical – just like the man who'd given them voice. And, as he got older, the more sense they made.

While he was sure that everyone who had died fighting tyranny and wickedness should always be remembered, some things were best forgotten. All the hate and evil, buried along with those who'd made it happen. A line had to be drawn;

a line that was the end. The accounts must be reconciled, the books balanced.

Hugh Machie struggled out of bed, took a couple of puffs of his inhaler and got dressed.

Now it was time to end his personal remembrance.

31

Shreya Dhar was incandescent with rage. She'd returned to the station as Daley had ordered, but sitting in her borrowed office made her feel like a toy that had been put away for the day by bored children.

And there was little doubt that Daley and his irresponsible, drunken companion were like children. She'd heard so much about this dynamic duo. Tired old stories of their forays against the impossible. But the reality was very different – the events of the previous evening had borne that out. She'd never witnessed such an immature, embarrassing scene as Liz Daley and Ella Scott rolling about on the floor at a dinner party. One thing was certain: she was no plaything.

Dhar left the office without a word to Sergeant Shaw, who said goodbye nonetheless. She walked down the hill from the police office and into the centre of the small town. Some locals were chatting in small groups, muffled up against the cold. Others were engaged in what looked like serious conversations over shop counters and through car windows. As Dhar walked down Main Street, she felt every eye on her. She hoped this was a product of her own imagination, but as she reached the hotel near the seafront she realised that her instinct had been spot on and no casual paranoia.

'Excuse me, dear.' An old woman with a blue scarf tied across grey hair beckoned her.

'Yes?' Dhar replied, the smile no representation of how she actually felt at this moment.

'I know you're a policeman.' The woman hesitated for a moment. 'Well, police lassie – och, you know what I mean.'

'Yes, I do.' Dhar was surprised that this woman she'd never seen before could possibly know her occupation. The joys of policing in a small community, she realised.

'We're all wondering – in the toon, I mean. They say a man was found deid doon at the shore. You know, at the causeway.'

Dhar adopted her official manner. 'I'm sorry, but I can't say anything about that.'

The woman lowered her head. 'Aye, I understand, lassie. But you see, my husband went to his work this morning. When I heard they'd found a body I called to make sure he was okay – you know how it is, I'm sure. But they say he never turned up for work.'

'Oh, I see.' Dhar didn't really know what to say. She knew the remains on the beach were likely to have been there for much longer than just a few hours, but still, she couldn't be sure. 'What's your name, madam?'

'Johnson – Emily Johnson. My man's name is Craig.'

'Mrs Johnson, I'd like you to do a me a favour. Could you pop up to the police office and tell the sergeant at the front desk what you've just told me, please?'

Mrs Johnson staggered forward for a moment. Dhar grabbed her by the shoulders.

'Are you okay?'

216

'I couldna bear it if anything happened to him, dear. We argue like buggery, but it's the only life I've known. Aye, for near on fifty years.'

Dhar spoke quietly to the older woman. 'Listen, I shouldn't tell you this, but I don't think you have to worry about your husband. That's all I can say. But I'm pretty confident.'

Mrs Johnson looked at her, initially with suspicion and then growing relief. 'Are you sure?'

'Very sure.' Dhar was aware that a small crowd had gathered around them. 'Can anyone take Mrs Johnson up to the police office, please?'

There was a murmur from the gathered townsfolk, then a tall man in a boiler suit stepped forward. 'My van's just round the corner. I'll take you up, Emily.'

'That's very kind o' you, Colin.' She smiled weakly.

Colin put his arm around Mrs Johnson and led her away to his van. 'Thank you, dear,' she shouted to Dhar as they disappeared.

A man with red hair eyed Dhar suspiciously. 'What's up wae Emily?'

'It's fine, she's just a bit worried about her husband.'

'Oh, aye. Is he deid?'

'No, I'm quite sure he isn't dead. Now, if you'll excuse me, I can't say any more.'

'You're thon new lassie. The one replacing Sergeant Scott, aye?' said a young woman.

'No, I'm just here for a short time.'

'You'll be here for a while, I'm thinking. That man's lost the place wae the drink. Running aboot the pubs assaulting folk willy-nilly.' This local was of late middle age. 'We were better back in the days o' Inspector MacLeod. Since thon

217

Daley and his drunken mate arrived, there's been nothing but bother.'

'Aye, and I'd keep my hand on my ha'penny if I were you,' said the younger woman. 'That's all I'm saying.'

'Sorry?' Dhar was bewildered by this impromptu gathering.

'What she means is that your boss has an eye for the ladies. Bugger me, he drove the last one to suicide. They say it was an accident, but I've never believed that. The lassie wisnae half his age.' The middle-aged man looked pleased with himself.

Dhar shook her head, excused herself and marched off down the pier.

'Aye, that's poor Craig Johnson lying deid doon at the causeway,' said a woman in the crowd.

'Could be,' said another man. 'Mind you, he could just as easily be in bed wae Peggy Sommerville.'

'Away, no' at his age. Mind, he's retired. They took him back for a couple o' extra years.' A tall woman looked unconvinced.

'Aye, but they wee blue pills work a treat, so they do.'

'You'll know, Alec – wae all the galivanting you're at.'

'Shut your face, Duncan, or I'll show you just how roused I can get.'

'The truth hurts, and you know it!'

The tall woman spoke up. 'Come on, you pair. There's poor Craig Johnson murdered in the sand. Have some respect. I'll need to look oot my black frock.'

And with that, the community of Kinloch decided they'd lost one of their own.

'What's going on?' said the latest arrival, a man with wood dust on his blue dungarees.

There was a gasp followed by a pregnant pause. Alec piped up. 'You'd better get yoursel' up to the polis station. Your Emily's been arrested.'

'Eh?'

'Just get up there, man!'

As Craig, now resurrected from his sandy grave, rushed off, Alec was in receipt of malicious glares from the small crowd that had gathered around. 'What else could I say? *We all thought you were deid, but it's good to see you?*'

Having lived through a life and death drama in no more than a few minutes, the little crowd dispersed, all with tales to tell when they got to wherever they were going.

32

Glasgow, 1987

Ella Scott stared at her wedding ring. She never tired of looking at it as it sparkled in everything but darkness. The ring was the envy of her friends and the girls at work. Her husband was a police detective, and with the money they were able to save they'd soon be able to start a family and buy a new house.

Ella was sitting in Brian's parents' flat. It was clean and tidy, but spartan. The TV was an old black and white set, while the rest of the furniture had its roots back in the nineteen fifties, or beyond. She placed her cracked coffee mug on a coaster bearing an image of Rothsay. The wallpaper that had once been white anaglypta was now stained brown after years in the company of heavy smokers. Instead of a fitted carpet, threadbare rugs were scattered across a bare wooden floor. There was little doubt that the domestic affairs of the Scott family had been severely affected by the man of the house's drinking and gambling.

'You'll need to hurry up, Willie. We'll no' make that appointment if you don't get a move on. And you know fine what that surgery is like. You'll wait a week for another one.'

'I'm just coming, lassie. Hold your horses!' The disembodied voice came from the bathroom along the hall where Brian Scott's father was getting shaved, ready for a visit to the doctor.

'You've got another couple o' minutes!' Ella was impatient now, beginning to regret having learned to drive. For a start, the car Brian had acquired for her was an ancient Mini with an automatic gear-box. It chugged along well enough on level ground, but faced with the slightest incline – of which Glasgow had a plentiful supply – it was a case of revving the engine as much as she could and taking a run at it. Ella consoled herself with the knowledge that few of her friends had cars – or jobs, come to that. And though four days a week working behind the bar at the local British Legion wasn't the most glamorous endeavour, it was a means to an end.

Willie Scott appeared in the living room. He was dressed in an old suit that looked like a gift from the Salvation Army. Judging by the cut, like the décor in the Scott residence, it too came from the fifties. His grey hair was thinning at the front and his face was pallid, with black shadows circling his sunken blue eyes. For a moment Ella shivered, wondering if this was a shadow of coming events. The resemblance between her husband and his father was clear, despite the older man's obvious decline. Though Brian eschewed gambling, he was too fond of alcohol – in Ella's opinion, at least. She resolved to work on her husband's drinking.

'You're a bit dressy, are you no'?' she said.

'I thought I'd let the doc see my funeral suit – to give him an idea o' where he's sending me wae all these pills and potions I have to take every day.'

'The pills and potions are keeping you alive. You're to blame for destroying your ain health.'

'Bugger me, but my Brian's got his work cut oot wae you, eh? A scold's tongue, right enough.'

'Maybe if your wife had a sharper tongue you'd no' be in the state you're in. And I'll no' thole any lip fae you, Willie Scott. I'm doing *you* the favour, remember?'

'Favour, you say?' Willie coughed as he lit a cigarette. 'Going in a car wae you is like a trip to the carnival at the Kelvin Hall. I've had mair comfortable journeys on the dodgems – aye, and the big dipper, come to that.'

Ella ignored this comment. She made sure her cigarettes and lighter were safe in the pocket of her jeans, her purse in her handbag. From the latter she removed a set of car keys.

'Fuck, chocks away,' said Willie as they left the flat and headed out into the dark close. The stairwell was cold and damp, the stone steps worn down by the passage of countless feet over many years.

'These wee bastards, again!' Willie stared at red graffiti sprayed on the close wall. 'I'm buggered if I know what the likes o' my Brian and his mob are doing. Where's the polis when all this stuff's going on, eh?' He began to cough loudly and had to stop his descent of the stairs, one bony hand resting on the banister.

'You never mind aboot that. Come on!'

'Mother Teresa,' Willie wheezed under his breath.

'I heard that,' said Ella.

'And lugs like a bloody bat, into the bargain.'

The mustard-coloured Mini was sitting at the close entrance. Ella opened the passenger door and, after more coughing, wheezing and groaning, Willie lowered himself into his seat.

'Put your belt on, Wille. It's the law now, remember. And I don't want to be pulled o'er – no' wae these tyres,'

Ella told him as she made her way round to the driver's side of the car.

'Don't worry, hen,' Willie said to himself. 'If there was a parachute available, I'd be strapping that on wae gusto.'

A youth across the street kicking a football against a wall whistled at Ella as she ducked into the car. Rather than being irritated, it made her smile. She had a good figure, fine features and deep blue eyes. It was nice to know that she was still attractive. Compliments weren't her husband's strongest suit. And now she was a married woman she was pleased not to be invisible. Lots of her friends had wedded young. They seemed to shrink into themselves, almost disappear. Invisibility wasn't for Ella.

She turned the key in the ignition and revved the engine.

'This is what it must be like for thon Jackie Stewart,' said Willie above the din. 'For the only time I've heard a noise like that, it's coming fae an engine o' a racing car.'

'Remember, this motor isnae so hot on hills, Willie. And there's a big one at the end of the street.'

'I know. I've fallen doon it enough times to be intimately acquainted wae the bloody thing.'

Ella took off, the Mini's tyres screeching on the tarmac. 'I hope we get a clear run at it,' she said, head forward over the wheel like the pilot of a Spitfire. So far so good – there was no sign of any cars coming in the opposite direction, which would have meant having to slow down or, worse still, stop.

Willie Scott gripped the handle on the door, knuckles showing white through his paper-thin skin. 'I could have caught the bus!'

'Aye, and we know fine how that turns oot, eh? The nearest you get to the doctor is that wee pub on the corner. I have my instructions, and I'm going to follow them to the letter. Like it or loathe it.'

'Look at the speed you're at, lassie.'

'It's the only way we'll make it up this hill, Willie.'

The road rose up to meet them as Ella hammered on. So steep was the incline that Ella had to put her foot to the floor in order to coax the vehicle onwards.

'It's times like this I wish I had they rosary beads.'

'Eh? You're a Protestant, Willie.'

'At least I'd have something to dae with my hands. It would maybe take my mind off pishing myself.'

Ella was all concentration now. The only had a few yards to go before they reached the brow of the hill. With the engine screeching, Ella was sure it was all plain sailing until, over the rise, the familiar yellow and green of a Glasgow Corporation bus appeared.

'Bugger!' With both sides of the road adorned by parked cars, she had two options: take her foot off the accelerator, in which case they'd roll back down the hill, or hope she could navigate the small space between the parked cars and the double-decker. There was also a chance that the bus driver was an amiable soul and would stop to let her pass, but it was soon clear that this one was not of the chivalric variety.

It was going to be touch and go. Ella aimed at the narrowing gap with a strained expression, almost certain she'd shortly hear the sickening crunch of metal on metal.

'Oh, you bastard!' shouted Willie, turning his head away, bracing for impact.

But as they reached the top of the hill the bus swished past with inches to spare. Soon, Ella was applying the brakes to arrest their acceleration down the other side of the incline.

'There, that wisnae so bad,' she said.

'Bad? Listen, I was in the war, but that's the maist frightening thing that's ever happened to me.'

'You were in the catering corps – don't exaggerate.'

In a mile or so, mercifully free of any significant gradient, they reached the health centre. Ella parked as near to the entrance as she could. 'Are you wanting me to come in with you?'

'I'm no' ten years old. You sit here and get a smoke. I'll no' be long. It'll be the usual lecture about drinking and smokes. I've heard it all before.'

'Well, maybe it's time to listen, eh?' Ella watched her father-in-law as he shuffled into the surgery. He would have passed for a man thirty years older.

'Well, Mr Scott, how are we today?' Dr Clarke sat behind his desk, a stethoscope draped over his shoulders like a badge of office.

'Apart fae my daughter-in-law near killing me in the car, I'm no' too bad – the usual.'

'Yes, that's what I wanted to talk to you about.' Clarke swept a strand of dark hair from his brow.

'What?'

'Killing *yourself*, Mr Scott.'

'Eh?'

'It's as simple as this. If you won't help me, there's nothing I can do for you.'

'Oh? Why's that, doctor?'

'It's the drink, I'm afraid.' Clarke shook his head dolefully.

Willie Scott raised his brow, a look of surprise on his face. 'I'm sorry to hear that, doctor, I really am.' He stood. 'I'll tell you what, I'll come back when you're feeling a wee bit mair like yourself.' He patted Clarke's arm. 'We've all been there, son.'

Dr Clarke looked momentarily bewildered. 'No, not me – you! If you don't stop drinking, Willie, you're going to die – it's as simple as that.'

Ella looked on as her father-in-law appeared from the surgery. If anything, he looked older and more stooped than when he went in. She lit one last quick cigarette. Even though Willie had only thirty or so yards to get to the car, there would be plenty of time for a few puffs.

Out of the corner of her eye, she saw movement. Three young men were running quickly towards the building. At first, Ella thought nothing of it. But then they halted beside Willie Scott. She was puzzled when words were exchanged. Out of the blue, one young man swung a punch that caught her father-in-law squarely on the chin. The old man went straight down, not even putting out his hands to arrest his fall.

By the time Ella was out of the car, the three of them were kicking Willie Scott as he lay unconscious on the ground.

'Stop it, you wee bastards!' Ella shouted as she reached the scene.

'Okay, that'll dae,' shouted a youth in a baseball cap. He sauntered towards Ella. 'You want a wee bit, darling, eh? You're a cracker.'

Ella raised her chin. 'Fuck off back to your mammy, wee boy!' She knelt over Willie Scott's motionless body.

As people who'd witnessed the attack from inside the surgery began to spill out of the building, the youths took to their heels. The one who'd spoken to Ella turned. 'That's a wee present fae Jay-Mac.' He bolted after his accomplices.

'Willie, are you okay? Willie!' Ella stared at her father-in-law. A huge lump was already appearing over his right eye, and his lip was bloodied.

'What happened?' Willie Scott's voice was little more than a whisper.

'Don't worry, the doctor's here.' Ella moved back to let Dr Clarke examine the old man.

'Fuck, it's you again.'

'Just lie still, Mr Scott.' Clarke looked round. 'Nurse Swanton, get an ambulance. This man needs to be in hospital.'

'Is he going to be okay?' wailed Ella.

'No, I'm no' going to be okay,' croaked Willie. 'This is it, my life's over.'

'Now, come on, Mr Scott. You've taken a blow or two, but you'll survive,' said Clarke.

'I wisnae on aboot that. Why bother recovering when I cannae even get a drink?'

33

Despite the cold, Ian Macmillan was sweating as he took the winding path up the hill above Kinloch. The bag he was carrying was heavy. The zip was locked with a small padlock, but that didn't really bother him. He had no interest in the contents. He just wanted the bag off his hands. He'd seen a few people on the way up the hill, and it was what *they* wanted.

He'd been sent a rough map, and he could see the roof of a cottage down in a hollow a few hundred yards away.

He turned to take in the scene. Kinloch, far below, looked tiny. The loch was grey and choppy, the island at its head almost a speck. Macmillan's time in the wilds of Canada had taught him a few things: he could always smell rain on the air. He pressed on, his stride lengthening as the climb became a short descent.

The cottage was tumbledown, but still looked watertight in parts. A yawning gap where once had been a door led inside. The smell within almost made him gag. It was clear that livestock had been housed in this place – the building stank of their excrement.

Macmillan edged further into the cottage, trying not to stand on tiny black balls of sheep shit. He held a hankie over his mouth and nose; the stench was so bad it made his eyes water.

The interior was dim, with one small window that had lost its glazing many years ago. But the shaft of daylight coming from the open doorway was good enough. He looked around. An old fireplace had collapsed into itself, and a broken pair of round wire glasses lay amidst the dust and decay, almost rusted into the tumbledown stones. Macmillan found it impossible to imagine that people ever lived here. He wondered if this was a summer hut like the places he'd seen in Switzerland. Animals were taken to the high pastures in summertime to take advantage of abundant grazing. But he realised that the hills that rose above Kinloch were accessible all year round. This wasn't a temporary hut, but a home. He shuddered at the thought, and tried to put himself in the shoes of the person to whom the rusted spectacles had once belonged, but couldn't. Then he thought about his own life. At the mercy of ruthless criminals to whom he owed more money than he could possibly hope to pay back.

Now he was a simple functionary – a patsy, if necessary, he was sure. Either way, he was a mere creature of the people who'd sent him here, though he couldn't fathom what they wanted with this place. The hotel, that was different. Fugitives, illegal immigrants, all manner of felons would be arriving in the dead of night and lying low until a boat could pick them up from one of the many nooks and crannies along the coast of the Kintyre peninsula. But surely nobody would be kept here.

There were basically two rooms in this small building. Macmillan was startled when a large black rat scurried past him as he made his way into the second.

Now it was simple: he just wanted to leave the bag and get out of this place as quickly as he could. An old black sink, cracked in two, sat against the back wall. Next to it was a workbench with hinged metal doors underneath. As instructed, Macmillan leaned forward and pulled at one. The hinges groaned and creaked, almost impossible to move. But when he gripped the door with both hands he managed to drag it open, revealing a small cupboard with a couple of wooden shelves. He recoiled as a host of bugs scurried away at the disturbance.

He thrust the heavy bag through the crack, then stood, clapping his hands free of dirt and dust, and kicked the door closed. His job was done.

Ian Macmillan stumbled out into the grey day. It looked bright to him after the gloom of the cottage. He stared up the way he'd come and strode back up the rise.

Looking down at Kinloch again, he filled his lungs with fresh air – a relief after the rancid cottage. As he stared at tiny cars heading round the loch, the dots that were people going about their business, he pondered on his own life. He'd been a success; life was sweet. He married a beautiful woman and they soon had their first child.

But then the rot had set in.

Why had he agreed to senseless overspending he knew could never be sustained? He supposed he was just carried along with it all, reckoning that every year would bring more income than the last – the way it had been for so long. How was he supposed to know that another big trucking company would shoulder him out of lucrative contracts? How was he to know that his wife had run up huge amounts of debt without his knowledge? But these regrets tumbled through his mind every day. The process was pointless.

Macmillan looked back again. The slate roof of the cottage was just visible. What was in the bag? By the weight and feel, he couldn't really tell. He didn't really care.

As he made his way back down the hill towards Kinloch, he tried to banish it all from his mind, but the exercise was futile. He was tired of being the victim, tired of twisting in the wind, a pawn for those who were rapidly making his life a misery.

He thought of Daley and Scott. On their first meeting he'd liked them both. Now he saw the mistrust in their eyes. He supposed it was an improvement on the sheer hatred and hostility he felt from the locals.

Why were people so curious? Why didn't he think before he opened his mouth?

A lack of forethought had always been his problem. But maybe what he knew was worth something. He was sure it was. He'd done many deals during his life – this was just another. Maybe there was a way out of the mess in which he found himself – a negotiation.

Staring at nothing now, his mind went back to a hot summer's night. Heavy footsteps on the stairs. A woman's muffled screams. Threats: being forced against a wall with a knife at his throat.

Then came the wave of deep, deep regret – the self-hatred.

He thought of the attractive detective he'd seen with Daley in the hotel. She wasn't part of the unbreakable duo that was DCI Daley and his faithful Sergeant Scott.

She was the key to the deal – there always was one.

Feeling a great weight rise from his shoulders, Macmillan strode back down the hill to Kinloch.

Just as he was beginning to feel better about himself,

a massive gull swept down in front of him, screeching. It flew close enough for him to see its baleful gaze. He watched as the bird soared higher, pivoted in the grey sky and, with a caw like a woman's scream, plunged towards him again, catching him on the cheek with its sharp beak.

Macmillan put a hand to his face. It was covered in blood. He looked up, but the great gull had disappeared.

34

Daley squinted at his watch as he and Scott made for the County Hotel. He supposed that they could have enquired anywhere down the pier as to the identity of the man lying dead in the sand at the causeway, but he wanted to keep things quiet and reckoned that if big Davie at the County could do the business it would be relatively easy to persuade him be discreet. He knew this place and wanted to get word out to the deceased's family before the jungle drums sounded.

The town seemed unusually busy. Daley couldn't find a parking place near to the hotel. 'Bugger it, Brian. We might as well park up at the office and walk back down,' he said, accelerating as he spoke.

'Dae we have to?'

'What's the problem?'

'For a start, that new lassie Dhar doesnae fancy the cut o' my jib one little bit. And what if they pricks are aboot already?'

'PIRC, Brian. The Police Investigations and Review Commissioner.'

'Aye, whatever.' Scott waved his hand dismissively.

'By the way, don't think for one minute you're getting a drink when we're in the County.'

'I could dae with a wee voddy or something – you know, that they cannae smell on my breath.'

The look on Daley's face spoke more than words.

'I guess that's a no, then?'

'It's an absolutely no way in a million years. What's wrong with you? Booze is why you're in this mess in the first place.'

'Aye, you're right.'

Daley didn't speak again until they drew up outside the police office. He switched off the engine and turned to his friend.

'You need help, Brian. And once we get rid of this ridiculous charge, it's time to find it for you.'

'Oh aye, just as easy as that. I hope you've got a magic wand, Jimmy. Aye, and it better be a big one.'

'There's no magic to any of it. We just work the problem, like we always do.'

'Only now the problem is that I'm a hopeless alcoholic and the powers that be see a perfect chance to get rid o' me.'

'Pull yourself together and stay here. I'll just go and check what's happening with SOCO – and our disappearing DS.'

Daley left Scott in the car and headed into the office. He made for the front desk to see if Sergeant Shaw knew of Dhar's whereabouts. But before he could talk to the desk sergeant, who was busy toiling over a computer with his back to the DCI, he heard a familiar voice.

Turning on his heels, he saw Hamish sitting on one of the seats reserved for those waiting to speak to an officer.

'Aye, it's yourself, Mr Daley,' said Hamish, a grim expression on his face.

'Sir, sorry I didn't see you, sir. Hamish is waiting for you,' said Shaw.

'Och, he knows that fine. I'm sitting right here.'

Daley and the old fisherman ended up in the glass box that was the nerve centre of Kinloch police office.

'What can I do for you, my friend?' said Daley.

'I'm a bit worried aboot a pal o' mine. I haven't seen so much as a glimpse of him since the day before yesterday. When I heard that a body had been found doon at the causeway, well, I worried. You know fine what it's like, Mr Daley.'

Daley bit his lip and reached into his pocket. 'Hamish, I have a picture here on my phone of the person we found. If you don't want to look at it, I'll understand.'

The old man stared into space for a few moments. 'When you're young you reckon you're immortal, so you do. But then – maybe in your fifties – folk you've known all your life start to die off. It's then you realise the perilous nature o' existence, right enough. I saw good men die at the fishing – long before their time, mark you. And every time it happened, the thought in your heid would be, is it me next? I don't think I've ever stood beside a grave and no' wondered what it would be like to be in the box. My faither, mother, Peeny, McKirdy, my auld skipper Sandy Hoynes . . .' He hesitated, a tear in his eye.

'Annie?'

'Poor wee Annie. Bright as a button – would take on the whole world to defend a friend.' Hamish swallowed back his emotion.

'I understand. There's no need for you to go through the trauma of identifying this person. Others can do it. Don't worry, Hamish.'

The old man sniffed. 'No, that's no' what I mean, Mr Daley. If I can help you, well, I'm pleased to be at it. Show me your picture.'

Daley removed the phone from his pocket, scrolled down to find the image and stopped. 'Are you sure?'

'I am.' Hamish reached out a calloused hand. He stared at the screen for what must have been a full minute, saying nothing. Daley sat back in his chair, worried that he'd had to inflict more sadness on the man he respected so much.

'Aye, I know who it is. The feeling I had in my stomach all day yesterday was a justified one.'

'Is it your friend?'

'It is. Danny O'May – an auld colleague, as well as a trusted friend.' Hamish lowered his head.

The door burst open. Brian Scott stood in the doorway. 'Bugger me, Hamish. What's up wae your coupon?'

Daley frowned. 'Hamish has just identified our dead man on the beach. One of his friends.'

'You're no' much o' a body for tact, Brian, and that's for sure,' said Hamish.

'Sorry. Jimmy said he was just popping in the office for a while. I was sitting oot there like a diddy.' Scott held up his hands, in a gesture that said *How was I supposed to know?*

'He lived just down the road from me, in one o' the fishermen's cottages. I dare say his is in better nick than mine. Danny is – was – a few years younger than me. Lost his wife to cancer aboot five years ago. Bonnie lassie, she was.'

'This has been a shock, Hamish. I'll have someone take you home.'

To their surprise, out of the blue, the old fisherman burst into a fit of loud sobs. Daley hurried round to the desk to his side as Scott moved awkwardly from foot to foot, not really knowing what to do.

'I'm sorry. I shouldn't have put you through that, Hamish.'

'A man o' your years shouldna be thinking aboot death – it so close by, an' that,' said Scott.

'Shut up, Brian,' said Daley.

But Scott's observation seemed to pull Hamish from his misery. He sniffed back his tears and wiped his eyes with a paper hankie. 'There was an auld police sergeant here – och, when I was a boy. He went tae Betty Muir's hoose – she was married to a fisherman at the time. Bobby was his name. "Are you the widow Muir?" says he, quite jocose, like.

'"No, I saw my man off to work this morning."

'"Well, I'm here to tell you, he'll no' be hame for his tea. For he got flattened by Jock McCallum's lorry. I'm sorry to be the bringer of bad news, lassie." Wae that, he just put his bunnet back on and buggered off.' Hamish shook his head.

'I'm glad to say that things have improved in that time,' said Daley.

Hamish turned round in his chair to face Scott. 'No' as far as I'm concerned, anyway.'

There was silence for a moment, before Hamish began to chortle. That set off Daley and Scott. Soon all three men were laughing heartily in Daley's glass box.

'Sheer hysteria, that's a' it is,' spluttered Hamish.

35

Glasgow, 1987

Brian Scott was standing at his father's bedside, his new colleague ADC Daley at his side.

'I'm so sorry, Brian.'

'Aye, it's a bugger o' a thing, man.' His words were calm enough, but the fury on his face was hard to disguise. 'Tell me again what these wee bastards said, Ella.'

'You calm down, Brian.'

'Just tell me!'

Ella looked at the tall young man standing beside Scott. He was dark-haired, trim and good-looking, but she saw sadness in his eyes, though she couldn't work out why. 'Can you tell him to behave, please?'

'He cannae tell me anything. I'm in charge o' him. No offence, Jimmy, son.'

'None taken. But I'm sure your wife is right. We should go back to Burns with this. He'll know what to do.'

'I know fine what'll happen. It'll be recorded in a crime report and bugger all will be done aboot it. It's always the same. You said they mentioned Jay-Mac, Ella.'

'Och, it might have been that. I cannae be sure.'

238

'Sure, my arse!' Scott's face was a mask of hatred, his eyes flaring with the need for revenge.

'You go after that bastard and he'll kill you, Brian,' said Ella.

'That'll be right.'

'Jay-Mac, as in James Machie?' said Daley.

'Aye, that's what he's taken to calling himself now. Some crapper thing fae America – I don't know.'

'Rapper, Brian. It's they boys that gie it big licks wae poetry, and that,' said Ella. 'No' a *crapper*.'

'I'm no' bothered what they call themselves – look at the state o' my old man.'

Willie Scott's face was virtually unrecognisable: bruised, bloodied, with a gash in one cheek stitched back together. His right eye was almost obscured by a huge purple lump, and his lip was burst, swollen and stitched. He was tethered to a bleeping heart monitor and a drip.

The door of the side room burst open and a middle-aged consultant in a white coat barged in, followed by a line of younger people, dressed likewise.

'Now, here we have an elderly male who suffered an attack earlier today.' As he pulled a pair of half-moon glasses from his top pocket, his students busied themselves writing notes. It was as though they were all oblivious of Brian, Ella and Jim Daley. 'Now, as you can see, face trauma, mostly superficial, apart from the stitches.' He turned to face a young woman with red hair and glasses. 'How should we be treating that head wound above his eye, Miss Blackley?'

The young woman was about to answer when Scott butted in.

'What's this, *General Hospital*?' he said. 'Who the fuck are you?'

'I'm senior consultant surgeon Walter Baird. And I don't take kindly to being spoken to in that manner.'

'Aw, I'm sorry. But see me, I don't care what way you prefer to be spoken to. Take your weans and dae one. This isnae a classroom, you rude bastard.'

'I beg your pardon?' Walter Baird looked nonplussed.

'I should think so too. Pardon granted, now fuck off,' said Scott.

'That's not what he meant,' Daley whispered.

'I don't know who you people are – relatives of this wretched man, I don't doubt.'

'Wretched man?'

'Indeed. His injuries are the least of his problems, let me assure you. He's spent too much time propping up a bar, by the look of his liver tests. Now, please leave, or I'll call the constabulary.' He angled his head in a haughty manner.

'You don't need to bother calling them, we're here. Show this prick your warrant card, Jimmy,' said Scott.

Reluctantly, Jim Daley produced his ID. 'I'm sorry, Mr Baird. This man is my colleague's father, and we're police officers.'

'My goodness. So this is what the force has become. I remember when police officers had manners – and knew their place.'

'Aye, and I don't remember when doctors had any manners, so nothing's changed.' Scott grabbed Baird by the collar of his white coat and pulled him towards the door. 'Yous lot too – come on.' Scott gestured to the door with his right thumb.

One by one, the student clinicians fled the room. When Scott ejected Baird, only one skinny youth with red hair and bad acne remained.

'You've no right treating Mr Baird like that. He's a great man.'

'And you're one ugly bastard, son. You'd better stick in at this, 'cos you'll never snag a woman wae a coupon like that. See you!' Scott gestured again towards the door.

The spotty youth eyed him for a few seconds then thought better of saying any more.

'Brian, you'll get intae trouble for that,' said Ella. 'And young Jimmy here. You need to think before you open your big mouth!'

Their attention was drawn back to Willie Scott. His eyes flickered open. He looked round at the three people at his bedside until his gaze rested on Daley. 'I hope you're no' a priest, son? Because you're barking up the wrong tree, by the way.'

'He's my buddy, Faither,' said Brian Scott.

Willie glanced over at Ella. 'Fuck, I've no' got to go back in a car wae her, have I?'

36

Hugh Machie was ready – it was time.

He'd dosed up on morphine to help kill the pain and his 'go faster' pills helped boost his flagging energy. Now he donned the old overcoat, the Webley in one of its deep pockets.

Looking out of the grimy flat window, he stared down at the street. The sun was out, something he'd never before witnessed during his short stay in Kinloch. It did little to lift his spirits. Even when he considered that it may be one of the last times he would see the great orb in the sky, it meant very little. Thinking was too hard – death was something he couldn't get his head around. So he simply concentrated on the matter in hand.

Kinloch was larger and more spread out than he'd anticipated. He'd always thought of the place as being little more than a fishing village. He'd been wrong. This changed his whole plan. He thought that police officers would be highly visible, coming to and from the police office. But that wasn't the case. Though he'd caught sight of his quarry on a couple of occasions, it was in a speeding car.

This in mind, Hugh had formulated a plan, something designed to attract the attention of the police. By no means was it foolproof, but he struggled to think of anything he'd ever done that was.

Yet again, he swept back his thinning har and looked in the mirror. If anything, he looked worse than he had the day before. His eyes were sunken further into his face, his pallor greyer than ever. There was a distinct tinge of yellow in the whites of his eyes – something the doctor had warned him would happen as his condition advanced.

None of this made him feel anything – certainly not sadness. His only goal was to finish what he'd come to do. He was here to draw a line under everything. He was here to make things right. The time he had left to do that was rapidly running out.

Machie sat on a chair in the hallway to catch his breath and gather his thoughts. There was a noisy argument going on in the flat next door. A man and a woman were screaming at each other. He couldn't remember how many times he'd been part of such a domestic disagreement. But thinking back on life with his wife, he wished he could take back every word. The woman had been nothing short of a saint. Her memory, as always, made him feel ashamed. He hadn't been a good husband – he hadn't been a good father. And the latter short-coming had come back to bite him hard.

Hugh took a deep breath, opened the battered door and headed out on to the streets of Kinloch.

Shreya Dhar, having managed to calm down, returned to Kinloch police office. She knew that any objection to Scott's reinstatement would be petty and futile. She was here to work, and nothing could get in the way of that, certainly not the seemingly unbreakable bond that tied Daley and Scott

243

together. Her storming away from a crime scene had been petulant and unprofessional. That made her angry with herself, for all sorts of reasons.

She forced a smile as she breezed in past the front desk.

'Oh, DS Dhar,' said Shaw, taking his attention away from a computer screen.

'Yes?'

'They've identified the body on the beach – a local man. I've been trying to get you on your mobile, but it appeared to be switched off.'

'Sorry, my fault, Alasdair. Forgot to charge the bloody thing – you know how it is.'

'I know how it is for sure, Shreya. I have so many things in the house that need to be charged up, I don't know where I am. Phones, tablets, laptops, e-readers – the kids keep on top of it much better than I can.'

'That's it, I must have some children.' Dhar laughed.

'It's not all win-win, I can assure you.'

'I'm sure. Certainly, from the stories some of my friends tell me.'

'Oh, just to let you know, PIRC are here.'

'Oh, not good.'

'No, I can't stand the sight of them. I'm the Federation rep, into the bargain. I'm just having a look at a few things before I take up the cudgels on Brian's behalf.'

'My goodness, I don't envy you that task.'

Shaw sighed. 'No, he's not the most conventional officer, that's for sure.'

'To say the least. Anyway, I'd better get through. The DCI's probably going to have my guts for garters as it is.'

'I think they're just pleased to have made a breakthrough

with the identification. A sorry business. Anyway, I ought to get back to saving Sergeant Brian.'

Dhar made her way into the CID office. She could see Scott, Daley and another man inside the glass box. Dhar knocked on the door and entered.

Scott was sitting biting his nails beside an elderly individual in a fisherman's jumper, who had an unlit pipe clenched between his teeth. Daley was leaning back in his chair, his face a mask of concern.

'Ah, Hamish, this is DS Dhar. She's with us here in Kinloch for a while.'

'Just in case Brian here gets the order of the boot, I'm thinking?' said Hamish.

'No, not at all.' She smiled and held out her hand. 'Hamish . . . what?'

'Hamish what?' The old man looked puzzled.

'Your surname?'

'Oh, aye – just Hamish will do. Everybody calls me that.' He grabbed Shreya Dhar's hand and shook it vigorously.

'You have a strong grip, Hamish!'

'Sorry, lassie. I was brought up to have a firm hand. A sign of trustworthiness, my faither always said. Before he drank himself to death, that was.'

'I'm sure you're more than trustworthy.'

'He identified our dead man,' said Daley.

'Oh – wow! I don't know quite what to say. Well done you!'

The old fisherman eyed her for a few moments. 'A man must do his duty as he sees fit, you know – and women are jeest the same.'

'May I speak to you about the ongoing situation when you have a moment, sir?' said Dhar, turning to Daley.

'Of course. I'll just get Hamish fixed up with a lift.'

'My goodness, you're a bit of a star, Hamish. You've been a great help.'

'I dae my best, lassie.' He looked down at his hands. 'Danny O'May was a fine man. I've known him since we were both young fishermen. Och, I remember him diving into the sea like a porpoise. Aye, fair agile he was.'

'Was he going for a swim?'

'Well, no' exactly. Let's say it was a wee misunderstanding with Her Majesty's Customs and Excise. Long before you were born, I hasten to add. You're very quiet, Brian. Man, it's no' like you at all.'

'You're no' facing the Spanish inquisition, Hamish.'

'Yes, I heard PIRC were here,' said Dhar.

'Aye, here wae bells on. Sitting up in the canteen plotting my downfall as we speak.'

'I'm sure it will all be fine.' She looked at Daley. 'I have somethings to write up, sir. Will you excuse me?'

'Absolutely. I'll come and fill you in with what's happening shortly.'

She nodded. 'Good luck, Brian. And lovely to meet you, Hamish.' Dhar left the office.

'I need a coffee, Jimmy. The condemned man, and all that.'

'Just don't leave the building.' Daley's look said more than the statement. The last thing he wanted was for Scott to go walkabout round Kinloch's pubs instead of facing the questions of those come to investigate his conduct. He was worried. Scott seemed determined that his time as a police officer was over. He'd never heard Brian talk like that – even during the worst of times. And there had been far too many of those.

'Keep the heid, big man. I know when it's time to screw the bobbin. See you later, Hamish.' Scott followed Dhar out of the glass box.

Hamish sucked thoughtfully on his unlit pipe. 'Poor Brian seems to have lost his spark, eh?'

'Yes, you're right. He's rarely been out of hot water ever since I've known him. But I've never seen him like this. He's really thinking of chucking it.'

'Man, you'd be like a fish oot o' water, the pair of you.'

'What do you mean?'

'Yous are a double act, for sure. It would be like Fran without Anna.'

'Flattering, Hamish.'

The older man leaned forward in his seat, his voice lowered conspiratorially. 'The lassie, do you know much about her?'

'DS Dhar?'

'Aye.'

'Why do you ask, Hamish?'

'Just a feeling, that's all. I feel a wee bit melancholy looking at her, if you know what I mean?'

Daley shrugged. 'Not really. Can you elaborate?'

'Och, you know fine what I'm like by now. I just think she's carrying a burden o' some kind. I had that same feeling no' that long ago. I ignored it, and I dearly wish I hadn't.' Tears brimmed in Hamish's eyes.

'When . . . what do you mean?'

'Annie,' the old fisherman replied quietly. 'I felt sadness coming fae her for a long time. I just put it down to all that carry-on at the hotel. Well, now we all know different. But I don't think it was the sadness o' someone who wanted to hasten her own end.'

247

'What then?'

'Mair like the sadness o' somebody who knew the end was coming – subconsciously, maybe.'

Daley considered this for a while. 'I know you never believed she killed herself.'

'I've never said it to a soul. Aye, and maybe it's the thought o' my auld friend lying dead doon at the causeway thonder. But I tell you true: I've never thought she did.'

Daley knew Hamish too well to just cast aside what he said. It could be called instinct or characterised as something more arcane. However, he was in no doubt that this man felt things that others didn't. Many of the notions he'd had could not be simply explained away.

'You have enough on your plate, Mr Daley. Just the ramblings o' an auld man.'

'You and I both know that's not true, Hamish.'

'Whatever you say.' Hamish got to his feet. 'I hope all goes well with Brian. Aye, and you see to Danny. But at the end o' the day, what's for you, me and everybody won't pass us by.'

'You think everything is preordained?'

'I do, Jim. But if you're quick enough, trust what you feel and act accordingly, things can be changed. The trouble is, we rarely know.'

The light was fading, the streetlights of Kinloch popping into life one by one. Hugh had brought his painkillers and the small bottle of liquid morphine with him. Darkness suited his purpose, even though he supposed that he should have stayed in his dingy flat. But he felt so ill, so tired, that he was frightened that he'd simply lie down, fall asleep and never reawaken.

He was sitting by Kinloch's harbour in his old Toyota. As the engine turned over, he had the heater on full blast and a CD of his favourite songs from the sixties playing in the background. The brighter day had brought even colder temperatures. Already, he could see clouds of breath form in the air from those who passed by. But clouds in the distance warned of a change in the weather.

Hugh Machie had always liked the winter. He'd been born in the teeth of a snowstorm on a December evening long ago. He supposed it had stayed with him.

He popped another two pills from the leaf, opened a flask of tea, poured a little into the plastic cup and washed the medication down. He'd have some morphine later. He was worried it would dull his senses now.

He looked at his watch; it was twenty to four. The winter nights on Scotland's west coast were long. Machie thrust his hand into the pocket of his overcoat. The very feel of the Webley was reassuring. He decided to wait a while longer. Maybe just as folk began to shut up their shops and leave their offices. That would be the best time.

He took another sip of tea as the loch darkened.

37

Glasgow, 1988

To anyone watching, the party of men and women were the same as any other group of revellers as they walked up Hope Street, laughing, giggling and shouting. Nobody paid them much attention.

Perhaps, had they known that this little band contained within their number some of the city's most violent, ruthless criminals, others under the acetylene glow would have given them a wider berth. But to those scurrying in the cold from late nights in the office or to early nights in the pub, there was nothing out of the ordinary at all.

'Come here, Mandy!' shouted Frank MacDougall. 'You're away the wrong way.'

The young woman in high heels and a short skirt almost fell as she halted her progress up the street and turned down the lane, a hand to her mouth covering her laughter.

'This is our new place, Frankie, eh? Right in the city centre, too. Good work, my man.'

'What better place to kick off your birthday celebrations, Jay?'

James Machie caught Frank MacDougall in a headlock and

rubbed his feather-cut hair with his knuckles. 'I don't need to think o' a thing. You've got it all covered, man.'

'Oh! Watch the hair, Jay. That Taylor Ferguson charges a fortune.' Once he'd been released from Machie's grip, MacDougall squinted down the dark lane. 'Third close doon on the right, that's where we're off to.'

'And what's so special about this place, Frankie?'

'The ground floor is an old shop that's been closed for yonks. The third floor's buggered because the landlord tried to rewire the place himself and fucked it up. We have both flats on the first floor. Aye, and room to expand, if we fancy it.'

'I want a toot. Hurry up!' shouted one of the girls. Big Gerald Dowie drained a half bottle of whisky as they headed down the lane.

James Machie stopped near the close next to theirs. The curtains of the ground-floor flat were closed, but a flickering TV could be seen through the thin material. 'We don't have the street to ourselves then, Frank?' he said.

'Come on, what dae you expect, miracles? It's the city centre.'

'Aye, I suppose so.' Machie stood before the window, swaying with the after-effects of the booze and drugs he'd already consumed. 'I should say hello to the neighbours, eh? It's only polite, after all.' Machie rapped the window with his fist. 'Hey, want to come to a party?' he shouted.

Inside, the TV was silenced, and the shadow of movement could be seen through the curtains.

James Machie unbuttoned his Levi 501 jeans.

The curtains twitched open to reveal an elderly woman in a nightgown. She looked horrified as she saw Machie urinating on her window. Quickly, she closed the curtains, and in seconds the lights in the room were switched off.

'Jay, leave it, eh? We don't want any trouble roon here. It's business. The lassies don't need the cops bursting in every two minutes because o' the neighbours, eh?'

James Machie shrugged as he buttoned his jeans back up. 'Any bother fae that auld bastard and you stick one right between her eyes, got it?' He turned to MacDougall.

'Aye, sure, Jay-Mac. Follow me.'

'She'll be hiding under the covers pishing herself.' Machie burst into a fit of manic laughter.

From the outside, the third close down looked dark and unwelcoming. But once MacDougall pressed a code into the entry panel, the large steel door opened on to a clean, well-lit stairwell, newly painted in red.

'Lead on, my man,' said Machie.

On the first floor, MacDougall opened the flat on the right side of the landing. 'Wait till you see this.' He flicked on a light.

The flat was warm and, like the stairwell, adorned in red. They all followed MacDougall through to the lounge. The floor was dotted with bean bags, a mirror-topped table, a very expensive sound system and a cabinet, painted black, standing ominously against the wall. Paintings of naked women in various poses hung round the room, while the smell of paint was all-pervasive.

'Happy birthday, Jay-Mac!' MacDougall swung the doors of the cabinet open to reveal bottles of whisky, vodka, gin and just about every spirit and liqueur imaginable. MacDougall knelt down. Having removed a metal strongbox from the floor of the cabinet, he fished in his pocket for a key and opened it.

The box contained nothing but a small mountain of white powder – cocaine.

Machie thrust his finger into the powder and sniffed back the coke from it. 'Woo!' he roared as the drug hit the spot.

MacDougall gathered everyone in a circle around the man who now controlled so much crime in Glasgow. 'Before we all get blasted, let's hear it for the guy who made a' this happen – Jay-Mac!' He sang the first few words before the rest joined in heartily. '*Happy birthday to you . . .*'

Machie smiled, grabbed a girl and planted a kiss on her lips. It made them all roar. 'Time we broke this place in, Mandy.' He pawed at her top, trying to unzip it.

Just as Mandy's black lacy bra was revealed, MacDougall cocked his head. Through a gap in the red curtains he saw a flashing light. He picked up the metal box of cocaine and made off with it.

'Oh, Frankie, what the fuck do you think you're doing, eh? You're no' going to tan all that yourself!'

'It's the polis!'

Sure enough, the crash of metal on metal could be heard from the front door of the flat. 'Flush that shit, Frank!' shouted Machie, still laughing and groping Mandy.

As he spoke, Frank MacDougall was busy doing just that. A mound of cocaine was dissolving in a toilet bowl. He cursed the plumber he'd hired as, after three attempts, he couldn't flush the cistern. The fourth time he tried, it worked. MacDougall watched as the water and cocaine bubbled up in the toilet bowl then disappeared down the drain. He rushed to the sink and turned on the tap, just as the metal door to the flat smashed open and police officers swarmed into the place. Then he remembered. There was another stash in one of the bedrooms.

253

James Machie was sitting on a beanbag, Mandy on his lap, her blonde hair cascading down her shoulders. While she and the rest of those present looked terrified, Machie's face was frozen in a rictus grin, his eyelids half closed as he gazed at the police officers who'd just burst into the room. 'Evening all,' he roared before laughing manically once more.

'Stay where you are!' A thin man in late middle age with greying hair stood in the middle of the room, six armed police officers behind him. 'I have a warrant to search these premises and arrest everyone here.' Police officers moved amongst the guests at James Machie's birthday party, forcing them into handcuffs. Big Gerry Dowie began wrestling with two hefty cops, but in his inebriated state he was soon subdued. James Machie sat on his beanbag, still in fits of laughter at the unfolding scene.

In the bathroom, Frank MacDougall was held down by two detectives. He had his back to the sink, shirt soaking following his attempt to rid himself of any trace of the cocaine.

One of the policemen was tall and thin, with dark hair. The other was of average height.

MacDougall screwed up his face in disbelief. 'Scooty – what the fuck?'

'DC Scott to you, Frank. Gie me your hands while I cuff you.'

'You're kidding on – this is a wind-up, right?' MacDougall stared at the taller of the two. 'Who's your pal, Darth Vader's wee brother?'

Scott forced MacDougall against the sink and whispered in his captive's ear. 'You should never have touched my auld man, Frank. I warned you.'

254

MacDougall, now handcuffed, stared back at him. 'You've got mair to lose than me, Scooty – know what I mean?'

'You think?'

'Oh aye. And you know it, too.'

Scott thrust his face in MacDougall's. 'You told me about this wee get-together, Frankie, remember? I was to make sure the shift boys turned another blind eye. There've been too many. I've got you on tape. In fact, I've got you on tape saying lots o' things, my old pal.'

Frank MacDougall glared back. 'Scooty, what's wrong wae you, man?'

38

Three men and one woman were in the main interview room at Kinloch police office. DCI MacPherson and her second in command, DI Donnelly, were consulting their notes. Scott and Sergeant Shaw sat across the table from them.

'DS Scott, this will be the first of three interviews we're going to conduct with you over the next couple of days,' said MacPherson. She was a small woman with light, short-cropped hair and an inquisitive face. 'For the tape, please introduce yourselves.' She nodded to Shaw.

'I'm Sergeant Alasdair Shaw, local Police Federation rep.'

'Aye, and you'd better be good at it,' said Scott under his breath.

'Sorry, DS Scott?' MacPherson cocked her head to one side.

'Just consulting my representative, ma'am.'

'If you must do so, please ask for permission first.'

'The condemned man ate a hearty breakfast. You've made your mind up about me anyway. This is just pish.'

'DS Scott, please refrain from these outbursts. We're not here to judge you. Our job is to do what you've done thousands of times – gather evidence. Whether it's favourable or otherwise for you doesn't matter to me. My colleague and I are utterly impartial.'

Scott looked round the room inquisitively.

'Is something bothering you, sergeant?' asked DI Donnelly.

'Aye, I'm just waiting for that flying pig tae land.'

'Let's get on with it, shall we?' MacPherson consulted her notes once more.

'Listen, I never touched the guy in the Douglas Arms. Well, I might have done, but it was in self-defence.'

'Whatever happened on Friday last is part of an ongoing criminal inquiry. For that reason, we won't be discussing it, unless it were to become the case that you were found guilty. Do you understand, DS Scott?'

'No, no' really. If that's no' the issue, why am I here?'

MacPherson leaned her chin on her hands, clasped beneath her face. 'You've had a colourful career, haven't you?'

'It's had its ups and doons, if that's what you mean.'

'I should say. Everything from colluding with an organised crime group to threatening to defecate in a member of the public's dinner. I would say "Technicolor" would be the most apt description.'

Shaw looked at Scott with an expression between horror and surprise.

'I didnae say this was going to be easy, Alasdair.' He shrugged. 'I was under cover for that first bit, ma'am.'

'For some of the time you were, yes. I must say, when I read about it all, I wasn't sure whether I was reading a report, a crime thriller or the synopsis for a television drama.'

'See, the ones that mix it up, they're the best writers, eh? All that depressive stuff you see on the telly now. It fair bores the shi— bores the life oot o' me, ma'am.'

'Unfortunately, this is real life – all too real. You're also the subject of a disciplinary inquiry involving Chief Superintendent Carrie Symington, I see.'

'Is that relevant at this time, ma'am?' Shaw piped up.

'Aye, you gie it to them wae both barrels, Alasdair,' said Scott.

MacPherson banged the table with her fist. 'I will not let you turn this into a sideshow, DS Scott. I know that's your trademark. We will focus on specifics in our next meetings. However, this investigation will concentrate on your conduct as a police officer going back to the nineteen eighties.'

'In that case, yous will need to book some extra nights in the hotel – like a year or two,' said Scott.

MacPherson pointed her finger at Scott, a silent intimation that this was his last warning. 'We're particularly concerned with the general lack of attention you pay to Force Standing Orders, your problem with alcohol, and the way you see fit to adapt the law to suit your own purposes. In the case of the alcohol, we require you to consult a medical specialist in the subject.'

'Excuse me, ma'am,' said Shaw. 'I'm not sure you have the power to require such action.'

'Really? I've only been doing this for ten years, so you must excuse me if I've failed to remember what powers are or are not within my remit.'

'She got the better o' you there, Alasdair,' Scott sighed.

Ignoring his intervention, MacPherson turned a page in her notes. 'Now, just as an example, here we have an incident from twelve years ago in Glasgow. I note that the use of pepper spray as a deterrent hadn't long been introduced at this point.' She cleared her throat. 'In front of witnesses, you – and I quote – say: "Gargle on this, you bastard." The incident took place at the moment of arrest as the suspect was being taken to the van, I believe.' She looked at Scott for a reaction.

'The bas— gentleman tried to stab me, ma'am. What would you have done? In any case, I wisnae just too clear aboot the protocols surrounding the use o' the pepper spray at that time. And anyway, that's been investigated already.'

'Yes, and you were officially reprimanded by ACC Cunningham.' She stared at Scott. 'DS Scott, you will be aware of cases in your time as a police officer where the sheer bulk of evidence against a suspect goes against them in court, yes?'

'Aye.'

'Well, this is kind of where we are with you. Not in a legal way – the investigation into the incident you mentioned earlier notwithstanding – rather with a view to your continued employment. In short, you're rapidly running out of rope in this job.'

'So, thanks for a' the memories, now bugger off, eh?'

'I do have a list of your achievements, commendations, your QPM awards. It's not all grim – just a lot of it. Too much, unfortunately.'

Again, Shaw looked at Scott with surprise. 'A Queen's Police Medal, Brian – impressive.'

'Two, actually, Sergeant Shaw,' said MacPherson.

'Aye, and I'd to get shot for one o' them.'

DCI MacPherson took a deep breath. 'It's getting late, gentlemen. We reconvene tomorrow morning at eleven. This was just an introductory meeting, as I've said.'

Scott looked unimpressed. 'Yous clock off at five. Might have known,' he muttered.

'Thank you very much, ma'am. We'll be here tomorrow, as requested,' said Shaw hurriedly.

MacPherson ended the tape, then Scott and Shaw left the interview room.

'What's up wae your coupon, Al?' said Scott.

'I can't believe you were involved with organised crime. How did you survive that?'

'It's a long story. It's no' what it seems. I was under cover – things she doesnae know.'

Shaw raised his brow. 'You are a man of great hidden depths, Brian.'

Hugh Machie had picked a particularly run-down close in which to linger, waiting for the right moment. Nothing illuminated the stairwell, and he'd noted that many of the flats above seemed empty, the windows unlit, or in some cases boarded up.

Main Street was now bright under the tall streetlamps as Machie huddled into his old overcoat. He could see a drizzle under these lights slanting up the street from the loch. It was so fine it looked like billowing smoke.

He was cold – very cold – and felt unsteady on his feet. Not because of any sense of dizziness, but from weakness. He knew only too well that, quite quickly now, his body was failing him, the sheer weight of the cancer rotting him from the inside, draining his very existence away.

As it was just after five p.m., the street was busy. Cars swished through the forming puddles as pedestrians hurried by crouched under umbrellas or dashed for the shelter of their vehicles. In short, the place was just as he wanted it – Machie couldn't have wished for better weather to be about his business.

He felt the weight of the revolver in his pocket. The metal

was cold and oily, the weapon maintained to perfection. He checked his watch – another couple of minutes.

Hugh Machie looked on as a young mother pushed a pram into the face of the rain, a toddler hanging on to her jacket, hood up, wide eyes taking in the world as though it was all fresh and new. He couldn't help but remember a similar scene, more than five decades ago, though instead of the child hanging on to his mother's jacket, his wife hung on to his. He was pushing a pram made for twins, but now it contained only one.

That grey winter's evening in Glasgow was much like this one. In fact, Kinloch often reminded him of Glasgow back in those days: rows of small shops under bleak tenements. Even through the rain he could see his wife's tears. They'd just given up one of their children. One infant would have been hard enough to support, two impossible. They'd discussed it and made the terrible decision, holding each other close in the damp flat in the East End as they did so. His wife had cried fit to burst, while he bottled up the ache in his throat as fiercely as a poor man grasped his last penny. It was the way in Glasgow in those days: men didn't cry.

When it came to deciding which child to give up – well, the choice was beyond them. They decided to leave it up to the authorities. Hugh had marvelled at the ease with which the woman in the plain, smoke-filled office removed one of his twins from the pram and handed him to another young woman who took their child away for ever – out of their lives. All the while, his wife's head was buried on his chest as their remaining infant howled. He remembered her tear-stained face looking up at him. 'It's James! They've left us James.'

Those were hard times, difficult days. What no one knew – could possibly have known then – was that the choice made by a social worker in a dingy Glasgow office on a dark, damp winter's day was the wrong one.

A bout of coughing pulled Hugh back into the present. He reached for the hankie in his pocket. It was soon dark with blood again.

It was now or never. Hugh eased his head out of the close mouth. The street was clear enough, the closest pedestrians far enough away on either side. He drew his head back into the close and took aim at a portion of dark sky between a streetlamp and the loom of a tenement. Leaning the Webley on his withered arm, he fired two shots, accurately and in quick succession. Their reports sounded loud down the street, carried on the wind, sharp and clear, echoing along the buildings on either side of the road.

First there was one scream, then another. Soon, the good folk of Kinloch were scurrying for cover. He watched as a young man in a dark raincoat rushed into his SUV, mobile phone to his ear.

Hugh Machie pulled up the collar of his coat, and as fast as his failing health would allow made for his old Toyota parked a few yards down the street.

At least this wait would be in relative comfort.

39

'So?' asked Daley. Scott and Shaw were sitting on the other side of his desk.

Shaw looked between the two old friends. 'Well, it appears that we're going to play host to our colleagues for a bit longer than we expected, Jim.'

'This isnae an investigation, big man. It's a witch-hunt. These buggers are going to have me oot o' here, and that's just a fact.' Scott looked downcast yet resigned to his fate.

'I don't see what they have to talk about. Whatever happened in the Douglas Arms is your word against theirs – at the moment, in any case. And we're doing our best to make sure it doesn't go anywhere near the courts. Even if it does, that MacConnachie will make the least trustworthy witness I've ever seen.'

'There's slightly more to it than that, sir.' Shaw shifted uncomfortably in his chair.

'Like what?' said Daley. He glared at Scott. 'What have you not told me?'

'If you don't mind, I'll take my leave,' said Shaw. 'I'd better get back to the desk.'

Before Daley could reply, Scott did it for him. 'Aye, good man, Alasdair. I'll see you later.'

Daley waited until Shaw had scurried from the room. 'Right, what is all this about?'

'They're no' just here to investigate the other night, Jimmy.'

'What, then?'

'It's a *career review*.' Scott nodded knowingly. 'They've even rolled me into the Symington thing – stuff fae years ago, too.'

'But you were just following orders – hers!'

'Aye, but I battered that Special Branch punter o'er on Gairsay, mind?'

'But he's dead. And in any case, he was bent. He raped Carrie, held what happened over her head for years!'

'True,' Scott nodded. 'But the main thing isnae any of that. It's the crocodile in the room, big man.'

'Elephant, Brian.'

'Elephant tae? Bugger me, it'll be like a zoo in here.'

'*What* elephant?' Daley was exasperated.

Scott was mumbling a reply when the door burst open. Sergeant Shaw looked pale.

'It's like the bloody hokey-cokey in here. You're either in or out, Alasdair,' said Daley testily.

'It's not that, sir. PC Duncan is reporting gunshots in Main Street. It's blind panic. There've already been two RTAs – folk trying to get as far away as possible.'

Daley stood up in a flash. 'Sign out firearms to myself and DS Scott, Sergeant Shaw.'

Shaw looked doubtful. 'Technically, DS Scott is still suspended, sir.'

Daley was about to let rip when Shreya Dhar's face appeared round the door. 'I can carry, sir. If that's any help.'

Daley thought for a moment. 'Yes, okay.' He looked at Scott. 'You stay here, Brian.'

'Nae chance. I'm coming with you, sidearm or nae sidearm.'

'I don't think you should,' said Dhar. 'PIRC are here – it's career suicide. For both of you.' She stared at Daley.

'I think she's right, Brian. You're in it deep enough, by the sound of things.'

'I'm coming and I'll wear a vest. It's been too long now, Jimmy. In any case, it's likely a car backfiring. You know the exaggeration that goes on in this place.'

'Right, come on. Let's get kitted out.' Daley made for the door.

Main Street was all but empty. One solitary figure tottered past Michael Kerr the bakers taking two steps forward and one back, clearly the worse for wear.

A woman called out of the window of her flat. 'Get hame, Neil! There's some bastard firing a gun!'

Neil looked heavenward. 'Betty, I was at the Cod War in the Navy, mind. I'm no' bothered aboot gunshots.' Unperturbed, he continued his faltering progress up the street until a police van, lights flashing, screeched to a halt beside him. The inebriated man stood his ground. 'Hey, I've no' got the car, honestly!'

Quickly, a police officer in uniform wearing a bullet-proof vest leaned out of the van and hauled the drunk man off the pavement, before the vehicle reversed back up the street at speed, the engine whining.

'Daley to all stations. Is Main Street secure, over?'

'*Two-ten. I'm at the roundabout, all clear from here, over.*'

'*Two-twelve. Same here in Long Road end, sir. Street also clear, over.*'

Daley listened as reports came in from officers positioned

around Kinloch. 'To all stations, we observe until we know what's going on, over.'

One by one, Daley's order was acknowledged. But then the radio crackled into life.

'*Sir, two-fifteen, over.*'

'Go ahead, two-fifteen.'

'*Four cars remaining in Main Street, sir. Three unoccupied. But I think someone is in the one parked north of Michael Kerr's. I can't make out the reggie, but it's an old Toyota, I think, over.*'

Daley, Dhar and Scott were in a marked car in Kintyre Road, almost at the head of Main Street.

'Shit, there's always one idiot,' said Dhar.

'Might no' be that stupid,' said Scott. 'Could be a victim – or the gunman.'

'More details, two-fifteen,' Daley shouted into the radio.

'*Do you want me to get closer, sir? Over.*'

'Negative! From where you are, over.'

There was a pause as the officer tried to look more closely at the Toyota. The radio crackled back into life.

'*Two-fifteen. Occupant looks to be slumped across the wheel, over.*'

'Bastard!' Daley swore.

'What now?' said Dhar.

'We can't leave it,' said Scott. 'Could be injured – heart attack wae all the fuss, maybe?'

'Could be the gunman,' Dhar retorted, turning Scott's words from moments ago against him.

'Daley to all stations. Can nobody get me the plate number?'

Again, one by one, the answer from each officer near the scene came one by one, all in the negative.

'We can't leave whoever it is there. Brian's right,' said Daley.

'Shouldn't we wait for assistance from Glasgow?' Dhar asked.

'And be here until midnight?' said Scott. 'I don't know what you learned at the college, but we learned to protect life and preserve order.'

'You drive, Brian,' Daley ordered.

Daley ducked out of his door and crouch-ran round to the other side of the car, while Scott did the same. Dhar looked on anxiously from the back seat.

'Stick on the blues, Brian.'

Scott drove to the end of Kintyre Road and edged the police car out on to Main Street. 'Here we go,' he said as he turned the car fully into Kinloch's main thoroughfare. Dhar crouched in the back, uncomfortable with the situation, but more so with the reckless Scott at the wheel.

Under the streetlamps, they could see the Toyota. Daley leaned forward and quickly shouted the licence number into his radio.

Shaw was quick with the information. '*Sir, belongs to a Tracy Millard, Bank Street in Alexandria. Not reported lost or stolen, over.*'

As the police car idled at the top of the street, Daley rubbed his temple, deep in thought. 'Right, we'll go down. Take it slowly, Bri.'

The drizzle was sheeting down now as they neared the car parked just yards from the white-fronted baker's shop.

'Give it the works!' shouted Daley. Soon the police car was emitting the familiar wail of the siren.

They were close enough to see – even through the drizzle – that the figure slumped over the wheel hadn't moved, despite the siren and flashing blue lights from the police car coming up behind.

'Okay, get us level with the car, then shift to neutral and crouch down as far as you can,' said Daley as he removed the sidearm from the holster at his side.

'What are you going to do, sir?' Dhar asked.

'We get beside the vehicle, I'll jump out and duck behind the car. Use the loudspeaker, Brian.' Daley pulled at his old friend's sleeve. 'At the first sign of anything wrong, reverse up the road as quickly as you can, okay?'

Scott stared at Daley without speaking.

'That's an order, DS Scott.'

'How can I crouch and drive at the same time, Jimmy?'

'You know what to do. This is no time to come the old soldier with me. Got it?'

'I'll come too,' said Dhar.

'You stay where you are, DS Dhar.' Daley turned to face her, noting her nod in response to the order.

'Okay, let's go!'

Hugh Machie was trying to keep as still as he could. Though he'd tried to make himself as comfortable as possible, his arms and chest ached with having to hold the position slumped over the steering wheel of the car. He really needed to cough but tried to swallow away the impulse.

He was aware of the blue and red lights flashing closer. He could see their reflection in the wing mirror of the car. So loud was the wailing of the siren, it was hard to tell how close or far away it was. But he knew they were nearby.

He wondered what he'd do. They weren't trying to be in the least stealthy. So, he reasoned, his plan had worked.

They must be treating him like a victim of the shooting. Machie reasoned that any haste could only be to save a life. But there was one aspect of his plan he couldn't control. Which officers were in the car? This wasn't some random act of violence against law and order. It had to achieve its aim or it meant nothing at all.

All it took was the whine of a brake to send Machie's plan into action. Knowing that the police car was now level with his own, it was time to move – maybe for the last time in his life. He crouched from the steering wheel out of the passenger door and ducked behind the nearside wing of the Toyota.

For Daley, as always in such a situation, everything seemed to be happening in silence and slow motion. As they drew level with the Toyota, he rolled out of the passenger seat, sidearm in his left hand. The ground was wet with the heavy drizzle and his right hand landed in a small pothole where rainwater had gathered.

Then everything returned to normal speed. He was about to push himself up off the ground when he heard a voice above the din. Brian Scott's head was poking out of the passenger door. The loud siren made what he was saying difficult to understand, but he could read Scott's lips.

'Get back in, Jimmy!'

Machie took a split second to scan the car to identify its occupants. A glimpse of recognition was enough.

He saw movement.

Just as he was about to let go with a round from the Webley, he began to feel strange. His hands were shaking as though the revolver weighed a ton, and he felt sick. Very sick.

But Hugh Machie had never given up – never. He blinked the smir from his eyes and squeezed the trigger. At first, the thought that the gun had jammed crossed his mind. But quickly he realised that the fault was his own weakness.

With all his remaining strength, Machie took aim and the Webley exploded into life.

The gun's recoil was like none he'd ever felt before. The power of the shot rippled through his whole body, sending him flying backwards.

If he remembered hitting the pavement, it was as a dull thud akin to falling into bed, dead to the world.

40

Glasgow, 1992

For Brian Scott, life was good. He was now the father of a beautiful daughter; his career was stable, and he loved his wife. In fact, under the guidance of Ian Burns and the calming influence of his partner Jim Daley, he looked to be in line for a promotion. As he drove to his parents' flat back in the East End, the world seemed rosy. He and Ella had managed to buy a modest bungalow in Kirkintilloch, away from the city and its problems – a great place to bring up children.

In short, he should have been happy. With Ella working part-time at a golf club while his daughter was in nursery, and his never-ending access to overtime, they were doing fine financially. Yet Brian Scott felt uneasy – had done for days – for reasons he couldn't explain.

Scott was a simple man with little time for the arcane notions of life that Jim Daley espoused. He didn't believe in ghosts, ill omens or coincidence. But at that moment, as he switched on the car radio, if he had thought about it at all, he might have reconsidered his uncomplicated view of life.

He caught the tail end of a man blethering on about roses and the best soil in which to grow them. For Brian, mud was mud, and he had little or no interest in the subject. But as the time ticked on to midday, the first item in the news had his full attention.

'*Glasgow gangland boss James Machie was released from custody at the city's Barlinnie prison today after serving almost two years on drug, extortion and assault charges. His High Court sentence, originally nine years, has been overturned by the Court of Appeal following the crusading work of investigative journalist Dougal Fenton, whose book* Scarer *revealed several apparent miscarriages of justice . . .*'

As the reporter droned on, Scott pulled the car into the first parking space available. He reached for a packet of Benson & Hedges, noting with dismay the trembling of his hands as he lit a cigarette. He tuned the radio to a music station and stared out of the window, not really seeing anything of the street in which he was parked.

Eric Clapton's line about shooting the sheriff was enough for him to hurriedly switch off the song. Coincidence? He wasn't sure now.

Scott stared into the middle distance, trying desperately to make sense of what he'd just heard. But in the end, there was little need for extended reckoning: James Machie was back – free to wreak revenge on those who had brought him low.

Though Scott had been instrumental in the initial arrest – merely doing his job – he was sure that would not be the way the gangster would see it. Yes, he'd been blackmailed into helping Machie and his cohorts, but Brian Scott knew that for those on the wrong side of the law, who lived by the directions set by a skewed moral compass, his actions would be considered as betrayal, plain and simple.

'Shit!' He banged his fists on the steering wheel, in fear as much as frustration. The faces of his wife, mother and daughter and particularly the gaunt features of his father passed before his mind's eye without beckoning. He finished the cigarette and stubbed it out in a flurry of sparks. He had to act quickly; he knew Machie would.

Minutes later his car was speeding through valleys of dark tenements. Scott was driving recklessly, and he knew it. Frank MacDougall had been released two years before and had taken the reins of Machie's criminal organisation. And though Scott and MacDougall could hardly be described as bosom buddies now, he knew the man he'd grown up with would never harm his family, that he'd been against Machie's threats to his father all along. But with Jay-Mac free, MacDougall too would be under pressure.

He parked outside the tenement in which his father and mother lived, with no idea how he'd reached his destination. He took the worn stairs two at a time and flung their front door open.

'Ma, it's me!'

Scott's emaciated father appeared from the bathroom, dressed in a pair of trousers held up on his skeletal frame by a worn pair of braces. His string vest did little to hide a chest which seemed barely there at all. He was holding a razor, his bony chin half covered in shaving foam.

'Your mother's down at the dairy. Where's the fire, son?'

'When did she go?'

'Aboot ten minutes ago. She's getting some rolls and milk for you coming. You know fine what she's like when her number one boy arrives. You'll likely get the good meat paste instead o' that Co-op own label shite she feeds me.'

Scott hurried his father into the living room. 'Fuck me, it's like nineteen fifty-four in here.' Brian stared at the grey suite as though he was seeing it for the first time.

'It served you well enough when you needed it, you ungrateful wee bastard.'

'Don't gie me the *we worked oor fingers tae the bone* speech. My mother did, while you were oot getting plastered or doon at the bookies.'

Willie Scott sat down wearily on the threadbare couch, gasping for breath after walking the short distance from the bathroom. 'Have you any fags on you, son? You know what your mother's like if I try to light up these days.'

'Fags? I might as well wallop you o'er the heid wae a mallet. You stay away fae the fags – you know what the doctor said.'

'Bugger him. These bastard doctors. They telt me I was dying six years ago. I'm still here!'

'Aye, like the ghost o' Christmas past.'

The front door opened, making Brian Scott start.

'You're jumpy, eh? On the bevvy last night, were you, son?'

'Ma, come on,' said Scott, hurrying to take the shopping bags from his mother.

'You're early, Brian.' She followed her son into the kitchen and watched as he unpacked a few meagre groceries.

'I want you to come and sit down,' said Brian when he'd finished.

'What's all the fuss? Is wee Martha ill?'

'No, she's fine, Ma. Go in and sit doon.'

In the living room, Scott's mother turned her attention to her husband. 'Why are you sitting there like that? I telt you to be ready for Brian coming. You look like a used lollipop stick.'

'Right, enough, you two!' shouted Brian as his parents began to argue. 'Ma, I want you to pack a bag – things for my faither and you. But you'll have to be quick.'

'I cannae just drop everything, Brian. For a start, it's my bingo night.'

'Forget the bingo, Mother.'

'And it's Charlie Stott's wake tomorrow,' said Willie. 'You've got to hand it to the Catholics, they know how to gie somebody a decent send-off.'

'And hand oot plenty free whisky, Faither.' Brian Scott kneeled in front of his mother. 'I want you to come wae me. It's a wee surprise.'

'You know fine I cannae stand surprises, Brian. No' since the Lodge's mystery tour your faither took me on. We were halfway to Saltcoats when the bus crashed intae a combine harvester. Poor auld Mrs Sheady near got baled.'

'Aye, she got a right surprise, that's for sure,' said Willie.

'Nobody's going to be turned into a hay bale. Come on, don't ruin this for Ella. She's fair looking forward to it.'

'I'm no' going anywhere in a car wae her. I've telt you before,' said Willie vehemently.

As Scott's parents looked at each other in the silent communication only those married for many years can achieve, the phone rang.

'See that bloody thing. It'll be Maria Martin. She'll be wanting to find oot what bus I'm catching the night to the bingo.'

'Nothing aboot the red barn, then,' said Scott as he rushed to the phone sitting on the sideboard. 'Hello.'

'Brian, is that you?' Ella sounded worried.

'Aye, I'm here, don't worry.'

'No, it's no' that. I just got a call for you.'

'Who fae?'

'Frank MacDougall. What's he wanting? You shouldna be associating wae scum like him – no' wae the job you're in!'

'What did he say, Ella?'

'He gave me a number – said it was urgent. What's going on, Brian?'

'Just gie me the bloody number!' Scott grabbed the stubby bookie's pen from the table and jotted the figures down on the back of his left hand. 'Right, I'll phone you back.' He ended the call then dialled Frank's number. It rang twice before the familiar voice sounded on the other end of the line. 'Frank, it's me. How did you get my number?'

'You should be thanking me, Scooty. You're the fucking grass. I don't know why I'm doing this for you.'

'Doing what?' Brian Scott felt his heart sink.

'You'll have heard that oor man's oot, eh?'

'Aye, against all odds.'

'Some cop made a backside of the evidence. I wonder who?'

'You can't blame me. But I'm sure you know fine who did it.'

'Nah, you're a good little boy, Scooty – can't be relied on. We had to think bigger.'

For a moment Ian Burns's face crossed his mind, but he quickly dismissed the notion. 'Just get on wae it, Frank.'

'Well, he's coked up doon the snooker club, and you've just turned into public enemy number one. Whatever you're doing, go somewhere – take the wife and your wee lassie. I'm only telling you this for auld time's sake.'

'Aw, cheers. I'm really touched.'

'I'm no' kidding, Brian. He knows where you live, he knows aboot the wean. You know what he's like. Do one – and quickly!' The line went dead.

Scott slammed down the phone. 'Right, both of you. Get packed – now!'

41

The scene on Main Street was quite different now. An ambulance carrying the unconscious Hugh Machie to hospital speeded off under the streetlights. People began to emerge and stand behind barriers at each end of the road in an effort to see what had happened, while uniformed officers maintained order.

Daley, Scott and Dhar were sitting in an unmarked car parked on Main Street, not far from where Machie had fired on them. Sergeant Shaw had appeared with hot coffee in two flasks. Scott drained his mug and looked unimpressed. Secretly he wished he was back home with access to what he really needed now: a dram – a few drams.

Daley was in the front passenger seat staring blankly as his officers worked away, securing the locus for further investigation. He was massaging his temple, a familiar act when he was deep in thought. Even in the car, the smell of cordite in the air from Hugh Machie's gunshot still seemed strong.

Dhar sat silently, simply looking at her trembling hands.

'First time someone's shot at you?' asked Scott.

Dhar looked at him as though she'd just realised he was there. 'Sorry?'

'You've no' been target practice for somebody until today?

Don't worry, hen. You'll get o'er it. You're still here, that's the main thing.'

'Oh, thanks, I'm sure,' replied Shreya Dhar, still looking bewildered.

Daley eyed her in the mirror. 'I'll get someone to take you up to the hospital. Shock shouldn't be taken lightly.'

'In the auld days you just got telt to get on wae it,' said Scott. 'But me and Jimmy have been shot at before, haven't we, big man?'

'Yes, too often,' said Daley.

'I don't understand what happened?' said Dhar. 'I mean, you didn't discharge your weapon, sir. How come he collapsed?'

'We'll take a wander up to the hospital soon and try to find out. The world will descend on us now. Any firearms problems these days and it's gold braid all round.'

'Just dandy,' said Scott. 'By the way, his aim wisnae so clever, neither, eh? The bugger used to be like Deadeye Dick.'

'That's a long time ago, Brian. He looks like a corpse.'

'Wait, you mean that you both know him?'

Scott saw Daley's eyes flick to his in the mirror. 'Aye, we know him okay.'

'It's Hugh Machie,' said Daley flatly. 'James Machie's father, and sometime hitman.'

Dhar shook her head, as though she couldn't believe what she was hearing. 'But James Machie's been dead for years. You shot him!'

'No' before the bugger shot me,' said Scott.

'Yes, it's been a bit of a saga between me, Brian and the Machie family. I thought that was a thing of the past – hoped, anyway.' Daley sighed. 'It seems some things are destined to go on for ever.'

Outside, the drizzle had almost abated, and the crime scene had been cordoned off. DC Potts made his way to the car and tapped on Daley's window.

'Yes, Potts,' said Daley as the front passenger window of the car buzzed downwards.

'That's us ready for SOCO, sir – everything secured.'

'Okay, I want three uniforms on this until they get here. Man the barriers, keep the street closed to all but residents and emergency vehicles. You're in charge, Potts.'

'Yes, sir.' The DC hurried off to follow his orders.

'Okay, we'll take a quick look at our motor, Brian – see how close we came.'

'I want to look too, sir. I know something hit the car. I'm just not sure where,' said Dhar.

Under the streetlights, they were soon examining the police car. The trajectory of the bullet Machie had fired wasn't hard to ascertain. A metallic gash began at the rear of the vehicle's roof and passed across the entire width of the car.

'Must have lost his touch, right enough,' said Scott. 'He missed me by about a foot.'

'And me by even more,' Daley added. He looked at Dhar. 'I know what's going through your head, Shreya. The bullet his just above where you were sitting. But it's best not to dwell on it. It's over, end of story.'

'Mind you, if auld Hughie had been twenty years younger, you'd be minus a head right noo,' said Scott.

Daley glared at him.

'But that didnae happen, so nae harm done, eh?'

Shreya Dhar was staring at the long scrape of metal across the roof of the police car. Her expression was a mix of fear and incredulity. Understandable under the circumstances,

Daley thought. 'Sir, I'd like to go home – well, back to the guest house, if that's okay?'

'I want you to have a check-up first. I'm sure everything's fine – but just in case. Brian and I will be coming too.'

Dhar cocked her head at Daley. 'Sir, with the greatest respect, please don't treat me like some little girl. I'm already unhappy that you recalled DS Scott from suspension when the body was found on the beach. I could have handled anything required of me just as effectively as him – and sober when I did it. Which is surely an advantage, wouldn't you say?'

'Oh! Cool your jets,' said Scott.

'Leave it, Brian,' said Daley. He turned to Dhar. 'I understand that you've had a shock. I know from bitter experience how unpleasant that is. But it's that experience that puts me where I am, with the rank I hold. Please don't challenge my authority or decisions, DS Dhar.' He looked at her levelly for a moment, then smiled. 'Now, we all go up to the hospital: it's procedure and we're going to follow it.'

The older detectives watched as Dhar got back in the car and slammed the door.

'You never learn when to shut up, Brian,' said Daley.

'And you never learn to listen to me, Jimmy. I telt you I saw Hughie Machie in the Douglas Arms that night. You chose no' to believe me. So, let's no' all get into the Brian-kicking competition.'

'You must forgive me, Bri.'

'Forgiven.'

'I was being sarcastic.'

'Eh?'

'I admit, you were right about Hugh Machie – as we've just found out. But not only were you drunk on the evening you reported seeing him, you were so pissed men had to be sent to arrest you. You might be able to work out why I thought what you were saying may just have been a little fanciful.'

'A few drams.'

'It was after a few drams you told me that you'd seen the ghost of Elvis in the old Apollo before it got demolished.'

'Okay, it was a bloke in a black safety helmet. But he was a dead ringer for him. Plus, it was dark!'

'Listen, we need to work out why Hugh Machie – of all people – is lying up in the Kinloch hospital having tried to shoot us.'

'You did kill his son.'

'They were hardly best buddies, were they?'

'Blood's thicker than water. You know that.'

'Who knows? Anyway, we'll get a quick once-over up there. We don't want you getting into any more strife. Then we'll find out how Hughie is, too.'

'He looked like shit when he was lying there. What's the odds on him having had something to do with that old bloke doon at the causeway?'

'Two psychos in the one family.'

It was Brian Scott's turn to think. 'He wasn't the psychotic one, Jimmy. Remember?'

42

Glasgow, 1992

Scott flung the Mondeo round another bend and caught sight
of his mother in the rear-view mirror. She was sliding along
the back seat like a plate in a ship's galley in heavy weather.

'Has that wife o' yours been giving you driving lessons?'
Willie Scott complained. 'The rate we're going at you'll likely
get hame and find that she's no' had the wean at all.'

'What are you on aboot?' said Brian distractedly.

'Time travel. I've been reading a lot since I'm no' allowed
to dae anything else. I saw it in some sci-fi novel. If you go fast
enough, you get younger and go back in the past.'

'In that case, Faither, maybe you can go back and refill those
pubs you drank dry. Aye, and bet on the right horses.'

'Always wae the smart comments. You get that fae your
mother, the poor bastard. Look at her in the back there, she's
like an Olympic skier.'

'Are you okay, Ma?'

'I'm feeling a bit sick, if I'm honest, son.'

'We'll be there soon. Just try and hang on.'

Scott took another bend at high speed as the last of the
city turned into countryside.

'Bugger me, that's us heading for Croy. A shithole o' a place,' said Willie.

'It looks okay to me,' his son replied.

'Nah, way back when, you had to be a bona fide traveller to get a drink on a Sunday we went there. The beer was shite and the place was adorned wae green jerseys. Shithole, like I say.'

'You should write one o' they travel guides. *Britain Fae A Thousand Pubs*. It would be a bestseller, nae danger.'

'Cheeky bastard.'

'How cheeky? The only thing you ever have to say aboot any place you've been to concerns the quality o' the pubs. Look at that time you and my mother went to Skye. You complained the whole time that the beer wasn't Tennent's.'

'Thon McEwan's poison. I remember.'

Scott shook his head and drove on, his mother still holding on for dear life in the back seat.

Ella was waiting for them on the front doorstep of the Scotts' new home in Kirkintilloch. She had the toddler by the hand and shook her head as her husband skidded into the drive.

Brian was out of the car in seconds. 'Right, get them in the Mini. Go to that sister of yours in Twechar, Ella. I phoned; she's expecting you. I telt her that my folks were visiting because oor boiler's broken.'

'Twechar?' said Willie Scott as he alighted gingerly from the front seat of Brian's car. 'So, that's the big surprise?'

'What's your problem, Faither? You never guessed you'd be off tae Twechar, did you? So, it's a surprise.'

'Shite pubs in Twechar, and all.' Willie shook his head as his wife struggled out of the back seat.

'Are you okay?' said Ella as she took in her dishevelled mother-in-law.

'I feel like I've been on a spin-cycle, lassie.'

Brian looked at his watch. 'Right, come on, get going! You're packed, aye?'

'I want to know what's going on,' said Ella.

'I don't have time for this, honey.'

'I could do wae a good shite, by the way,' said Willie.

'The wean, Faither! Anyway, you'll be there in no time at all,' shouted Brian.

'Wae her driving, you're no' wrong, son.'

'You're going in the back seat, Willie. I'm no' going through that again.'

'My pleasure, dear. You've a better chance in the back wae her at the wheel.'

Martha looked up at her mother and took the dummy from her mouth. 'Shide!' she uttered with a grin.

Seeing his nearest and dearest safely on the road to Twechar made Brian Scott feel less ill at ease.

He rushed back into the house and picked up the phone. 'DC Daley, please,' he said to the desk officer at Stewart Street police office. After a few clicks, Daley's voice sounded on the other end of the line.

'Brian, where are you?'

'Listen, Jimmy, you've heard that Machie's oot, aye?'

'Yes. I can't believe it. Neither can anyone else.'

'What's Burns saying?'

'Nothing.'

'Eh? I thought he'd be spitting blood.'

'He probably is, but he's not here. Down at a senior

285

detectives' conference in Harrogate.'

'Fuck!'

'Better still, they chose today to replace Inspector Wallace.'

'Who wae?'

'You'll never guess.'

'That bloke fae Rainbow.'

'What?'

'Zippy.'

'I don't get you, Brian, sorry.'

'Just tell me! Things aren't good here. I had to uplift my folks and send them, Ella and the wean off to Twechar. I'd a call. I'm Machie's public enemy number one, Jimmy.'

'Shit, I never even thought about that. But why you, in particular? I mean, we were all involved with the arrest.'

Scott bit his lip. 'Who knows wae that bastard.' He hated the deceit, but Burns had hammered into him the need to keep the truth about his enforced relationship with Machie and his crew away from Daley.

'Okay. You being from the old neighbourhood, maybe?'

'Aye, something like that. Who's the new DI?'

'John Donald – can you believe that?'

Brian Scott felt his stomach sink. He knew Donald was on the take – most likely in Machie's pocket. He'd realised it long ago. The deduction wasn't a difficult one, as Donald had all but handed him Machie's orders in the past. 'When does he start?'

'He's here now: new suit, thin, tanned, smart haircut. I barely recognised him.'

'Brilliant.' Scott was desperately trying to work things out in his head. His family were safe, though that solution could only be a temporary one. And though DCI Burns was away, he'd be back soon. In any case, he had nothing concrete on John Donald. He reasoned that the former uniform sergeant would be anxious to impress in his new role. If that was the case, the last thing he'd want to do would be to rock the boat. Scott could picture Donald licking Burns's arse: it was his default position, after all. 'Okay, Jimmy. I'm on my way in.'

43

The staff at Kinloch hospital had Hugh Machie attached to wires leading to two monitors. A nurse and a doctor were by his bed in one of the hospital's side rooms when Daley arrived. He cracked the door open and looked inside. Though he'd known Hugh Machie for so many years, the cadaverous figure in the bed bore almost no resemblance to the man he remembered.

'DCI Daley. Can I come in, please?'

The young doctor emerged from the room and closed the door behind him. 'I'm Dr Malton. This man is in no condition to be interviewed, if that's what you want to do, DCI Daley. In fact, I'm not sure we'll be able to hang on to him at all.'

'Meaning?'

'*Meaning*, he's a very sick man. The tests we've managed to run on him, combined with the medication that was found in his pockets, all point to the same thing.'

'Which is?'

'He's dying, and quickly. We're trying to stabilise his condition. That would allow us to helicopter him out to Glasgow, at least. But I'm not sure even that's going to be possible. We're trying to contact the oncologist who's been treating him, but that's a painstaking process via the name of the chemist on his meds, and our database. I presume he is a Glasgow man, as far as you know?'

'He was at one time. I haven't seen or heard of him for years – until today, that is.'

Dr Malton glanced at his notes. 'Well, he won't be anywhere for much longer. Looking at his general condition, I'm surprised that he's lasted this long. Never mind having the energy to shoot at people in the street. Quite remarkable.'

'Oh, he was quite a remarkable man, trust me.'

Daley parted company with the doctor, turned on his heel and made for the assessment unit where Scott and Dhar had gone to be checked over. As he expected, DS Scott was on a chair, dozing.

'Right, Bri, up and at 'em, eh?'

'You near shifted my heart, Jimmy. What's the word on Hughie?'

'Not long for this world, apparently. Cancer.'

Scott looked puzzled. 'So, he's dying of cancer but decides to come all the way doon here and shoot us. Does that make sense to you?'

'What makes sense ever, Brian? You know what it's like. Some of the drugs – chemo, radiotherapy – they give cancer patients. It can turn folk a bit odd. Who knows what was going through his mind?'

Scott stared into space for a moment. 'Brings it all back, doesn't it?'

'Yes, it does. I thought we'd seen the last of this shit on that beach.'

'See, guys like James Machie. You never see the last o' them. The bastards are in the walls for the rest of your life – whether they're dead or alive.'

Daley looked around. 'Where's DS Dhar?'

'Oh aye, I meant to tell you. They're giving her more tests. Her blood pressure was through the roof, apparently. They seemed quite concerned. It's likely down to all the nightmare on Main Street.'

'She's never been through that before. Not the least stressful thing in the world.'

'Water off a duck's back, as far as I'm concerned. You can get used to anything.'

Daley raised his eyes. 'I don't know. Sometimes I wonder if your idea of getting out of all this isn't a bad idea.'

'Aye, and then you remember we've got work to dae. The ballistic results from those shell cases they found on the beach should be in soon. How much do you bet they match Hughie's shooter?'

'It's a reasonable conclusion, Brian. But what was he doing frightening some old fisherman from Kinloch to death?'

'Like you said, maybe the effects of the cancer, the drugs – who knows? Could just have been for entertainment.' Scott shrugged.

'Come on, Hugh Machie was never like that. A killer, yes.'

'But you have to admit, I never forget a face, Jimmy.'

'Even though you're pissed and getting arrested. Aye, well done. Must be a commendation there, at least.'

'Aye, right. What do we do about the lassie?'

'*DS Dhar* will have to get her treatment. I don't think it will do her any harm to take it easy for a while. I remember how I felt when I was fired on the first time – not good.'

'It's even worse when they hit you, trust me.' Automatically, Scott's hand darted up to his shoulder.

Leaving Dhar at the hospital, Daley and Scott returned to the office, to find Campbell the lawyer waiting for them at the front desk.

'Gentlemen, glad to see you're both okay after your adventures this afternoon.'

'Well, we could have done without it, but all part of the job,' said Daley. 'What can I help you with, Mr Campbell?'

'Oh, I don't know. It's something that's been troubling me. Normally, I'm bound by confidentiality, but in this case . . .' He threw his arms in the air. 'I must confess, I don't really know what to do.'

'Are you sure you're not after a priest?' said Scott. 'I'll away and get a coffee and let you confess to Father Daley.'

'He doesn't change, whether he's been shot at or not,' said Campbell ruefully, as he watched Scott disappear down the corridor.

'You don't know the half of it,' said Daley.

They made their way to the glass box. Campbell kept muttering excuses, as though he was about to be placed under investigation.

'Take a seat,' said Daley.

Campbell took up the offer, sitting beside the DCI's large desk. Daley noted he was playing nervously with his tie.

'So, what is it you have to tell me? Not an unpaid parking ticket from nineteen sixty, I hope?' The detective smiled.

'No, not that – though such a thing may exist, even if it's not from as early as the sixties.' Campbell shuffled in his chair. 'The other day a gentleman came to see me. He was elderly

– didn't look well, to be honest – but there was something menacing about him, nonetheless.'

'Did he threaten you?'

'No, he didn't. In fact, he wished to avail himself of my services. He made a will.'

'Is that menacing?'

'No, of course not. I've done thousands of the bloody things. But this one was different. And given what happened this afternoon, I felt it appropriate to let you know.'

'This afternoon? How does that have anything to do with a will?'

'It's quite simple, really: you're one of the beneficiaries. Well, you or your next of kin. So is DS Scott, under exactly the same conditions. Both of you have been left a considerable amount of money.'

Daley looked at Campbell, a smile playing across his face. 'If this is a joke, I'm afraid it's in very poor taste. I have a body down at the causeway, one officer and an old gangster in hospital. So I'm not really in the mood for humour, as I'm sure you can see.'

'I'm a professional, DCI Daley. I'm not in the habit of playing practical jokes on police officers. You, DS Scott and others stand to inherit a great deal.'

Daley eyed the lawyer. 'This man, what was his name?'

'Forsyth.'

Daley shrugged. He couldn't think of anyone of that name. 'Can you describe him for me?'

'Old, late seventies or early eighties, at a guess. Though he could have passed for someone much older. Long face – wrinkled as you'd expect for a man of that age. Short grey hair. But he'd obviously lost a lot of weight. His clothes were hanging off him – especially his overcoat. Could have fitted a much more robust individual.'

Daley stared at Campbell for a moment, barely believing what he was hearing. He pressed his computer into life and typed on the keyboard for a few moments.

'Are you taking a statement, DCI Daley?'

Without replying, Daley turned the screen round to face the lawyer. 'This is from twenty years ago, or thereabouts. But given that, is this the man who made the will?'

Campbell fumbled inside his suit jacket and produced a pair of glasses, which he perched on the end of his nose before leaning forward and peering at the image on the screen. 'My goodness. This man looks very different, obviously, but there's enough of a resemblance to say yes, that's him. Not Forsyth, I take it?'

'No, his real name is Hugh Machie.'

'Not one of *the* Machies?'

'Father of James Machie. You'll remember we ran into him a few years ago.'

'Oh yes, who could forget? It was all over the TV and newspapers.'

'I know you have responsibilities to your client, whoever he is. But I'm in the middle an attempted murder investigation, Mr Campbell. I must ask you for a copy of this will. You can say no, of course. But you know I'll just get a warrant.' Daley shrugged his shoulders apologetically.

'I will make a copy available to you immediately, no question. With all the usual caveats, I'm sure you'll understand.' He hesitated. 'If there's a hint of criminality here, my work is probably not worth the paper it's written on.'

Daley smiled. But behind the expression his mind was

working overtime. Why try to kill people when you've left them money in your will? Or maybe Hugh Machie's mind really was simply befuddled by his illness and the drugs used to treat it.

44

Glasgow, 1992

Brian Scott's drive back to the centre of Glasgow from Kirkintilloch was a nervous one. He kept checking the rear-view mirror to see if he was being followed. At one point, just as he was reaching the outskirts of the city, a white Ford Transit van appeared to be tailing him. Only when Scott took off down some side streets and through a run-down industrial estate was he sure that the vehicle was no longer behind him. But the detective knew that paranoia had well and truly set in.

Brian Scott knew James Machie – had done since he was a kid. The boy who had set his teacher's car on fire, stabbed a boy in his class and beaten an elderly lollipop man half to death had travelled the route most of those who knew him expected. He'd led a charmed life as a teenager, walking away from violent episodes as though they'd never happened. Even then, people were becoming too scared to speak against this dangerous young man.

Only when DC Brian Scott turned off the motorway and was wending his way along Cowcaddens did he feel that he was safe. He parked his car beside Stewart Street police office and rushed in, anxious to speak to his partner Jim Daley, and avoid the eye of his new inspector John Donald.

Daley was at his desk working on a crime report when Scott appeared. The detective took in the man who had been his designated mentor with surprise. Usually, Scott had more than a hint of devil-may-care. Today, however, his face bore a pale, haunted look that made him look young and vulnerable, something Daley had hitherto thought impossible.

'Right, big man. What's the scoop?' said Scott.

'Our man wants to see us.' Daley checked his watch. 'In about half an hour. He was asking where you were. I palmed him off with a story about you running an errand for DCI Burns. He'll ask, so don't forget.'

'You know him better than me, Jimmy. He was your shift sergeant. Dae you remember much aboot him?'

'I do. And I'll never trust him, that's for certain.'

As though his ears had been burning, John Donald appeared in the general CID office, scanning the place with a beady eye. His transformation had indeed been a spectacular one. Along with his uniform, his jowls, beer belly and unruly thick black hair had all disappeared. The new John Donald could have stepped from the pages of a magazine. He was trim, his hair neatly cut and slicked back. His face was tanned, and his dark grey suit expensive. In short, he bore very little resemblance to the uncouth uniformed sergeant both Scott and Daley once knew.

'Bugger me, he's had one o' they makeovers that my Ella's always on aboot,' Scott whispered to Daley.

DI Donald raised his head. 'You two, in my office. Now!'

'I thought you said half an hour, Jimmy?'

Daley shrugged. 'You don't know him, right enough.'

Obediently, the pair followed the newly minted detective inspector down the corridor to his office, situated just along the corridor from DCI Burns's.

Donald's office took Daley by surprise. He remembered the clutter of the old sergeants' room just across the corridor from where they were now. In his mind's eye, he could see the much more rotund figure of John Donald reclining with his feet on the table, the remains of a half-eaten sandwich on his desk amid a scatter of empty coffee cups, untidy bundles of paper and other detritus. Now, this place was as immaculate as the man who occupied it. The desk was neat and tidy, a computer screen at one end, a black tin containing pens, pencils and a pair of scissors on the other. In front of his large office chair was a blotting pad upon which sat a black desk diary and two telephones. Instead of the reek of the cigars he used to smoke, the office smelled of expensive aftershave. John Donald's transformation clearly hadn't ended at his personal appearance. It was the full package.

'The dynamic duo, eh?' Donald sneered at Scott and Daley. 'Where have you been, DC Scott?'

'I was running a wee errand for DCI Burns, sir.'

'Of what nature?'

'I think it's something he'd rather keep to himself, sir. But I'm sure he'll tell you if you ask him.' Scott said this confidently, as he'd already come to the decision to make his suspicions about Donald known to the DCI on his return.

Daley was even more taken aback by the man who sat before them. His accent was almost gone. He sounded like someone brought up in one of Glasgow's most exclusive areas.

Donald opened the desk diary. 'I know you're more than well acquainted with the Townhead, DC Daley.'

'Yes, sir.'

'Good. I want you to go to Patterson's garage in Swan Street tonight. Keep a low profile and observe what's going on.'

'What do you reckon is going on, sir?' Scott asked.

'I think it's a cut and shunt shop. Two stolen cars coming in, all serial numbers removed, cut in half and turned into new vehicles. I assume you know the process, DC Scott.'

'Do we know who's doing it, sir?' said Daley.

'If I knew who was doing it, I wouldn't be sending you up there, would I?'

'No intel, sir?'

'If you listen for a few moments and stop asking stupid questions, I'll be able to impart any *intel* we have.' He glared at Daley.

'Sir.'

'We think the eponymous Mr Patterson is behind this. He's hit hard times. Car repairs aren't what they were. Most vehicles go back to the dealerships with whatever fancy new kit they have now. The small garage's days are numbered. He's working with McGarrity from Castlemilk – or that's what we surmise. Your job is to confirm these suspicions and shut this business down. McGarrity is a big fish. It'll do your careers no harm.'

'Sir, I have a question,' said Scott.

'Put your hand down, Scott, this isn't primary school.'

'Aye, bang on, gaffer.'

'*Sir.*'

'Sir, sir – aye, nae bother.'

Donald shook his head. 'What's your question? Hurry up!'

'This ebony mouse, sir. Is that a nickname, or what?'

'What are you talking about, man?'

'I think he means *eponymous*, sir.'

'I'll leave you to explain that to this bloody illiterate. I wonder how you managed to get into this job at all, Scott, never mind the CID.'

Daley noticed a look pass between the two. It puzzled him.

'Visit the collator, he'll fill you in with more details.' Donald closed the book. 'Right, get on with it. Sergeant Ramsay will brief you and the four uniforms you'll have at your disposal at seventeen hundred hours in the muster room. Got it?'

'This is an official operation, sir?' Daley asked.

'What do you think?'

'Just seems to have been put together very quickly. I'd have thought DCI Burns would have been involved.'

'DC Daley, I know you worship the very ground on which DCI Burns walks, but you may be surprised that policing goes on when he's not here, as it will when he's gone and forgotten.'

'Yes, sir.'

'Crime doesn't operate on a schedule to suit DCI Burns. While he's busy imparting his unmatched breadth of knowledge to the uninitiated in Yorkshire, our work continues. I hope you understand – both of you?'

As they stepped back out into the corridor Scott grinned. 'At least he's no' changed completely, eh?'

'Why do you say that? He looks like an entirely different person to me.'

'He still remembers what a collator is. They all refer to them as Divisional Intelligence officers these days.'

'I can't see Alec liking that.'

'Nah, he hates it. Come on, Jimmy. Let's find oot what the score is fae him.'

'I hope he knows about the ebony mouse.'

'Aye, on you go. You try going to school where I did. Survival was mair important than vocabulary.'

Daley was deep in thought as they headed off to see the collator. He'd been unsettled by two things: Donald's complete transformation, and the apparent haste with which this operation had been put together. Neither he nor Scott had been involved in the investigations that presumably led to tonight's deployment. It worried him. As did the spectre of the newly released James Machie.

45

As always when an operation was on the cards, the wait seemed endless. Scott and Daley had a meal in a pub at the top of Hope Street and passed the time people-watching, something that seemed to galvanise Scott.

By the time they'd eaten their burger and chips, the pair felt they'd worked out what just about everyone on the bar did – or didn't do – for a living. It was all based on observation; though Scott's theory that the three elderly men sitting along from them were all retired firemen couldn't be reasoned out logically.

'It's shite when you cannae get a pint,' said Scott as they waited for Sergeant Ramsay's briefing in the muster room. 'The time flies by wae a drink in your hand.'

'Don't get too fond of it, Brian. You know the number of alkies floating about in this job.'

'Wae my Ella in charge, no' likely.'

Sergeant Ramsay arrived. He was a small, neat man in an immaculate uniform, apparently destined for the fast track as he was studying part-time for a law degree at university.

'Scott and Daley. You'll be in an unmarked car, Zulu-one, for the purposes of this exercise. 'You four' – he pointed to the uniformed cops – 'you'll be in a Sherpa round the corner from Patterson's garage – here.' He pointed to a small lane on the map behind him. 'Remember, the purpose of this exercise is to catch McGarrity or his men bringing in a motor. Intelligence points to the fact that – if it happens at all – it is likely to be between twenty hundred and twenty-three hundred hours. Method of transportation is via a flatback lorry, with the cars covered in a tarp, okay?'

Daley put up his hand. Ramsay nodded for him to speak. 'Sir, have you been on this case for a while?'

Ramsay shook his head. 'No, not me. I was just briefed today. I'm only a part-time cop these days, remember. I spend more time in the students' bar in the QM than I do in a uniform.'

'I'm into that,' said Scott.

'Trust me, it's not all it's cut out to be, son. You pair sit parked up here,' he continued, pointing to another lane. 'You have a view right down the street, but stay as unobtrusive as you can, for obvious reasons. We have the impression that these guys aren't too bright when it comes to precautions, but you never know.'

'What about control, sir?' said Daley.

'We'll have our own channel, but keep another radio on the divisional frequency. We have a controller on station, and I'll be there with DI Donald.'

'Superb,' said Scott sarcastically.

'I'm glad you approve, DC Scott,' said Ramsay.

The briefing went on for another twenty minutes, mainly taken up with pictures of suspects being passed round the team, and a brief risk analysis.

'Okay, we're all set, yes?' Ramsay was bringing the briefing to an end. 'Listen, this will probably be a no-show job. But you never know. Good luck!'

In a few hours, Scott and Daley were in place in an unmarked car, hidden up a lane in the relative gloom of Glasgow's Townhead.

'Did you get Ella?' Daley asked.

'Aye, and I wish I hadnae bothered. She was in a right bad yin,' Scott replied.

'You can hardly blame her, Brian. Whisked off to her sister's at a minute's notice.'

'At least I know they're all safe, Jimmy. Burns is back tomorrow. I'll speak to him then.'

'You could have spoken to Donald this afternoon.'

'Aye, much good that would have done.'

'You don't trust him, Brian. Why?'

'Ach, just instinct, Jimmy. You'll get the knack one of these days.'

Daley smiled to himself as Scott shifted in his seat.

They had been in position since just before eight, and almost an hour and a half had passed. One radio was tuned to their own dedicated 'Zulu' frequency. It had been silent since the call had been made, to make sure everyone was in position. On the general channel, the usual chatter of divisional radio traffic burbled on: a disturbance here, a break-in there. It was normal fare for a weekday night in Glasgow's Central division.

Scott was speaking about football when Daley hushed him.

'*A-Alpha to all stations. A code twenty-one, repeat code twenty-one at North Frederick Street opposite the university. Officer in urgent need of assistance, over.*' The controller's voice was calm, but it belied the frantic activity that would undoubtably be taking place right now around the division as cops made for the locus to help a colleague in danger. Meal breaks would be disturbed as every available man and woman grabbed a lift in the handiest vehicle in order to reach their colleague as quickly as possible.

'That's just doon the road, Jimmy,' said Scott.

'You know what our orders are, Bri. We stay put.' Just as Daley said this the 'Zulu' radio burst into life.

'*Zulu control to Zulu-two, over.*' Their frequency was on talk-through, so Scott and Daley heard the uniforms located in the van at the other end of the street reply.

'*Zulu-two, go ahead, over.*'

'*Zulu-two make for North Frederick Street, locus of a code twenty-one, over.*'

'*Roger, Zulu control. Attending, over.*'

Scott lifted the mouthpiece. 'Zulu-one to Zulu control, over.'

'*Go ahead, Zulu-one.*'

'Do you want us to attend this code twenty-one, o'er?'

There was a pause, then, '*Negative, Zulu-one. Remain in position, over.*'

'Aye, roger,' said Scott as he looked at Daley. 'That's us on our Jack Jones, Jimmy.'

Daley bit his lip. 'So it appears, Bri.'

Both Scott and Daley could hear distant sirens, no doubt making for the stricken officer in North Frederick Street.

'Kind o' makes you feel a bit guilty,' said Scott. 'I think this is the first shout for a twenty-one I've no' attended on shift. What aboot you?'

'I've been to a few. Thankfully uneventful, in the main.'

The pair sat in silence for a while. With Scott's window cracked open to get rid of his cigarette smoke, the rumble of the city was just about all they could hear: a car horn, a dog barking, the echoing yell of a reveller.

After a few minutes of this, Scott put the radio to his mouth. 'Zulu-one, o'er.'

'*Go ahead, Zulu-one.*'

'Any outcome for the code twenty-one, o'er?'

'*Negative, Zulu-one.*'

'Sounds bad, Jimmy.'

Daley shrugged. 'Nothing we can do. I dare say if they need us, they'll shout.'

'Oh! Hang on, Jimmy. Look.' Scott raised a finger and pointed down the street.

As Daley stared down the dark road, illuminated only by a streetlight at either end, a lorry was making slow progress, showing only sidelights. 'What do you think?'

'They've got something on the back, no doubt about it,' said Scott, again lifting the radio to his mouth. 'Zulu-one, o'er.'

'*Go ahead, Zulu-one.*'

'We have a vehicle that matches our subject, o'er.'

'*Roger, Zulu-one. Plate number, over?*'

'Negative. But they've just parked outside Patterson's garage, o'er.'

This time it was Inspector Donald's voice on control. '*Move in with caution. Observation only, over.*'

Scott looked at Daley. 'Here we go, Jimmy.' Without waiting for a reply, Scott ducked out of the car and made his way into the shadows of the street. He began edging along a wall, Daley in his wake. Scott plugged an earphone into his radio, as did Daley. They were well away from the nearest streetlight, both standing still as a clattering noise echoed on the night air.

'They're lifting the roller-shutter, Brian,' said Daley.

Though silhouetted by the light at the end of the road, it was clear that the flatback lorry was carrying something covered in a tarpaulin.

'That's a motor,' whispered Scott. Then into his radio, 'Zulu-one. We have a lorry carrying a vehicle covered in a tarpaulin. Looks like this is it. Require assistance, o'er.'

There was silence from Stewart Street for a few moments. But soon an instruction sounded in their earpieces. '*Proceed with caution into the premises, over. First available assistance will be routed to you, over.*' Normally, every controller sounded calm and authoritative, just as the divisional controller had sounded during the code twenty-one shout. But this time, Daley was sure he could hear a hint of uncertainty. He made up his mind that it was his imagination, triggered by the fact that – for now, at least – he and Scott were very much alone, unarmed and unsure as to what they faced.

The lorry's engine revved, and it began to turn into the garage. The roller-shutter door was two-thirds of the way open, enough to allow the lorry and its cargo to fit through. A bright light spilled on to the street from within.

'Okay, we go to the door. Stay close to the wall, Jimmy,' said Scott.

'You're the senior man, Brian,' whispered Daley.

'I'd be happier if I wisnae.' Scott shrugged. Staying close to the walls of the buildings that led to Patterson's garage, they made their way towards the light.

46

Ian Macmillan was looking at the certificate he had on his office wall. *Licensed to sell alcoholic beverages. Thomas Ian Macmillan, the County Hotel, Kinloch.* He'd been annoyed by the way people addressed him as Tom when he'd first arrived. It was the name his mother had given him, and, true to form, it was the name the people of Kinloch wanted to call him by, regardless of his protestations. Many remembered his visits as a small boy. He very nearly decided to leave it like that. But soon he reckoned that he deserved what little control he had left of his life. He became Ian again.

He thought about his life in an abstract way. He'd been reasonably clever in school: not top of the class, but in the top third. Despite this, his mother and father forced him to study in order to catch up with the best. So, instead of being out playing ball with his buddies, he spent what seemed like every free minute studying in his room.

Macmillan resented spending the long summer days of his childhood trying to please his parents rather than simply being a kid like the rest of his peers. But it had worked – to an extent, at least. He'd managed some good grades and a place in a decent college, studying business management.

He looked round the dreary office, then at the pictures of

his family under the dim glow of the anglepoise lamp on his desk. They didn't give a shit, that was for sure. He was just an unseen provider, a worker bee, a drone. What did they care that to keep his wife upsides with her fancy new friends he'd had to over-extend himself, first at the bank, then with anybody who'd lend him money?

He'd thought that the loan company was legit. It had been recommended by a friend. But when he was forced to pay outrageous rates of interest, he quickly realised that he'd made a dreadful mistake. When he was unable to make these payments, a well-dressed, polite man had come to call. His shoes were of Italian leather, his camel coat of the finest cut – he even smelled good. But what he had to say didn't match his demeanour.

'You're in deep, my friend.' Though he did his best to hide it, this man, who introduced himself as merely a *representative* of the Bucco Finance Company, had an underlying New York drawl. 'The office here tells me you've asked them for more time. What was it again?' He stroked his chin, as though trying to find the words it was obvious he knew. 'You want a *payment holiday*, is that it?'

Macmillan remembered stammering, 'Yes'.

The response was as clear as it was chilling. The representative from Bucco Finance quietly reeled off his children's schools, their friends' addresses – same with his wife's club, gym and beautician and the times she attended them all.

The threat was inescapably implicit. His visitor hadn't raised his voice. He'd smiled throughout their meeting. But, even taking his most recent brush with organised crime into consideration, it was the most unsettling encounter Macmillan had ever had.

The phone rang, making him jump. It wasn't his direct hotel line but the burner they'd given him. It was as though every time he thought of his tormentors they appeared, as if by magic, to torture him further. And these days, he could think of little else.

'Yes.' Macmillan's voice was no more than a whisper.

'We need the space – soon.'

'How soon – how many?'

'One. It could be any time.'

'But I can't just shut the hotel at a moment's notice. Surely you understand that?'

'You'll do what you have to do. Just be ready.' The call was ended abruptly.

Macmillan puzzled over this – not just the logistics of hiding someone on the premises, but what could be behind this sudden flurry of activity. He knew there had been an incident in Main Street – the hotel had been cordoned off from one end. But he knew the man involved was very ill in the local hospital. Then again, there was the ruined cottage in the hills. It all made him sick to the stomach.

Macmillan got up from his desk and left his private quarters at the top of the County Hotel. But instead of turning left down the hall to the stairs, he turned right. There was only one door at the end of the corridor; it was the room that had once belonged to the hotel's general manager – Annie.

Macmillan fumbled with the bunch of keys he had on a chain attached to his belt. The one with the red tape affixed to its head jumped out from the rest. He pushed it into the Yale lock and the door slid open across the thick carpet.

Apart from her personal effects, the place was much the same as it had been when Annie lived there. Macmillan fancied he could still smell her cheap perfume on the air. Otherwise, the room was musty, like a house opened after a long holiday. The bed was neatly made, the dressing table, wardrobe and chest of drawers lying empty. But to Macmillan the place felt cold. Not because it hadn't been aired or heated; it had. But there was something about the room that gave him a shiver.

He could see the bathroom door lying ajar. He pushed the switch which sent the lights flickering into life. In the bathroom, he looked up. The small square in the roof was almost invisible. He knelt and pulled a panel from the side of the bath. It came away easily. Reaching underneath, he laid his hand on a wooden pole. Carefully, he took it out from the space under the bath. The pole was a couple of metres long with a hook on one end. He pushed it up against the square in the ceiling, and a tiny portion gave way. He worked the hook until it clicked into place. One pull was enough to set the steep steps on their slow progress to the floor, the hydraulic system working beautifully as it was designed to do.

Macmillan made his way into a loft. Again, he turned on a switch to illuminate the space. The roof was low – just high enough for someone to stand, if they weren't too tall – but the floor-space dimensions matched the room below. In one corner sat a bed, in the other a long couch. The bathroom was a small affair, with a WC, tiny sink and tight shower unit hunched under a sloping roof.

It was a room that only one person had known of, apart from Macmillan himself. But that person was now dead.

He descended the stairs, pushed the steps back up into the roof space and replaced the pole under the bath. The panel reattached with a couple of clicks. Ian Macmillan stepped out of the bathroom and closed the door behind him.

Somehow, Annie's perfume – so distinctive and vulgar, he'd always thought – smelled stronger now. He sighed at the stupidity of his imagination, his irrational fears. It was more than likely that guilt was responsible for his false perception of the odour. After all, the bedsheets and curtains, even the carpet, had all been replaced since Annie died.

It was only when he felt a cold breath on the back of his neck that he turned round, eyes wide, goosebumps on his skin.

But the room was still empty.

47

Brian Scott was in Hugh Machie's flat with Jim Daley. Despite Machie's alias, Campbell had confirmed his odd client's identity. While Hugh had always been a criminal to be reckoned with, he lacked the guile and ruthlessness possessed by his son James. The job of finding this place would have been much harder had it not been for the set of keys discovered in his overcoat at the hospital. The flat's location was written in small, neat letters on a plastic fob attached to the key ring.

'Bastard ran oot o' time, Jimmy. Hughie would have been away fae this hovel quick smart if he'd managed to kill us.'

Daley looked round. The flat was certainly basic: old, worn furniture, peeling wallpaper, patches of damp dotted everywhere. It wasn't the kind of domicile most would have desired. But something caught the detective's eye. There were photographs placed along the mantelpiece.

As a police officer, Daley had known plenty of colleagues who ended up living on their own following separation or divorce. The break-up of marriages was endemic, not just in his job, but across the emergency services and the NHS. The shift system could almost have been designed as a tool to end relationships; Daley knew this from both ends of the spectrum.

Spouses felt neglected, bored and alone when their partners were taken away by an occupation that could, at times, be all-consuming. On the other hand, people thrown together in stressful situations, encouraged to bond as a team and rely on each other, would regularly form attachments that threatened any marital union.

The face of Mary Dunn passed before his mind's eye. He always tried not to think about her, but that was something he just couldn't do. Idly, in the very basic space that had, up until recently, been the home of Hugh Machie, he wondered what would have happened if she'd lived – how his life would have changed.

'Take a look at this, Jimmy.' Scott handed him a small monochrome photograph in an old frame.

A pretty young woman was standing beside a tall, light-haired man. She was in a floral dress, its colours lost to time in the black and white image. She was holding a baby, swaddled in woollen blankets, a neat little knitted bonnet hugging its tiny head. She looked happy; her smile was wide as she gazed adoringly up at the man beside her.

Not only was the man tall, but he also almost filled the doorway in which they were standing. In his shirtsleeves, his shoulders were broad, and the knots of muscles in his forearms were plain. He too cradled an infant. He smiled straight into the camera, a man proud of the family who surrounded him. Daley felt a twinge of sadness, for he was well aware how the story of all those in the picture ended.

'Hey, lucky it wasn't that version o' big Hughie that was doing the shooting, eh?' said Scott. 'I remember that hoose. Two streets away from where we lived. It was her mother's. They moved in when she died. Frankie MacDougall's was three doors away from ours. Happy days. I've been thinking of it a lot – well, for obvious reasons.'

'You were in the melting pot there, right enough, Brian. It was a brave thing to join the job surrounded by that mob. Hats off to you. I've always admired you for it. I'm sure nobody in our street gave a toss what I was doing.'

Scott grunted. 'Aye, it wasn't easy.' He bit his lip.

Daley took in the photograph. The couple and their new-born twins seemed like the happiest people in the world. They had no way of knowing what was in store. He studied Hugh Machie's face: broad, full, with high cheekbones and eyes that looked bright even in monochrome. 'You just don't know what's in front of you, Brian. Nobody does.'

'I know what's in front o' me if I don't stop the bevvy. I'll fade away like my faither. Buggered for years before I die. A life o' misery.'

'You're doing okay . . . well, you seem to be.'

'I could murder a drink – you know that. Look at me, for fuck's sake.' Scott held out his trembling right hand.

'I told you, you need help. Proper help. You can't just do this on your own.'

'Nah, I suppose not. Remember, I'm due to see that mob again in an hour.'

It took Daley a few seconds to work out who *that mob* were, before he realised it was the officers who seemed to be placing Scott's entire career under scrutiny. 'I want you to leave that with me. We'll go back to the office now. Get Potts and two or three bodies down here. I want this place gone through with a fine toothcomb.' He looked again at the photograph. 'How do any of us really know?'

'Aboot what?'

314

'Our families – anything. What about my boy – your kids? What road will they take?'

'I don't think any of oor offspring are going to end up like James Machie. And anyway, last time I saw oor Martha, you'd locked her in the productions cupboard.'

'And what about this?' Daley gestured round the room. 'What's all this about? Why on earth would a man fit to drop want to come all the way to Kinloch, rent a flat, place all his photographs about, leave us a fortune in his will, then try and kill the pair of us?'

'Unless we just got in the way, Jimmy.'

'In the way of what?'

'See if I knew that, I'd be the chief inspector and you'd be me.' Scott smiled. 'Anyhow, we'd better go back and let me face the music. It's like a really shite version o' *This Is Your Life*.'

'I said, leave it to me. We have an active attempted murder inquiry. It's enough to be going on with. I can't have my right-hand man weighed down with all that shit.'

'What about your right-hand woman?'

Daley hesitated.

'What's up?' Scott had known and worked with him for so long that every pause and tick meant something.

'I've not been entirely honest with you about DS Dhar, Brian.'

'Shit, I knew it!' Scott flung his arms in the air. 'She is here to replace me.'

'No, nothing like that.'

'Well, what then?'

'She's here to investigate Ian Macmillan.'

'Eh?'

'It's a long story.'

'Annie, you mean?'

'No, not Annie. There was no foul play there, you know that.'

'Aye, but the bastard might as well have killed her.' Scott's expression turned dark.

'Yes, that I admit. But it's obvious that she'd been unhappy for a long time.'

'Him throwing her oot the place she'd lived in for years didnae help – never mind losing her job.' He thought for a moment. 'Bugger. That's what's going to happen to me.'

'I told you, I'm going to fix that.'

'Aye, I believe you. Anyway, what's Macmillan been up to?'

'Intelligence from Canada points to mob connections.'

'Why's he here, then – on the run? I cannae see much scope for organised crime in Kinloch, unless it's something to dae wae fish.'

'Well, whatever. They wanted a subtle approach. Dhar's from OCU. Just testing the waters.'

'We could have done that, Jimmy.'

'We could. But I think we're considered old hat.'

'Huh. I could out-investigate her any time.'

'Well, we'll start here with Hughie Machie. Because right now, I haven't got a clue.'

48

Glasgow, 1992

Scott edged himself to the doorway, Daley just behind. He could hear voices echoing from inside the garage. He wanted to lean his head round the corner but knew that would be reckless.

'Where's this back-up, Jimmy?' he whispered.

Daley shrugged and cupped his hand against Scott's ear. 'We should go back to the car, tell them properly what's going on. The two of us can't handle this alone.'

'You go. Tell them we need bodies here, pronto. Argue wae that bastard Donald if you have to.'

Daley nodded. 'You should come too, Brian.'

'Nah, I can maybe clock somebody. The worst thing is if they fuck off and we're left here wae nothing. Man, we'd have been in there and rounded up the bastards by now if the boys hadn't been called to that thing in North Frederick Street.'

Suddenly Daley felt uneasy. He couldn't explain the reason for this, but the night felt somehow colder and darker. He shivered.

'What's up wae you?' whispered Scott.

'Nothing, just ignore me.' Daley turned, but he wasn't faced by an empty street. A man dressed in black, with a balaclava covering his face, was standing behind him and Scott. His well-oiled pistol shone black in the dim light like a slick, prowling cat under a full moon.

The control room in Stewart Street police office was hushed. A beat officer had been attacked and badly injured in North Frederick Street, a thoroughfare thronged with students during the day, but almost empty at night.

Luckily, Constable White had managed to get the urgent call for assistance out before he was overpowered by his attackers. Now, officers were all over the locus searching for those responsible, who'd had little, if any, time to escape.

John Donald was stroking his chin, deep in thought.

'Sir, we should pull out the remaining Zulu unit,' said Ramsay.

'Why? They might be able to gather some intelligence, if nothing else. The priority is the search for PC White's attackers.'

'But we promised them back-up, sir.'

'You promised them back-up, Sergeant Ramsay, not me.'

'I should tell them that has been amended and just to maintain a watching brief, sir.'

'I thought that's what they were doing?'

'They're expecting assistance. Who knows what they're doing?' Ramsay's face was red under his fair hair.

'No need for raised voices. You get on the search team. I'll deal with Scott and Daley.'

'But, sir . . .'

'But nothing! I'm in charge of this operation. In fact, I'm the senior officer in the building right now. I know you seem destined for greater things, but you're not there yet. And as our bard might say: *There's many a slip twixt cup and lip*. Just do as I've ordered, *Sergeant* Ramsay.' Donald passed his hand across his slicked-back hair. 'I have to step out for a moment. Take charge, but follow my instructions, do you understand?'

'Yes, sir,' said Ramsay, not turning to face him.

Scott and Daley were pushed into the bright garage. Being off the dark street made them blink into the light.

Four figures were standing beside the lorry. Like the man who'd forced them into the place at gunpoint, their faces were covered by balaclavas.

'Shit,' said Scott under his breath. But his blood ran cold when he heard a familiar voice emerge from behind one mask.

'On your knees, hands behind your heads, gentlemen.'

The detectives knelt on the oily floor.

The man who'd ordered them to kneel spoke again. His voice was heavy with the accent of Glasgow's East End. 'I've never felt safe knowing that Glasgow's finest were loitering aboot every doorway. Kind o' creepy, don't you think, men?'

He walked towards his captives. 'Right, I recognise one o' you. But no' this big streak o' a lad.' He aimed a kick at Daley's stomach that sent the policeman lurching forward with a strangled groan.

As his colleague struggled with the pain of the blow, Scott spoke up. 'I don't know why yous are wearing they balaclavas. I know fine who you are.' He scanned the room. One of the men was standing behind the rest. He was taller, well-built. Something about his stance made Scott think he was older, somehow not comfortable with the situation. Or perhaps that was only his imagination desperately searching for a way out of this mess. Thoughts of his wife, their new daughter and his parents flashed before his mind's eye. It was enough to make him want to scream out for mercy, for he had no doubt what was going to happen to him and Daley.

'Right, you're on!' Their captor looked over his shoulder at the man who'd been lurking in the shadows. 'Come on, we agreed about this. This is what you're for from now on.'

One of the marked men beside him leaned in to his ear and said something that neither Scott nor Daley could hear.

'What? This is like a meeting o' the women's fucking guild!' With a gloved hand the leader pulled the mask off his head. James Machie's eyes flashed under the strip lights of the garage.

'Surprise, surprise,' said Scott, more boldly than he felt. Daley, meanwhile, was still hunched over, coughing and spluttering, trying to recover his breath.

'Brave wee Brian. What happened to the spotty lad we once knew, eh?'

The man who had whispered in Machie's ear spoke up. 'This is too much, Jay. How did you even know it would be this pair?' Scott recognised Frank MacDougall's voice immediately.

'I know much more than you think I dae – much more than these poor bastards, that's for certain. Anyway, why have yous turned into a Girl Guide pack? Fuck me, what's been happening since I've been inside, Frankie?'

'I'm saying enough is enough, Jay. These are polis.'

'They'll be deid polis shortly, so don't worry.' Machie smiled wickedly at Scott and Daley. 'Time for the lights to go out, my little rat friend.'

In the distance, the ring of a telephone sounded.

'Get that,' said Machie to a man at his side. 'Maybe it's your auld ma, Scooty. Phoning to say goodbye, so she is. Mind you, knowing your family, it's mair likely to be your faither looking for a tap until his Giro day.'

Scott's fear had turned into something else: rage. The injustice of it all had been building up inside him for years. These were the boys he'd grown up with. In most cases, he was sure, old schoolfriends would meet up for drinks and the remembrance of old times. He was equally sure that kneeling on a concrete floor waiting for a bullet between the ears from your old pals wasn't the way things should be.

The man hurried back from the phone and whispered something to Machie.

The gangster responded by throwing his head back and laughing manically.

As soon as Inspector Donald had left the control room, Sergeant Ramsay called over one of his junior colleagues. He spoke to him quietly, and the young constable nodded and hurried out of the room. Ramsay had served in the traffic division before turning to his studies and all but part-time work as a police officer on the street. It was his old friends to whom he turned now – he needed a favour.

Ramsay picked up the mic, took a breath and spoke.

'Control to Zulu-one, come in Zulu-one, over.'

Daley, his earpiece still in place, lifted a hand to his chest, desperately hoping that Machie wouldn't notice. But the sharp-eyed gangster thwarted his attempts to open a channel between them and Stewart Street.

'Oh! What are you at, lanky?' Machie shouted as he made for Daley and patted him down. 'Look at this, oor boys are listening to the wireless!' He leaned in to Daley's face.

'Anything good on? I cannae stand all that rave shit they're playing these days. Gie me a good Jam track any time.' Machie pulled the radio that was hidden under Daley's jumper off him and examined it with a sneer. 'Cutting edge, boys, cutting edge.'

Still masked, Frank MacDougall stepped to his side. 'See, fuck knows what the cops have heard, Jay. Just end this now!'

'You should listen to your pal, James,' said Scott, sheer anger giving him strength. 'There's only one place you're going now, and it's no' the Costa del Sol.'

'Shut up, rat!' shouted Machie, flecks of spit spraying from his mouth, the veins on his neck standing proud like cords of flex. He took a step towards the man he'd grown up with, raising his hand to strike him.

But Brian Scott was too quick. He pushed himself forward on his heels and threw himself at Machie, his forehead catching the gangster square on the chin.

Machie flew backwards. Taken by surprise, he landed heavily on the hard floor. The man who'd answered the phone stepped forward and launched a blow at Scott, catching him in the midriff and doubling him in two. Another blow, this time on the face, sent him flying backwards in much the same way Machie had, to the sickening sound of bones breaking in his nose.

Machie was struggling to his feet, screaming at the top of his voice. 'Now! Now! Come on, you owe me, remember!' He was shouting at the older man still standing in the shadows.

'No!' The reply was emphatic. 'That's Willie Scott's boy. I've known him since he was a wean. Aye, and his faither and mother are one o' us. You've no sense, boy, no loyalty. Once you turn on your own, it's over – over for us all!'

He and Machie were now face to face, the taller of the two staring at the gangster through holes in his balaclava.

'Dae it!' screamed Machie. 'Kill them both now!'

'Nah, you dae it, you little shit. I'm done wae your dirty work. You don't tell me what to dae any more, got it?' The big man turned on his heel, Machie still screaming at him as he went.

'You're a coward! My ain father is a fucking coward!'

The man stopped in tracks and turned to face his son. In a flash he pulled out an old handgun and held it out before him. 'You ever call me that again and, son or no son, I promise I'll kill you.' Hugh Machie turned away from his offspring and was soon eaten up by the shadows.

Scott was on his hands and knees, breathing heavily; a mix of anger and the after-effects of the blows he'd taken was making him feel suddenly disconnected from the very real peril he and Daley were in.

'Can you hear that, Jay?' Frank MacDougall cocked his head.

'What the fuck now?' said Machie, still smarting from the encounter with his father. But as he spoke the words, the wail of sirens became plain.

'Right, we're out of here!' MacDougall shouted at the top of his voice. He grabbed Machie by the arm and began to pull him away.

'You're all fucking cowards, every one o' yous!' Machie's face was scarlet with anger now.

Scott was struggling to his feet, Daley still on his knees.

As the sirens grew louder and louder, Machie broke free of MacDougall's grip. He reached to his side and brandished a handgun.

Scott, now on his feet, stared helplessly on as Machie took aim. Just before Frank MacDougall managed to grab him again, he had time to fire one shot. It hit Scott, swinging him round like a kite in the wind, a spray of crimson blood erupting from his shoulder.

'Brian!' shouted Daley as he struggled to his feet.

The men dressed in black disappeared into the darkness, Machie still roaring at the top of his voice.

'Die, you rat bastard, die!'

49

Hamish was sitting at a table in the Douglas Arms staring balefully at a half pint of beer. The fruit machine was making a racket and those gathered at the bar were shouting at the TV in the corner as it blared out the horse racing.

'Hamish, it's yourself,' said a man in a stout jumper, yellow oilskin trousers and pair of green wellington boots.

'Aye, Peter, it's me right enough. Man, you look like you've just been through a storm.'

'Aye, it was rough up at the Minch. I'm fair glad to be hame, I can tell you that.' Peter Murray walked to the bar. 'What can I get you, Hamish?'

'A dram would be graciously received, and that's a fact, Peter. Take my advice and stay well away fae the beer. Man, it's like puddle water in here, so it is.'

Murray leaned on the bar and was quickly served by a bespectacled barman. He delivered a large measure in a small glass to Hamish, pulled over a chair and sat down beside the old fisherman.

'Your good health, Peter. You're a fine man, just like your faither, God rest him, poor auld Peeny. I thought he'd live for ever. But at my age, there's nothing but death all around.'

'Twenty years ago,' said Peter. 'I miss him to this day.'

'Aye, and you always shall, young fulla. It's jeest the way o' things, and that's a fact.'

'Is what I'm hearing aboot Danny O'May true?'

Hamish lowered his voice. 'I don't know who telt you, but you have the right of it. Stone deid, buried in a shallow grave doon at the causeway. A hellish thing, so I hear.' Hamish sighed and took another draw of his unlit pipe.

'I can hardly believe it. My son called me on the mobile to tell me.'

'The spitting image o' your faither, he is.'

'Danny O'May? No, you've no' got the right o' that, Hamish, no' at all.'

'No, you daft bugger. I mean your ain son. I can see your faither in him. He was in here yesterday, and the thought crossed my mind the minute I set eyes on him. It's something aboot the cant o' his heid, the shoulders. It's strange how the likeness is passed doon the generations.'

'He's a good lad. We've never had a day's trouble from him. But he wants nothing to dae wae the fishing, mind you. He's in his second year up at university.'

'Aye, notions o' heading to California, he was telling me.'

'That's his plan, right enough.' Murray shook his head. 'Och, I cannae blame him. Who wants to be braving the ocean's wrath at any age? Aye, wae precious little to show for it neithers. We never had the choices that young folk have now.'

'The world turns, Peter. None o' us knows in which direction. Ach, but aren't the weans always miserable? I don't see any joy in them. I canna mind the last time I saw anyone under thirty getting carried oot o' a bar, and that's the truth. It makes you doubt everything.' Hamish sucked at his unlit pipe, thoughtfully following this less than intuitive branch of philosophy.

'Och, I think it always goes roon all the time, Hamish. We can be pretty certain o' that. Let's hope that in years to come there's young folk enjoying a good drink and no' sitting wae their faces stuck to some screen or other. My boy was talking to his pal on his phone last night – face to face, mark you.'

'It's amazing what they can do now, right enough.'

'Aye, true. But the lad only lives next door. It would have been jeest as easy for him to go and chap his door and save the money that he spent on thon slate, or whatever they call them.'

'Tablets,' said Hamish.

'I'll get them for you. Where are they? Dae you need a glass o' water to wash them doon?'

'No! I'm no' needing tablets. It's what they call they wee things – the devices. Tablets, no' slates.'

'Like you, I don't know which way the world is turning. It could be spinning oot o' control, for all we know.'

'No, I don't mean in the natural sense. I'm talking figuratively, Peter. As fishermen, we'd be in some state if we didna know which way the world was turning. I dare say there'd be tidal waves, earthquakes, all manner o' calamities.' Hamish frowned at his drinking companion.

'Talking o' calamities, it's obvious why you're in here.'

'That's very true. It doesna take thon Columbus to work it oot.'

'Columbo, dae you mean?'

'It doesna matter which language you're at, he's the same man. You're just being pedantic, Peter.'

Ignoring this, Murray carried on. 'A County man for sixty-odd years, they tell me, Hamish.'

'Aye, and the rest. My faither before me, too. Mind you,

he'd have done well to stay oot o' any licensed premises, as the drink did for him when he was just a young man.'

'Aye, I think I heard that story fae someone.'

Hamish looked unimpressed. 'It's Kinloch. I don't doubt you were well informed aboot every step o' his demise. Aye, and some he never took, into the bargain.'

'If it's any consolation, they tell me the place is like the grave.'

'A rather unfortunate illustration, if you don't mind me saying. Considering what happened to poor Annie, I mean.'

Murray considered this and apologised. 'Unfortunate illustrations aside, they tell me that Macmillan has aged ten years in the last while. No doubt he has money troubles now there's nae bugger in his hotel. Taken to the hills now, so he has. It's a man in trouble that finds solace up thonder. Any normal soul would work through his problems by fair staring out to sea.'

'What dae you mean, taken tae the hills?'

'Just that. My boy is at the exercise. He's taken to running up and doon hills.'

'Oh, for any's sake, what on earth for?'

'You know how it is, Hamish. We got exercise aplenty at oor work. Too much o' it, many a time. But the young folk sit at the computers a' day, wae only their hands at the go. I suppose they need to get some o' the frustrations oot wae the exercise.'

'Has he no' got a girlfriend?'

'Aye. A lassie fae Tarbert. Bonnie, so she is – cannae be a native o' the place. Why dae you ask?'

'Och, jeest a passing thought.'

'They have all kind o' notions these days.'

'He saw Macmillan, you're saying?'

'Aye, struggling up Ben Saarnie wae a bag o' some description. Making heavy weather o' it too, by the sound o' things.'

'So the bag must have been a fair weight, eh?'

'Aye, must have been.'

Hamish sucked at his pipe again, in his mind's eye picturing Ian Macmillan hefting a bag and trying to work out what he could be carrying, and to where. 'There's nothing up there these days. Man, he's likely burying evidence!'

'Evidence o' whoot?'

'You know I think the man's nothing but a murderer.'

Murray shook his head. 'He didnae kill Annie, Hamish. The lassie was depressed. She'd lost her job and her home. Man, that place was all she had in her life. It's jeest a pity none o' us knew aboot it beforehand. Maybe we could have done something.'

'One way or another, that bastard took that lassie's life, I'm telling you.' Hamish's face was suddenly filled with hatred. 'I wouldna be surprised if he'd something to dae wae that maniac in the Main Street. Him that shot at the polis.'

'Maniac in the Main Street. That's good,' said Peter Murray.

'Ach, it's the headline in today's paper.'

'The *Kinloch Herald*?'

'And the twa Jocks were banging on aboot it on the wireless last night, too. Of course, they'd make a fire oot a wisp o' smoke, that pair.'

'Very true. But what can you expect fae sons o' the soil?'

'They tell me the gunman was a fair age. Up in the hospital under police guard. No' but a few puffs o' breath left in him.'

'But what can that have to dae wae Macmillan at the County?'

'The man's like a spider, trust me. A web o' criminality and deceit likely crossing the globe.' Hamish got to his feet and donned his threadbare pea jacket.

'Where are you off to in such a hurry?'

'I'm away to put a stop to Ian Macmillan before he does for some other innocent wee lassie. I'll return that dram the next time I see you, Peter.'

Peter Murray watched Hamish rush out of the Douglas Arms, a man on a mission.

'Aye, and there's to be green snow and yellow hailstones the day I get my dram back.' Murray smiled, drained his glass and headed wearily back to the bar.

50

Shreya had showered and dressed, and should have been on her way to work, but she was lying on her bed deep in thought.

She hadn't expected to be shot at within a few days of arriving in the remote town, nor had she expected that her landlady would search through her things. Dhar was suspicious by nature, and always set a trap for unsuspecting prowlers when she stayed in a guest house or hotel. Her mother had warned her about it when she was a child, and her daughter never lost the habit. She used an old trick, but it still worked, unless the person keen to look through her things was trained to look out for such basic traps.

Before putting her small valise at the bottom of the wardrobe, she'd placed a single hair across one of the locks that had to be clicked open in order to access the case. When she'd arrived back in her room it was the first thing she'd checked. The only item of her luggage left unlocked. The hair was gone; and checking the bag – which only contained some paperwork, her chargers and a notepad – she knew that things were not as she'd left them.

As far as she knew, Dhar was still the only guest at Shandy's. She'd heard proprietor Shona MacBride humming tunelessly outside her door. Was this woman simply nosy or was there something more sinister about her rifling through the detective's personal belongings? It was always a point to be considered.

Dhar decided to ask for some breakfast – nothing more than some toast and coffee. It would give her time to assess whether the owner of the guest house had any intent other than bland curiosity. The thought that Daley could be having her quietly checked out crossed her mind, but she soon dismissed the idea. Why would he? She supposed that paranoia was just another part of the life she'd chosen for herself. But nonetheless, she was determined to confront Shona MacBride, just to be sure.

Dhar descended the spiral staircase. The place reeked of furniture polish and the little baskets of potpourri that were dotted about.

'Oh, good morning, Miss Dhar. I hope you slept well?' said the proprietor.

'I did, thank you.' Dhar smiled. 'I was wondering, would I be able to have some breakfast? Just toast and coffee.'

'Of course, dear. I'd be happy to make you a full breakfast. I reckon you need it, if what I'm hearing is true. Poor Danny O'May lying dead in the sand, and a gun battle in the Main Street. I don't know what the world is coming to.' MacBride eyed her for a response.

'It was hardly a gun battle, Mrs MacBride. A poor old man – dementia, I suspect – just letting off a firearm. It was frightening for the people in the street, I'm sure. But all's well that ends well.'

'And Danny O'May?'

Dhar shrugged. 'I'm not at liberty to say anything. I'm sure you understand.'

'Yes, yes, of course.' MacBride was all apologies. 'Now, just take a seat through here. I'll have you some toast and coffee on in no time.' She led Dhar through to the dining room. The place was airy and tastefully decorated. Perhaps the product of Mr MacBride's imagination rather than his wife's, she thought uncharitably. Like Dhar's room, the bay windows afforded a great view across the loch and the hill behind.

Dhar was shown to a table covered by a spotless white cloth, some coasters and the usual sugar bowl and condiments at its centre. The photographs of Kinloch that hung around the white walls were interesting. She spotted places she recognised, even after such a short acquaintance with the town.

'Now, brown or white toast?'

'Brown, please,' Dhar replied.

'Good idea. There's nothing like keeping regular.'

'Sorry?'

'Oh, you know, roughage and the like. Maybe it's no' the best conversation for the breakfast table.' Shona MacBride coughed with embarrassment. 'What about coffee? It's freshly brewed.'

'Will that help me with my bowels too?'

'Oh, I'm not sure about that.' MacBride was blushing.

'Black, please.'

Watching her host bustle off to the kitchen, Dhar pulled the mobile phone from her pocket and scrolled down her emails and messages. She hesitated over one and replied quickly, using her thumbs to type. She placed the phone on the table and gazed at one of the images on the wall. It was of Main Street at night, and the County Hotel was lit up and looked quite the place. Dhar stared at it for a while, a look of determination on her face. The spell was broken when her phone bleeped into life. She read the return message and smiled.

It didn't take MacBride long to bring the coffee and toast. She set a porcelain coffee pot down on the table, the toast beside it.

'Now, can I get you some jam or marmalade? It's all homemade. Most of the guests seem to love it.'

'And the rest don't rate it?'

'Oh, they just don't like jam or marmalade.'

'No, thanks. I'm not a big fan either. Just butter for me.'

'That's there in the wee packets. Use as many as you want.' MacBride forced a smile. She wasn't happy after Dhar's comment about the preserves.

'Why don't you join me, Mrs MacBride? I eat alone too often.'

Surprised by this unexpected invitation, Shona pulled up a seat and sat down at the little table. 'You don't mind if I have a wee cup of coffee with you, eh? I've plenty more in the kitchen.'

Shreya Dar was buttering a slice of toast. 'Not at all. Be my guest. I'll only drink one cup anyway.'

'It makes me a bit jittery if I drink too much o' the stuff.' MacBride was pouring herself some coffee. 'Nothing like it for keeping you going, though.' She took a noisy slurp.

Dhar regarded her landlady for a few seconds. Her face was slathered in far too much make-up, the lipstick a gawdy shade of pink. 'Still no other guests, I see.'

'No. As I said, it's a quiet time of year. I suppose folk don't like the weather. It can be cold and wet wae that wind coming off the Atlantic all winter.' Shona MacBride slurped again at her coffee.

'Must be quite a long day for you?'

'Ach, I keep myself busy. There's always a wee task or two to be at.'

'Like looking through your guests' luggage?' The question was from nowhere.

'Sorry, what do you mean?' MacBride's mouth flapped open and a sliver of dark coffee dribbled down her chin and landed on the white tablecloth.

'You opened one of my bags yesterday – the only one that wasn't locked, though I assume you tried them all. What were you looking for?' Dhar's voice was calm, but there was menace in it.

'Oh no, you're mistaken, Miss Dhar. I would never do a thing like that to one of my guests.' Tears were welling up in the landlady's eyes.

'I'm a detective, Mrs MacBride. This is what I do for a living. I don't understand what your motivation was; I assume mere nosiness. I hope there was nothing more than that behind your actions.'

'Like what?' Shona MacBride now looked quite alarmed.

'You seem very curious about the cases I'm working on. You were fishing for information about them just now, despite the fact I told you I couldn't discuss my work when I arrived.'

MacBride sat back, her chin set. 'You're a police officer, so you know you require evidence when such accusations are made. I'm no' some daft wee lassie, by the way.'

'Fingerprints,' Dhar lied. 'Yours are all over the catches on the red bag at the bottom of my wardrobe.'

MacBride's mouth gaped, but no words were forthcoming. 'Do you still deny it?' Dhar took a sip of coffee.

Finally, the proprietor broke down. 'Yes, all right, I did take a look inside your bag. I wisnae going to steal anything, honestly. Like you say, I'm nosy – I canna help it. I'm mortified.'

Shreya Dhar chewed thoughtfully on a piece of toast before washing it down with the last of her coffee. 'I could report this, you know.'

'No, please! I'm sorry. My husband would have a fit if he found out.'

'Does he help you go through people's property when he's here?'

'No! He doesna know anything aboot it, I swear.'

Dhar leaned back in her chair, wiping her mouth with a napkin. 'I don't know, Mrs MacBride. This kind of thing – well, it's just not right, is it?'

Shona MacBride shook her head as tears streamed down her face. 'Please, I'm begging you, Miss Dhar. You canna understand what it's like for me stuck here day after day. Truth be telt, I haven't got many friends. They were all jealous when I married into a bit o' money. When my husband's away, all I have is these four walls. I take a walk doon the street and folk are just talking behind their hands aboot me. *There's the wee lassie fae the Glebe Fields wae her nose in the air.* I know fine what they say.'

Dhar supposed she should feel sorry for this pathetic woman, but the emotion was entirely absent. 'Try growing up being called names, spat at, having shit posted through your letterbox. That's what happened to us when I was a child.' Dhar opened her mouth to say something else, but quickly thought the better of it. 'You should count your blessings, not get your kicks from nosing around other people's possessions.'

'What are you going to dae?'

Dhar had no intention of taking her discovery any further. But for some reason, the wretched woman reminded her of the mothers of the children who had bullied her at school: the same caked make-up, dropped vowels and cheap perfume. 'I'll have to think about it.' She got up and headed out of the guest house, leaving Shona MacBride shaking at the table, head in her hands.

As Shreya Dhar drove down the steep, winding drive to the road, she suddenly remembered the day when the bullying stopped – the day it stopped for ever.

51

Hamish took the steps up to the front door of Kinloch police office and made his way to the reception desk. Instead of the familiar figure of Sergeant Shaw, a small, spare woman with short hair and wearing a blue trouser suit was bent over a computer typing furiously.

'Who are you?' said Hamish.

The woman stopped, a disgruntled look on her face. 'I'm a police officer. Who are you?'

'I'm a fisherman.'

The pair stared at each other for a moment until Shaw appeared back behind the front desk with a mug of tea.

'Hamish, what can I do for you?'

'Hello, Alasdair. I'd like to speak wae Mr Daley, if he's aboot. I've some important information for him.'

The woman in the trouser suit snorted, got up from the computer and stomped off.

'She got up on the wrong side o' a haddock this morning, I'll wager.'

'Yes, long story, Hamish. She's not having a good day. One of her witnesses has decided that something he thought happened didn't happen at all.'

'Aye, that'll be MacConnachie, I'm thinking. I'd a wee word

in his ear yesterday. He's been a chancer since he was a boy. You jeest canna let folk get away wae that kind o' stuff. And never gie the bugger a rock bun. He's bound to choke on the bloody thing.'

'You spoke to him alone?'

'Och, myself and some younger friends o' mine. Just a wee chat, it was – nothing more.'

Marvelling once more at the old fisherman, Shaw picked up the phone and dialled Daley's extension number.

DCI MacPherson burst into Daley's office just as the phone started to ring. He listened for a few seconds, eyeing his visitor.

'Tell Hamish I'll see him shortly.' He put the phone down and addressed MacPherson. 'I know we're the same rank, but I'd have thought you'd still have done me the courtesy of knocking.'

The discipline investigator didn't address his point. Instead, she folded her arms and looked at Daley with a malevolent expression. 'I know you think you and that alcoholic friend of yours are impervious to anything. But let me tell you, Daley, I'm not finished with this – not by a long chalk.' She tapped her foot on the floor with irritation.

'I don't know what you mean. All charges against DS Scott have been dropped. In fact, I'm considering charging the gentleman concerned with wasting police time. I'll let you know what happens.'

'I don't know what goes on down here, but I'm going to find out. My next case is your erstwhile chief superintendent's. I'm sure she has plenty to say.'

'Chief Superintendent Symington will be cleared. I've no doubt about it.'

'After seeing the evidence, I don't share your confidence.'

'I don't think I'm the right person to complain to, do you?' Daley smiled.

'Huh! And so the Jim and Brian show rolls on, eh?'

Daley shrugged. 'If you mean that we will continue to do our work bringing criminals to justice, yes, it rolls on. I'd rather that than spend my life trying to dig up dirt on my own colleagues.'

'We'll see, DCI Daley. Your luck won't run for ever.'

'I'm sure. If this is what you'd call lucky.' He gestured airily round the glass box.

DCI MacPherson made to leave but turned on her heel. 'Oh, I think your investigation around your dead fisherman may be over. The victim just walked into the office.'

'Sorry?'

'Or is it your star witness? If that's the case, he's old and he stinks of fish. Good luck with that!' She stormed out of Daley's office and slammed the door.

The DCI barely had time to sigh before he had another visitor. Hamish entered on his call and stood framed in the doorway.

'Hamish, good to see you,' said Daley.

'And you too, Mr Daley.' Hamish took a seat opposite the detective. 'Aye, that's a woman I widna like to cross in a hurry. Is she the one who was trying to put Brian on the dole?'

'I'd rather not say.'

'When I arrived in the office, I could smell her wrath. Fair strong it was too.'

'I don't doubt it. She's having to pack her things now she's lost a witness.'

'Young MacConnachie saw sense at last. About time, for his heid is fair empty of anything but chance.'

'And you know this how?'

'Ear to the ground, Mr Daley, nothing more.'

As Daley considered this, Hamish pulled out his pipe and clamped it between his teeth.

'So, what have you got for me?'

'Well, I don't stick my beak into places it's no' desired.'

'And?'

The old fisherman went on to tell the tale Peter Murray had related to him in the Douglas Arms. 'Evidence to be trusted, mark you. The young man who witnessed this chicanery is off to California to work wae they fruit folk, no less.'

Daley was mulling over what he'd heard. There was no law against carrying a heavy bag up a hill. But somehow he found it hard to picture the well-dressed, urbane Ian Macmillan doing it. 'The fruit folk?'

'You see them all o'er. Selling a simple thing like an apple for outrageous prices. Man, and some o' the names they gie stuff – och, the mind fair boggles, so it does. What's wrong wae a Cox's Orange Pippin?'

'Ah, those fruit folk,' said Daley with a smile.

'Anyhow, what are you going to dae to bring this bugger to justice at last? You and I both know fine that poor lassie would be alive if it wisnae for him.' Hamish's eyes blazed with a mixture of sadness and hatred.

'Okay, it's interesting. But don't mention a word to anybody, okay? And don't get carried away, either. I don't want a posse of angry locals burning him at the cross.'

'You have my word, Mr Daley. And I think you know me

well enough to know that my word is my bond. And in any case, we've no' burned anyone at the cross since the war.'

'Though I'm pretty sure you're joking, it's only ninety-nine per cent. But thank you – for everything.'

'What everything?'

'Let's just say that you helped a friend of mine.'

Hamish sucked at his unlit pipe. 'I have to say, I'm jeest no' sure what you're on aboot. But I know you're a busy man. I'll leave you to your toil.'

Daley watched his friend leave. He chewed his lip. The detective didn't like Macmillan, that was for sure, though he still couldn't work out what the Canadian could possibly achieve in a town like Kinloch.

Daley left his glass box and went in search of Dhar. He found her speaking to Scott in the canteen, both of them smiling, which surprised him.

'Now, I know what Brian is grinning about, but what about you, Shreya?'

'I'm pleased that DS Scott is out from under his cloud. We're having a celebratory cup of tea.'

'Tea is good,' said Daley with a glance at his old friend.

'I've no' touched a drop for a couple o' days, Jimmy. You know that.' Despite his smile, Scott looked tired, drained.

'I have some news, too,' said Dhar. 'I want to go and have another word with Ian Macmillan.'

Daley took in the young woman. The disgruntled expression she'd adopted since he'd brought Scott back from suspension to help with the investigation into O'May's death was gone. He'd met many police officers in his time, and they all had their own foibles. He presumed that sometimes going around with her noise out of joint was Dhar's. 'Okay, what is it?'

'Only a theory for now – a piece of unexpected intelligence. It came from HQ. But I want to see how he reacts when I ask him about it.'

'Is this to do with his hillside activities?' said Daley.

'I'm sorry?' Dhar looked confused.

'I have it on good authority he's parading about on Ben Saarnie with a heavy bag.'

'Oh, that's interesting.' Dhar looked preoccupied, no doubt trying to process this latest information. 'But no, it has nothing to do with that, sir,' she said absently.

'I thought we could go up there and see if we can get a clue what he was up to. It's pretty isolated, not much about but sheep, gulls and crows. If he was burying anything, for example, it would be quite easy to spot disturbed ground.'

Dhar thought for a moment. 'Can we go and see him first? I'm anxious to try him with this new information. He seems to me a man who wouldn't be able to stand up to too much scrutiny – he'd crumble, I mean.'

Daley nodded just as the phone went off in his pocket. He answered it, listened and nodded to Scott. 'Yes, thank you, doctor.'

'Is that you got the all-clear fae the clinic, big man?' Scott quipped, while Dhar looked less than amused.

'It's Hugh Machie. His vital signs have improved slightly. They're going to be able to fly him up to Glasgow.'

'Great.' Scott looked unimpressed. 'The boys are still going through his stuff. They've just about got it all up here now.'

'No, you don't understand. He's going to be conscious. They want to speak to him before they move him. I want you to do the same.'

52

Two big men, a woman and a smaller man with his back pressed firmly against the door were in the room.

He could hear his heart beating.

The woman was motionless. Her eyes were closed, but he could see her chest moving up and down as though she was struggling silently for breath.

He wanted to look away, but somehow it seemed as though he was drawn to the gruesome scene playing out before his eyes. It was like watching a horror movie between his fingers, or passing an accident: not wanting to miss anything but appalled at the same time. An unfathomable human trait.

Suddenly, she was still. One of the large men gently pushed back her neck with his gloved hand. He placed something in her open mouth and then reached for a bottle. As though feeding a child he carefully measured amounts of clear liquid into her mouth, massaging her throat to encourage the swallowing reflex in the unconscious woman.

He could feel the bile rising in his throat. His stomach was churning as he watched the man repeat the process, feeding her with something then washing it down by pouring small dribbles from the bottle. Somehow the oh-so-gentle massage of her throat was the most disturbing part of it all.

The unconscious woman stirred, then her body began to convulse of its own accord. Just as quickly, she was still.

He swallowed back the bile he could taste in his own throat as again something was placed in her mouth and the man massaged her throat. The same process, over and over.

Her body tensed, but this time didn't convulse. The large man and his companion stepped back; their job was done.

He could see her clearly now. The slight figure in the dress was taut, as though she was braced in a horizontal attention.

Her eyes flicked open. He could see the terror in them.

She stared straight at him, and then they glazed over.

Macmillan woke with a start and almost shot out of his office chair as the phone on his desk burst into life. He answered the call and, following a brief exchange, slammed down the receiver.

The Canadian leaned on the desk in front of him, his head in his hands. He wanted to scream, to call for help he knew would never come – could never come.

He walked through to the washroom and splashed water on his face, patted it dry with a towel and vigorously slapped some colour into his cheeks in an attempt to regain a semblance of normality. The man he saw in the mirror was almost a stranger. He opened the bathroom cabinet and removed a packet of pills, pushed one from the blister pack and washed it down with a handful of water from the tap.

He remembered the dream and shuddered.

*

345

The detectives were in the deserted bar of the County Hotel. The barmaid looked thoroughly bored as she rubbed at pint glasses unenthusiastically with a towel.

'Quiet, isn't it?' Daley remarked.

'Aye, there's no guests right now.' The woman's accent was Scottish, but not from Kinloch.

'Nobody just drop in off the street for a drink any more?'

'Nah.' She picked up another glass. 'I've only seen a couple and I started a week ago.' She thought for a moment. 'Hey, are yous fae here, like?'

Daley nodded, while Dhar seemed preoccupied with something on her phone.

'Some guy told me this place used to be pure jumping, man.'

'It did,' replied Daley.

'Hard to believe.' She looked about the bar and continued polishing.

Macmillan appeared in the doorway. He looked pale and his face was puffy. 'Go and check the upstairs bar please, Melody.'

The young woman sighed, discarded her polishing towel and disappeared from behind the bar.

'You feeling okay, Mr Macmillan?' Daley asked.

'Well, yes. Just not sleeping very well.' He took a seat at their table.

'Why so?' asked Dhar.

'Take a look round. I'm haemorrhaging money in here. The place is like the grave.' He hesitated, raising his eyes as though he regretted the phrase.

'Can't be easy,' said Daley. 'You've done a lot of work. Must have cost a pretty penny. It's a shame the business isn't seeing the benefit.'

346

Dhar changed the conversation. 'Sol Zietner, Mr Macmillan. How well do you know him?'

'Sorry?'

'You heard me. I know you know the man.' She picked up her phone and held it before Macmillan's face. Daley couldn't see the screen, but he reckoned that Dhar's surprise tactic was a good one. Certainly, the hotelier's face, if anything, became even more wan, and his eyes widened as he stared at the screen.

'He's a well-known gangland figure back in Toronto. Gambling, racketeering, prostitution, things like that. But you know that already, don't you?'

'I don't know anything about such affairs, only that he uses our trucks from time to time – as a customer, that is. He fabricates roofing materials.' The reply was rushed and, to Daley at least, sounded rehearsed.

'I have information that he's not only a customer.'

'I don't know what you mean.'

Dhar raised her brow. 'Forensic accountants working for the Toronto police have uncovered potential cash transfers into Mac Logistics. That company belongs to you, doesn't it, Ian?'

Daley was impressed by the way Dhar was pushing Macmillan's buttons. It was clear to him that she didn't have enough information from Canada in order to arrest him, otherwise this conversation would have been taking place in Kinloch police office. She was trying to break the man, force him to confess. It was an old technique, but Dhar used it like a pro.

'I'd rather not say any more until I've sought legal advice,' said Macmillan hesitantly.

Dhar sat back in her chair, perhaps unconsciously revealing that her plan to pressure the hotelier hadn't worked.

'I have every right,' said Macmillan, looking at Daley.

'Listen, you're in deep, whatever you do. You tell us, confess, or . . . well, who knows?' Dhar's face was expressionless.

'What do you mean?'

'Don't think you're safe here in Kinloch. Guys like Zietner have the whole world in their hands.' She pushed her chair back, as though readying to leave. 'Last chance, Ian.'

Macmillan glared at her. But the tremor in his voice was plain. 'I say again. Unless you arrest me, I want to seek legal counsel now.'

'Your funeral.' Dhar paused for a few seconds. 'Right, sir. If you're ready?'

The detectives made their way out of the hotel on to a bright but cold Main Street. Daley looked at the sky and then at his watch.

'We've got plenty of time to take a wander up that hill I was telling you about. What about it?'

'Yeah, sure. How do we get there?'

'It involves a bit of a trek, I'm afraid. We can take my SUV so far, but after that it's Shanks's pony.' He patted his stomach. 'Anyway, I could do with a bit of exercise.'

They made their way back to where Daley had parked the car. 'I wonder how Brian's doing?' said Dhar.

'I'm sure he'll be handling everything with his usual aplomb. He's a good man, you know. Not perfect, but which of us is?'

Dhar stared ahead as they pulled away from the kerb. 'Listen, I'm sorry I was a bit pissy about you bringing him back – you know, down at the causeway. Being a woman in this job still isn't easy, despite what they tell you.'

'Things are changing for the better, I'm sure.'

'I know you've probably seen a lot of change in your time, sir. But nonetheless, I still feel as though I've got to be twice as good as a man to get ahead. That may be real or imagined, but I'm not the only woman who thinks that way.'

Daley shrugged. 'I've met some fine people in this job over the years. But I've also met some real idiots – not worthy of putting on a uniform.'

'I'm sure. I've met quite a few like that myself.'

'Why did you join?'

Dhar thought for a moment. 'Oh, I suppose the fight against injustice. I've seen plenty of that. When I was a kid – when we first came to this country – our lives were hell.'

'It can't have been easy.'

'I think about it every day. The blows, you can take. It's the casual, off-hand stuff that really hurts.'

'An old boss of mine told me that it was always the throwaway remark that got you in trouble. He was right. And I agree, they can be the most hurtful, too. Did things get better?'

'They did. My mother met a man who helped us a lot.'

'I'm glad. Where is he now?'

There was silence for a moment. Daley could see tears brimming in Dhar's eyes.

'I'm sorry. I didn't mean to upset you.'

She brushed away a tear. 'No, just me being silly. He died a few years ago. I miss him – every day. He was the only father I ever knew, really. Not my real dad, but it felt like he was. But we all suffer it. Loss, I mean.'

'Yes, we do. I still miss my folks. I still see things and think, I must tell my mother. She's been gone for years.' He gazed at the road, his mother's face passing before his mind's eye. He heard Dhar groan and turned to the DS. She was holding her head, her face screwed up in pain.

'I'm sorry, it'll pass. I get migraines. They come from nowhere.'

'Me too. Listen, we'll get the hill tomorrow, if you're feeling better. I'll take you back to the guest house now. You can have a lie-down – take the day. Migraines are hell.'

'It's okay, sir. I'll be fine in an hour or two.' She screwed up her face again in obvious distress.

'You've been shot at. That can have all sorts of after-effects. It's back to Mrs MacBride's for you'

'Okay, but I'll get back as soon as I can.'

'Don't worry about it. We know what happened to poor O'May. Natural causes – confirmed by the pathologist. He was living with a bad heart – could have happened any time. Brian's in the clear – for now, at least. And it doesn't look like Machie will last much longer.'

'He's probably been pumped full of all sorts. I can't think he'll have much to say to DS Scott.'

Daley reversed into a side street and turned the car round. 'He's known Brian since he was a kid. You never know. If anyone can get any sense out of him, it'll be him.'

Dhar groaned again as Daley drove along the esplanade towards Shandy's guest house.

350

53

Scott was waiting in a corridor at Kinloch hospital for a chance to speak to Hugh Machie. Though the staff were reasonably confident that they would be able to helicopter him out to Glasgow, they weren't sure how lucid he'd be. The combination of the pain medication he'd been given and his general state of health had likely rendered him incoherent. In any event, it was clear that he wasn't being taken to Glasgow in an attempt to save his life, rather for the palliative care that Kinloch could not offer.

Scott thought back to his childhood. Hugh Machie, big, strong, with a shock of blond hair. On some doors you knocked and ran away for a laugh. You didn't knock on Machie's door. Not only was he respected, that respect was tinged with fear. Everyone knew that Hughie was a hard man, and his son James, slightly older than Scott, was gaining a very similar reputation. But in addition to the toughness, the son was cruel, stopping at nothing to get his own way. Even spells in borstal did nothing to change him for the better. They served only to make him worse.

For Scott, little was left of what had once been his younger life. Jay-Mac was gone, as was Frank MacDougall. His parents had passed away long ago. And he was now in Kinloch, far away from Glasgow's East End. All that remained was the man dying in a bed not too far away. A shadow of the battering ram he'd once been.

Scott leaned his head against the cold wall. He felt sick, tired and paranoid. His hands shook, and he found himself jumping at shadows. But these were classic signs of withdrawal, something to which he was more than accustomed. Getting sober was like joining the police, he reckoned. You had to go through the pain and discipline of basic training until you were out on the streets doing the job. The pain he was feeling due to his yearning for alcohol would eventually fade. But, having slipped off the wagon many times in his life, he knew they'd never disappear – not ever. The temptation would always be there.

He squeezed his eyes tight and tried to think about recovery. But that place seemed far away. The antiseptic smell of the hospital made everything seem worse. For Brian Scott, hospitals were places of sadness, the end of the road – of many roads.

Footsteps outside caught his attention, and he turned to face the double doors at the end of the corridor. The bottom halves of the doors were solid, while large glass panels in the top halves allowed people inside to see who was coming. As he struggled to focus, all Scott could see was a long neck covered in brown fur and a small head with pointed ears. A shiver of fear caught his heart.

'Shit, no' this again,' he muttered to himself. Suspecting that the DTs had returned, he screwed up his eyes to banish the hallucination.

As the doors squeaked apart he tentatively opened one eye, hoping to see something normal. Instead, a kangaroo was bounding towards him, its head nodding to and fro as it came nearer and nearer, tail flapping behind.

Scott forced himself back in his seat, praying the illusion would vanish. He wasn't sure he could go through another period of terrifying visions brought on by delirium tremens. He felt sick, really sick, his heart beating fit to burst.

'Excuse me, do you know the way to ward three?'

As Scott stared at the marsupial, a human head poked out from behind a massive stuffed toy's backside. A diminutive woman of middle age smiled at him.

'My wee nephew broke his leg, so he did. He loves kangaroos. We found this in Glasgow. Thought it would fair cheer him up.' She looked up. 'It's a big bastard, right enough.'

Scott was still breathing heavily. 'Just doon there on the right, dear.'

'Aye, cheers. The sooner I get tae put this thing doon, the better. My arms will be longer than my legs in a minute. Hey, are you okay? You look right pale. See waiting to get seen in here, shite so it is.'

Scott watched the tiny woman's legs stomping off in the direction of ward three, the head of the kangaroo nodding rhythmically with each step.

'Oh, ya bastard,' he said to himself, hand on his chest, feeling his heart rate slow.

'Are you quite all right, DS Scott?' Staff Nurse Kelly, a solid, formidable woman, approached.

'Aye, just a touch o' wind. We'd broth for tea last night, hen.'

'*Staff Nurse* will do, thank you, not *hen*. I don't know about wind, but I remember the fuss you made when that peanut hit you in the eye a couple of years ago. I've seen swaddled infants behave in a more mature fashion.'

'When are yous going to forget aboot that? What happened to the hypocritic oath you all bang on aboot, eh?'

'It's Hippocratic, and when it comes to peanuts, all bets are off. Mr Machie is awake. I'd come now, if I were you. The poor man doesn't look as though he'll last long enough to make it to Glasgow.'

Dutifully, the detective followed the nurse down one corridor after another until they came to a ward of single rooms reserved for the very ill. Staff Nurse Kelly stopped outside room three and leaned her head through a gap in the door.

'How is he?' she said in a gentle voice to a nurse sitting by Machie's bed.

'Stable, but I don't know. I wish the helicopter would come,' the nurse replied.

Kelly looked over her shoulder and beckoned Scott to follow her into the room. She put her finger to her lips in a hushing gesture as they approached the old man's bed. His exposed chest was covered by sensors attached by wires to the machines that were monitoring his vital signs. To Scott, his ribs looked like the remains of dead animals he'd seen on nature documentaries, picked clean by scavengers. It was as though the skeleton could burst through the grey parchment skin at any time.

The detective looked at Hugh Machie's face. His cheeks were hollowed, his eyes sitting so deep in their sockets that it was easy to picture the shape of his skull. All told, the dying man looked infinitely worse than he had when he'd been carried from the cold, wet pavement on Main Street following his attack on their car.

Scott pondered on this as the nurses checked the monitors,

speaking quietly to each other as they went about their business. In his mind, he was in a run-down garage in Glasgow's Townhead. Though it seemed like a lifetime ago, he could still picture the place as though he'd been there yesterday; he could smell the smells, taste the fear.

The conundrum was, why would a man who'd point-blank refused to shoot him that day have chosen to wait all these years for a second chance? Of course, James Machie was dead. But the pair hadn't spoken for years, and it was common knowledge that father and son detested each other. So was revenge really the motive?

Scott recalled standing beside his own father's deathbed. He was hugging his mother, while Ella lifted their son – named after the dying man – into her arms. Martha was at school. She was old enough to be impacted by watching her grandfather die, and both he and Ella didn't want that for her. She'd have time enough to face up to the grim realities of life and death.

His mother had shrunk into a tiny, frail old lady, he remembered. Looking at her, he knew she wouldn't outlive her husband by much. Willie Scott, his body ruined long ago by drink, cigarettes and hard living, was hanging on to life for no reason. Though Scott hated the thought of his father no longer being there, what was the point of seeing a man pushed to the limits of his very existence with the aid of drugs and oxygen?

Just let him slip away. He recalled the thought. It still sounded callous, but it was the right thing to do. He hadn't changed his mind. Everything came to an end. It was best for that end to be as swift and painless as possible. Scott had witnessed too much agony in his time as a police officer.

Looking at Hugh Machie, he felt the same. What purpose was served by prolonging this man's life? He should have been allowed to die as nature intended, not preserved for a few final hours of pointless misery. There was nobody here to hold his hand, nobody to bid him farewell.

As he stared, Machie's eyes flickered open. It made Scott take a step back with surprise.

'Mr Machie, how do you feel?' Staff Nurse Kelly gently placed her hand on the old man's forehead, as he struggled to draw in breath, the wheeze in his chest so loud that it sounded like a whistle. His lips moved, but no words would come.

'I'm sorry, I didn't hear you,' said Kelly.

Scott watched as Machie closed his eyes and, through the pain, drew as much air into his lungs as he was able.

'Shite!' The sound was like a cross between a curse and a whisper.

'Oh, yes, indeed.' Kelly looked embarrassed. 'They're going to take you to Glasgow, Mr Machie – where you can be more comfortable.'

Scott knew that this was shorthand for *we're going to take you to Glasgow, where they'll fill you with morphine until you die, because we don't have the balls.* But he said nothing. This was the final dance of death, and every step had to be choreographed perfectly until the music stopped.

Kelly turned to Scott. 'It's against my better judgement, but if you want to speak to him, now is probably the last chance.'

Brian Scott took her place at the bedside and leaned over the man he'd known for so long.

'No' so good, Hughie, eh?' To his surprise, Machie pulled one withered arm from under the sheets and reached for his hand.

'It's good to see you, son,' he said, before coughing weakly.

Scott froze for a moment, thinking that, in his distress, Hugh thought he was James Machie – his son. He was about to point this out when Hugh spoke again.

'Willie's boy – the polis.'

'Aye, that's me, Hughie – Brian Scott.'

'My son hated your fucking guts.' He gasped for breath once more. 'But that bastard hated everyone.' A waspish expression crossed his face until another bout of coughing wracked his broken body.

Kelly held a white tissue to his mouth. It was soon spattered black.

'I don't think this is serving any purpose aside from distressing my patient further. Don't you agree, DS Scott?'

The detective furrowed his brow. 'Aye, you're right.' Whatever was behind Hugh Machie's stay in Kinloch, his attack on them and his last will and testament, would now remain a mystery.

'No!' Machie's voice had surprising strength. He held up his hand. 'I want to speak to him.' With every gasp of breath, his wheeze became louder. He waved Scott towards him. 'Listen, Willie.' Machie's eyelids were flickering as he used up his last reserves of strength to address the policemen.

'It's Brian, Hugh. But on you go.'

Hugh Machie grabbed Scott's hand. His skin was almost translucent, every thin vein showing, the bones of his knuckles white and gnarled. 'I know who you are.'

Scott looked at Kelly with a grimace.

'It has to end, understand? There should be nobody left who remembers. It stops wae the last.'

As Scott tried to process this, the old man's eyes rolled back

357

in his head, and the machine monitoring his heart pinged alarmingly. Staff Nurse Kelly pushed the detective aside.

'Get help, nurse!' The junior member of staff ran out of the room as more machines pinged and bleeped. 'I want you to leave – now!' she shouted at Scott.

He hesitated for a second, torn between the desire of leaving a man privacy in his death throes, and wanting to know what he had tried to say.

'Out!' Kelly pointed her finger at the door in a gesture that brooked no argument.

Scott was back in the corridor as more medical staff rushed into Hugh Machie's room. He could feel the urgency, but there was nothing he could do. Though, with the door open, Scott could hear the long, mechanical whine, the dread lament that signalled the end of Hugh Machie's last battle. His heart had stopped before the rest of his body gave up on life.

54

Daley looked on as cases and boxes were hauled into the CID suite at Kinloch police office by Potts and his team.

'Where on earth has all this come from?' asked Daley, amazed that the run-down flat in the town that Hugh Machie had rented could possibly contain so much.

'Every cupboard and drawer was full. Boxes under the bed, on top of the wardrobe.' Potts heaved a cardboard box onto a desk. 'I don't know how he managed to carry it all, sir.'

'He must have had help. The Hugh Machie I knew was a resourceful man. Clearly he never lost the knack.' Daley picked a bundle of papers out of one box. He turned over a few pages, looking puzzled. These were bank accounts from Switzerland, Panama and the Cayman Islands. Each page documented large amounts of money. 'Potts, get everything in then go through it all. Starting with this box.' Daley pointed to the box of statements. 'I want every address, phone number, email, name – the lot. I'll put everyone I can on it to help you. This is one for up the road.'

'Yes, sir.'

Daley was still deep in thought when he sat down in his glass box. What was Hugh Machie doing with such documents?

And, more importantly, to whom did the huge sums mentioned in the statements belong?

He thought about his last conversations with Frank MacDougall. The senior members of Machie's gang were all dead. The founding notion regarding organised crime was that there had to be someone to organise it. He couldn't see Machie senior having the ability to manage such a wealth of funds. Even in his heyday he'd been muscle, a hired hand there to keep – or more often than not – enforce the rules. He was no criminal mastermind.

Daley thought back to James Machie's reappearance. That he'd gone to ground, everyone knew, even if they didn't know where he'd gone, or what he'd been doing. But surely his only reason for raising his head above the parapet was to seek revenge on his erstwhile number two Frank MacDougall, and the police officers he blamed for his criminal demise.

He was still working this through in his head when Scott burst in.

'He's away, Jimmy. Big Hughie, I mean.' Scott looked flushed – upset, even.

'To Glasgow?'

'Nah. He's *away,* away, if you get my drift.'

'Dead?'

'Aye! It's no' like you to be so slow, Jimmy.' Scott took a seat on the opposite side of Daley's desk.

'Did he say anything?'

Scott related Hugh Machie's last few minutes alive. 'Felt quite sorry for him in the end. Reminded me o' my ain faither dying.'

'But what did he mean, *There should be nobody left to remember*?'

'How should I know? He was in some state, Jimmy. Nothing left o' him. Like a skeleton in clingfilm. I'm no' sure he knew what he was talking aboot. He called me Willie – my father, you know.'

'You're not *sure*? That means you're not certain either way.'

Scott shrugged. 'I don't know what to think. He knew who I was at first.'

'Well, the end of a legend, eh?'

'Aye, it is that. The last man standing.'

'Or was he?'

'Eh?'

'Come with me and have a look at this. You're in for a surprise, Brian.'

Shona MacBride fussed over her guest. When she'd seen Daley's car pull up in front of the guest house, she was sure that Shreya Dhar had reported her for searching through her things. The truth was that she was tidy to the point of compulsive obsession. She hated the thought of bags or suitcases lying at the bottom of the wardrobe, dust gathering underneath. And, she acknowledged privately, she was inquisitive. If something was unlocked – well, she had a look inside. Not in a malicious way, for she never intended to steal or even talk about what she found. It was a compulsion. One she'd tried to break but couldn't. Ultimately, Shona MacBride was bored and lonely. Looking through the property of a guest gave her a frisson of excitement. The temptation was always too much. It had become a habit, like drugs or alcohol. She never once considered that she'd be caught.

'Can I get you anything – a cold flannel for your head, or that?'

Dhar was stretched out on the bed, her hands covering her eyes. 'You could draw the curtains, please.'

'Aye, no bother. What about a drink of something – a nice cup of tea, maybe?'

'A glass of water, please. But I just need to be alone, really. I don't mean to be rude. The migraine will ease in an hour or two. It always does.'

'Right, a glass of water it is.' The landlady bustled off, closing the door gently in her wake.

Dhar sighed, staring at the ceiling. The migraine was mild. But it had been the perfect excuse not to take to the hills with Daley, and probably Scott. She'd had enough of the double-act to last her a lifetime. It was clear that these men would only be separated by death. He and Scott protected each other. She wondered whether they would even be able to function apart. Her experience with the dead fisherman on the causeway rather proved the theory.

She beathed deeply, the ever-present smell of furniture polish strong in her room. She had enjoyed seeing Shona MacBride when Daley had delivered her to the front door of the guest house. It wasn't punishment enough for rifling through her things, but satisfying, nonetheless.

She closed her eyes for a few moments, then a passing thought sent her bolt upright in the bed. Dhar padded over to the bag that she knew Shona MacBride had opened. Inside the lining was a hidden pocket. Dhar searched it with her long fingers. She pulled out a piece of paper folded in two, opened it up and examined it. Her neat handwriting was easily legible. But what she noticed was the fold. She was also obsessed by symmetry; she always folded paper exactly in half, or quarters, running her nails along the paper to make sure it was crisp.

But this little note was no longer folded neatly in two. The crisp line she'd executed was still there, but there was another, slanting alongside.

There was a knock on her door. 'That's me with your water. Are you decent?' shouted Shona MacBride.

'Just a second, please.' Shreya Dhar hurried back to her bed and slid under the duvet.

'Okay, Mrs MacBride, come in.' But her thoughts drifted to Ian Macmillan. *How well do you know him, Mrs MacBride*? she thought.

55

Glasgow, 1992

Brian Scott was lying in a hospital bed, his shoulder heavily bandaged, arm held up in a metal frame. Ella, his mother and Jim Daley were sitting round the bed. He looked particularly disgruntled as he took in his visitors.

'This is what you get for being honest and decent, eh? They didnae mention this in the police recruitment leaflets, did they?' said Scott irritably.

'Now, son,' said his mother, a look of concern spread across her face. 'You're lucky, the shot could have hit you right in the heart.'

'Missed all your major arteries, too,' said Daley.

'Yous call this lucky? Lucky is wining the pools, nipping a good-looking lassie at the dancing. Trust me, this isnae lucky.'

'I know,' said Ella. 'They should have shot you through the heid. That way they'd have missed anything of any consequence. And if you'd been lucky enough to nip a good-looking lassie at the dancing, *I'd* have shot you. So, count your blessings!'

Scott looked at Daley. 'See, dae you get this fae Lizzie?'

The detective shook his head. 'No, to be fair, that's not one of our issues. But there are others, trust me.' He smiled ruefully.

'But you're getting a commendation from the chief constable, at least.'

'And you're no' getting one. How does that work? You've got to take a bullet before they gie you any credit? He can stick it up his arse!'

'If what I read in the paper's true, that might not be a problem,' said Daley.

'Eh?' Scott looked bemused.

'Just you concentrate on getting better, son. You've had a terrible shock.' Scott's mother patted his hand.

'No' as big a shock as getting wakened up at six in the morning for a bed bath. I'd be better back at work. You get no peace in this place. Lights on, hoovers oot in the middle o' the night. Aye, and I've got to pee in a cardboard bottle.'

'I'm glad o' the peace,' said Ella.

'On the bright side, I passed my sergeant's exam,' said Daley.

'You better be careful wae all that, Jimmy. You know fine if you pass your next ticket you'll be back on the streets as a uniform sergeant. I don't fancy a' that again. Oot in the freezing cold on a Monday night in February. This promotion lark isnae for me. I'm in oot o' the rain and that's fine and dandy.'

'You just get shot, instead,' lamented Ella. 'What's wrong with your face, anyway? You've been moaning since we arrived.'

'Och, it's this arm. I've got an itch right doon by my elbow. Pure murder, so it is. I'm glad you're here. Can you get it wae a knitting needle, Ella?'

'Would you rather a ruler or maybe a yardstick?'

Scott thought for a moment. 'Might work, though the ruler might be a wee bit on the short side.'

'That's just as well, because I don't have any of them. When did you ever see me knitting?'

'When the wean was born. You knitted that nice wee white cardigan – wae the boots and bunnet, mind?'

'That was me, son.'

'I telt you that was your mother. You never listen. Jimmy here could have knitted the damn things and you'd no' be any the wiser.'

'So, I'm left wae this bloody thing to itch all day. It's driving me mental.'

'Ask the nurses. They maybe carry aboot knitting needles – you know, in case of cardigan emergencies.' Ella pursed her lips.

There was a light knock at the door.

'I hope that's no' the physiotherapist. Man, they're rough bastards. Can you see who it is, big man?'

Daley opened the door to find Inspector John Donald standing there, a basket of fruit in one hand.

He checked his watch. 'So, this is where you are, Daley? I've been looking for you half the morning.'

'I was taking statements from witnesses in the Kennedy Path incident, sir. Thought I'd take a quick look in on Brian while I was in the Townhead.'

'Well, visiting time is over. Get back to work.' He pushed past Daley into the room.

Scott smiled, though Daley could see it was forced. 'Mum, Ella, this is my boss, DI Donald.'

'My goodness,' said Donald. 'You barely look old enough to have a son this old, Mrs Scott.'

'That's because I'm his wife, inspector.' Ella crossed her arms in disgust.

Donald grinned. 'Only my little joke. I must tell you how relieved I am – we all are – that Brian is on the mend. This has been the most worrying few days of my career.'

Daley gave Scott a knowing look from behind Donald's back.

Picking up on this, the inspector turned to Daley. 'Why are you still here?'

Ignoring his boss, Daley wished the Scotts farewell and headed back to work.

Donald placed the basket of fruit on the table at the end of the bed. 'From us all at Central CID.'

'Was it too early to buy a bottle o' whisky?' said Scott.

'Hardly what you require in order to recover, Brian. Fruit is the very thing.' He picked an apple from the basket and sunk his teeth into it. 'Hope you don't mind.'

'Right,' said Ella. 'We better get a move on. I'll need to get your mother home, then back and make something for the tea before Martha finishes school.'

'Right, Ella.' Scott's mother kissed her son on the cheek. 'You take it easy, Brian.'

'I'm pinned to the bed, Mother. I'm no' off to the dancing, if that's what you're worried aboot.'

She turned to Donald. 'I hope he's no' as cheeky to you, inspector?'

'No, he isn't.' Donald's tone was sharp.

When wife and mother had departed, John Donald closed the door.

'How's Constable White?' said Scott.

'My next stop. He's been lucky – a bit like you.'

'Aye, lucky that Traffic turned up when they did. If they hadnae, me and Jimmy would be on a slab right now.'

Donald took another bite of the apple and chewed it noisily, discarding what was left in the fruit basket. 'You appear to be a marked man, DC Scott. I wonder why?'

Scott did his best to shrug but winced with the pain. 'You tell me, sir?'

'I think it's the old "if you play with fire" maxim.'

'I don't know what you mean.'

'Don't get too close to the sun, then. Anyway, I'm perfectly aware you know exactly what I mean.'

'With the greatest respect, sir – the fire or the sun? You're talking in riddles. But I have a question.'

'Which is?'

'That night – you know, when me and Jimmy were in that garage.'

'Yes.'

'Why didn't you send back-up like we requested?'

'I had a code twenty-one to deal with, as you know. And anyway, we had no intelligence that you would be in any real danger. Is that good enough for you?'

'That's no' what Sergeant Ramsay says, sir.'

'You and Ramsay have built up quite the rapport, I see.'

'Eh?'

'You appear to be very friendly, all of a sudden.'

'Good bloke. Knows his job.'

'I see.' Donald walked round the bed and examined Scott's plastered shoulder. He examined the frame holding up Scott's arm. 'Must be sore – at least uncomfortable?'

'Aye, what do you think?'

In one quick movement, Donald caught Scott's injured arm and twisted it. Brian Scott yelled in pain. He felt the room swimming before his eyes. 'Ya bastard!'

Donald leaned over him. 'Perhaps worth remembering who's in charge, DC Scott.'

'Fuck you!'

'Most of all, better not to go running to DCI Burns at the first opportunity with these ridiculous tales.'

'Who's going to stop me – no' you!' Scott's face was still contorted in pain.

'I must say, your wife is a good-looking woman. Fuck knows why she chose to get hitched to you.' John Donald's newly acquired accent and manners suddenly deserted him. 'And such a nice wedding ring. That must have cost you a pretty penny, eh?'

'I don't know what you're talking about.'

'Oh, I think you know exactly what I'm talking about, Brian. And you must be watchful. Machie will have to lie low after this. But he has so many friends – dangerous ones too, I believe.' He sneered at the stricken man.

The door to the room swung open, and a nurse rushed in. 'I heard a scream. Is everything okay, Mr Scott?' She glanced at Donald warily.

'Brian had a spasm, nurse. I'm his superior, Detective Inspector Donald.' He held out a hand, which she ignored.

'Aye, I'm okay, nurse. You know, just turned the wrong way.' Brian glared at his boss.

'Right then. As long as you're feeling fine now.' She left the room, looking back with a worried glance.

'Well, I'd better be off. "A" Division CID doesn't run itself, you know.'

Scott turned his head away. 'What's the news on Machie, anyway?'

'It's been a few days since your little escapade. Everyone is pushing, of course. But a hardened criminal like him . . . well, he'll have had a plan in place. I doubt he's even in the country by now.'

'Huh, you don't say.'

'As I *do* say, Brian. Be careful. In fact, I think you'll have to be *very* careful . . . for a very long time.'

Suddenly, the young detective felt vulnerable – very vulnerable indeed.

56

The next day dawned cold. A thin line of frozen mist hung over the loch as folk hurried to and fro in thick coats and heavy gloves. The harbour was quiet, only a few fishermen working on their boats or their nets, or standing chatting, their collective breath rising in clouds in the freezing air. The sun, if it existed at all, had yet to show its face on this Kinloch morning.

In the police office, Daley was busy in the production room helping the team who were going through the late Hugh Machie's possessions with a fine toothcomb. He picked up a box of rounds that fitted the old Webley revolver the dead man had used in so many criminal enterprises over the years. He stared at it for a while, wondering how Machie had managed to conceal himself for so long, and where all the money fitted into the picture. Not just the bundles of notes in his possession, but the documents describing far greater sums.

Scott leaned round the door. 'A word, Jimmy?'

'I need a coffee. We can do this in the canteen, right?'

'Aye, sure,' Scott replied. In fact, he'd spent another sleepless night. Perhaps the third in a row. His abstinence from alcohol had induced all the stages to which he was so accustomed. But knowing what was to come didn't make it any easier to endure.

They grabbed two coffees and sat at a corner table in the canteen. Daley watched as Scott held on to his beverage with both hands but still struggled to put the mug to his lips.

'You're suffering, Brian. You shouldn't be here.'

'Aye, you keep saying, Jimmy. I should be in the hands o' the professionals. I've heard it – a lot.'

Daley sighed. 'You know you're doing the right thing. But it could be so much easier with proper support.'

'Nah. I got drunk, so I can get sober.'

'What have you got?'

Scott laid a file on the table and opened it. He struggled to place his reading glasses on the bridge of his nose with his trembling hands, but eventually managed to manoeuvre them in the right direction, albeit at a jaunty angle.

'Right, this list o' benefactors that Hughie gave to Campbell the lawyer.'

'Including us?'

'Aye, including us.'

'Okay, what about it?'

'Everyone – I mean all of them – are victims of Machie junior in one way or another. In some cases – quite a few, in fact – the money has been left to next o' kin. Sons, daughters, wives, that type o' thing.'

It took Daley a few minutes to take this in. 'So, old Hughie was trying to right wrongs using his son's ill-gotten gains?'

'Looks like it.'

'What about the foreign bank statements?'

'All scanned and up the road. Oor financial crimes boys are on it. They're being circulated, too. Bugger me, I think those statements are halfway roon the world, from what I hear.'

Daley sipped at his coffee. 'Takes you back a bit, Brian, doesn't it?'

'Patterson's garage?'

'Yeah. If he'd done what Jay-Mac wanted him to do, well . . .' He hesitated. 'Neither of us would be here. The cavalry would never have arrived in time.'

Scott nodded, gave up on his coffee and put it back on the table with a thud that sent the beverage spilling over the side of the mug. 'I know. I've been playing it over and over in my mind for years. You must be the same.'

'Yup.'

'Then I'll ask again: what changed from then till now? He doesn't kill us all those years ago then tries to gun us down here, just after he left us a pile of dosh. Doesnae make sense, Jimmy.'

'I killed his son.'

'Hughie hated him. Surely his will shows that, and remorse too. For his own actions, but mostly for the son who caused so much pain to folk.'

'But can you really hate your own flesh and blood?' Daley tried to imagine having such feelings for his own son and couldn't.

'You can if he's a psychopathic murdering scumbag, Jimmy. He cracked his faither o'er the heid wae a half brick when he was in his teens. Near killed him. I remember the whole scheme on aboot it. They went at it in the middle o' the street in broad daylight. You didnae need TV where I came fae.'

'I suppose. We'll have to send your conclusions up the road too, Bri. But I'll make sure they know who worked it out.'

The pair sat in silence for a while. Two uniformed officers helped themselves to hot drinks and sat nearby, cradling the mugs to warm up their hands.

'Mind those days? Freezing your bollocks off a' winter. Bugger that.'

'I remember you saying that a long time ago. Just after I passed my sergeant's exam, I think.'

'I've been saying it for years. Aye, and I've no' changed my mind, neither.'

The canteen door swung open again. This time DS Shreya Dhar swept in and looked round the room. Spotting Daley and Scott she headed to their table and took a seat beside the latter.

'It's bloody freezing out there.'

'You're in the countryside. Wait till the gales start,' said Scott.

'How's the head?' Daley asked.

'Fine now, thanks, sir. Just needed to lie down in a darkened room for a while.'

'Good. So, you're up for a little wander in the hills?'

She smiled. 'Yes, of course. Let's see if we can pin anything on this bastard Macmillan.'

'Great. If we leave at eleven, that should give us plenty of daylight to have a poke about. Hamish was quite specific about where he'd been spotted. Will you give Potts a hand, please, Brian? They have another third or so to go through.'

'Do you mean Hugh Machie's things, sir?' said Dhar.

'I do. Some big surprises there, let me tell you.'

'I'm sure.'

'Do you not want me to come up the hill wae you, Jimmy?'

'Nah, it's just a two-person job, Brian. Your turn to stay in the warm.'

'Admirable attention to inclusivity,' said Dhar.

'Sorry?'

'*Two-person.* I like it.'

'What it always should have been.' Daley got to his feet. 'I have some calls to make. We'll head off after that. Get yourself a hot drink, Shreya. You'll be glad you have when we get up there.'

In his apartment at the County Hotel, Ian Macmillan was sitting with his head in his hands. His mobile phone was lying on the floor at his feet, a large crack across its screen. He'd thrown it down in frustration after reading a message half an hour before.

He'd heard of people paralysed by fear and hopelessness, but he had never realised that it was an actual thing. But that was his condition now. He didn't know whether to stick or twist. He was literally and metaphorically stuck in the middle of something he was sure would cost him everything, perhaps even his life.

It was strange, really. He'd grown up with lots of advantages in life. Good looks, a decent brain and parents who could afford to make sure that he had a top education. Until his wife began to spend cash like a drunken sailor on shore leave, it had all seemed so easy – effortless, almost. He ate at the best restaurants, drove the nicest cars, dressed in designer suits. But he'd been through this so many times in his head. Now he was sure that it would all end here, in this small town, thousands of miles away from the place he called home.

He had to force himself from the couch to pick up the phone. In the time that had elapsed since he'd pitched it there, Macmillan had tried to tell himself that perhaps he'd misread the message. That the stress he felt had somehow rearranged the words on the screen. But when he read it again, there was no room for misinterpretation.

Macmillan looked at his watch. He swore under his breath as he picked a bottle of whisky from a cabinet. There was no point in bothering with a glass. He put the bottle to his lips and glugged down a few mouthfuls. It made him retch, but he managed to swallow back the mixture of bile and spirit that burned his mouth and throat.

His window looked out over Main Street. Freezing fog made it almost impossible to see the other side of the road. The town looked odd, ethereal, as though he'd suddenly been deposited in another place entirely. But Ian Macmillan was all too aware of his circumstances and location.

The Canadian had often watched films where people were left with few choices: cornered victims of their communities, or at least of some of the people who lived there. *Run away, why don't you run away?* he remembered thinking to himself. But the reality was different. There were some things from which one could never escape. Situations that almost seemed to have been preordained, so bizarre were the circumstances that led to their creation. Macmillan had never believed in fate, or chance – any of the things that people would use to cover their own flaws or regrets. In many ways, he still felt he was right. But now it seemed that destiny was inescapable; the inevitability of fate appeared to be immovable.

He took another glug of whisky, more measured this time. He didn't want to make himself sick again, but he needed to be anaesthetised against his own reality. It was what people did, wasn't it?

In the bathroom, Macmillan doused his face with handful after handful of freezing water in an attempt to clear his head. But no clarity would come. In truth, he was a lemming, bounding quickly and determinedly to his own demise.

He made his way to the bedroom. Perhaps he still had options; maybe the course of his life was still in his own hands. He removed a bottle of strong painkillers from a drawer in his bedside cabinet. He'd been given them after sustaining a shoulder injury playing tennis. He'd kept hold of the tablets – handy things to have around, he thought.

It was then he reasoned that maybe this was all part of the plan, the plotted conclusion to his own story. He grabbed the bottle and returned to the whisky. He sat back on the sofa with the pills and the alcohol. This was it. His destiny wasn't to kill innocent people. It was to die here on the couch in this miserable place with nobody at his side.

He had no illusions about his family. He was a human cash machine, a mere functionary. His existence only served to keep them fed, watered, clothed, housed – and all the rest of the shit that he'd showered on them over the years that had brought him to this very place. This was the price of kindness.

Ian Macmillan poured a handful of pills into the palm of his right hand. He stared at them for a moment before thrusting the tablets into his mouth and washing them down with two gulps of whisky.

He looked at his watch – just after ten. He gazed round the room as tears spilled down his cheeks. This was the end. Macmillan closed his eyes. It took a few minutes, or so it seemed, but soon he could feel himself drifting. His troubled mind began to calm; the fear was draining away.

He was pulled from this slow tumble into death by two hands on his shoulder. It felt as though he was being pulled backwards and forwards, roughed up.

'Okay, okay!' Macmillan shouted, his eyes still pressed shut, not wanting to leave the place of growing calm he'd just entered. 'Leave me alone, please!'

The hands disappeared from his shoulder. He opened his eyes and turned round. There was nobody in the room.

For the second time that morning, Macmillan felt the bile rise in his throat. He rushed into the bathroom and was violently sick. His body convulsed again and again, as though consciously purging itself of the poison intended to end its existence.

He wiped his face clean, stomach aching, throat burning, and looked at his watch: ten past ten. He couldn't believe that so little time had elapsed since he'd swallowed the tablets. He ran from the bathroom into the lounge and looked out of the window, convinced that he must have slept for twelve hours. The pills hadn't killed him. It must surely be night-time.

But outside on Main Street, the freezing fog still hung in the air like a curse.

He sniffed the air like a dog in a field of sheep. He recognised the smell but couldn't place it. Then it dawned on him.

Macmillan ran out into the corridor on the top floor of the County Hotel. He didn't make for the stairs. Instead, he turned right and headed for the last door on the landing. He pulled the bunch of keys from his waist and fumbled one of them into the lock.

The room was the same as on his previous visit – virtually as she'd left it. All he could smell was the lingering aroma of Annie's perfume. Was it just his imagination?

He fell to the floor, sobbing.

57

Hamish had woken early, as always. No matter how much whisky he'd consumed the night before or how tired he'd been the previous evening, his body was stuck to an alarm set long ago for early starts at the fishing.

He had seen the day dawn over the island. It seemed to emerge in the cold, grey light like some hulking colossus, thrusting up from the dark, still waters of the fog-bound loch.

Hamish hated these kinds of days. A cold, misty morning took him back to the day his mother had died. He could still see her lifeless face staring up from the scullery floor, a pan of fish stew boiling dry on the hob. He pictured the men in their dark uniforms as they carried her down the stairs from the flat and into the ambulance, their breath like a pall as they went. He'd known Dougie and Donnie well. They were mechanics at the Argyll Garage. But, in this small community in those long-ago days, they doubled as ambulance drivers when circumstances required.

It had been one of the saddest days of Hamish's life.

So it was with maudlin thoughts that the old man broke his normal habit and returned to the warmth of his bed, happy to sleep the cold and mist away until the sun broke through once more.

He was tired, and soon felt himself drifting back to sleep.

'Hamish.' The voice was soft, familiar but distant, as though he was being addressed from another room.

'We're no' going oot the day, Mother. The engine's fair buggered. I telt Sandy often enough, but he widna listen. She's up on Galbraith's slip. Let me lie a whiles.'

'Hamish.' The voice again. This time louder, more urgent.

The old fisherman opened his eyes, blinking the sleep away. He forced himself from his side on to his back and stared at the woman at the end of his bed.

'Annie. It's you, lassie.'

She smiled at him, the mist she'd brought in with her swirling all around the tiny bedroom. Her red dress was like a bright light on a stormy night at sea.

'I never got to say goodbye, Hamish.'

'No, you broke my heart.' Hamish felt a fat tear meander down his leathery cheek.

'I'm sorry. But there was nothing I could do.' Her words swirled, as though modulated by the mist. 'You were gone. I was sad.'

'Aye, but you had so many folk who loved you. Man, the whole toon was near cried dry the day we lost you.'

'I'm sorry.'

'Stop saying sorry, for you've nothing to be sorry aboot.'

'I tried, but they were too strong.'

'Whoot?'

'I should have tried harder.'

'I canna follow you at all, lassie. Tell me!'

Through the shimmering mist he could see her smile. The smile that he'd seen so many times on the face of the woman he loved like a daughter.

'Follow your heart, Hamish. Just follow your heart. The truth is there.' She held up her hand to wave.

'Wait! You're no' going to fly off, you've only jeest arrived. I canna take it again, Annie. The pain's too much.' Hamish could feel the sob shake his shoulders.

'Goodbye, Hamish. I love you – love you all. Kinloch, my friends, everyone. But don't be sad, for I'll see you soon.'

The mist closed round her like a curtain. She was gone.

'Lassie, no!' He shot bolt upright in his bed. Hamish the cat, curled at his feet, looked at him balefully, hissed and tucked his head back under his tail. There was no mist to be seen, only the cold light of morning as it seeped through snags in the old curtains. It might have been a dream, but it seemed all too real.

Daley and Shreya Dhar were kitted out in warm jackets, stout boots, gloves and hats. It was cold, but both were anxious to see if they could find any trace of Ian Macmillan's recent trip up the hill.

'I'm no' going, and me called Scott, tae,' said Brian.

'We're going now; we may be some time,' said Daley with a wink.

'Be as long as you like,' said Scott, missing the reference completely.

They tramped through the office and out into Daley's SUV.

'I'm looking forward to this,' said Dhar, taking in the still all-encompassing freezing fog.

'No cliffs to fall off, just rolling hills. As long as we're careful, we'll be fine.' Daley started the car. 'Gets us out of the office. Though, to be honest, I'm not sure he'll have left much behind. Certainly not if he's the criminal genius everyone seems to think he is.'

They were nearing the roundabout at the bottom of Main Street when Daley spotted a figure in his wing mirror. A man was standing on the corner waving his arms frantically.

'It's Hamish. I'll go round here and see what he wants.' Daley pulled the car through a full circle on the roundabout and stopped by the kerb on which Hamish stood. 'What's up, my friend?'

'It was him!' Hamish's voice was shrill, his expression as dark as night.

'Who?'

'Macmillan. That bastard killed oor Annie. I know it for a fact.'

Dhar leaned over Daley to speak to Hamish. 'How can you know this?'

'A dream, simple as that. She came to visit me. Clearer than this day, it was. She was wearing her red dress. Aye, and by the sound o' it he wasn't alone when he did it. They must have held her down – killed that beautiful lassie.' Tears filled Hamish's eyes.

While Dhar looked momentarily preoccupied as she tried to take in this information, Daley put his hand out of the window and grabbed Hamish by the shoulder. 'Listen, I know you're upset, I understand. But it was a dream. You shouldn't be out in this weather – it's freezing. Get back home and have a nice mug of tea. Put a dram in it.'

'No, I'm no' going back home. I'm off to confront that murderer myself.'

'You can't do that, Hamish.' Daley looked at him sternly. 'I know how you feel – what you feel. But this isn't your fight.

And remember, the pathologist found nothing suspicious about Annie's death when she . . . well, when she died.' He cursed his awkwardness.

'You'll forgive me, but I canna understand why you haven't brought this evil man to justice yet. I'm sorry, Mr Daley, but you're wrong. You know me, the things I see. You must trust me this time, too.'

Daley lowered his voice as someone passed by. 'You have to listen to me. We're on his case this minute. If you go and do something stupid, it could ruin everything. The last thing we want is to warn him. He'll take off, and there'd be nothing we could do about it. You know how this works: we have to gather evidence, make a case. You could set him free if you interfere. You have to trust me, Hamish.'

The old man shivered as he gazed at Daley's face. He looked smaller, more vulnerable somehow. It was as though the sorrow of Annie's death had worn him down, left him diminished. 'I know you to be an honest man, Mr Daley. And there's no' many good honest folk aboot these days.' He nodded. 'Aye, I'll do as you say. But any inkling this devil o' a man is going to escape justice – well, I won't answer for my ain actions.'

'You have my word, I promise.' Daley held out his hand and Hamish shook it firmly.

'That's good enough for me. I'll head to the Douglas Arms for a dram or two. Jeest to take the chill off, mark you.'

They said their goodbyes. Daley drove off with Dhar frowning in the passenger seat.

'Problem?' asked Daley.

'If I'm being honest, sir, yes.'

'Go ahead. I believe in open discussions in this job.

How many have walked free because thoughts or instinct haven't been passed on?'

'I'm sorry, but I just don't understand why you see fit to divulge so much information to this old man. He's not a police officer. He shouldn't be apprised of our every move. If there is a case against Macmillan, well, we try to find proof. But making empty promises to an old drunk is dangerous. At least as far as I'm concerned.' She looked away, choosing the view from the passenger window instead.

'How long is your service, DS Dhar? Eight years, something like that?'

'Nearly ten.'

'Can I give you the benefit of my experience?'

Dhar shrugged.

'That *old drunk*, as you call him, saved my life.'

'Oh, I'm sorry. I didn't know that.'

'No reason you would.' Daley sighed. 'All I'm saying is, try not to rush to judgement. There are things in the world none of us can explain. Hamish – and yes, he likes a drink – has a talent for seeing stuff that I can't see. I never write him off, no matter how outrageous. As a police officer it pays to listen – listen and remember.'

'If you say so, sir.'

'Thank you.'

They drove to the hill in silence. Daley took the car to the end of a steep lane. The fog up here was even thicker – so bad, in fact, that the town below was only an outline in a sea of white, a bit like a colouring book. It was almost as though Kinloch was slowly being erased from the face of the earth.

'Wow, it's bad, right enough,' he said.

'But you said it would be okay.'

He looked at his watch. Almost twelve. 'It should thin soon. I haven't seen a fog like this here, but I can't think it'll last all afternoon.' He pointed ahead. 'We go through that gate and follow the path until we get to where Macmillan was spotted. Then we can have a poke around.'

'Okay, I'm up for that.' She touched the sleeve of Daley's thick jacket. 'I'm sorry. I spoke out of turn.'

'No need to apologise. I'd rather hear what you have to say than for you to bottle it up.'

They left the car and were soon eaten up in a swirl of mist.

58

It had been days since Brian Scott had touched alcohol, and he was feeling it badly. Really badly.

He couldn't keep his hands still, even if he tried to hold one in the other. His whole body was trembling, or so it seemed. His mind was a scramble of paranoia, fear and gut-churning sadness. It was the lot of the heavy drinker; with no alcohol to blunt the sharp edges, the world seemed an almost impossible place to face.

His thoughts turned to his father. He remembered him holding the grandson who bore his name. Willie Scott was yellow; his skin, the whites of his eyes – even his fingernails bore the tinge. His liver and kidneys were failing and there was nothing the doctors could do.

As Brian Scott gazed through bloodshot eyes at his reflection in the mirror, he knew he had to stop drinking for good. He also knew that Daley was right, he should seek professional help. But he couldn't face that either. The thought of being locked away for weeks, the process, the cold, lonely nights away from Ella.

He'd watched Hugh Machie die. The man he'd known since childhood had been reduced to a grey ghost in an antiseptic room, with only a nurse and a police officer to watch his last few moments. Hell wasn't just waiting for him to arrive, it was there, ready to consume his soul.

Scott was well aware that Jim Daley, his oldest friend, suffered these bouts of melancholy without over-indulging in drink. He didn't envy him. It was hard to concentrate when even holding a cup of coffee without spilling it seemed like a Herculean task.

The door to the men's room flew open.

'Right, here you are.' Potts was reflected in the mirror.

'I cannae even get peace in the bog. What is it?'

'We've found some stuff I don't get – among Hugh Machie's things, I mean.'

'Like what?'

'Kids' stuff. You know, crayon drawings, wee keepsakes, that kind of thing. I thought you might want a look.'

'Can I have a pee first?'

'Of course.'

'That's really kind o' you, Potts. You'll make a great gaffer one day.'

'You kidding? I don't know what rank I am from one day to the next. My career seems tied to yours. If you go get a bump, so do I. Aye, and the other way round, too.'

'Don't hold your breath for that. You've mair chance at a shot o' playing for the Rangers than relying on me to help you up the ladder. Doon, aye, that's nae bother.'

'I don't support Rangers.'

'See, there you go. That's your problem.'

'St Johnstone's my team.'

'My case rests, your honour. Now bugger off and gie me some peace for a minute.'

Alone again, Scott held his hands out in front of his eyes.

'Bugger me, jazz hands,' he said to himself before splashing some water on his face.

The narrow path was steeper than Daley remembered. He and Liz had trudged up this way not long after they'd arrived in Kinloch. He'd been on one of his endless drives to stay fit and lose weight. He recalled how Liz had positively skipped up the hill. DS Dhar was doing likewise. The joys of youth and good health, he thought as he felt a twinge in his chest. The wisdom of this little jaunt was less and less obvious the further they climbed.

'Look,' said Dhar, pointing back the way they'd come. 'You can't see Kinloch at all now.'

'No,' Daley replied as he fought to catch his breath. The combination of cold, fog and exertion didn't make for pleasant exercise, he decided.

'So, where are we, roughly?' Dhar removed a smartphone from her pocket and checked their progress on GPS. 'Looks like there's a slope coming soon.'

'Yes, it's a false summit. When you look at it from below the hill it doesn't look that way, but it's down and up to reach the top.' He was bent over now, propping his arms on his knees.

'How far are we from where Macmillan was spotted?'

Daley thought for a moment. 'Well, he was heading down the slope into the little glen. We can't be far away.'

'We go down the slope?'

'Yes.'

'Do you want to take a moment or two?'

Jim Daley was many things, but he'd never been keen on showing weakness, regardless of his physical condition.

'No, we plough on. The going will be easier when we start walking downhill.'

'I'm not looking forward to getting old,' said Dhar.

'Why? It's fabulous. Everything stops working, you can't remember why you walk into rooms, every part of you aches and instead of going to parties you get to attend funerals. What's not to like?'

She laughed. 'I thought Brian was the witty one.'

'Don't let reputations fool you.'

'Talking of things stopping working, the bloody phone signal's gone.'

'Now that is an advantage of getting old. You can remember the happy days when our lives weren't predicated on the strength of our 5G.'

'If you say so, boss. Are we good to go?'

'Yeah, absolutely.' With legs felt feeling like great blocks of stone, Daley pressed on in the wake of DS Dhar.

Hidden by the fog, a man stood down in the little glen. He could hear the voices from above. They were muffled, distant. Knowing what he had to do, he retreated from the path and was careful to stay out of sight.

For Ian Macmillan, there were no choices left. A mixture of fate and stupidity had brought him here. Now there was only one way back down the hill, both literally and metaphorically. He cursed his weakness, every mistake he'd made along life's long road. Up here, in this cold, white world, it was almost the way he'd imagined death: endless nothingness.

He tried to remember everything he'd been told. But even if all went as planned, the best outcome would still leave blood on his hands. The overwhelming feeling that he should have had the courage to take his own life earlier that day was almost unbearable. He weighed up thoughts of the living hell he'd been through in Kinloch. The lies, the deceit, the cunning – none of which he was good at.

As he made his way to where he'd been told to wait, he tried desperately to think of anything to mitigate the actions he'd have to take in order to stay alive. The more he tried to persuade himself that it was survival of the fittest, the less the notion convinced him.

One thing he couldn't force from his mind was the sight of the woman's eyes, wide with desperation as she was pinned down in the bed and so gently force-fed the drugs that would take her life.

Suddenly, impossibly, there was that scent again.

Macmillan clenched his teeth. 'Leave me alone, you bitch,' he muttered, but he knew she never would.

59

Hamish was sitting in the pool room of the Douglas Arms. This part of the pub was only busy at nights. Though he didn't particularly want to be with other people, he felt as though he couldn't bear his own company. The sensation was a strange one. He had lived for years quite happily in the little cottage with only Hamish the cat to talk to. But Annie's death had changed all that.

The old fisherman had been through a lot in his life; he was too old to suffer more sadness and loneliness. Now, the bad times didn't recede the way they once had. They said time was a healer, but now it just seemed like a burden. The grating pain of losing the ones he'd loved had faded when he was still young, though little spikes, like the thorns of a rose bush, pricked his memory from time to time, just enough for that sadness never to be completely forgotten. But now Hamish reckoned that the quota of misery he could endure in one lifetime had reached its limit. He was like a huge glass of whisky, filled to the brim. The loss of Annie had forced his spirit over the edge, letting it spill to the floor and into oblivion.

In his hand he had a large dram. He took a gulp and leaned his head back against the wall. The usual noises of a quiet bar on a cold day washed over him: the fruit machine burst into a life of its own from time to time just to remind people it was there; bottles clinked in their cases as the barman restocked the shelves; the till bleeped open and closed as a handful of customers bought drinks; the TV blethered away, but the muttering voice had no meaning for Hamish.

Having had a disturbed night, he felt tired, drained almost. A mix of sleep and whisky washed over him. He closed his eyes.

He was on the pier, and the boat he was stepping on to wasn't his little lobster vessel, but a proper fishing boat. The *Girl Maggie* looked as though she'd been newly painted, everything spick and span. This puzzled Hamish, as this was by no means her natural state.

'Where have you been? A big night on the whisky, no doubt.' The voice was familiar at once.

'I was in my bed by nine.' Hamish heard himself speak, but the voice had a higher, clear, youthful pitch and felt odd on his tongue. 'Man, you've got her in fine fettle, Sandy.' Hamish took in the polished brass, the varnished wheelhouse and shiny new funnel. 'Must have cost a few shillings.'

Hoynes stroked his beard and puffed on a new pipe. 'When you embark upon your last voyage, it's important to make sure everything is right and proper.' Another puff of tobacco smoke drifted into the white sky. 'Comes to us all, Hamish.'

'We canna go oot in this, skipper.'

'You canna.'

'What dae you mean?'

'I have to skipper this journey myself, for it's one from which I'll no' return.'

'Don't say that, Sandy.'

'I've jeest said it. That was a stupid statement if ever I

392

heard one. The booze is having a fair impact on your intellect. Aye, an' no' for the better, neithers.'

'Och, your backside. I like a few, but it's only social drinking.'

Sandy Hoynes burst into fits of laughter, his fat cheeks wobbling under an ample white beard. 'That's the same thing your ain faither used to say. Aye, you'll be taking this trip before long, I'm thinking.'

'You used to be a cheery bugger. I'm no' sure jeest what's happened to you at all.'

'Nae wonder. You never came to visit me – well, hardly. Och, I saw you staring doon at my stone noo and again. But it was just in the passing when you were away to lay somebody else under the turf. I never thought you'd turn oot such a scunner – especially wae me leaving you the captaincy o' this fine vessel.'

'Aye, and I sailed her until she'd sail no more. I kept my promise to you and made sure Mrs Hoynes never wanted for anything.'

'You did, and it's to your credit, right enough. Even though you could never make it into the Smuggler's Hole without battering her off thon sandbank. But I forgive you.'

'That's a piece o' nonsense. In any case, you'd burned your boats long afore.'

'It was the feasting hall for me, right enough.'

'Valhalla, you always said.'

'Better than sitting in the County Hotel wae the sad eyes and an empty glass in your hand. I warned you aboot that. Why you never found the right lassie, I'll never know. Man, you would have had a happier life – shorter, likely, but happier all the same.'

'Shorter?'

'You'd have been kept on your toes by a wife. None o' this mooning aboot like a wet weekend in Blaan telling tales o' the future, like some washed-oot seer ready to rob decent folk o' their coin.'

'I never took as much as a penny. And I shut my mouth aboot maist o' what I saw, into the bargain.'

'Well, you missed this one, Nostradamus.'

'Eh?'

'I'm waiting on my passengers. Ach, there's mair money in ferrying, these days. No' a fish to be had, they tell me.'

'What passengers?'

'Take a look up thonder.' Hoynes pointed up Ben Saarnie with the stem of his pipe.

Hamish grabbed a pair of binoculars which was hanging from a hook on the side of the wheelhouse. It took him a few moments to set the focus to suit his own eyes, but when he did, the sight before him made the bile rise in his throat.

Standing side by side, their heads bowed, arms outstretched, were Daley and Scott. Though neither was nailed to a cross, they were hanging there, as blood and gore dripped from their pale corpses.

'Hamish!' The owner of the Douglas Arms was shaking the old man's arm.

'Have you hit on a proud shoal, Sandy?' The old man blinked into wakefulness.

'What? You were screaming. You must have drifted off to sleep, you stupid auld bugger. Aye, and you spilled your dram into the bargain.'

Hamish thought for a moment, then a look of panic crossed his face. 'I need to be off, my friend.'

'Take a wee drink to calm doon, why don't you? It's hellish weather to be aboot the day.'

'No, there's no time for that.'

Hamish rushed to his feet and out of the Douglas Arms as fast as his old legs would carry him.

60

Scott returned to the productions room, where the search of Hugh Machie's belongings was almost complete. Papers were stacked in neat bundles, as were photographs. Scott picked up a few and looked through them. He recognised the younger Hugh and his wife standing at the door of a council house. By the look of things – cars, fashions and hairstyles – Scott reckoned he'd have been in short trousers when this picture was snapped. It brought back memories of his own home, not far away in those days.

'Sir, this is what I was talking about, here,' said Potts.

A cardboard box was filled with all sorts. There were little paintings, clearly wrought by a child's hand. He picked out a piece of yellowed paper, a long line of the same letter, written over and over again down half of the page. It was a youthful attempt at writing practice. Scott remembered doing something similar himself at school. He smiled at a rough watercolour of a rainbow over a field of sheep. The animals looked like fluffy clouds with stick legs and broad smiling faces.

'My weans did all this stuff,' said Scott. 'Do you not remember doing it when you were at school?'

DC Potts shrugged. 'I suppose so.'

'There's no doubting your long-term memory, son.' Scott shook his head as he picked out another painting. A man with blond hair was holding a little girl by the hand. He towered over her, but both had the same bold smiles as the painting of the sheep and the rainbow. 'It's certainly someone close. Might well be early masterpieces by James Machie himself. The old boy kept them all these years. Touching, in a way. But I'm surprised.'

'Why?'

'Because they hated each other. Jay-Mac was a problem even when he was a kid. It wisnae happy families in that hoose, let me tell you.'

'How many years ago would that have been?'

Scott thought for a moment. 'I don't know – fifty odd. That evil bastard was a bit older than me – only two or three years in it, mind.'

Potts produced another sheet of paper. 'Look at this.'

'Aye, what aboot it?'

'It's long division and multiplication, right?'

'Good for you! Amazing powers of detection, Potts. Imagine you recognising this kind of stuff. I'm impressed. You'll be sitting in Jimmy's seat before you know it.'

Potts rolled his eyes. 'No, this way of doing it – the way they work out these sums. It's not the way I was taught. My kids bring this stuff home. It's like double Dutch to me. My wife sorts it out.'

'What are you saying?'

'There's no way that James Machie learned this way. And anyway, the paper would be older-looking. Pencil wouldn't last this long. It would be much more faded.'

'Aye, I suppose you're right.'

397

'Did he have any other children – much younger, I mean. Other than James?'

'No, no' younger. Not that I know of, anyway.'

'Could be grandkids, I suppose.'

'Could be nieces and nephews, for all we know – or the boy next door. You know what old folk get like. James was his only son, remember.'

'I don't think it's a wee boy.'

'Why?'

'Look at the picture of them holding hands. That blue triangle on the child is a skirt.'

'Right enough,' said Scott.

The phone in the room burst into life. Two short rings, an internal call.

Scott picked up the phone. It was Shaw at the front desk.

'Brian, you have a visitor. A very agitated one, at that.'

'Who is it, Alasdair?'

'Just come through, will you?'

Daley and Shreya Dhar were almost halfway down the hill heading into the little glen when Daley lost his footing on a wet piece of ground. As he tried desperately to regain his balance, the toe of his boot caught on a loose boulder, pitching him forward and sending him head first down the slope.

'Sir!' shouted Dhar as she hurried after him, being careful not to take a tumble herself.

Daley had come to a stop in a little dip on the muddy hillside. He was groaning with pain. Dhar hurried to his side.

'Sir, are you okay?'

'I think I've sprained my ankle,' said Daley, reaching for it desperately.

'Stay still, I'll take a look.' She kneeled over him and gently pulled his trouser leg away from his right ankle. 'Oh, I think rather more than just sprained.' Her expression was serious.

'Broken?'

'Yes, it looks like it, Jim.'

'Bastard!' Daley swore loudly then apologised to Dhar for the outburst. 'Sorry. Too used to being with Brian.'

Dhar didn't reply; she was studying the screen on her phone. 'On the map it looks as though there's a building of some kind. It's not far, a bit off the path.' She looked out into the fog. Visibility was no more than a few yards. 'It's in this direction.' She pointed to the left of where Daley had landed.

'How far, do you think?'

'A hundred yards, no more.'

'Funny, I can't remember seeing a building when I was last up here.'

Dhar showed him her phone. 'You know what it's like these days, sir.'

Sure enough, a satellite image showed the roof of a structure nearby.

'It may be hidden from sight from the path.' She shrugged.

'And if I can get there?'

'I don't know. At least I can find you easily, and you'll be inside out of the elements.'

'You'll retrace our route until you get a phone signal?'

'Yes, exactly.'

'I could try and get back to the car.'

'With the greatest of respect, sir, you'll never make it back up the hill. I'll try and get you back up on one foot. I can be a crutch until we make it to this – whatever it is.'

'Okay, we'll give it a go.'

It took a few moments of agony for Daley, and sheer effort on Dhar's part, before the detective was upright. 'Put your arm round my shoulder, sir. It shouldn't take us long,' Dhar said breathlessly.

The first few steps were agony. But with Daley hopping along while leaning on Dhar, they started to make progress. It wasn't long before a building began to take shape out of the mist.

'Not far now, sir.' Dhar was sweating with the effort of helping her bulky colleague. Daley himself looked white as a sheet, his face contorted in pain.

Another couple of minutes found them standing outside a small steading. At one time a family might have called this home, but even with an intact roof it would have been a cramped, unwelcoming one. As it was, it would serve as a temporary shelter while Dhar sought help.

With Daley propped up against a broken door jamb, Dhar pulled forward a wooden crate with the word *Feed* stencilled on the side, now barely visible. She pushed down on it with both hands until she was confident it was sound enough to take some weight. Athletically, she levered herself up on to it, then jumped back to the hard earthen floor.

'It's okay to sit on, sir.'

'You mean it'll take my weight?' Daley did his best to laugh but winced instead.

'It's not a sun-lounger, sir, but it'll be more comfortable than standing there. Even when I raise the alarm, they won't get here for a while.'

'True.'

She pushed the crate against a stone wall, and with no little effort on either part managed to help the detective inspector on to it.

'Okay, sir.' Dhar was panting. 'I don't know exactly where we lost signal, but I'll head back up there until I can call the office.'

'Okay,' said Daley. He looked at his watch. 'We have another two hours of light left at the most.'

'Don't worry. I'll be back as soon as I can. It's not as though we're miles away from anywhere. The town's just down there.'

'Yeah, you're right. I'm sorry about all this, Shreya. Maybe it wasn't the best idea I've ever had.'

She smiled. 'Hang in there, Jim.' With that, she was gone.

Daley tried to manoeuvre himself into something resembling comfort. But his ankle was throbbing with pain, and the wall against which his back rested was cold, helping to chill him to the bone. Daley began to shiver and, despite his best efforts, could not stop. Though he tried to focus his mind, his whole body trembled, making his ankle throb all the more.

It was then that he heard movement from outside. Dhar had only been gone for a few moments.

'Hello! Who's there?' Daley shouted. He held his breath awaiting a reply, but no response was forthcoming.

61

Brian Scott was sitting in Daley's chair in the glass box, Hamish seated opposite. The box containing the child's drawings and other bits and bobs was on the desk. For some reason, its contents fascinated Scott.

The old fisherman blew his nose loudly on a tattered old hankie.

'Now, you must listen to me, Brian. I don't know how this all works, but you're going to have to dae something.'

Scott sighed. 'I can't just send officers all over the place based on your dream, Hamish.'

'But you'll acknowledge that I've been right before. And no' jeest once or twice, neithers.'

'Yeah, I get all that. But see me and you, we've no' been oor normal selves for a while, have we?'

Hamish stared into space. 'I dare say you're right. The world isnae the same place it was, that's for sure.'

'Right. Neither o' us is thinking straight. Me wae the bevvy and you wae the dreams.'

'That's where you're wrong, Brian. It's the feeling, no' jeest the dream. I've never had a dream o' Sandy Hoynes that wisna a happy one. Until this day, that is.'

'See, it is the dreams.' Though Scott said the words,

he doubted them almost immediately. The fact that Hamish had pictured both him and Daley 'crucified' on the hill made him uneasy. He didn't know why, it just did. 'I'll gie Jimmy a call.' Scott dialled Daley's mobile number from memory.

Hamish looked on until Scott ended the call. 'You see, no answer. That can only be bad.'

'There's no signal up there. It's no' confirmation o' your abilities to see into the future.'

'I'm telling you, go up there. But go up there in numbers wae your shooters at the ready.' Hamish pointed one gnarled finger at him.

'Shooters? This isnae *Bonanza*.'

'Whatever it is you call guns these days.'

'Guns,' Scott replied.

'Well, no' like the polis to call something by its name. Man, I've been watching that thing on the telly. All initials and the like – talking in riddles. I'd tae switch it off.'

'Okay, here's the deal. You take a lift home from the boys, and I promise to let you know the minute we get in touch with Jimmy. Okay?'

Hamish looked doubtful.

'I know you have these feelings, Hamish. But if I'm to draw firearms, for example, the procedure dictates that I must have a reasonable excuse in order to get permission from the bosses. I can't just say *An auld friend o' mine had a dream*.' He blew out his cheeks. 'And I'll be honest wae you. They're no' likely to look on such a request from me that favourably in any case.'

'Right enough. The way your hands are shaking, you'd be fair spraying bullets all over. There's no saying who'd get hit in the crossfire. And apart from that, you just said firearms, no' guns. I knew fine you'd have a fancy name for them.'

'Hamish, much as I'd like to spend the rest of the day with you, I've a lot on my plate.' He gestured to the box on the desk.

'Very well, I'll be off. I'll no' take your kind offer o' a lift home, mind you. But promise to keep my heads up.'

Scott frowned. 'Up where?'

'That's what they say these days. There's always some bugger getting his heads up.'

'Right, I get it. Don't worry, your head will remain firmly up.'

'That's good to know, Brian.' Hamish got to his feet and stared at the detective who had become his friend. 'I don't care what folk say aboot you, you're a good man.'

'What people? What are they saying?'

'Ach, the usual – you must have a handle on this place by now. Just that you're a drunk and you've no place in the polis. Nothing slanderous or that.'

'Cheers! Good news is always welcome.' Scott could just picture locals huddled around in pubs and cafés discussing his fitness for duty.

'You be careful, that's all I'm saying. If that bastard Macmillan can do for my dear friend Annie, he can do for you – aye, and Mr Daley.'

'Yes, so you said.'

Hamish left. Scott was aware that though he'd done his best to mollify him, the old man was like a dog with a bone when he was of a mind.

He balanced his reading glasses on the bridge of his nose and began to sift through the contents of the cardboard box on his desk. It was all much the same: paintings, drawings, little poems, school jotters and daft doodles.

Scott pictured the Hugh Machie he'd known, not the shadow of the man he'd just watched die. Though he was a better man than his son, the detective hadn't had him down as someone of an overly sentimental nature. And as Potts had pointed out, though the items they'd found weren't new, neither were they venerable enough to have belonged to James Machie.

Near the bottom of the box, he discovered an envelope. It was addressed to a Mr G. Harding at an address in Singapore. As it was written in English, Scott tried to mouth the street, but couldn't get his tongue round the unfamiliar name. He opened the envelope and looked inside. A small letter was contained within.

The letter was in two distinct hands, the smooth script of an adult, followed by more childish writing.

My dearest James, the letter began.

At first, Scott wondered why the writer was addressing Mr G. Harding as James. But as he read the note, everything began to make more sense.

Brian Scott's throat started to dry. He could feel his tongue sticking to the roof of his mouth. Suddenly, he knew to whom this letter had really been sent. There was no other James in whom Hugh Machie could have an interest.

With his hands trembling so much, he found it difficult to focus on the second part of the letter, written in a child's hand. But when he reached the neat little signature at the bottom, his heart froze.

Scott rushed out of Daley's glass box, sweat pouring from his brow.

'Potts, come with me.' He looked round the CID office. A young detective who'd only arrived in the town the day before was busy at her computer keyboard. 'You too, DC . . . sorry, I've forgotten your name.'

'Mearns, sergeant. Alice Mearns.'

'Right, DC Mearns, follow me!'

Daley took in the scene. Shreya Dhar was standing in the doorway, a gun to her head. Behind her, Ian Macmillan, his eyes wild, was staring at him.

'I'm sorry, sir,' said Dhar.

The gun was shaking in Macmillan's grip. 'What's up with him?' He prodded Dhar in the head with barrel of the pistol, making her gasp.

'I fell,' said Daley. 'My ankle is broken.'

'That's okay. You won't be needing it for much longer.' Macmillan's voice was as unsteady as his hand.

'Why don't you tell me what this is all about, Ian?' Daley tried to reason calmly with a man he could see was desperate.

'It's about you – her. All of you. Don't think I haven't seen you all poking about the hotel. Do you really think I'm stupid?'

'No, I don't. But I don't know what you mean, either.'

'You all think I killed Annie. But she killed herself.'

'I know. I was at the inquest.'

'No, not the way you think.'

Daley noticed Dhar's brow furrow.

'Tell me how she died, Ian. We all know you can't kill us. You're not that stupid. Trust me, whoever is behind this, we'll bring them down.' The pain in Daley's ankle was excruciating now. He felt as though he might faint away. But for Dhar's sake he had to stay with her.

'You think you're smart. I noticed it right away. You love

parading your pretty wife about the place like some trophy. And Brian Scott – nothing but a panhandler with a badge.'

'I wish you would tell me what this is all about,' said Daley. Sweat was pouring down his forehead despite the cold.

A strange look passed over Macmillan's face, as though he didn't know what path to take. He looked down at Dhar. He still had her by the neck, gun to her head. He tightened his grip. She flinched.

'There's so much you don't know, *chief inspector*. I read you were one of the top cops around. That's shit. If you really want the truth, it isn't very far away.'

'Sorry?'

Just as Macmillan opened his mouth to speak again, Shreya Dhar caught him in the solar plexus with her elbow. The blow winded him, but he still managed to keep hold of the gun. As Dhar struggled to break free from his grip, Daley tried to get to his feet, but his broken ankle wouldn't support him. He tumbled to the floor with a heavy thud and a yelp.

62

Scott dashed into the bar office, Potts and Mearns following close behind.

'Alasdair, I need you to break oot the weapons – now!'

The bar officer looked doubtful. 'You know I can't do that, Brian. Neither you, Potts or DC Mearns have current certificates. I needn't tell you the way things have been.' He took in the DS doubtfully.

Scott threw the letter across the high desk. 'Is this enough to persuade you?'

Sergeant Shaw read it, wondering why he was doing so – until he came to the end of the note. 'It can't be, surely?'

'Aye, it can. Your man James Machie got about. Until he turned up like a ghost, he'd been on the run for years.'

'I still can't issue you with a firearm, Brian. We'd all be out of a job.'

'Are you kidding? Oor Jimmy will die, and you're worried aboot paperwork! See if you don't give me the key to the weapons cabinet, I'll arrest you myself.'

'That won't be necessary. Potts, I need you behind this desk.'

'Sergeant?'

'You know how this works, son. I can carry a weapon,

even if DS Scott and DC Mearns can't. I need you here to get help and mind the ship.'

Potts nodded as Shaw hurried off to arm himself. He looked at Scott, who was clearly agitated. 'I don't understand, sergeant. What did you find in that letter?'

'Here, read it for yourself.' Scott pulled the letter off Shaw's desk and handed it to the DC.

My dearest James,

We've missed you so much. But you've been as good as your word. The man arrives with money every week, and we want for nothing.

When will we be able to join you?

Potts looked up at Scott. 'Must be James Machie, right?'

'Spot on. Who else could it be? Why would Hughie send such a thing to another James?'

'But I still don't get it.'

'Read the bit in pencil.'

'The wean's writing?'

Scott nodded. There was a pause.

'It can't be!' Potts looked astonished.

'Aye, it can – it is. Your man Machie had a soft spot for children. It was the only decent thing aboot the bastard. Probably thought he got a raw deal fae his ain faither.'

'The car,' said Potts.

'Eh?'

'When Hugh Machie shot at you in Main Street.'

'Aye, what aboot it?' Scott thought back. The bullet hit the roof just above the driver's back passenger's door. He remembered Hugh Machie's last words: *There should be nobody left who remembers. It stops wae the last.* 'Hughie wisnae after us. He was trying to save us!'

Shaw appeared, a weapon in his hand. He thrust a spare clip into his pocket. 'Come on, Brian!'

'Potts, find out who was given James Machie's belongings after his death – what there was of them,' said Scott.

Leaving the DC behind the desk, Scott, Shaw and Mearns rushed from Kinloch police office, the letter to James Machie stuffed into Scott's pocket.

Daley looked on helplessly as Dhar struggled with Macmillan. The Canadian was tall and strong, but the detective was quicker. She caught Macmillan's left wrist with both hands and forced it against the stone wall of the steading. Then she thrust her knee into his groin. The pain was enough to dislodge the weapon from Macmillan's grasp.

As he cried out, Daley tried to force himself up, but his broken ankle left him rooted to the spot. Frustratingly, he was only a few feet from the pistol, now lying on the earthen floor.

Dhar was panting with the effort of wrestling with the hotelier. He managed to break free of her grip and caught her a glancing blow to the chin. Dhar fell backwards, landing with a thud.

'Shreya!' Daley cried. The detective sergeant looked as though she was down and out, knocked unconscious by a combination of the blow and the fall. 'You give up now, Ian!' he said through gritted teeth.

Macmillan was on his knees, gasping for breath. 'Listen to me! Annie didn't kill herself: she was murdered. I was there – I know!'

'What?' Daley looked at Macmillan in disbelief.

'She heard something – at least, they thought she did. Me on the phone. I should never have said anything to them.'

'Who are you talking about?'

Macmillan took a deep breath. 'I don't know who they were, but I know who they were working for. You have to believe me. They've got me by the balls.' His words were rushed, sheer panic in his voice.

'I don't believe you, Mr Macmillan.'

'I'm telling the truth. It's a conspiracy – I don't know. I owed money to people I shouldn't have. It was stupid, but I'd no choice. But I know who is pulling the strings now.'

Daley was about to ask the obvious question when he saw Dhar move. In a flash she reached behind her head, recovered the pistol from the floor, took aim at Macmillan and fired two shots in quick succession.

The Canadian fell backwards as though he'd been pushed by a massive hand, two holes in his chest weeping dark blood. His head crashed against the stone wall of the building. Now spread out on the floor like a discarded rag doll, he blinked at Daley, eyes wide. As his life drained away, his eyelids flickered, the tension in his body eased and he died.

'I'm sorry, sir. I had no choice. He would have killed us both.' Dhar was still on the floor, propping herself up with one hand. A large bruise was already forming on the end of her chin.

He looked at her, astonished by the events of the last few minutes. 'It's easy to judge. I don't know what I'd have done if I'd been you.' He frowned. 'I'd like to have had the chance to get more from him, though.'

'It was life and death, sir.'

'Yes, you're right. Did you hear what he said?'

'Yes. I was just waiting for the right moment – when he was off-guard, I mean.'

'I wonder what this conspiracy is all about, and who's behind it all? I just can't get it.'

'He won't enlighten us now. But it ties in with what we know up the road. We thought the hotel was going to be used as a safe house for criminals ready to flee the country. That must be the conspiracy, surely.'

'You never said.'

'Orders from above. Sorry, sir.'

'But from what he told us, he certainly wasn't acting alone.' It suddenly dawned on Daley that, despite the fact that their attacker was lying dead a few feet away, he might not have been alone on the foggy hillside either.

Dhar was catching her breath, staring at the dead man. 'There must be a leak – in my department, I mean. He lured us here when the attack on Main Street failed. He must have known we were close – that I was close.'

Thoughts of Hugh Machie, huge sums of money and Annie's death all crowded Daley's head. James Machie's whereabouts before his dramatic return to take revenge on all those who wronged him were still unknown. Was it possible he'd salted money away from his gangland empire in Glasgow and begun another nefarious enterprise somewhere else? Daley supposed it wasn't impossible. But if that were the case, why had this information ended up in the possession of Hugh Machie, the father who hated him?

'What will we do now, sir?'

Daley pulled his thoughts back to the present. 'We still have to get word back to Brian. Are you fit enough to go and find this mobile signal?'

'Yeah, I'm okay. Just a bit battered and bruised.' Shreya Dhar got to her feet. 'Here, sir. Take this.' She offered Daley the pistol.

'No, you keep it. I'll take my chances. You're the one out in the open.'

Dhar looked out of the door into the white world. 'The fog hasn't lifted. It must be to our advantage.'

'Yes. Get a call in to Brian. He'll know what to do.'

63

'I don't know what to dae,' said Scott. He parked the car at the gate beside Daley's SUV.

'Well, we know they made it this far, at least,' said Shaw.

They stared out of the car at billowing fog, obscuring everything more than a few feet away. Shaw produced an iPad. Using an app, he pulled up a detailed map of the area.

'It's fine having a map, Alasdair, but how do we know where they're at?'

Shaw pulled two Airwave radio phones from a bag. 'The phone signal is crap up here. That's why we can't raise DCI Daley. I thought we could use these. Hopefully they'll be more useful.'

'No' bad for a desk jockey, buddy.' Scott looked at the iPad. 'Okay, we go up this hill then into the wee glen.'

'Yes, that's the idea,' said Shaw.

'DC Mearns, I want you to relay anything you hear on the radio in the car back to Potts. He's busy getting a few bodies together and putting the gaffers up the road in the picture. First sign o' bother and you're oot o' here, right?'

'But what about you two?'

'We cannae cover as much ground if we buddy up. You agree, Alasdair?'

Shaw shrugged. 'We have no idea what we're walking into. It's a real bear trap.'

'I'll go by myself.'

'Don't be stupid. But keep the radio on.'

'Okay. You go left, I'll go right.'

'Sounds good, Brian.'

'And I'll be in intensive care afore you.' Scott smiled.

'You really do have a brilliant turn of phrase, Brian.'

As they were about to leave the car, Scott's phone rang.

'Potts, what is it?'

'Sir, I've been speaking to ACC Cunningham. You've to stay put until they can get some reinforcements.'

'Fae where? They cannae send a helicopter down in this pea-souper.'

'By road, I suppose.'

'That's fine then. They'll be here in four hours. Just say you couldnae get me. The signal's bad up here, Potts.'

'ACC Cunningham was very clear.'

'Eh?'

'He was very clear about what you were to do, I mean.'

'You're breaking up, son. Sorry.' Scott ended the call.

'How you've kept your job this long, I'll never know,' said Shaw.

Scott shrugged. 'People have been saying that to me for years.'

'I'm not representing you the next time.'

They left DC Mearns in the car as a temporary controller and took to the hill.

Had Jim Daley not been nursing a broken ankle he'd have felt less vulnerable. As it was, the pain was so great he was fighting to remain conscious. The biting cold didn't help, either. He was shivering with a mixture of pain and shock as he looked across the dim space at the lifeless body of Ian Macmillan.

To try to take his mind off the discomfort, Daley concentrated on recent events. He recalled Macmillan's last words. Another corpse, another wasted life. It had been his lot for so long, but the misery of it never left him. Instead, it piled on, year after year, breaking him down like a great boulder being worn away by the elements over millennia.

Dhar's speed and strength had impressed him, even though he wished that she'd subdued Macmillan rather than killing him. Still, he was a big man, and she'd prevailed in the end.

Daley thought of the life she'd had. The misery of facing up to an entirely different culture. The taunts of other children – and the ignorant adults who filled their children's young minds with bile and pointless hatred.

My mother met a man who helped us a lot.

He wondered at the relief Dhar and her mother must have felt when this guardian angel appeared in their lives. The man must have been formidable to stand up against the bullies and bigots. He knew, for he'd faced people like that throughout his career.

Only then did instinct kick in. Only then did the picture in his mind resolve like a telescope suddenly focusing on a distant object.

Hugh Machie had said that there should be *nobody left who remembers.* He was sure that was how Scott had related the dying man's last words.

Through biting cold and the agony of his broken ankle, Daley now felt fear – genuine, stomach-churning fear.

64

Scott and Sergeant Shaw struggled up the hill together. Scott looked back. Instead of thinning out, the fog was worse. There was nothing of the town below to be seen now.

'Okay, this is where we go our separate ways, Brian. Give me your phone.'

Scott did as he was told and looked on as Shaw located the maps feature on Scott's device. 'Okay, that's you good to go. See that building?'

'Aye.'

'You have a look there. I'll head for this area of bushes over here.'

'How far apart will we be, Alasdair?'

Shaw thought for a second. 'No more than a few hundred yards. But in this, it's more like two miles.'

'Aye, tell me about it. Right, see you.' Scott disappeared into the freezing fog.

'Keep your radio on!' Shaw called out but heard no reply. He shook his head and veered off the path to his right, keeping an eye on the digital map.

For Brian Scott the whole thing was like something from one of his fevered alcohol dreams. Nothing made sense. He wasn't sure if it was the ongoing impact of his over-indulgence or just fear of the situation. But the hairs on the back of his neck were standing on end – the primaeval instinct that told him he was being watched. But who could see through this?

He looked at his phone, reckoning he was less than a hundred yards from the building displayed on the map on the screen. He began to tread more carefully. It was odd to be so close to something and have no sight of it whatsoever.

In a few minutes he saw the rough outline of a building through the fog. 'Right, got you,' he whispered under his breath.

As he came closer, he could see this was a broken-down farm steading, the like of which he'd seen before in the hills around Kintyre. The roof was caved in on one side, while a tumble of old stones suggested that a wall had collapsed.

He edged round the side of the building, holding his breath as though he was under water. Listening for a few seconds, he was sure he could hear a moan coming from within.

Scott edged further round the corner. Instead of a weapon, he held the Airwave radio in one hand, ready to alert Shaw at the first sign of life.

Instead of a doorway, there was only a hole. Scott paused. There it was again, the gasp of somebody injured or in pain. Quickly, he dashed through the gaping doorway into the darkness inside. He could just make out the figure of Daley, who seemed to be sitting on the hard earth floor, but before he could speak he felt a sharp pain in the back of his head and he tumbled, unconscious, into his own blackness.

Having pistol-whipped Scott, Shreya Dhar stood back in the doorway.

'Funny, I didn't think it would be this easy. The dynamic duo. The crime fighters extraordinaire, with nothing to offer.

You don't know how long I've waited for this day.'

As she spoke, the Airwave radio lying beside Brian burst into life.

'*Brian, any luck, over?*'

'That's your nice bar officer,' said Dhar. She picked the radio up and pressed the transmit button, making low noises to imitate a man's voice broken by poor reception.

'*Brian, repeat, over.*'

This time Dhar merely clicked the button a couple of times, mimicking a signal almost entirely lost.

'*Listen, in case you can hear me, I'm just going to have another poke about here. There's more to these bushes than I thought. I'll head your way when I'm done, over.*'

'My goodness, it gets worse. Like some really bad comedy.' Dhar laughed as Scott began to stir.

'What now, Shreya? Your little escape plan is lying dead in the corner.'

'Macmillan? He was always just an excuse. A way to include my associates. It was easy to put pressure on such a weak man. But looking at the pair of you, maybe all men are weak.'

Scott forced himself half off the floor. 'What the . . .' When he turned to face Dhar, he sighed. 'You.'

'Me, yes. All these years with ignorant men and stupid women in this shit job, just to get to this moment. Funny, it all seems rather anticlimactic.' She cocked her head. 'We'll have to wait for your intrepid Sergeant Shaw. I'm sure he won't be long. Unless he falls and breaks his neck like his clumsy boss nearly did.' She glared at Daley.

'I don't know why you're doing this, Shreya,' said Daley.

'She's doing it for James Machie, that's what, Jimmy.'

'Yes, I'd worked that out, Bri. But how can you bear a

grudge on behalf of a dead man? A real bastard, at that. You've been in this job for years. Didn't it mean anything?'

'Ha! You should have tried it. Moving to this country: the prejudice, the hatred. The idiots whose only ambition was to find the next drink, burger or drug. I hated it – still do. James Machie may have been a criminal, but he was worth thousands of people like you.'

'Oh, aye,' said Scott. 'He was a really enlightened guy. Right good bloke. Just ask the families of the folks he killed. Better still, the ones he left behind. They all love him.'

'But you didn't reckon on Hugh Machie, did you, Shreya?'

She shrugged. 'He's dead.'

'He stole your little inheritance, didn't he? I wonder, how will your new business partners react when they hear that all their little secrets are out in the open?' Daley saw her expression change. It was only for an instant, but he knew what it meant. 'Oh yes, Hugh Machie had gathered more than you thought. Bank statements from Panama, the Caymans – you know the score. We have all that now. I wonder how much they stand to lose, these fine people … and the heir of the man you so idolised.'

She shrugged. 'My aim was never money. It was to kill you and this drunk.' She spat the words, the hatred plain in her eyes, even in the gloom.

'You won't have seen this for a while, eh?' He reached into his pocket and watched Dhar flinch. 'No need to worry, lassie. It's only a letter.' He screwed it up and threw the paper in her direction.

With the gun still trained on Daley and Scott, she knelt down and read it, squinting in the gloom, with regular glances at the page. Her eyed filled with tears. 'I remember writing this. I was just a little kid.'

'Really? Shame you grew up. You're just as worthless as James Machie now. You can't resist the grand gesture. The big picture ending.' Daley shook his head.

Scott squirmed on the floor, intending to rush her. Instantly, she pointed the weapon in his face. 'But I guess he failed where I'll succeed. In fact, a little change of plan, I think. Your lovely sergeant is bound to hear the shots that will kill you both. Then it's simple. He comes running to the rescue and is the next to go.'

'He's armed,' said Scott.

'I thought he would be. I know they won't let you have a weapon. Very wise, in my opinion. He won't be a problem, trust me. Well, time to say goodbye to each other. I wonder how your airhead wife will take it, Jim. Or yours, Brian? Her of the flashy wedding ring and glottal stops. Ah well. Pity your pal here will never know the truth, Brian, eh?'

Shreya Dhar backed away slightly, the pistol now held out before her.

65

Daley's heart was beating in his throat, while at his feet Brian Scott looked defeated. A broken man about to die. Dhar took aim.

'Aye, that'll be enough.' The voice came from nowhere and took all three of them by surprise.

Scott and Daley peered out into the white shadows behind Dhar. Two figures emerged from the fog. Hamish was standing beside Shaw, who had his gun trained on the back of Shreya's head.

'I warn you, Ms Dhar. Put down your gun. You'll kill nobody else this day.' Shaw was only two feet away from her.

'Jeest blow her away,' said Hamish, much to Shaw's surprise.

'Oh, yes. The old fisherman who wants to know too much, and the man who makes his living behind a desk, to the rescue.' Dhar didn't turn to face them, but remained standing, her pistol still pointed at Daley and Scott. 'You'll find that shooting somebody isn't quite the same as pushing paper, sergeant.'

'Every man has a point beyond which he canna be pushed, Ms Dhar,' said Hamish. 'I had a wee chat wae your landlady. She telt me enough to be able to work oot what you were at. My dreams tell me the rest. I found Alasdair here just in time.'

Dhar sniggered. 'Dreams. What next?'

'You killed a beautiful woman. Like my own wean, she was. And you did it just to avenge an evil man. You can believe me or not. But right this very moment nothing would give me greater pleasure than seeing the good sergeant blow your heid clean off.'

Scott shook his head at Dhar. 'Trust me, he's no' joking.'

'And I'll make sure he gets away with it,' Daley added. For the first time he saw indecision on Dhar's face as the pistol lowered fractionally. He tried to move again but yelled out instead. Dhar took aim at his head.

But she was too slow. Hamish caught her with a kick to the back of the leg. She fell forward, almost into Scott's lap.

'Go you, Hamish!' said Scott as he pinned Dhar to the ground.

'The good Lord looks after the righteous, and that's a fact.' The old man looked up into the endless white sky. 'God rest you, Annie.' Tears flowed down his sunken cheeks.

Epilogue

Two weeks later, Kinloch

The restaurant was busy. Waitresses and waiters carried food and drinks to tables as the happy buzz of conversation sounded just above the classical music being played over speakers placed around the room. For it was well known that the good folk of Kinloch didn't like to be disturbed when they were at their chat, and overly loud music, no matter how ambient, would have been met with a cacophony of complaint.

Five people sat round a side table: Jim and Liz Daley, Ella and Brian Scott and Hamish. Who, despite pleas to the contrary, refused to remove his bunnet.

'Here, I hope yous lot aren't going to be at the battling like you were a few weeks ago.' He looked round the table.

Daley coughed with embarrassment before answering. 'How on earth do you know that?'

'Och, you know fine. This is Kinloch. I heard Ella had the upper hand, Mrs Daley.'

'That's not true!' Liz looked astounded.

'It's o'er, Lizzie,' said Ella. 'It should never have happened in the first place. We're grown women – aye, o' a certain age, too. How long have we been friends?'

Scott sipped on his Irn-Bru. 'Maybe there's a lot o' us should be taking stock of ourselves right now.'

'You still want to retire, Brian?' Daley asked.

'I'm no' going to some pub in Spain,' said Ella before her husband could reply.

'I don't know. It seems like this is the end o' something.' He shrugged.

'There's never an end, Brian,' said Daley. 'Look how Shreya's – James Machie's – associates just disappeared like snow on the river. All those accounts were closed before our financial people could find anything. There's always work to do. You know it.'

'Aye, for sure there is,' said Hamish. 'Folk are strange. I've never harmed as much as a fly in my life. But if I'd killed thon woman it widna have bothered me. I tell you true. If my head can be turned, so can anybody else's.'

'She's not saying anything,' said Daley. 'But she'll have a long time behind bars to think about things.'

'Death would have been too easy for her,' said Hamish.

'And in any case, what would you do wae yourself, Brian? Fighting crime is all you've ever known.' Ella took her husband's hand.

Scott looked at her expensive wedding ring. 'Aye, I suppose you're right, dear.' But in his head, all he saw was the dying figure of Hugh Machie. They were all gone: Jay-Mac, John Donald, Frank MacDougall, Hugh – all the faces from his past. He, Brian Scott, was the only one left to remember. 'I need a smoke. Are you coming, Ella?'

'Are you kidding? It's snowing outside. I'll just wait here and get a good grip o' Lizzie's hair.'

'I'll keep you company,' said Daley. 'It's good to move about after a big meal.'

The pair made their way through the maze of tables. Scott opened the door, and soon they were in the chilly domain of the dedicated smoker – the snowy street outside.

Daley watched as Scott lit a cigarette, his hands still trembling. 'How are you feeling, Bri? Enjoying your time off, I hope.'

'I'm just doing it my way, as Ol' Blue Eyes would say.'

'I know. You and I are too old to be guided on anything, I think.' He looked down a Main Street devoid of people, apart from a man staggering from one lamppost to the next in the snow, drunk as a lord. 'I've been thinking.'

'What aboot?'

'Dhar – you know, up on the hill.'

'Aye.' Scott took a long draw of his cigarette.

'*Your pal will never know the truth*. That's what she said, wasn't it?'

'She was meaning Macmillan. Must have been.'

Daley shrugged. 'Maybe. I don't know. I just thought it was strange, that's all.'

'The lassie's deranged, Jimmy. That's bloody obvious.'

Daley studied his old friend as he took another draw on the cigarette. He remembered DCI Ian Burns telling him that Scott was special. It was something he'd wondered about for years.

Scott was stubbing out his cigarette when Daley's mobile rang.

'Yes, Alasdair,' Daley said, answering the call. He listened for a few moments. 'Right, I see. Thanks for letting me know. I'll see you in the morning for the gory details.' He clicked off the phone and sighed.

'What's that aboot?' said Scott.

Daley sighed and hung his head. 'Shreya Dhar. She's dead. She hanged herself in her cell at the remand centre. Another wasted life.' He shook his head, grieving silently for the woman who would have killed him if she could. It never ended. The good, bad and indifferent – it always ended with the spare, cold hand of death.

Scott looked up into the falling snow. 'Hughie was right then. It's over.'

'We thought that before, Brian.'

'Shame, just a young lassie. Mind you, she was going to blow oor brains oot, so fair play. But every bugger that really knew aboot Machie's deid, Jim. He *was* right.'

'We'll keep it light in there, eh? No need for folk to know before they need to.'

'There's no folk left that need to know, Jimmy. Nobody cares. Nobody remembers.'

Daley looked on as Scott rubbed his hands to banish the cold then pushed the restaurant door open. There may be one person left who remembers, Daley thought.

'You coming back in, big man? It's brass monkeys oot here.'

Daley smiled. 'Yes, I'm right at your back, Brian. As always.'

Acknowledgements

I know it's a cliché, but the last ten years have flown by. During that time, a core of people has been instrumental in bringing Daley to the page.

Hugh Andrew and Neville Moir at Polygon saved the day right back in the beginning. I wish the latter a long and happy retirement. Alison Rae has been a constant editorial presence, overseeing the many processes every book must go through before it sees the light of day. And for the last few Daley novels, I must also thank Nancy Webber for her thoughtful copy-editing. So, too, the rest of the team in Edinburgh, headed up by Jan Rutherford. Their collective efforts are much appreciated.

A big shout-out to all the hardworking booksellers who put so much time and effort into getting the books into the hands of readers. And to those who toil away in the digital domain. For all the dedicated librarians everywhere, who work under growing constraints. Those who govern us should realise how important libraries are. I thank you all.

Huge thanks to my old pal David Monteath, who has become the voice of the Daley universe for audiophiles. He does a fabulous job ensuring the books are hugely successful on that platform. And a big thank-you to my SBooks podcasting partner in crime Douglas Skelton. A man who regularly has his legendary 'bad feeling' about nearly everything. Give us a listen!

I owe a great debt of gratitude to my tirelessly enthusiastic agent Jo Bell. She sprinkles everything with *can do*. Everyone should have a Jo in their lives.

I must, as always, thank the people of Kintyre. Ten years ago, they got behind the first in the series, *Whisky from Small Glasses*, and now, as we move into a new and exciting phase, they're still there. It will always be home – *always*.

And to all of you, my dear readers. I thank you all for investing in my work. Long may it continue!

And lastly, my lovely wife Fiona. She's been with me every step of the way, including the dark days of 2017 when I feared I wouldn't be around to write another book. I love you.

The DCI Daley thriller series

Book 1: *Whisky from Small Glasses*
DCI Jim Daley is sent from the city to investigate a murder after the body of a woman is washed up on an idyllic beach on the west coast of Scotland. Far away from urban resources, he finds himself a stranger in a close-knit community.

Book 2: *The Last Witness*
James Machie was a man with a genius for violence, his criminal empire spreading beyond Glasgow into the UK and mainland Europe. Fortunately, Machie is dead, assassinated in the back of a prison ambulance following his trial and conviction. But now, five years later, he is apparently back from the grave, set on avenging himself on those who brought him down.

Book 3: *Dark Suits and Sad Songs*
When a senior Edinburgh civil servant spectacularly takes his own life in Kinloch harbour, DCI Jim Daley comes face to face with the murky world of politics. To add to his woes, two local drug dealers lie dead, ritually assassinated. It's clear that dark forces are at work in the town.

Book 4: *The Rat Stone Serenade*
It's December, and the Shannon family are heading to their clifftop mansion near Kinloch for their AGM. Shannon International, one

of the world's biggest private companies, has brought untold wealth and privilege to the family. However, a century ago, Archibald Shannon stole the land upon which he built their home – and his descendants have been cursed ever since.

Book 5: *The Well of the Winds*

As World War Two nears its end, a man is stabbed to death on the Kinloch shoreline, in the shadow of the great warships in the harbour. When DCI Daley comes into possession of a journal written by his wartime predecessor in Kinloch, he soon realises that he must solve a murder from the past to uncover the shocking events of the present.

Book 6: *The Relentless Tide*

When Professor Francombe and her team of archaeologists find the remains of three women on a remote Kintyre hillside – a site rumoured to have been the base of Viking warlord Somerled – their delight soon turns to horror when they realise the women tragically met their end only two decades ago.

It soon becomes clear that these are the three missing victims of the 'Midweek Murderer', a serial killer who was at work in Glasgow in the early 1990s. DCI Jim Daley now has the chance to put things right – to confront a nightmare from his past and solve a crime he failed to as a young detective.

Book 7: *A Breath on Dying Embers*

When the luxury cruiser *Great Britain* berths in Kinloch harbour, the pressure mounts on DCI Jim Daley. The high-powered international delegates on board are touring the country, golfing and sightseeing, as part of a UK government trade mission. But within hours, one of the crew members vanishes and a local birdwatcher has disappeared.

Book 8: *Jeremiah's Bell*

Teenager Alison Doig disappeared from Kinloch over thirty years ago under mysterious circumstances. Her reclusive family still live in a remote part of the Kintyre peninsula, amidst rumours of wrecking, smuggling and barbaric cruelty.

Now rich American hotelier Alice Wenger has arrived in town, determined to punish those who made her suffer in the past. But someone has vowed to keep hidden sins concealed for ever.

Book 9: *For Any Other Truth*

When a light aircraft crash-lands at Machrie airport, DCI Jim Daley and his colleague Brian Scott rush to the scene. But it soon becomes clear that both occupants of the plane were dead before take-off.

Meanwhile in Kinloch, local fisherman Hamish is unwittingly dragged into danger when he witnesses something he shouldn't have, and hotel manager Annie is beginning to suspect her new boss may not be as he first appeared. And just as Chief Superintendent Carrie Symington thinks she has finally escaped the sins of her past, she finds herself caught in an even deadlier trap.

As the action spills across the sea to County Antrim – all under the scrutiny of the Security Service – the search is on for any other truth.

Short Stories and Tales from Kinloch

One Last Dram Before Midnight: The Complete Collected DCI Daley Short Stories

Published together for the first time in one not-to-be-missed volume are all Denzil Meyrick's short stories. Discover how DCI Daley and DS Scott first met on the mean streets of Glasgow in two prequels that shed light on their earlier lives. Join Hamish and his old mentor, skipper Sandy Hoynes, as they become embroiled with some Russian fishermen and an illicit whisky plot. And in present-day Kinloch Daley and Scott investigate ghosts from the past, search for a silent missing man, and follow the trail of an elusive historical necklace.

Dalintober Moon: A DCI Daley Story
When a body is found in a whisky barrel buried on Dalintober beach, it appears that a notorious local crime, committed over a century ago, has finally been solved. However, the legacy of murder still resonates within the community, and the tortured screams of a man who died long ago still echo across Kinloch.

Two One Three: A Constable Jim Daley Short Story
Glasgow, 1986. Only a few months into his new job, Constable Jim Daley is pounding the beat. When he is seconded to the CID to help catch a possible serial killer, he makes a new friend, DC Brian Scott. Jim Daley tackles his first serious crime in an investigation that will change his life for ever.

Empty Nets and Promises
It's July 1968, and fishing-boat skipper Sandy Hoynes has his daughter's wedding to pay for – but where are all the fish? He and the crew of the *Girl Maggie* come to the conclusion that a new-fangled supersonic jet which is being tested in the skies over Kinloch is scaring off the herring.

First mate Hamish comes up with a cunning plan. But they will have to face down a vindictive fishery officer, a suspicious exciseman and the local police sergeant – not to mention a ghostly piper and some Russians.

Single End: A DC Daley Short Story
It's 1989, and Jim Daley is now a fully fledged detective constable. When ruthless gangster James Machie's accountant is found stabbed to death in a multi-storey car park, it's clear all is not well within Machie's organisation. Meanwhile DC Brian Scott must revisit his past in an attempt to uncover the identity of a corrupt police officer.

A Large Measure of Snow: A Tale from Kinloch
It's December 1967, and the town of Kinloch is cut off by heavy snow. The only way to feed and water the townsfolk is for the fishing fleet to sail to Girvan for much-needed supplies. But the skipper of the *Girl Maggie*, Sandy Hoynes, has a problem. First mate Hamish has, to everyone's astonishment, been chosen as Young Fisherman of the Year by a Glasgow newspaper. Marooned in the town and with one eye on a scoop, their reporter decides to join the fishing crew on their mercy mission.

As the blizzards worsen, the crew of the *Girl Maggie* embarks upon a trip like no other, encountering ghostly Vikings, gigantic crustaceans and a helpful seagull.

A Toast to the Old Stones: A Tale from Kinloch
It's 1968, and the fishermen of Kinloch are preparing to celebrate the old New Year on the twelfth of January. The annual pilgrimage to the Auld Stones is a tradition that goes back beyond memory, and young Hamish, first mate on the *Girl Maggie*, is chuffed that he's been invited to this exclusive gathering.

Meanwhile, it appears that the new owners of the Firdale Hotel are intent upon turning their customers teetotal, such is the exorbitant price they are charging for whisky. Wily skipper Sandy Hoynes comes up with a plan to deliver the spirit to the thirsty villagers at a price they can afford through his connections with a local still-man.

But when the Revenue are tipped off, it looks as though Hoynes and Hamish's mercy mission might run aground. Can the power of the Auld Stones come to their rescue, and is the reappearance of a face from Hoynes' past a sign for good or ill?

Ghosts in the Gloaming: A Tale from Kinloch will be published in October 2022.

For up-to-the-minute news
and information about
Denzil Meyrick's books
and projects find him here

f DenzilMeyrickAuthor
t LochLomonden